Five Weeks
to *Jamaica*

DOUG OUDIN

iUniverse®

FIVE WEEKS TO JAMAICA

iUniverse books may be ordered through booksellers or by contacting:

iUniverse
1663 Liberty Drive
Bloomington, IN 47403
www.iuniverse.com
1-800-Authors (1-800-288-4677)

ISBN: 978-1-4917-6303-2 (sc)
ISBN: 978-1-4917-6302-5 (hc)
ISBN: 978-1-4917-6301-8 (e)

Library of Congress Control Number: 2015903895

Print information available on the last page.

iUniverse rev. date: 03/30/2015

Acknowledgments

Special thanks to my editing ladies; Pamela Norcross/Sherrick, Vicki Miller, Sharon Bison, and especially the love of my life, my wife Maureen Oudin. Each of you helped me tremendously, and I am grateful to all of you for sharing your skills, insight, and suggestions.

I would also like to thank my wife Maureen and my sons Trevor and Troy, and daughter-in-law Lauren for supporting me through the process of writing both this book and my first book, 'Between Two Harbors, Reflections of a Catalina Island Harbormaster'.

Your understanding, encouragement, and tolerance allowed me to achieve my goal.

Thanks also to Lani Battey of Grants Pass, Oregon for my author cover photo.

DEDICATION

To every person that has ever stepped aboard a boat with me, thank you for being there on our journey, no matter how long or how short, and for helping me reach my destination.

This book is also dedicated to every person with the dream, the fantasy, or the wanderlust to sail the high seas, find that perfect beach, or survive that violent storm. Congratulations! You too have known at least a part of the ocean mystique that I have tried to share in these pages.

Wishing you calm seas.

Journey of the motor vessel Explorer
And sailboat Cozy
(5,780 nautical miles)

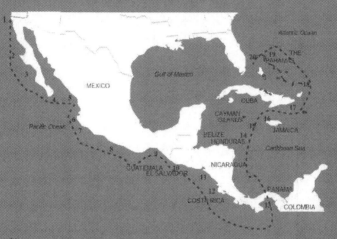

Legend:

1) Ensenada, Mexico
2) Cedros Island, Mexico
3) Seammons Lagoon, Mexico
4) Cabo San Lucas, Mexico
5) Mazatlan, Mexico
6) Isla Marias, Mexico
7) Manzanillo, Mexico
8) Acapulco, Mexico
9) San Jose, Guatemala
10) Acajutla, El Salvador

11) Puerto Corinto, Nicaragua
12) Puntarenas, Costa Rica
13) Panama Canal, Panama
14) San Andres Island, Columbia
15) Seranilla Bank, Columbia
16) Montego Bay, Jamaica (on sailboat Cozy)
17) Windward Passage
18) Great Inagua Island, Bahamas
19) Nassau, Bahamas
20) Bimini Islands, Bahamas

Chapter One

Kurt watched appreciatively as his girlfriend Madison walked across the patio bricks, involuntarily twitching his eyebrows at the motion of her hips under the short restaurant skirt. Madison had an unusual method of movement, almost manly in nature, but somehow always sensual. Kurt turned back to his workbench, and placed his tools in the center of the table. He had hoped to finish the job he was working on by nightfall, but a cold beer sounded really good. Maybe he would go back out after dinner and complete the project. He rolled down the garage door and went into the house.

Madison waited for him in the kitchen, popped open two Pacifico's and grabbed his hand in an effort to lead him into the living room.

"Hang on a minute," he said, "let me wash up." He scrubbed-up quickly and joined her.

Seated together on the small, front-room sofa, Kurt turned to Madison and gave her a brief kiss on the lips. She grinned. He loved her lips. They were soft, and the upper lip was nearly as full as the lower—one of the many things about her that he adored.

Kurt had noticed the unusual fullness of her upper lip one evening a couple of years before, when she was lying on her back on the kitchen table drying her hair. She liked to let her thick tresses hang down nearly to the floor while drying. Lying on the table, she would run her fingers through the long golden locks, spreading them outward and let air between the strands to help them dry. On that particular evening, he was struck by the beauty of her heart shaped face in the upside-down position. With a cat-like slant to her eyes and a narrow bridge across her nose, her face appeared even more intriguing and lovely than when right side-up. That memory made him grin.

He stood and walked behind the couch, and leaned over to kiss her from that upside-down angle. She responded coquettishly, and smiled happily at his seemingly childlike captivation. "Oh Kurt," she whispered, "Sometimes you are so silly."

Both of them jumped in surprise when the phone rang. "Darn," said Kurt.

"Let it go," said Madison.

He shrugged and told her, "I'm expecting a call from work that I need to take."

It was a phone call that would change their lives.

∞

Kurt picked up the telephone. "Hello?" He was expecting a call from his boss, but instead it was his brother Larry.

"Hey Kurt," Larry asked, "want to go to Jamaica with me and Marcos?" It was so typical of him to get right to the point.

"What?" Kurt replied, frowning because his brother had once again managed to disrupt his usually imperturbable state of mind. "What are you talking about?"

"We found a luxury yacht selling a five-week, all-inclusive cruise to Jamaica, and we're leaving in ten days. Want to go? It's only five hundred dollars per person, and they still have space available."

Kurt's immediate reaction was one of slight annoyance, partly because Larry had interrupted his dalliance with Madison, and partly because he would not have answered the phone if he had not been expecting an important call. Pausing for a moment before responding, Kurt tried to focus. *'A five-week cruise to Jamaica for five hundred dollars?'* It was a little too much to wrap his thoughts around.

"Larry," Kurt responded slowly, "I'm kind of in the middle of something right now. Besides, I can't just stop my life to take off on a five-week cruise."

"Okay, not a problem. I just thought I would ask. Go ahead and get back to what you were doing and I'll talk to you later." With that, Larry hung up.

Madison sat with a puzzled expression. "What was that all about?"

"Oh, you know Larry. Apparently he and Marcos found a five-week cruise to Jamaica for five hundred dollars and he called to ask us if we wanted to go."

Madison looked at him for a long moment, then asked, "Can we?"

Madison rarely strayed beyond her comfort zone. She grew up in the tiny desert community of Barstow, California. She had lived there for the first eighteen years of her life, never venturing out of the State, much less the country. Her life was basically predictable and routine. For her to express even a faint interest in taking off on the spur of the moment on a potentially life-changing excursion seemed well outside of her conservative nature. But as Kurt searched her face, an expression of quizzical interest was evident.

"Seriously?" You are actually contemplating an adventure like that?" Kurt asked.

Madison paused for a moment before answering, "Why not? After all, what do we really have going here? I don't like my job very much. I've never had the opportunity to visit other parts of the world. Both of us are more or less just living day by day without any real goals, plans, or serious ambitions. Why couldn't we just drop everything and take off on a cruise?"

Kurt did not expect her reaction. Her eagerness intrigued him, but he needed a little time to try and digest the direction this was beginning to take. Like most men, he tended to categorize everything in his daily life into neat little compartments that could be opened, reacted to, and closed in systematic order. To have something like this pop up out of the blue caused him some serious consternation. He stared at Madison for a long moment before answering, "Okay, if you like, I'll call Larry back in a little while and ask him for more details about the cruise."

"That would be great." Madison whispered as she stood and moved toward him, wrapped her hands behind his neck and stretched her five foot-three inch frame onto her tiptoes to brush his lips. "Now can we get back to where we were before the phone rang?"

∞

Afterward, they dressed and went back into the kitchen to prepare some food. Kurt caught a couple of decent size surfperch the evening before, and he prepped the filets while Madison fixed a salad. Casually, they talked about their day, Kurt told her about the excellent body surfing he enjoyed that morning and Madison filled him in on some of the current gossip going around the restaurant.

Seated at the dining room table and eating their food, both of them were quiet. Kurt's thoughts lingered on Madison's reaction to the cruise conversation. Madison's face exuded a rare mix of pensiveness and restrained energy or enthusiasm. Her cheeks were slightly flushed, while her eyes sparkled as if they were lost in some far away Shangri-La. He wasn't sure what to make of her mood. He believed that she was truly engrossed and captivated with the thought of taking off on the cruise. At the same time, he was reluctant to bring up the conversation, simply because he was still trying to come to terms with even considering such a bold and outlandish move. They finished their meal in silence and cleaned up the mess.

Then Madison asked, "Are you going to call Larry and find out more details about the trip to Jamaica?" There it was. Obviously, she was serious, and evidently she was anxious to pursue the possibility.

"Sure, but I'm going to make my work call first, then I'll call Larry."

Kurt and his boss spoke briefly about everyday things, and he assured his boss that he could have everything wrapped up by the following afternoon.

After hanging up, he asked, "Are you sure this is something you want to do?" He had pondered the matter enough to become more curious and was beginning to warm to the subject.

"Yeah, I'm pretty sure," Madison replied, "but there are a lot of things we'll need to know before we can really consider it completely."

Kurt nodded. "Yes, there is a lot to consider, but things like this don't come up very often in one's life; and hey, what's life without a little adventure?"

They smiled at each other for a long moment, and then Kurt picked up the phone and dialed Larry. "Hey Larry, what's this thing about Jamaica?"

"Like I told you earlier, Marcos and I found an ad in the local paper, advertising a five-week cruise to Jamaica for five hundred dollars, and we booked passage. The cruise is due to depart in ten days. We're going to downtown L.A. tomorrow to get our passports and our shots." He paused for a minute, and Kurt interrupted.

"So, what kind of a boat is it? Do your really think it's legitimate? That seems like a really cheap ticket for a luxury cruise ship."

Larry said, "Well, it's not a real cruise ship, more of a yacht. It's about one hundred-fifty foot long; and they're selling passage for thirty-five people. I think they are just trying to cover some of their expenses to get the boat delivered to Jamaica. It's scheduled to go into service as an inter-island excursion boat between Jamaica and the Cayman Islands. I spoke with the captain of the boat yesterday, and it all sounds legitimate to me. The captain said we could have our money back when we arrive at the boat if we are not satisfied with what they have to offer." He paused for a breath, "So, do you really think you and Madison might want to go? They told us at the Passport Office that if we got applications in by tomorrow, we should receive them back by the first of next week. That gives us about a five-day leeway. As for shots, I think we need malaria, typhoid, and maybe hepatitis. There is a travel vaccination office near the passport office we are using, and they will know what we need."

Kurt asked, "Okay, do you have a number to call where we can find out a few more things?'

"Sure, I'll give you the number, and I'll also give you the number for the captain. He said that anyone interested could call him for details. Give me just a second." A moment later, Larry read off two phone numbers.

"This is great!" Larry exclaimed, "I really hope you guys decide to go."

"Yeah," said Kurt, "it does sound pretty exciting."

"Great. Give me a call and let me know, and say hi to Madison."

After hanging up, Kurt filled Madison in on all the details. Rubbing the scar on his cheek—a habit of his whenever his thoughts are fraught with anything he is unsure of—Kurt grinned a sheepish smile and nodded at Madison. "Okay kiddo, I guess we've got a lot to do if we're going to try and make this happen."

For the remainder of the evening, Kurt spent a lot of time on the phone. He contacted the gal in charge of booking the cruise, finding out the details for payment, anticipated departure time, a basic itinerary of ports and stops along the way, and information about meals, sleeping accommodations and other amenities. Most of it sounded good, although there was some vagueness about the sleeping arrangements on board.

Kurt took notes of all the details, with Madison looking over his shoulder as he wrote. She questioned him about the sleeping quarters, and he told her that he would discuss that more with the captain. When he called the captain's number, there was no answer. He told her he would try again later.

He reached over and pulled Madison to his side. "If we're really going to make this happen, I think we had better try and get to the Passport Office tomorrow. My passport expired about two years ago, and I know you've never had one. If we get that done, and the shots, at least we've got those steps out of the way." Reflexively, he rubbed the scar on his cheek and continued, "Financially, I'm not really sure we're prepared for an adventure like this. We have plenty to cover the basic passage, but I think we will need quite a bit more for other things. Also, we will need to fly back from Jamaica at our own expense. Right now, I think we have about twenty-eight hundred put away. I'll bet we need considerably more than that. How is your own personal stash?"

Madison saved the majority of her tips, using them only for special occasions. She responded, "I think I have about one thousand put away. Of course, I still have an account with my mom that I can draw from if I really need to. It's close to five thousand, so I'm not too worried about money."

Seated together on the couch, they quietly shared their excitement and concerns about taking off and virtually disappearing for five weeks. They had no children to be concerned about, no pets, and no seriously binding ties. But there was the house, rent, and Kurt's pickup truck that needed to be on the right side of the street every Tuesday and Thursday or it would get ticketed. They also had to consider their jobs and possible lack thereof once the trip ended. Kurt was sure that his boss would agree to let him pick up where he left off upon his return, but Madison could lose her job. She told him that it did not really matter that much, she knew it would be easy to find another job. At nearly midnight, Kurt commented that the following day would come early and be a busy one.

∞

The first vestiges of dawn lit the window in the bedroom. Madison lay quietly with her head upon his chest as Kurt watched the arrival of 'the gray'; that condition between darkness and daylight when time always seems to be in slow motion.

Kurt thought back to the first time they met.

It was a balmy evening in 1973. Kurt lived in a small bootlegged unit in the back of a three thousand square foot home in Pomona, California, a place that he rented from the homeowner. He worked at a Mattel Toy manufacturing plant in nearby Baldwin Park. He played pickup basketball games twice a week with a few buddies from school and from the nearby neighborhood.

They had just finished a three-game set of hoops and were cooling off with a cold beer when a light green Volkswagen Beetle pulled to the curb with a flat tire.

A young lady got out of the car and walked around to inspect the problem. She looked baffled. Excusing himself from his buddies, Kurt walked over to the car.

"Hi," He said, "It looks like you've got a problem."

She stared at him, as if trying to determine if he was a potential threat, or merely friendly and helpful.

"Hi. Yeah, I seem to have a flat tire, and it's not my car. It's my brother's."

"Okay," Kurt smiled. "Do you have a jack and a spare?"

She replied, "I know this looks like I'm a real idiot, but I have no clue."

"Well, do you mind if I have a look?" Kurt questioned casually.

"I'm sorry," she responded. "If it's not too much trouble, I could use some assistance. I'm supposed to pick my brother up in fifteen minutes, and I really would appreciate a little help."

Kurt opened the hood and found both a jack and a spare tire. A few years previously, he had worked in a service station; so he was very adept at changing tires. The task was completed in less than ten minutes.

Finished, Kurt put the jack and the flat tire into the trunk. "Okay, that's that," he stated, stepping back onto the sidewalk. "You're good to go."

She looked slightly bewildered, blushed timidly, and stammered, "Thanks so much. I...I...can I offer you some money?"

Gazing at her innocent, yet tantalizingly provocative face, Kurt sensed that a connection was taking place. He chuckled lightly. "Of course not, it was my pleasure to be of service. If you wouldn't mind though, I would like your phone number."

She looked at him for nearly a minute before responding, "I don't have a phone, but I work at the Bob's Big Boy Restaurant on Ganesha Boulevard if you'd like to stop by sometime. I'll buy you breakfast. I work mornings, every day except Tuesday and Wednesday."

"Deal." said Kurt, and almost as an afterthought asked, "By the way, what's your name?"

"Madison."

"Okay, Madison, I'm Kurt."

He walked around the car and opened the door for her. "Guess you'd better be going, it sounds like your brother may not like to wait."

As he watched her drive away, Kurt knew that something special had just occurred in his life. A few weeks later they were seeing each other regularly, and two months after that they packed up their things and moved into the little beach bungalow in Hermosa Beach.

Kurt snapped out of his reverie, leaned over and kissed Madison on the lips and said, "Hey doll face, I think it's time to rise and shine. We've got a lot to do if we're going to make this journey happen."

The ensuing few days brought about a frenzy of preparation. Together they visited the Passport Office, the immunization clinic, and the local library to gather information about the countries they would be visiting. Kurt had heard rumors about the political climate in a couple of the Central American nations, and he wanted to know more about the Panama Canal and Jamaica.

It took a number of phone calls, but Kurt eventually contacted the captain of the boat to find out more information. The captain was friendly, but slightly aloof and vague about particulars aboard the ship. From their conversation, Kurt determined that the 'luxuries' aboard the boat were minimal, but the captain and crew would do everything possible to make everyone comfortable and ensure an enjoyable and positive experience for their guests. The captain put a lot of emphasis on the journey itself, and the opportunity to see and experience places and things that few people ever have the chance to encounter.

Packing for the journey was a challenge. Luggage would need to be minimal. On the other hand, having the essentials for five or six weeks of travel required some definite planning. Dress codes should not demand anything special. Once they reached the tropics, shorts and swimsuits would likely be the daily attire, along with light tops. Coats and jackets would probably not be needed in the warmer climates. Still, there were the personal items that nobody wanted to be without, extra toothpaste, deodorant, and other essential toiletries. They would also need towels, books to read, a camera, snorkeling gear, and other personal comforts.

For Madison, the list was longer. There were cosmetics and other female items necessary for her. Her hair alone required special combs, brushes, and shampoos. There was also her lingerie. On this matter, Kurt tried to subtly reassure her that most of those items would be unnecessary. She settled on a few select items.

Meanwhile, they kept in close contact with Larry and Marcos, compared lists and reaffirmed the departure time from San Diego—where the boat would be docked—and discussed a multitude of other questions they all had about the pending journey. During each phone call, Larry remained philosophical about the trip, equating it with an extended campout, albeit to faraway exotic ports. His enthusiasm was infectious.

At the close of one conversation, Larry told Kurt, "I know the whole thing sounds just a bit shaky, but it also sounds like a real adventure. A journey like this could really be life altering."

They had no idea how prophetic that comment would become.

∞

The year was 1976, a Leap Year. America was celebrating its bicentennial—two hundred years of independence from Great Britain.

Two days before their expected departure their passports arrived. However, so did a phone call from the boat captain that left both Kurt and Madison intensely concerned.

"Due to some unexpected problems with the delivery of the boat and with U.S. Immigration," he told them, "we have to postpone our departure date by two days and move the embarkation point to Ensenada, Mexico."

According to the captain, the ship encountered a gale force storm off Point Conception and had to hole-up in Port San Luis for two days, delaying its arrival in San Diego. Further complicating the matter, port authorities in San Diego—for undisclosed reasons—would not approve clearance out of the U.S. for the vessel. That bit of news disturbed Kurt. The idea of having to go to Ensenada did not bode well at all.

Kurt felt troubled. They had set all the wheels in motion for the trip, including giving the assurance to their respective employers that they would be back in six weeks. The two-day delay could mean an extension of the trip, but the captain told him that the lost time could be made up along the way.

But there were other things that disturbed him as well, particularly the apparent clandestine switch of the embarkation point from San Diego to Ensenada. The switch had a certain 'ring' of illegal action, as if the boat was trying to evade normal channels of operation. Kurt had spent enough time in Mexico to recognize that things were often done quite differently below the border, and the reason for the boat's change of departure to Mexico could possibly be an effort to avoid U.S. port authority scrutiny. He and Madison discussed the situation at length.

Together, they reached a conclusion that they would cancel the trip and ask for a refund. The decision was difficult, but they both agreed that it seemed prudent.

Kurt called Larry to inform him of their decision; he held the phone so they could both hear what Larry had to say.

Larry immediately began trying to persuade them to reconsider. "It's not a big deal," Larry reassured. "I already have a ride to Ensenada arranged, and there's really no reason to worry about switching the point of departure."

Kurt wasn't convinced. "Look Larry, there's something wrong with this whole thing. If a legitimate operation offers a trip like this, these types of issues would be arranged and taken care of well ahead of time. It looks to us like this whole trip is disorganized and not very legitimate. Neither of us wants to get involved with something that looks like it is falling apart before it even gets started."

Larry's response was immediate. "I understand your concerns, but think about how cool this trip will be if things work out. It's really a great opportunity, and something you might never have a chance to do again. Besides, you've already committed; give it a chance. At least go with us to Ensenada, see the boat, meet the other people; and if you still don't like how it looks, then back out. After all, what do you have to lose at this point?"

"Well, a thousand dollars, for one thing," Kurt retorted. "To say nothing of the time and energy we have already put into this whole thing."

"That's my point exactly." Larry replied. "Why give up now? If nothing else, go with us to Ensenada and check it out in person. If you're still convinced that you're making a mistake, take an extra day or two to enjoy Ensenada, then go back home. Look at it like a mini-vacation. But I really think you'll decide to go if you'll just give yourselves the chance to check it out."

His arguments were very upbeat, perhaps a little pleading. Kurt looked at Madison with a questioning lift of his eyebrows. "What do you think?"

She shrugged. "Okay, we'll go as far as Ensenada."

"Great!" Larry enthused. "I know you won't be sorry."

Chapter Two

Three days later they were on their way to Ensenada. Upon arrival, they parked in the nearly empty parking lot of the Ramada Inn and went inside. Directed to a large room setup for reception of the cruise passengers, about thirty people stood around in isolated little groups talking quietly.

Looking for anyone that seemed to be in charge, Kurt and Larry focused on a man of medium stature with his back turned to them. He wore what appeared to be a nautical cap. Approaching him from the side, Larry got right to the point.

"Hi. Are you Captain Ellis?"

The man gave an engaging smile, pleasant, and sincere. Everything else about him seemed very ordinary: medium build, medium height, light brown hair, indistinguishable brown eyes, and a quiet, unassuming voice. "Yes, I am Captain Ellis, but please call me Herb. And you are?"

Reaching out and clutching his extended hand, Larry exclaimed, "I'm Larry Decker. This is my brother Kurt."

Larry stood about two-inches taller than Kurt, with broad shoulders, a narrow waist, and an abundance of freckles. His dark brown eyes always seemed to shine, almost blackly; and his infectious laugh came easily and rather loudly. Often he laughed at things that nobody else seemed to find funny, or understand, but that did not seem to matter to Larry.

"Larry, Kurt, I'm happy to meet you both. Please make yourselves comfortable." Pointing to a nearby table, Captain Ellis continued, "There are soft drinks in that bin. There are also cookies and chips in the basket.

Help yourselves, and please introduce yourselves to some of the others. I will be speaking with all of you shortly." He turned back to the two other men, resuming their conversation.

Larry and Kurt went back over to Marcos and Madison. "Well," Larry observed, "I think everything is going to be fine."

Looking around the room, Kurt could not help but wonder what brought these other individuals to this place. It was a very eclectic mix of humanity. The ratio of male to female appeared to be almost equal; but from there, the comparisons differed greatly. Some of the passengers were young, others middle-aged, and a few elderly. Some appeared well to do, or at least conveyed the attempt to look well off. Others appeared very middle class. This trip, thought Kurt, could be very interesting.

Turning toward a couple standing nearby, Kurt introduced himself by beginning, "Hi, I'm Kurt, this is Madison, Marcos, and Larry."

The couple appeared to be about thirty years old, casually dressed, and (like all the others) seemed to be unsure of the whole situation. Smiling, the young woman responded, "Hi, I'm Tiona, this is Charlie."

Kurt recognized immediately that Tiona took the lead role in the relationship. He saw her cat-like yellowish eyes roam from him to Larry, and then linger fixedly on Madison. Reaching up to flip a strand of her medium length auburn hair from her cheek, Tiona appraised Madison from head to toe, settling on her hair.

"Beautiful hair." she commented, her eyes roaming up and down Madison's body. "You are truly quite lovely."

Madison looked flustered, as if she did not know how to respond; so she quickly changed the subject. "Well, um… thank you. We are waiting to hear from the captain. He said he would be updating us all soon."

Kurt picked up immediately on the undertones of Tiona's interaction with Madison, thinking that it would be wise to try and steer clear of this one. He laughed lightly, attempting to alter the awkwardness of the moment and emphasize his possessiveness of Madison. "We," he intoned as he draped his arm comfortably around Madison's shoulder, "are also a little concerned about this whole venture. It seems there are a lot of unanswered questions. Hopefully, the captain will enlighten us all and help clarify some of the ambiguity surrounding this trip."

Tiona looked him over, as intently and purposefully as she had appraised Madison. "You appear to be in very good shape. Do you work out a lot?"

Trying to maintain his composure, Kurt responded casually, "No, I swim a lot. Play some hoops. But I don't really work out much." Turning, he changed the subject. "So Charlie, what's your line of work?"

Kurt could see that Charlie was not surprised by Tiona's brazenness. Slightly overweight, balding, with thick bristly eyebrows, the neck of a wrestler, and dim blue eyes, Charlie looked over at Kurt. Before he could answer, Tiona interjected, "Oh, he doesn't work. My mother left me a lot of money; so I take care of him."

Charlie nodded, looking to Tiona as if getting permission to speak. She gave him a small nod and Charlie turned back to Kurt. "Yeah, I must admit I've got it pretty good. She takes good care of me. We do a lot of traveling, and we have a nice home on the beach in La Jolla." Stopping as if he didn't want to say too much, Charlie looked back over at Tiona.

"Yes, Charlie, I do take good care of you." She smiled.

Before anything further could be said, a sharp ringing resounded through the reception hall. Captain Ellis was tapping a spoon against the rim of a tall glass. He looked around the room, his reassuring smile infectious.

"Welcome. I know a lot of you have questions. Please bear with me for a few minutes, and I will update all of you on where things currently stand and what we expect. I will also attempt to answer any questions you may have." Pausing for a moment, he turned to a pleasant looking woman standing nearby. Crooking his finger, he beckoned her to his side.

The woman was everybody's girl next door and a female reflection of Captain Ellis. She stood about five foot four, with light brown hair and brown eyes, wore little makeup, but conveyed an all-around combination of both womanliness and young girl innocence.

"Allow me to introduce my wife Dawn. Dawn will be accompanying us on the trip, cooking meals, planning activities, and helping with all of the daily shipboard duties."

He turned back to the gathering. "I want to thank you all for coming. First of all, I apologize for the change of departure point and the delay. The delay was unavoidable due to a severe gale off the coast of Central

California. As for the change from San Diego to Ensenada, the immigration officials in San Diego were simply being difficult. There are no problems here in Ensenada, and we fully expect to depart on schedule tomorrow morning. Of course, as some of you are aware, the ship has not docked here in Ensenada just yet; but we are expecting it to arrive at any time."

This comment elicited a low grumble from the people in the room. Captain Ellis raised his hands, open palmed, to try and calm the reaction. "There is absolutely nothing to be concerned about. The crew stopped in San Diego Bay to refuel and take on a few more supplies. They should have completed all those tasks yesterday afternoon and gotten underway this morning."

He was interrupted. "Do you mean to say that you haven't heard from them yet?" asked a voice in the back of the room.

"No. But there is no phone aboard; and without a radio here at the hotel, our lines of communication are limited. I will personally make a visit to the Captain of the Port here in Ensenada Harbor and make contact with the boat as soon as I have answered all of your questions."

A bevy of hands went into the air, and numerous shouted questions became garbled in the uproar. Regaining control, Captain Ellis began slowly, reassuringly answering the barrage of questions. It soon became obvious that a small handful of people were completely disgruntled with the entire situation, and they were demanding their money back. Turning to Dawn, he asked her to take them aside and advise them how to go about requesting a full refund. Five individuals left the room with Dawn.

When the questions slowed to a few isolated inquiries, Captain Ellis excused himself to try and make contact with the ship. He promised to return within the hour, imploring the remaining guests to be patient and enjoy themselves. One of the men in the crowd asked that they be provided with cocktails while they waited. Captain Ellis somewhat reluctantly agreed to pay for up to two drinks per person.

Kurt, Madison, and Larry stuck together, moving from one little cluster of people to another, introducing themselves and trying to size-up and evaluate the others in the room. Marcos, always somewhat of a loner, excused himself and wandered off, ostensibly to find the restroom.

It soon became obvious that every single person in the room had some misgivings about the pending trip. Several of them commented that they were only waiting for the five people that had already backed-out to reassure them that refunds were being given. Shortly thereafter, when they were informed that refunds would only be done through the mail, their disgruntlement and suspicions grew stronger.

The anxiety and discontent in the room became almost palpable. As tensions mounted, Larry made the effort to calm the growing fervor. "Hey, everyone," he implored above the building din that continued to spread through the ranks of the uncertain crowd, "lets not jump to conclusions. The captain is trying to find out where the boat is; and once it gets here, everything should be fine."

"Yeah, right!" blurted an angry voice from beside the bar. "Those five people just found out that they will not get their money back like we were told. Who's to say whether they will ever get it? Or if we can too!"

Larry looked around. All of a sudden he was the focus of attention in a situation that he really had no control over. "Well," he remarked, "I really don't have any answers. But I'm excited about going on a five-week cruise to Jamaica and that's why we are all here. So let's at least give it a chance."

Thankfully, the lobby door opened, and Captain Ellis walked back into the room. "The boat is in the harbor now. It will be docking within minutes. If everyone will gather their things, we have taxis waiting outside to transport us all to the docks. I will get the porters to help any of you that may need assistance."

Uncertainty prevailed. At first, nobody moved. Then Larry turned to Madison and Kurt and started laughing. "Hey, that's great! Lets get our stuff and go checkout this boat."

There was little conversation. Nearly everyone in the large, expansive space seemed to be uncertain, but slowly the clusters of people began to gravitate toward their luggage. It was eerily quiet; but following Larry's lead and enthusiasm, snippets of muted conversation began to emerge. As the group moved outside to the waiting taxis, the prevailing sour mood eased. One by one the taxis were loaded and headed out for the six-block drive to the harbor.

∞

Kurt had to stifle a rueful smile as he gazed around Ensenada Harbor. It wasn't very impressive. Rotting fish smells permeated the atmosphere. Several rust-bleeding purse seiners and shrimpers were tied side-by-side along the quay. Piles of nets were haphazardly strewn all along the concrete landing.

On the end of the dock, its narrow bow extending into the bay, was tied an old wooden yacht. The *Explorer*, three hundred ninety-five gross tons, one hundred forty-seven feet long with a relatively narrow beam of twenty-three feet, ten inches, had obviously seen better days. She drafted eight feet, six inches, and was powered by twin, straight sixteen-cylinder diesel engines. Built in 1938 in Seattle as a luxury yacht, her double-planked cedar hull and ribs were still solid; but neglect was evident along her topsides and hull, despite a recent slapped-on coat of white paint.

Bleeders of rusting fasteners seeped down the sides of the hull; and in several locations, chunks of cedar had obviously been filled with a wood-filler. On her port side, a large section of rail stanchion was ripped loose, sloppily tied together with some grungy looking rope that looked like it had spent several months in a dirty bilge.

In her heyday, the ship must have cut a shapely figure. Her long, full-displacement hull carried the sleek lines of wooden yachts of that era; and the fine woodwork visible in the superstructure adhered to the craftsmanship of a long line of wooden shipbuilders. An indulgent extravagance for the upper class, the *Explorer* likely served to entertain many a fine socialite in her day. Quite obviously, she was now suffering from general neglect.

Madison looked questionably at Kurt. He lifted his brows in response, trying to read her thoughts. He accurately realized her anxiety was due to the condition and appearance of the 'luxury yacht' they were seeing for the first time. Taking her hand, Kurt murmured quietly, "Let's go take a closer look."

Chipped paint and flaking varnish exposed parts of the dark mahogany and teak rails and trim. A second deck had been added at some point. Unlike most of the ship, the add-on was of poor craftsmanship, constructed of plywood and rough-cut fir. The added structure was evidently built to add more decking and perhaps provide shade for the main deck. Had it been part of the original structure, it would likely have added character and usefulness to its lines; but built as it was, it detracted from the appearance. As they looked it over, both Madison and Kurt felt the same disillusionment that all of the other passengers must be feeling.

Captain Ellis stood at the rail. "Welcome to the *Explorer*." He addressed the approaching individuals. "Please come aboard. I realize that our fine little ship has been neglected somewhat over the years; but I assure you that she is sound, comfortable, and well maintained throughout the power-train system, which is the most essential element of any ship."

As he waved them aboard, the intrepid group followed him gingerly across the gangway and onto the main deck. He opened the cabin door to the main salon and stepped inside.

Unlike the outside of the ship, the main salon looked quite impressive. Beautiful wooden cabinets, counters, tables, and nautical furnishings filled the large and comfortable lounge area. Paintings of ships at sea and tropical islands hung from the walls. Polished brass portholes, counter rails, and door and cabinet hinges lent another touch of comforting ambiance to the room. Captain Ellis looked around at their faces as they took in the impressive décor of the main lounge, then he moved to another doorway on the starboard side of the ship. Opening the doorway and fastening it open with a bronze latch, he beckoned the group to follow.

Moving into another space that was slightly larger and setup with three impressive mahogany tables, Captain Ellis announced, "This is the dining hall. We will be serving daily meals at precisely eight a.m., twelve-thirty p.m., and six-thirty p.m., starting this evening. Please feel comfortable in casual attire; however, we do request that shirts and shoes or sandals be worn in the dining room."

He paused and looked around at the expectant faces. "I realize that all of you are wondering about sleeping quarters and accommodations. Unfortunately, we do not have cabins for all, but there is more than enough room on the main and upper decks for everyone. Once we are in the tropics, I do believe that most of you will prefer the upper deck where it will be much cooler for sleeping. There are eight staterooms aboard. Four of those have individual bunks. The other four have a double-size berth. Those cabins are below the main deck. Additionally, we have cleared out two storage rooms in the aft quarter of the ship that have adequate space for two individual berths. There will be an additional charge of one hundred dollars for the enclosed cabins. I would suggest all of you wander around the cabin areas and go to the upper deck and inspect the areas that have been set aside for sleeping quarters. I will go below decks; and Dawn will go above to answer your questions."

For the next hour, the ship bustled with activity as every one of the thirty passengers inspected the ship and talked amongst themselves about the obviously limited accommodations. There were several couples aboard, Kurt and Madison among them. There were also two families, one family with two teenage boys, and a middle-aged woman with a twelve year-old grandson. A consensual agreement was reached that conceded two of the staterooms to those families. Two other couples, one in their mid-sixties, the other a pretentious looking pair dressed in gaudy outfits and draped with layers of flashy jewelry, demanded their own private quarters or they would not stay.

Kurt and Madison staked out an area on the top deck above the fantail that looked suitable for a pair of deck mattresses. It was partially closed-off on three sides, with enclosed rail standards providing a forty-inch barrier of semi-privacy. The fourth side was open toward the stern, on the opposite side of the stairwell. Kurt's biggest concern was that they would not have enough privacy. Madison expressed similar concerns.

Larry identified his own space on the forward upper deck on the port side of the exhaust stack. Marcos chose the opposite space on the starboard side of the stack. Other passengers selected areas on both the main deck and the upper deck that they felt would provide as much comfort and privacy as possible.

For all, the general consensus was 'you get what you pay for'—and five hundred dollars for five weeks at sea, with meals, was certainly a bargain.

∞

By five p.m., everyone had selected a spot on the boat, loaded their luggage, and resolved to try and make the most of what they would be living with for the next five weeks. Nearly all of the thirty passengers had gathered on the top deck where plank benches and about a dozen folding lawn chairs were setup. Most were drinking; and some had been drinking all day.

There was still grumbling from some guests about the condition of the boat, the overall accommodations, and the delays.

At precisely six-thirty, one of the deckhands bounded up the stairwell and announced, "Dinner is ready."

Everyone migrated to the dining room where Dawn had prepared a tasty stew, sourdough bread, and a salad. After the meal, most of the passengers went to their 'private areas' to try and establish some sort of a 'nest' for themselves and, if they had one, their partner.

Kurt had secured a couple of plastic milk crates to use as 'cabinets'. He secured them to the rail stanchion with a piece of line to prevent them from sliding around in the event of rough seas once they were underway. Placing their mats side by side, they lay down next to each other and talked quietly about the day, the odd mix of people aboard the *Explorer*, and their 'new home' for the next five weeks. For the most part, they remained philosophical and in good spirits. They, as well as the others aboard, were not pleased to discover that two of the four restrooms (heads) aboard the boat were unusable. That created an extremely uncomfortable and awkward dilemma for nearly all aboard, but particularly the ladies. Captain Ellis reassured everyone that the problem was temporary and would be repaired the next day.

At midnight, the ship was quiet. Everyone had settled into their own individual spaces for the night, several of them passed-out drunk.

∞

In the morning, Kurt awakened to the sound of diesel engines and working machinery. The sun was not yet up, but it was light enough to see. Several of the commercial fishing boats were getting underway, firing their engines and lifting nets from the docks onto their vessels. He looked over at Madison. She slept soundly.

Kurt climbed out of his sleeping bag and went quietly to the lower deck to use the toilet. Nobody else moved around yet, although there was one gentleman sitting in the main salon staring out at the harbor. Kurt approached and said, "Good morning, I'm Kurt."

"Hi, Kurt," the man responded, pointing toward the counter where a large stainless steel coffee maker emanated a fine mist of steam and the rich aroma of fresh brewed coffee, "Want a cup of coffee?"

Kurt picked up a cup and filled it about three-fourths full. "Is there any milk or cream?" he asked.

"In the refrig against the wall," the man answered.

Kurt filled the remaining one-fourth cup with milk, sipping to keep it from spilling.

"So, what's your name?" Kurt asked the man, as he sat down on one of the comfortable lounge chairs.

"I'm Sam. Sam Gilford."

Sam had a ruddy complexion, short-cropped reddish hair, and appeared, from his sitting position, to be quite tall. His voice carried a deep, resonating southern drawl that indicated he was from perhaps Texas, or one of the gulf coast states.

"Good to meet you, Sam," Kurt replied. "What brings you aboard this ship?"

Sam cocked his head slightly. "Well, Kurt, like most everyone else that's here, I reckon I was just ready for an adventure and thought I'd found a good deal." He paused briefly. "Now I suppose, like many of you, I'm not so sure about this whole thing."

Before Kurt could respond, Sam continued, "Of course, I'm not complaining too much, nor giving up. I think this journey could be a whole lot of fun if things work out. Besides, I'm a trucker. Just finished a run that kept me on the road for nearly three straight months; and I'm ready for a little break. How about you and the little gal?"

Obviously, Sam had seen Kurt and Madison together the day before.

Kurt smiled pensively before replying, "About the same, I guess. My brother told us about this opportunity. We didn't have any major commitments; and it sounds like we thought about the same things you did. Now I suppose we also have the same questions and wonder if we made the right decision."

"Oh," Sam drawled, "I wouldn't be too concerned about the decision. This cruise could be something special."

Before Kurt could respond, Captain Ellis walked into the cabin. "Good morning, gentlemen," he greeted them. "Glad to see you found the coffee and have made yourselves at home." Filling a cup for himself, the captain was dressed in coat and tie, not the attire one would expect aboard the ship.

Remaining standing, he turned to the two men seated in the lounge area. "Could you do me a favor?" the captain asked. "Would you tell my wife Dawn, when she comes out, that I have gone to the Immigration Office to secure clearance out of the port?"

"Sure," Kurt responded. "Is there anything else that we can do to help?"

Captain Ellis flashed his charming smile. "Well as a matter of fact, if you wouldn't mind, my deckhands Phillip and Paul should be coming out soon. Can you give them this list of projects and let them know that I'll be back as soon as I can?" He handed Kurt a sheet of paper with several things written in a neat, numbered manner.

"Sure. Whatever we can do to help," Kurt replied, taking the paper and setting it down on the deeply varnished tabletop.

They watched the captain walk out the door and down the gangway. Sam turned to Kurt, and commented, "Well, looks like we won't be leaving Ensenada first thing this morning after all."

∞

As the morning progressed, others began to join them in the salon. The word quickly spread that they would not be departing early, as previously thought. Once again there was grumbling.

A while later, Dawn and Phillip brought a heaping dish of scrambled eggs with sautéed onions, mushrooms, and avocados to the table. While Dawn served the tasty dish, Phillip informed the group that they were expecting Captain Ellis back before noon, and the ship would depart soon thereafter. In the meantime, he asked if anyone was willing to help out with a couple of projects that he would be starting after breakfast.

Several men in the group agreed to help out with the work, offering their own individual skills in order to make things better for everyone. One of the passengers, a retired plumber traveling with his ex-schoolteacher wife, offered to work on the heads. Another gentleman worked as an electrical contractor and agreed to help Gus, the Chief Engineer, repair the windlass. Kurt and Marcos offered to put together a couple of showers on the second deck.

At noon, there was still no sign of Captain Ellis. The gaudily dressed couple that had boarded the *Explorer* decided they had had enough of the whole thing and informed Dawn that they were leaving the ship. As with the other five that opted out at the Ramada Inn, they were informed that there was no immediate refund available; but they were given a phone number and a contact person in San Diego.

During lunch, Dawn informed the remaining twenty-eight passengers that Captain Ellis was still encountering problems with immigration officials. She assured all that he was doing his very best to resolve the issues and expected to be underway before the end of the day. She suggested that it would be okay to leave the boat for a few hours, but to be back aboard not later than four p.m.

A number of the passengers went ashore to pick up some last minute supplies (especially more booze), or to visit the fabled Hussong's Cantina on Avenida La Primera, the main street running through Ensenada. Afterward they returned to the ship with a tequila-buzz, as well as some memorable images from Hussong's.

Everyone was back aboard by four, anxiously awaiting any sign of Captain Ellis. Meanwhile, Dawn had withdrawn to her cabin, evidently weary from the constant barrage of questions and concerns voiced by the people on board. Paul and Phillip, the hard-working and dedicated deckhands, continued to perform maintenance and make repairs to the ship. Nearly all of the passengers sat around on lounge chairs on the second deck, talking amongst themselves about their personal lives and backgrounds while, for the most part, avoiding the lingering doubts about their impending journey.

At five p.m., Captain Ellis rushed up the gangway, and barked instructions to Phillip and Paul to prepare to cast off. Evidently, the *Explorer* was finally going to depart.

Kurt, who had been working with Phillip to complete a few minor details on the deck showers, offered to help cast off. He worked with Phillip to hoist the gangway, and then jumped onto the dock to release the mid-ship spring lines from the dock bollards. Paul and the chief engineer, Gus Thomas, were below starting the engines and checking instruments. Tossing the bow and stern lines over the rails, Phillip and Kurt jumped up onto the gunnels; and the ship was finally (with great relief from everyone) on her way to Jamaica. No one had an inkling of what lie ahead.

CHAPTER THREE

Departing the Port of Ensenada, Captain Ellis seemed somewhat nervous. He glanced repetitively at shore, as if expecting something. His urgency to depart left Kurt wondering if there might be a problem. However, as the vessel slowly picked up speed and churned through the murky waters of Bahia de Todos Santos, a sense of relief and excitement filled the air.

The *Explorer* cruised at about eight knots. Fitted with twin-screw straight-sixteen cylinder diesels, the propellers rotated directly from the flywheel without the benefit of reduction gears. From stationary to cruising speed required about a half-mile of distance, as did coming to a stop. Fitted with a single rudder, maneuverability was also somewhat lessened due to the absence of prop wash directly onto the rudder stem. Those limitations meant little when at sea but would pose challenges when docking or transiting in confined waterways.

Kurt, Madison, Larry, and Marcos stood on the bow of the vessel with about a dozen others, gazing out to sea. In the distance, the two small islands of Todos Santos soon came into view. On the larger of the two islands, a dilapidated lighthouse cast an occasional, muted flash of light. Moderate Pacific swells could be seen breaking on the rocky northwest shore, tossing spray onto the rocks from the light onshore breezes. A low haze blanketed the horizon, blending the sea and sky into one. The prevailing winds blew over the starboard bow and created a wind chill factor that dropped the temperature to the low sixties. Kurt left the foredeck briefly to get sweatshirts for him and Madison. Most of the others did the same.

Rounding the northern end of Islas Todos Santos, they changed course toward the south. Once out of the bight of the wide, expansive bay, it wasn't long before the coloration of the sea changed from a murky green to the deep blue of the Pacific. With the sun dropping in the western sky, a purplish hue spread across the horizon and onto the surface of the ocean.

The mood on board was electric. Gone were the furrowed eyebrows of consternation that had prevailed earlier, replaced with eager expressions of anticipation and wonder. For many, it was the first time out on the open ocean. On the port side of the boat, the low distant outline of Punta Banda and the Baja Peninsula merged into the sea, a fine white line marking the surf zone. In the background, the darkening shadows of the imposing Sierra Juarez mountain range lent a desolate image to the scenery. Cruising downwind, the temperature, though unchanged, felt warmer, infusing the feeling of a definite change in the air. The trip to Jamaica was underway and, at least for now, there was no turning back.

As the sun dipped below the horizon, its yellow/orange glow lingered for a while. Temperatures dropped, and most of the passengers moved inside to the salon.

Slow rolling Pacific swells pushed the vessel on its way, gently rocking the ship as the waves rolled under her hull. Several people on board felt the nauseous pangs of seasickness beginning to form. For a few, the mix of the ship rolling, together with their consumption of alcohol compounded their discomfort, sending them to the rail, or the nearest head to relieve themselves of their daily food and beverage intake.

At six-thirty, Dawn rang the dinner bell. Table fare for the evening was thick-sliced roast beef with mashed potatoes and whole kernel corn. One rogue swell disrupted the meal, causing a large dish of corn to slide off the tabletop and crash to the teak deck. Paul pulled out the broom and mop and cleaned up the mess.

After dinner, Captain Ellis joined the passengers in the dining hall. He addressed the group, "I know this has been trying for most of you, and I want you to know that I appreciate your tolerance and forbearance. Now that we are underway, there are a few things that everyone needs to know and comply with. Unfortunately, we lost a couple of crew members in northern California; so we are short-staffed. If anyone among you might be willing to help out with some of the operational duties on the ship, it would be much appreciated. We could use some help with standing watches and with periodic engine oiling. In addition, Dawn will be sorely taxed in trying to prepare all of the meals with only one galley helper available." He paused and looked expectantly around the room.

"I'd be willing to help out with the engine room in any way that I can," offered Sam. "I'm knowledgeable about diesel engines and don't have much else to do while we're underway. I reckon I could do about anything that might help."

Captain Ellis thanked Sam then turned back to the others. "Anyone else that could help?" he asked.

Kurt spoke up. "I've spent a lot of time on boats and on the water. I would be more than willing to help out with watches or assisting with routine things on the boat. My only request is that I have free time to check out some of the places we visit along the way."

"Of course," stated Captain Ellis. "We would not expect you or anyone to commit any of your time while we are in port. Once we have cleared Customs at our various destinations, all of you will be free to leave the ship and explore at your leisure. Obviously, we will have deadlines and schedules to adhere to. Beyond that, your own time is your choice completely."

Both Larry and Marcos chipped in to let the captain know that they too would help out with things, admitting to having little experience aboard anything bigger than a ski-boat.

A few others volunteered to assist in various ways, although most admitted a complete ignorance of most things nautical. Madison and a young woman named Sally offered to help in the galley. Sally, on board with her boyfriend Peter, informed Dawn that she had lived in a commune for several years in Big Sur, California, where she helped to prepare meals and run the kitchen for about forty communal dwellers. She also volunteered Peter's help, although he was currently below decks suffering from seasickness.

Captain Ellis then went on to inform the group of a few safety precautions, imploring everyone to always be careful, and in the event of rough seas, to refrain from going on deck alone, or moving about the ship needlessly. He also informed everyone where the life-saving equipment was stored: life-jackets, flares, man-overboard rings, the two small skiffs that were on the foredeck, and three foam rafts attached to the overhead canopy that were rated at a twelve-man capacity. All things considered, if anything serious should happen and the ship needed to be abandoned, the life-saving gear was minimal.

Soon the group started to disperse. A few of the passengers along with Captain Ellis adjourned to the main salon. Once there, the group talked in more detail about watches and other ship duties. For Captain Ellis and First Mate Leonard Fitzpatrick—the two men responsible for the running of the ship— their hours would be long and strenuous. Beginning that first night at sea, Kurt, Larry, Marcos, and Charlie would divide helm watches into two hours on, eight hours-off shifts. Captain Ellis and Leonard would each carry eight-hour shifts until they were comfortable that the others learned the nuances of standing watch, and then one or the other of them would always be on-call.

Kurt's first watch was the midnight to two a.m. shift—one of the worst. At ten-thirty, when the group dispersed, there wasn't much sense in trying to sleep before his shift started. He went up to the second deck and found Madison seated in one of the lounge chairs talking with another female. They were both bundled up in fuzzy, dark gray shipboard blankets, warding off the cool night air. Both had their knees curled onto their chests and had their hair bundled into woolen caps.

"Hi, Kurt," Madison said, "This is Linda."

"Hi, Linda," Kurt offered his hand, impressed with the firmness of her handshake.

There was a brief moment of uncertainty in the air. Kurt realized that he had interrupted a conversation of some sort; so he made an effort to back out gracefully. "Excuse me, I didn't mean to interrupt."

"No. No. That's okay," Linda responded affably, "We were just talking about how much more difficult it is for us girls to try and adjust to this shipboard thing. We're used to having our own private spaces, bathrooms and mirrors, and all the things that a girl usually has for making herself pretty and for doing the personal things that we like and need to do."

Kurt flashed a grin. "I totally understand. I know it's easier for us guys, but in time, I think we'll all find ways to adjust to the inconveniences. In the meantime, it's a lot like camping out, except that here there is almost always someone standing in line waiting to use the head. The point is, I think that we all expected better accommodations when we signed up for this cruise."

Linda nodded, "Yeah, I think we did."

Linda's beauty exuded the dark, sensual characteristics of her Mediterranean heritage. Kurt had noticed her several times prior to this meeting, but had not yet had the opportunity to talk to her. She gave Madison and Kurt a brief background of her life.

Her grandparents had emigrated from Italy to New York City, and both her mother and father were of pure Italian descent. An only child, they had raised her in downtown New York, where her parents ran a small bakery and Italian sausage shop. Growing up in a devout Catholic home, she had gone to a small, private Catholic school and had lived a rather strict, severe childhood, rarely mingling with other children. After graduation from high school, Linda attended and earned a Bachelor's Degree in Design from the City University of New York, landing a job in fashion design with a distant uncle. She looked at this sea-going venture as an eye-opening experience.

They sat and chatted as the ship chugged steadily southward toward their first scheduled stop, Cedros Island. Between the rail cap and the overhead canopy, clusters of glittering stars filled the dark sky.

Linda explained that she was on board with her parents. At twenty-four, she had recently, and rather painfully, learned to live her own independent life. She and her parents had learned about the trip to Jamaica from a mutual friend; and since they were retired, and she was not deeply committed to anything special, thought it might be fun to travel together. She seemed to be a very intelligent woman, engaging and friendly, and the time passed easily as they talked.

Soon Kurt realized it was nearing midnight and time for his first watch. Leonard was on duty and greeted him with a handshake when he entered the wheelhouse. Charlie helped cover the ten p.m. to midnight watch; so they exchanged brief salutations before Charlie headed for his bunk.

Leonard didn't talk much, but he did show Kurt the basic duties for watch coverage. The ship was equipped with autopilot, making physical steerage unnecessary. Their course was currently set at one hundred sixty-eight degrees, cruising speed seven point nine knots, and distance to their next waypoint one hundred eighty-eight miles. Dashboard gauges were illuminated with dim internal red lights, minimizing the glow inside the cabin and maximizing visibility. Outside it was very dark. Ahead of the slightly elevated bow, the ocean reflected an occasional indistinct glow from the running lights. Except for the stars, there was nothing else to be seen. The drone of the engines and the muted sloshing of the hull as it ploughed softly into the two to three foot westerly swell was all there was to hear. Several times, Kurt attempted to engage Leonard in conversation, but each time his efforts were thwarted by Leonard's preoccupation with checking a gauge, the compass heading, or a prolonged visual sweep of the horizon.

Kurt decided to forego any further attempts at conversation until Leonard showed an interest in talking. Instead, he immersed himself in absorbing the strange and fascinating nuances of offshore cruising in the dark of night. Oddly enough, despite the lingering realization that they were nothing more than a tiny speck in the immensity of the ocean, the overall sensation was soothing and relaxing. An illusory sense of vastness prevailed. His thoughts wandered randomly, strayed briefly to personal things in his life, but returned always to the present and the vibrant emptiness of his immediate surroundings.

The time passed very quickly; and before Kurt knew it, Larry entered the cabin to assume his two to four a.m. watch. Kurt thanked Leonard for his time and information, to which he received a cursory nod. Shrugging his shoulders, Kurt left the helm and headed for his sleeping area.

Madison was sound asleep. He used the head, brushed his teeth, and crawled into his sleeping bag.

∞

Kurt slept through breakfast, a rarity for him. He was usually an early riser, awakening to the dawn and eager to start his day. Madison had made him an egg sandwich, wrapping it in a napkin. There was coffee available in the galley.

Overnight the swells had increased, although the duration between swells became longer and in effect improved the ride. By about ten a.m., the outlines of Cedros Island became visible; and by eleven-thirty, they were dropping anchor in the lee of the Island.

Isla Cedros, approximately two hundred fifty miles south of San Diego and thirty-five miles offshore, is one of the larger islands along the Baja coast, nearly twenty-four miles in length. Its dry and arid terrain looked rugged, covered extensively with the omnipresent cacti of the Mexican deserts. On the higher mountaintops, small stands of scrub juniper and wind-lashed pine dotted the skyline. Along the northeast shores, date palms lined parts of the coastal plains, transplanted from the mainland at some distant time. Numerous fish camps lie scattered around its shores.

In the cove where the *Explorer* dropped anchor, there wasn't much to see. A few clapboard shacks erected by transient fishermen dotted the dunes. Barking sea lions and elephant seals lolled lazily in the lee of the northern end of the cove.

Kurt had brought along two breakdown fishing rods and two reels, along with an assortment of lighter tackle and heavy gear for trolling. As soon as the ship settled onto the anchor, he rigged one of the rods with a leadhead jig and tipped it with a thin slice of chicken that he begged from the galley. Making a cast toward the nearest kelp bed, he hooked-up immediately and landed a fat five-pound calico bass. 'Awesome,' he thought to himself. If the fishing is going to be this good, we'll have plenty of fresh fish for meals. Unfortunately, that was not to be.

He and Larry fished for the next two hours and caught nothing more than a couple of very small bass, one tiny little turbot, and an even smaller sheephead. Not one of those fish was large enough to keep.

Around two p.m., after attending to periodic engine inspections, Captain Ellis ordered the anchor hoisted; and the ship was again underway.

After covering a midday watch, Kurt found himself seated in the salon with Madison, Larry, and a middle-aged woman named Emily. Emily was traveling with her nephew, a precocious twelve-year old from Arizona. He was in their cabin reading, his primary passion.

Emily was English, very conservative in appearance, and always conveyed a proper demeanor. As the group sat and chatted idly, she somewhat stoically and without preamble informed the room, "My ex-husband asked me to help him get his pecker up the first time we met."

Everyone in the room burst out in laughter. "Yes. That's correct," she continued, "but that was in Britain where the phrase 'get your pecker up' means to perk up your spirits. Of course, when we moved to America, we discontinued using that phrase because it carries a distinctively different meaning in the States." The others looked at her expectantly, assuming she would continue with some explanation of her off-the-wall comment; however, she had nothing further to say.

As the *Explorer* cruised southward, a distinctive change developed in the atmosphere. The air became much drier, and temperatures rose considerably. Sweatshirts and light jackets disappeared. Shorts replaced long pants on most of the passengers.

Rounding Punta Abrejojos, at roughly twenty-six degrees latitude, the first whales of the trip were sighted near the entrance to Bahia Balenas (Whale Bay). In late winter and early spring, between sixteen and eighteen thousand California Gray Whales make the roughly twelve thousand mile round-trip migration from the Arctic Circle to the calving grounds of Baja California. This annual migration is the longest of any animal on the planet, and the *Explorer* was arriving at the breeding grounds at the most opportune time of the year. Recognizing an opportunity to provide a diversion for his passengers, Captain Ellis ordered a change of course to nearby Scammon's Lagoon at the entrance to Bahia San Ignacio. Setting the anchor in the lee of Punta San Ignacio, the Captain asked who would like to go ashore to hike up to viewing areas where they could watch the whales 'doing their thing' in the shallow bay.

Nearly everyone aboard expressed a desire to go.

After launching the two aluminum skiffs, Captain Ellis informed the group that he and Phillip would operate the skiffs. He warned that although it looked manageable, the surf could be tricky; so he advised that gear such as cameras and other items of value be left aboard. Unfortunately, not everyone heeded his advice.

The first group, with Captain Ellis at the controls, had no problems accessing the beach, although it did require getting wet up to the waist. When Phillip made his approach to shore, he slightly misjudged the swell pattern, and the skiff was caught in the break. As it turned sideways on the rolling wave, two of the passengers panicked and decided they would try to jump out of the skiff. Their mistake was in trying to jump out on the down-swell side of the skiff, which not only put them in a position where the skiff could run into them as it propelled toward the beach, but it also imbalanced the small boat in such a manner that it caused it to broach. Tipping over onto its port side, the small skiff collided with the man who had jumped, then with the woman. Both were struck in the chest and attempted to fend-off; however, the weight of the skiff and the force of the water pushed them under, and they both disappeared beneath the wave as the skiff tumbled toward shore.

For a brief moment, the two passengers could not be seen, and those already on shore began to rush out into the surf to try and find them. Fortuitously, both of the dunked parties popped to the surface and signaled they were okay. Wading ashore, it was discovered that both had suffered minor scrapes but were otherwise uninjured.

Captain Ellis advised those on shore to bail the water from the skiff and push it out to his position. After a few minutes of bailing, the skiff was re-floated and pushed out to the other skiff, then towed back to the *Explorer*. As a result of the dunking, Captain Ellis also advised everyone that he would be discontinuing any further landings. He promised to return within the hour to pick up those already ashore.

∞

On the beach were twelve of the ship's passengers, including Marcos and Linda who had been on the second skiff that flipped in the surf. Those two decided that since they were already ashore, they would stay and explore, even though they were now all wet and had lost one camera (Linda had tried to take hers in a small bag).

In the past two days, Linda and Marcos had become interested in each other. Marcos, a biochemist by profession with curly red hair, thick glasses that he always wore, and a receding hairline, looked to be the antithesis of what one normally expected from the 'scientific-type.' His piercing blue eyes and habit of staring—without wavering—directly at those he spoke with, was unnerving for most people. He and Larry had gone to high school and college together, still shared an apartment in Huntington Beach, California, and remained best friends. Marcos was usually content to be alone, read scientific journals, and rarely do anything other than work, workout at the gym, or surf, his only recreational passion. He did have his surfboard along, anticipating that he might have opportunities along the way to engage in his favorite sport.

When Marcos first saw Linda at the dock in Ensenada, he felt intrigued, After she landed on the beach soaking wet, with her clothing clinging tightly to her body, he gaped in amazement at her voluptuous figure. At nearly six-feet tall, he was well aware that she was a large woman and seemed to possess a shapely figure, but seeing it revealed for the first time made him gasp. In the wet clothing with her full shape clearly outlined, she looked stunning; and he was left nearly breathless.

He felt a bit intimidated by her presence, thinking that she was very self-assured and confident. He had no idea that she actually considered herself unfeminine; with an unusually large and out of proportion figure that she considered an oddity. In reality, most men were so overwhelmed by her statuesque figure that they felt intimidated, and therefore rarely approached her, but almost always stared. It was the stares that made her feel as if she was an oddity.

"Wow," Marcos blurted, "You're incredible!" It was the perfect thing to say.

Linda looked at him closely and smiled broadly. "Thank you, Marcos."

He could not take his eyes off her body. She seemed fully aware that he was enthralled, and her eyes took on a feminine glow.

"Shall we get out of these wet clothes?" she asked. "I have a bathing suit on, how about you?"

Although diffident, Marcos felt very comfortable in Linda's presence. "No, I don't have my swim trunks with me; but I'd sure like to wring-out this wet shirt and soak up a little sunshine. If you want me to, I'll wring out your wet clothing for you."

Slowly, she began shedding her clothing, lifting the loose-fitting top over her head. Next, she slid the full skirt she wore over her broad hips and down to her ankles. Stepping out of the skirt and standing in her bikini, she looked at Marcos. His beaming face flushed. "Wow!" He shook his head from side to side as he said again, "Wow! I apologize for staring and making a fool of myself, but I've never seen anyone so beautiful."

Her olive skin radiated in the sunlight and her dark hair framed her classical Italian features. To Marcos she was a true vision, a vivid remarkable embodiment of what a woman should be. He was captivated.

He removed his shirt, exposing his own physique. Since high school, when he became absorbed with the fascinating world of chemistry and biology and became known as a bookworm, Marcos had determined to get into good shape. He began working out at the local gym, pumping iron and honing his body. On weekends, he went to the beach to surf, spending hours cultivating his skills at the pier in Huntington Beach and below the oilrigs along Pacific Coast Highway. The results were impressive. His chest, covered almost completely in fuzzy red curls, was well defined. He shaved regularly, always removing his shirt and shaving to an area just above his collarbones so that a distinct line of shaved/unshaved hair arced from shoulder to shoulder, almost as if it were a collar of its own. His muscular arms, covered from the wrist to the shoulder in a thick matt of curly red hair, had turned golden from the sun. His hours at the beach gave his skin a burnished glow, and Linda seemed impressed with his physicality.

They wandered casually around the desolate shoreline, chatting comfortably about their impressions of the trip they had embarked upon. Both of them seemed oblivious to the harshness and desolation of their surroundings as they walked hand in hand over the dry cactus-dotted terrain—almost as if they were on a casual stroll through a verdant park.

Lost as they were in their own world of discovery, Marcos and Linda eventually decided they should join the others, who as a group had wandered over a series of nearby sand dunes and disappeared from their view. Backtracking to the point where they had shed their wet clothing, they gathered their clothes and traipsed up the sand. When they reached the crest, they saw the others standing together about one hundred yards away. The others were absorbed in watching something in the distance.

Both Linda and Marcos gasped as, not more than two hundred yards away, a large gray whale rose into the air, its mottled grey shape shooting skyward until twisting, it crashed back into the water with a massive splash that sent wavelets spreading outward. Again the animal rose, higher than before, its long angular pectoral fins spread like small wings from its rippled torso. Again it crashed back into the bay, sending out yet another circular wave that spread for several hundred yards before dissipating.

For the next half-hour, the passengers from the *Explorer* stood atop the sandy dune and watched the antics of dozens of California Gray Whales as they splashed and cavorted in the warm waters of Scammon's Lagoon. To see the magnificent creatures spy hopping, breeching, and seemingly having a wonderful time was quite inspiring for the entire group.

Captain Ellis had given them only an hour to stay ashore. Someone suggested they should probably return to the beach. Once there, to everyone's dismay, the currents had changed; as a result, the surf appeared more treacherous. When Captain Ellis approached the surf-line, he was reluctant to attempt the beach landing. As the skiff bobbed atop the swell just outside of the breaking surf, a panga fisherman arrived on scene.

Mexico has an abundance of panga fishing skiffs plying beaches and bays along the Baja coast, its islands, and on the mainland coast. The pangas are ideally suited for moderate surf launches, their flat bottoms, long narrow hulls, and high bows allowing them to traverse in and out of the surf zone with relative ease.

In his adequate Spanish, Captain Ellis explained that the dozen people on shore were from his ship anchored nearby and they had already swamped one of their skiffs during a launching effort. He made a deal with the grinning fisherman to ferry the group off the beach in the panga. Two uneventful trips later, everyone was back on board the ship, and the panga fisherman was one hundred Pesos, two T-shirts, and a Dodger baseball cap richer.

∞

Back onboard, Marcos and Linda told Larry, Kurt, and Madison about their adventure on shore. All three had missed the excursion, expecting to go ashore on one of the runs that were cancelled. As they listened to the animated story of the beach swamping and the subsequent discovery of the frolicking whales, both Kurt and Madison realized that there was another story developing: the infatuation between Marcos and Linda.

As the group chatted amiably on the foredeck, Captain Ellis rang the ship's bell, indicating a meeting of the crew and passengers. With most of the passengers already assembled on the foredeck, Captain Ellis informed everyone that fresh water supplies were extremely diminished due to overuse, and water rationing would be required until they reached the next port. The rationing edict limited water use to about a gallon per person per day until the ship's tanks could be filled in Cabo San Lucas about twenty hours away—if everything went smoothly.

His announcement was not well received. Six of the passengers had been tossed into the sea during the swamping episode and felt they needed showers. Others in the group had plunged into the water simply because it was inviting. They too wanted to take showers. When he informed them that there simply was not enough fresh water for anything more than drinking and cooking, the entire ship was in an uproar. He explained that there simply had been too much water used, despite his admonitions during the introductory briefing when they first boarded the ship. Many in the group began to protest, claiming they had used water sparingly and under the guidelines he had given; but they soon realized they had no choice other than to comply.

∞

As they departed Scammon's Lagoon, Kurt and Madison pulled a couple of deck chairs onto the bow and sat together quietly staring out onto the ocean. For Kurt, being on the water was nothing new. He had spent many days fishing along the southern California coastline and near the Channel Islands, as well as taking a few overnight fishing trips below the border in Mexican waters. But he had never spent successive days at sea. Madison had done very little boating, just a couple of short day trips with Kurt, in and around Redondo Beach on small boats.

Sitting there on the bow of the boat gazing out into the endless blue sunshine along the Baja Coast, they each slipped into a pensive mood, quietly absorbing the seeming emptiness of the vast Pacific. But for both of them, the scene was anything but empty.

Kurt pondered the expansive panorama of the ocean, the sky, and the few streaks of contrasting white stratus clouds that hung suspended in the unending vastness. Kurt could feel the ocean like a feminine presence, her breath pulsating softly in sync with the slow, undulating pulse of the southerly swells. Like an everlasting canvas painted by a master artist, the scene filled him with a profound sense of wholeness and awareness.

His thoughts encompassed the wonders of life, the enormity of nature, and the role that man plays in the vast scheme of life and death. He was mesmerized and felt fulfilled and stimulated. A warm feeling of belonging and gratification coursed through his veins, filling him with hope and love. He glanced over at Madison. She sat staring out to sea, as he did.

Madison also seemed absorbed by the vast expanse of the ocean. She stared at the horizon, but a furrow creased her brow. Her eyes darted back and forth between the dazzling sea surface and the curling white tips of the bow-wake rolling endlessly from the prow and disappearing beneath the hull. She looked somewhat daunted and intimidated. Without realizing it and despite the warmth of the sun, she shuddered and wrapped her arms tightly around herself.

She turned toward Kurt and saw him gazing fixedly upon her. Smiling almost forlornly she whispered, "This sure is overwhelming, isn't it?"

Kurt laughed lightly. "Overwhelming?" He replied after considering her comment. "No. I don't think it's overwhelming at all. Maybe awe inspiring, or maybe even arousing, but not overwhelming."

Madison looked back at Kurt and stated. "It just makes me feel so small. It's just so immense, and it makes me feel small and vulnerable."

He slid his chair a little closer to hers and leaned over to wrap his arm around her shoulder. Kurt spoke to her softly. "I recognize what you're saying. I just don't see it the same way." He paused briefly in order to respond without putting her on the defensive or seem condescending. "The ocean, for me, is a soothing influence. I feel whole and alive out here. When I look around, I see much more than just water and sky. I feel as if I am looking into an unfolding story that encompasses the past, the present, and the future. It makes me feel larger than life and strong. It makes me feel manly."

Kurt breathed deeply and looked at Madison.

She smiled wanly, nodded almost imperceptibly, and looked back out to sea. "I can see that, Kurt, and I think I have a sense of what you are saying and feeling. It's what makes you who you are, and it helps me to appreciate why you love the ocean like you do. However, it is still intimidating to me. I hope that as we continue on this trip and see and experience more, then perhaps I will eventually begin to see and understand the affinity that you feel for the ocean. But for now, I feel very small."

Kurt nodded and stroked her long, golden hair. "It is a huge thing, this ocean, and it does tend to be intimidating at times; but it is also very peaceful, very beautiful, and very inspiring. I hope that with time you really will come to appreciate it like I do."

They sat together quietly, looking out at the ocean. The endless swells rolled languidly beneath the boat. The horizon formed an obscure but distinctive separation between sea and sky. The sunlight danced lightly across the rippled plane of the shimmering ocean.

He slipped his arm around her waist. Kurt felt strong, powerful, and protective of the fragile young woman with her fingers involuntarily digging into his brown forearm. He could see that she seemed confused and exposed, and he hoped that she would get used to being at sea.

∞

Kurt had shown himself to be fully competent and qualified for shipboard duties; and both Captain Ellis and Leonard considered him capable of overseeing a watch without their needing to always be there. On his ten to midnight helm-watch, he relieved Captain Ellis, who informed him of the compass heading, and told him to rouse him from his cabin if anything out of the ordinary occurred.

Charlie served as the second man on watch and was unusually quiet. For the next two hours, Kurt reveled in the pleasure he derived from standing watch. He felt fulfilled when he was at the helm, aware of the responsibility of the position, the all-pervading enormity of the ocean, and the wondrous authenticity of nature.

At midnight when Leonard and Guillermo arrived for relief, Kurt made the customary exit entry in the Ship's Log, noting the sighting of a single set of running lights that eventually disappeared to the west as the only incident of the watch. He bid Leonard and Guillermo goodnight, took care of his evening rituals, and curled up next to Madison.

When he awakened in the morning, Madison was gone. He went to the dining area where most of the passengers and crew sat at the tables, eating pancakes.

"Good morning Kurt." The calls rang out from several individuals.

"Coffee's hot, and there's plenty of batter left," called Madison. "How many will you eat?" She stood at the stovetop in a white apron, helping with the morning meal.

Looking at the generous size of the cakes stacked up on a couple of plates, Kurt replied, "How about three?"

"Your wish is my command," Madison responded, using a tone and a penetrating look that seemed to convey a deeper meaning.

After breakfast as the *Explorer* steamed southward, a rare pod of sperm whales was sighted about half a mile away, their peculiar blunt heads distinctive even from that distance. Frigate birds circled high above the placid sea and plunged like rockets toward the surface as they spotted potential prey. They abruptly pulled up from their dives just before hitting the water; but every once in a while, they could be seen plucking an unsuspecting fish from the sea with long extended talons. When they captured a meal, they soared back into the sky where they often encountered another frigate or two trying to take their catch away, high up in the atmosphere. Often the birds dropped the catch, which plummeted downward only to be plucked from the sky again, either by the frigate that dropped it or by one of the others attempting to steal the meal. The antics appeared to be an airborne game, testing the birds' agility and stealth. It was fascinating and mesmerizing.

Below the twenty-fourth parallel, south of Magdalena Bay, Larry and Kurt set heavy trolling lines off the stern of the ship. Using three-hundred pound test manila line rigged with one-hundred-eighty pound monofilament leaders, two large tuna feathers with large treble hooks were set about twenty yards off the stern. Using two bicycle inner tubes tied together as a shock cord, they guessed that the rigs were heavy enough to handle fish up to about thirty pounds. Since the ship could not reasonably stop to pull fish in, anything larger than about thirty pounds would likely snap the lines, straighten out the hooks, or rip the jaws right out of a fish's mouth.

Late that afternoon, the wind picked-up from the west, and the air chilled. Jackets and sweatshirts were pulled out of bags and storage areas. A general disgruntlement continued to prevail. The biggest complaint was the lack of water; but food supplies were also diminishing, and meals were becoming less appetizing. Starchy foods were the predominant table fare—simple dishes with various forms of pasta or potatoes. All of the fresh fruit was gone, as was all of the fresh milk. Someone dubbed the *Explorer* the 'Ship of Fools,' a popular movie that had recently graced the big screen. Nerves were beginning to fray, and attitudes were getting ugly. There was a distinct faction of extremely unhappy passengers, and then there were those that were enjoying the cruise despite the problems and limitations aboard ship. It didn't help that the winds were up and the seas were becoming rougher than at any point thus far. Several people became seasick. To make matters worse, something in the food did not settle well with about half the people on board. There were several suffering from diarrhea. It was not a pretty picture.

Throughout a rocky-rolling night, the vessel slogged its way down the Baja Peninsula. Both Kurt and Larry had to forego their helm watches due to their frequent need to use the toilet. That left the helm watches to Leonard and Captain Ellis, although they too were suffering from the turistas epidemic.

∞

At daybreak, the rugged and picturesque tip of Baja California came into view, a scenic vista that is one of the most photogenic landscapes in the world. The fabled Cabo Arch stood majestically at Lands End, the turquoise colored surf roiling in and out of its jagged contours.

As the ship rounded the tip of the peninsula and entered the bay, all aboard marveled at the wide expanse of brilliant white sand beach that stretched nearly uninterrupted for miles in an easterly direction. Tucked under the austere bluffs that tapered ruggedly toward the Baja tip, several more isolated little beaches sloped into the turquoise waters. Above the high jagged peaks of the craggy hills, frigate birds soared on the updrafts that formed where the deep waters of the Pacific met the calmer wind-protected waters of the Sea of Cortez. The tiny settlement of Cabo San Lucas baked under the warm tropical sunshine, its silhouette low and unassuming against the stark contrast of the surrounding desert and mountains.

The town appeared to be quiet and sleepy, with only a few trucks, busses, and autos moving on the dusty roadway that led off toward the northeast. At the base of one of the stark appendages that lead to 'Lands End,' an imposing concrete structure graced the shoreline, its chalky looking walls broken only by a few small windows. A long wooden pier adjacent to the building led into a murky embayment. Inshore of that pier, several rusting pieces of marine equipment belched smoke into the air, their un-muffled diesel engines clanging loudly as they worked to dredge out what was destined to become Cabo's new small craft marina.

Everyone aboard the ship stood on deck, roused by the boisterous clamor of the port.

Captain Ellis ordered the anchor dropped in about forty feet of water. He put a radio call out on Channel 16 to the Captain of the Port, who advised him to keep everyone on board until Immigration arrived.

Larry, Kurt, and Marcos pulled out their fishing gear while they all awaited the immigration officials. Nearby, small schools of sardinas could be seen shoaling on the surface, occasionally breaking into a boil as a larger predator fish ripped into their mass. Casting small surface lures, the fishermen hooked into a few small needlefish but could entice nothing larger than about fifteen inches. Larry switched tackle and dropped down to the bottom with chunks of leftover Spam from the previous night's casserole and immediately brought up a couple of two-pound red rockfish. Larry and Kurt switched over to the same rigs and began landing similar fish of their own. There would at least be a nice change on the menu for the evening meal.

∞

When Immigration arrived in a large gray skiff a short while later, it quickly became obvious that something was amiss. Three uniformed officers stepped aboard and met with Captain Ellis, while four others armed with M-16 carbines stood stoically at the base of the boarding ladder. The interaction between the captain and the officials could be overheard from most parts of the deck; and from the tone of their voices, there was obviously some disagreement.

Larry translated what he could from the muffled discussion, advising those near to him that the port officials kept repeating, "Your papers are not in order," or something of that nature. He stated that they also kept referring to Ensenada, while Captain Ellis responded that he had permission from the Captain of the Port in Ensenada. In the meantime, the two deckhands, Paul and Phillip, were preparing to launch the two skiffs so that the passengers and some of the crew could go ashore. The armed officers advised them not to launch the skiffs. With weapons raised, a certain amount of tension charged the air.

For nearly two hours, discussions between the officials and Captain Ellis continued; and several of the passengers became even more frustrated and vocal. Eventually, Captain Ellis boarded the skiff with the immigration officers and a large bundle of papers, including everyone's passports, and went ashore. The officers told everyone on board—in no uncertain terms—not to leave the ship.

Temperatures rose as the day wore on. Most of the passengers, and part of the crew, jumped into the water to cool off. The water was warm, about seventy-eight degrees, and felt delightful. For all, it would have been nice to rinse off with fresh water; but until the ship was cleared to go into the dock, replenishing the water tanks would have to wait. Dawn and Madison made lunch for everyone, another pasta dish with beans and Spam. It was edible, but could not be considered savory cuisine.

For the remainder of the afternoon, the frustrated passengers and crew passed the time as best they could. Most spent a lot of time in the water. A few continued to fish, taking turns with the rods and reels. Others lay out on the deck chairs reading and soaking up the sun—way too much sun for some of them. Occasionally, small skiffs and dinghies filled with brown-skinned locals cruised near their boat. The locals waved and shouted at the passengers, admiring the women in their swimsuits, particularly Linda and Tiona. Those two were now very comfortable parading around in their bikinis, especially Tiona who seemed to get great pleasure from posing on the foredeck whenever a small skiff came by.

Linda (less self-conscious now that she and Marcos were obviously connected—at least on some level) had completely forsaken her matronly attire and seemed very comfortable in front of everyone in her multi-colored bikinis, short sarongs, and other scanty clothing.

Tiona, while not as statuesque as Linda, also exhibited quite the figure on deck. Her skimpy bikini was way ahead of its time by American standards, sporting the European style of bottom that left very little to the imagination. Her top, the same color of orange but with a small white star placed strategically in the center of the minimal fabric, barely contained her ample breasts. Perhaps her only flaw was an area of stretch marks across her flat stomach.

Captain Ellis finally returned to the ship around three o'clock, bearing good news. Immigration had cleared the ship and its passengers to go ashore. His first act was to maneuver the boat into the docks and take on water. As he prepared to hoist anchor, he advised everyone that shore leave would be permissible until noon the following day, when he intended to depart for mainland Mexico. Several passengers elected to stay somewhere on shore overnight, where they could enjoy the comforts of a real room and a real shower.

After hauling anchor, the *Explorer* slowly made its way to the old wooden pier where deep-draft ships could load and offload supplies and take on fuel and water. Once the ship was secured to the pier, Captain Ellis explained that when they were back out on anchor, the skiffs would make runs back and forth to the ship on a two-hour schedule, ending at midnight. and starting up again at seven a.m.

Chapter Four

Almost everyone disembarked to go ashore. Captain Ellis, Dawn, Phillip, and the chief engineer were the only ones to remain aboard. Everyone else wanted to feel solid land under their feet, and to visit the local hotspots.

Kurt, Madison, Marcos, Linda, Tiona, Charlie, Sally, Peter, and Larry, all went together to get fish tacos and beer at one of the local fish taco stands. With fish tacos costing twenty-cents (American) each and cold Dos Equis for thirty cents, they feasted and drank with gusto.

While joking around with the taco stand operators, Jesus and Maria, Larry asked about where to go for a little nightlife. Jesus suggested the Roadhouse Café on the main highway out of town. He offered to fetch his cousin Jesse for the ten-minute taxi ride.

All nine of the partiers piled into Jesse's 1959 Chevrolet Impala for the short ride to the Roadhouse Café.

Once there, tequila and cerveza began to flow freely. Charlie and Tiona started dancing, together at first, but Charlie lasted only a dance or two. Tiona was not about to stop. Dressed in a pale blue, loose-fitting, lightweight dress pulled tight at the waist and cut about halfway up her thighs, Tiona was creating quite a stir. She was braless, and it didn't take those watching long to realize that she also wore no panties. Her trim figure and sensual dance moves had the house rocking. When one of the local girls, a deeply browned young woman in her late twenties dressed in a thin white cotton dress, joined Tiona on the dance floor, the noise levels of the club increased impressively. She too danced with abandon, her long brown legs, shapely bottom, and ample bosom captivating every male in the room and attracting more patrons as the dancing continued. It was as if a call had gone out: 'hot dancers at the Roadhouse.'

For nearly an hour, the two ravishing women danced and entranced a growing audience. It didn't matter what music played, the two women performed equally well to American Rock and Roll as they did to Mexican Salsa. Before long, both of them were sweating profusely; and their sweat added even more fervor to the scene. Both of their light dresses became soaked with perspiration and clung to their curves. The entire room became energized, the men eagerly anticipating the next seductive movements. It was the most provocative display of carnal dancing in public that many of them had seen; and it was very close to getting out of control when Tiona abruptly stopped and moved to the table with her friends.

"Holy Shit," said Charlie, "what got into you?"

Tiona turned directly toward Charlie, a glazed look in her shining yellow eyes. "I want to screw. Let's get out of here," she blurted.

Charlie looked dumbfounded. He seemed to be at a total loss for words.

She watched him for a long moment, and then turned to Kurt. "Okay, how about you, Kurt?" she asked pointedly.

Kurt started laughing, partly from embarrassment and certainly because he was shocked by Tiona's boldness and directness. Glancing toward Madison, he realized that he was entering treacherous waters and better be careful with his response.

"Tiona," he replied, "all of us loved your dance. I'm sure that Charlie enjoyed it as much as any of us. If the two of you want to take off, find someplace where you can be alone, I'm sure that we could find a taxi driver to take you back to town."

His calm demeanor and matter-of-fact suggestion had a sobering effect. Tiona took a few deep breaths, and the glaze in her eyes faded. She laughed lightly. "Oh, you men," she commented, "can't any of you just go with the flow when the offer is put on the table?"

When her question went unanswered, Larry jumped into the silence. "Hey," he advised the group, "it's nearly eleven o'clock, and the last ride back to the boat departs in an hour. If we're going to go back aboard, we'd better hit the road."

Paying their bill, and much to the chagrin of the men in the Roadhouse Café, the group piled back in the taxicab and headed back into town.

At the Embarcadero, Tiona and Charlie, along with Marcos and Linda, excused themselves from the group and informed the partiers that they would be taking rooms in town for the night. The others stumbled drunkenly back to the quay near the fuel dock to await the last skiff from their ship.

∞

Tiona and Charlie, and Marcos and Linda rented rooms for the night at the Mar de Cortez Hotel in the center of town.

After checking in, Tiona bid Marcos and Linda a mumbled good night as she nearly dragged Charlie by the hand toward their room.

Their rooms were adjacent to each other and through the thin walls Marcos and Linda could clearly hear Tiona's vocal sexual urgency. Her carnal pleas passed clearly through the thin walls of the room, and there was no mistaking her coaxing and subsequent cries of pleasure and satisfaction.

Marcos and Linda listened and giggled together as they heard the commotion through the thin walls. Up to that point in time, their physical connections had been limited to some restrained touching, holding hands, and a few brief kisses.

Their urges may have been as intense as those of Tiona and Charlie, but were held in check by their mutually restrained demeanors. After Tiona and Charlie could no longer be heard, Marcos and Linda began exploring each other.

Marcos tended to show restraint in his approach to sexual activity. He had a great deal of pent-up anticipation, having hungered for Linda for days, but he controlled his eagerness and initiated their intimacy with remarkable patience.

Linda seemed eager, but remained somewhat submissive. They stood together at the edge of the bed, kissed tenderly and explored each other with patience and sensitivity. Eventually Marcos pulled back and sat on the edge of the bed.

Slowly and methodically he unzipped her dress and let it drop to the floor. When all of her clothes were off, he stopped to gaze upon her nakedness.

"My God," he uttered huskily, "You are an absolute vision. I have never, ever, seen a more beautiful and perfect body."

Smiling, she stepped toward him, her dark eyes shined brightly in the dimly lit room. Her hands reached out and grabbed his t-shirt, lifted it smoothly over his head and dropped it onto the floor. Marcos helped her by slipping out of his loose cotton pants.

He whispered endearing words, teasing and fondling her in the most sensitive places. She let her head fall back and closed her eyes, allowing him to explore her femininity, and she reveled in the tantalizing pleasure of his words and the slow, methodical exploration of her body. Finally she used her own considerable strength and flexibility to push him onto his back and mount his rigid manliness as she uttered a slow sensuous moan.

Watching her ride him, Marcos marveled at her wondrous form, her size, and her beauty. With a couple of days of sunshine turning her skin dark, the skimpy tan lines of her bikini stood out boldly. Looking up at her as she lifted and plunged, he felt his ultimate fantasy was taking place. Not only was she beautiful, she was completely wanton, immersed in her own selfish act of passion. She rode him with unchecked abandon and together they neared that blissful place where man and woman reach the pinnacle of sexual joy.

Their intense pleasure coincided with the bed crashing to the floor.

Dazed and disoriented, they lay atop the broken bed, gradually realized what had happened and began to laugh at the situation. Blanketed in sweat, her moist form draped atop his manly torso, they laughed together until tears flowed.

Eventually, they disengaged and climbed off the broken bed to assess the situation. There wasn't much that could be done—all four of the once sturdy-looking wooden legs were splintered and crumpled under the frame. They were surprised that no one came to the room to investigate the commotion. When a reasonable amount of time passed without any intrusion, they decided there was really nothing they could do to rectify the situation. They lowered themselves back onto the bed, giggled together for a while, then initiated another bout of sensual, but slightly more subdued lovemaking, with Linda assuming the submissive role and Marcos skillfully displaying his own animal-like prowess. Much later, they melded together and drifted into a deep and satisfying sleep.

∞

Back at the docks, Madison, Kurt, and Larry, along with the hippies, Sally and Peter, caught the last skiff back to the *Explorer*. Sally and Peter tended to their evening ministrations and disappeared to their little nest near the galley.

Kurt and Madison found themselves alone on the second deck. All the other passengers were either on shore or bunked down in the cabins.

"Wonderful!" Kurt exclaimed, "A chance to be alone."

She looked at him with the sultry gaze that he immediately recognized. Kurt always relished that look. It was as if she evoked a sense of complete and total submission, ready and willing to yield to his whims and desires.

In his inebriated state, Kurt could not keep his needs in check. His sexual appetite was urgent and he nearly tore her clothing from her body in his haste. It was over quickly.

After a few quiet moments where he was lost in that space-less frame of mind and body that immediately follows orgasm, Kurt gradually returned to the present. Recognizing his hedonism, he refocused his attention on her. He was still quite drunk, but was sober enough to try and make amends.

Rising onto one elbow, Kurt looked into Madison's eyes. That look of submission was still there, and he felt guilty for taking advantage of her. "Thanks for letting me get that out of the way." He whispered. "Now that I've gotten control of my urges again, how about another try?"

She looked up at his face and nodded almost imperceptibly.

This time Kurt began tenderly. He kissed her softly, lovingly.

He took his time, relishing her touch, her taste, and her femininity.

As her body responded to his lips, tongue, and gentle fingers, Kurt kept his own urges in check, focusing solely on her pleasure. Her body quivered to his touch, his kisses, and his tongue. Moisture built on her skin.

With an increasing urgency, she shuddered, and finally uttered a deep, sensual moan that left her quivering and spent.

Kurt waited patiently as her breathing slowed and her body relaxed. His head nestled in her lap.

When he sensed that she had returned to the present, he started again, touching and licking softly.

"Please". She whispered. I want you inside of me."

He raised himself to her level, smiled down into her milky blue eyes, and positioned himself above her, pushup style. She grasped his manhood and guided it into her wetness. She moaned, deeply.

Both of them turned their eyes downward to enjoy the visual effects. They watched spellbound, absorbed with the images and fantasies, entranced, until they reached fulfillment together. Afterward they drifted off to sleep, wrapped in each other's arms.

∞

Early the following morning, Dawn, Madison, and Larry went into town to pick up a few food items. Around eleven a.m., they returned with fresh fruits, bolillos (Mexican rolls), milk, and assorted vegetables and meat.

Captain Ellis announced that the ship would be hoisting anchor at noon to head across the Sea of Cortez for Mazatlan. He sent the skiff to shore for the last pickup of passengers. At eleven-thirty, Tiona, Charlie, Marcos, Linda, and one of the couples that always stayed below in one of the lower cabins, Mr. and Mrs. Blanchard from San Francisco, and their young daughter, returned to the ship. Missing were Mr. and Mrs. Adams, a quiet couple from Arizona. Nobody had seen or heard anything from them since the previous afternoon.

By noon, there was still no word from the Adams'. Captain Ellis got on the radio and asked the Captain of the Port if he had any information as to their whereabouts. He had none, but said he would make an inquiry. About an hour later, the Port Captain called on Channel 16 to report that the Adams' had booked a flight to Los Angeles. Some of their belongings were still on board in their berths, but it seemed evident that they were not concerned about those items. Captain Ellis ordered the anchor hoisted, and the ship was off to Mazatlan, approximately two hundred ninety miles across the Sea of Cortez on the mainland coast of Mexico.

The seas were calm, pale blue with an oily looking sheen on the surface. Dozens of frigate birds followed the ship as it chugged slowly out of the bay of Cabo San Lucas. Once out a few miles, an abundance of sea life became evident, feeding terns, soaring pelicans, pods of dolphin, distant splashes from airborne manta rays, and a few boils created by feeding pelagic fishes. Larry and Kurt set out the trolling lines; but despite evidence of feeding fish, there were no jig strikes.

A low haze filled the air, and the silhouette of Cabo San Lucas and the southern tip of Baja gradually faded from view. A long rolling groundswell from the south kept the vessel rolling sluggishly in a broadside trough. A few passengers again began feeling woozy and left the deck to lie down in the shade or in their bunks.

The frigate birds, pelicans, and terns took turns entertaining the passengers. The frigates were particularly entertaining, their dark expansive bodies gliding gracefully in the draft of the ship's motion, soaring effortlessly behind the exhaust stack and above the stern in the hopes of snatching a morsel of discarded food scraps tossed from the boat. Large flocks of pelicans appeared occasionally, flying in a v-pattern toward some unknown destination, their long wingtips spread majestically to catch the updrafts from the gentle sea breezes. Frenetic terns dipped and dived erratically in search of some tidbit of sea life from the rich and fertile ocean surface. On a couple of occasions, the surface erupted with a frenzy of activity as schools of Sierra chased shoals of sardinas to the surface, only to be harassed even further by the diving terns, pelicans and frigates. In a two-mile stretch, several dozen huge Manta Rays leaped and splashed from the water, their huge wingspans flashing white as they turned back-flips twenty-feet into the air. Some of the rays were as large as ten or twelve feet across, and their splashes threw huge sprays of water as they crashed back to the surface.

Most of the passengers had picked up fresh supplies of beer and booze while in Cabo, and the mood on the decks became loose and friendly. Calypso music played from the deck speakers, and a festive atmosphere prevailed, perhaps the first really relaxed and contented time since the *Explorer* left Ensenada.

As the sun settled in the west, high cirrus clouds helped create a beautiful tropical sunset. With the ship steaming steadily across the Sea of Cortez, the booze, music, and sunset filled everyone with a feeling that perhaps—just perhaps—this trip was going to be something special after all.

∞

The next day arrived with another titillating rainbow of colors in the eastern sky, the aftermath of a weak tropical depression that turned inland as it pushed northward toward the Mexican coast. Vivid red streaks mixed with undulating grays across a pastel blue background. The effects looked stunning, and most of the passengers aboard the boat climbed groggily out of their bunks to witness the spectacle.

Around noon, the first glimpses of mainland Mexico came into view. Positioned at about the twenty-first parallel, the brightening coastal landscapes appeared more varied than those in lower Baja. As opposed to the relatively flat, arid Baja Peninsula, the coast of mainland Mexico is lush, considerably more developed, and features towering mountain ranges that run nearly the entire length of the country.

As the ship neared the coast, small fishing pangas and bulky looking shrimp boats could be seen plying the coastal waters in search of the rewards of the sea.

At the entrance to Mazatlan Harbor, it became immediately obvious that it was a thriving commercial port. The hustle and bustle of commercial shipping and fishing enterprises materialized. Large sea-going ships lined concrete wharfs on both sides of the harbor, with dingy gray concrete and drab brown wooden structures constructed all along the water's edge. The boat slowed to idle-speed, and the passengers stared at the dreary looking bay. It was not at all what they expected. Most had envisioned swaying palms, crystal clear waters, lush tropical jungles, and thatched native huts; but there were none.

Suddenly, those standing at the rails were nearly thrown to the decks. Traveling at idle-speed of about one and a half knots, the *Explorer* had come to a sudden and immediate stop. The passengers looked around, but the cause of the abrupt halt was not immediately evident.

Several passengers began asking the others, "What happened? Why did we stop?"

Kurt, made a quick assessment of the situation, looked over the side of the ship into the murky water and offered his guess. "I think we ran aground."

Sure enough, despite the fact that they were almost dead center in the middle of the harbor, the vessel had run aground on a submerged sandbar. Approximately two hundred yards ahead, the faint markings of a SHOAL buoy could be seen. However, the shoal extended farther to seaward than Captain Ellis, expected.

On the bridge, Captain Ellis could be heard barking orders to his chief engineer. "Full reverse." he beseeched, "Give it all she's got."

Soon the decks began to vibrate, and the rumbling whine of the engines could be heard and felt from every location of the ship. For several minutes, there was a roar and resonant throbbing as the engines worked desperately to turn the five-foot diameter propellers under the fantail of the ship. Dense black smoke poured from the smokestack, and the deep rumble of the diesel engines winding to full rpm reverberated across the harbor. It was to no avail. She was stuck solidly on the seafloor in Mazatlan Harbor.

Within a few minutes, several small pangas circled the stranded vessel, their occupants waiving and shouting in indiscernible Spanish. Even Larry and Captain Ellis could not translate the shouts. There are many native dialects along the mainland coast, a result of the socialization between indigenous Indians and Spanish colonizers. As a result, the dialects from region to region vary considerably, to the point that even local Mexicans often require a translator to communicate with some of the coastal inhabitants.

After a while, a large tugboat arrived on scene, standing a good distance to starboard in what was obviously the main channel. The tug launched a small wooden skiff, and a distinguished looking mariner stepped aboard the small pram and was transported alongside the *Explorer*.

"Hola, amigos," the tall, handsome looking fellow called out in Spanish, switching smoothly into English. "It appears that you have run onto one of our unmarked sandbars. Can I be of assistance?"

Captain Ellis strode to the rail and responded, "We would appreciate some assistance. Do you feel that you can pull us free?"

"Free?" The mariner laughed haughtily, "Nothing is free my friend; but perhaps we could provide assistance for a small fee. Does two thousand pesos sound fair?"

Captain Ellis did a quick calculation in his mind. Two thousand pesos equated to almost two hundred dollars American, an amount that he could not afford. "Excuse me a moment," he said to the man in the skiff as he turned to his first mate, Leonard, instructing him to go into the wheelhouse and check the tide charts. However, he knew full well that the tides were working against him. He was not sure exactly when the tides changed, but he knew they were falling as they entered the bay a short time ago. He was hoping that they might be able to wait an hour or two, and then float loose as the tide rose.

"It's not good, Captain," Leonard informed him. "We're at about four feet right now. It will continue to fall to a minus one point seven as the afternoon wears on. High tide is not until around eight this evening. It's a five-five high; so we can probably free ourselves by then. But if the hull sucks deep into muck, it might make it tougher to break loose."

"Thanks," Captain Ellis murmured, turning back to the man in the skiff. "That price seems a little steep. Do you think you could find a way to reduce your fee to say, one hundred dollars American?"

The mariner pondered the question for a moment, and then replied seemingly without rancor, "Because you are such a fine gentleman, I will assist you for that amount. Understand that payment must be made now, and there can be no assurance of immediate success. It is possible that we will need to await the high tide this evening."

"I understand," replied Captain Ellis as he turned toward his stateroom. "I will be right back."

Returning to the deck, the Captain passed down five twenty-dollar bills.

After receiving payment, the man aboard the skiff gave his instructions. "I will send my assistant back shortly with a cable. Please attach the cable securely to your stern post and be prepared to engage your engines in reverse when you hear two short blasts on the horn."

"Understood," replied Captain Ellis.

Everyone watched as the small skiff slowly made its way back toward the stricken vessel. There were now three men in the skiff, the original operator and two barefoot men wearing dirty, tattered t-shirts. Those two men were manhandling the end of a cable that dragged through the murky water toward the ship. The small ten-horse Johnson outboard engine on the skiff was obviously taxed to the limits of its horsepower as it whined and spun the small propeller in an effort to pull the heavy cable. Recognizing the struggle, Captain Ellis grabbed a coil of line and heaved it toward the skiff, impressively landing the line in the center of its deck. One of the men grabbed the line and tied a quick bowline into the loop of the cable. Captain Ellis called out to lend a hand, and several passengers and crew on deck grabbed the line and helped hoist the cable over the port rail, then dragged it to the stern.

Once the cable was looped over the stern bit, Captain Ellis hoisted a thumbs-up to the tugboat, and then instructed his engineer to restart the engines. Everyone watched as the tugboat repositioned slightly to the starboard and astern of the vessel. When two short blasts sounded from the tug's air horn, Captain Ellis ordered, "All power full astern!"

For a few agonizing moments, all was quiet except for the building roar of the tug's powerful engines and the thumping groan of the boat's twin diesels. As the cable tightened, it began to lift from the water, springing free from its catenary with shimmering rivulets of water flying into the air as it shook and twisted taut. Almost imperceptibly, the ship began to slide backward, and then gradually the movement became more noticeable, much to everyone's relief.

With a roar of approval, she was suddenly floating free and moving rapidly astern.

"Halt all engines!" Captain Ellis bellowed. But concerned that the ship's momentum was destined to create another problem by ramming into the tugboat, he revised his first order. "Full ahead, full ahead!" He instructed, "but be prepared to disengage."

His instructions were handled smoothly by his chief engineer, who slowed their aft propulsion to avoid ramming into the tugboat, and then just as smoothly halted their forward movement before they drove themselves once again aground. They were free of the sandbar, and Captain Ellis looked relieved.

Again underway, Captain Ellis hailed the Captain of the Port for instructions to navigate into their wharf space. He was pleasantly surprised when the crew aboard the tugboat waved their arms in a signal to follow. Maneuvering into place behind the tug, Captain Ellis followed it up the channel for about half a mile, then cut across the channel to a long commercial dock on the west side of the bay. Dockworkers stationed between two large container ships waved their arms to indicate where the vessel should approach. As the ship eased alongside the wharf, the crew (which now included Kurt and Larry as dependable deckhands) secured lines to the dock bollards; and the *Explorer* was shut down, safe and secure alongside the wharf in Mazatlan Harbor. Looking around, the vista brought disappointment to the passengers.

∞

All had expected a vastly different scene than the one they now looked upon. Secured smack in the middle of a large commercial wharf, the vessel lay sandwiched between two large container ships; the bow of one and the stern of the other towering high above the decks of the *Explorer*. There was not much to see from any angle other than the rust-streaked hulls fore and aft, the murky bay to port, and an old concrete structure lined with rusting bay doors to starboard. It was certainly not a tropical paradise.

Captain Ellis called a general meeting of the ship. Standing on the foredeck, he began "I apologize for the grounding. My charts indicated a water depth of twenty-two feet through the entire channel. There was no indication of a shoal existing on the course we maintained, although it was marked a few hundred yards ahead."

Pausing briefly, the Captain continued, "I know this docking location is not the greatest. We had hoped to enter the scenic recreational area farther south; however, we are in desperate need of additional supplies, ship-stores, and other parts and equipment for the ship. The Canadian owners have assured me that those things have been either shipped or will be ordered here in Mazatlan and should be delivered within twenty-four hours. In the meantime, please give me time to check-in with the port authorities; and afterward, you may all go ashore and enjoy your day."

"Enjoy our day?" railed Tiona, "This is a flipping warehouse depot. What are we supposed to do, load boxes, or maybe chase rats? And what's that horrible smell? It's making me sick!"

"Again," reiterated Captain Ellis, "I apologize for the surroundings and the location we must use for docking. We hope to be here for only about twenty-four hours, and there is a very beautiful beach just across the bay that I highly recommend to all of you. There is a shuttle boat that will take you to it for a reasonable price. As for the smell, it is likely emanating from the grain warehouse behind us. I do believe that the winds will switch later on and the stench will go away. Also, if any of you are inclined to stay onshore, there are a couple of very nice, inexpensive hotels just a couple of blocks from here."

"What about after this?" one of the passengers asked. "Are we ever going to see some of the islands or scenic destinations that were promised when we signed on for this trip?"

Patiently, Captain Ellis assured them that there would be stops at several exotic ports and islands. He also promised that there would be additional supplies and equipment brought aboard that would enhance the entire experience. Amidst a general sense of doubt and skepticism, the meeting ended.

∞

The Port of Mazatlan bustled with the activities from freight terminals, a large commercial fishing fleet, industrial complexes and a couple of luxury ship terminals along the waterfront. In the nearby foothills live the residents of the city, a population of some two hundred thousand. Many of those residents make a living from the port operations; but there is also a widespread farming community that produces cotton, vegetables, and grains.

As the passengers made their preparations to go ashore and explore the sights of the city, Captain Ellis approached a group that was standing on the foredeck and asked if one or two would mind standing watch that evening. He explained that he had been unable to pay the crew since they departed San Diego, so several of the crew threatened to jump ship unless they received their pay and were given some shore leave. He said that he was going to be meeting with one of the ship's owners, who was flying in from Canada later in the afternoon. Kurt and Sam Gilford volunteered to serve deck watch.

A few of the passengers and crew disembarked almost immediately upon clearance by the port authorities. The rest stayed on board in anticipation of the evening meal, which saved them the expense of dining out. Dinner that evening was another pasta dish, heavy on the tomato sauce and light on the sausage. All hoped that the Canadian owner would provide additional funding, as well as the additional equipment and supplies that had been promised.

Madison, Tiona, and Linda, accompanied by Charlie, Marcos, and Larry, headed off after dinner to explore the nightlife of Mazatlan. Along the northern shore of the bay was a street lined with restaurants and bars. The group took a taxi into town, making brief stops at several bars before winding up at Mazatlan's most popular spot: Senor Frog's.

At Senor Frog's, Tiona once again put on an impromptu dance performance for the group, but it was considerably more subdued than her last performance at the Roadhouse Café in Cabo. Although they stayed out drinking and partying until nearly one a.m., their outing culminated without any notable histrionics.

Returning to the ship, all of the women felt similar sexual urges. Whether it was something in the drinks, the tropical atmosphere of Mazatlan, or merely a coincidence, each of them made their physical desires perfectly clear to their respective partners. As a result, the evening culminated with a bevy of eager lovemaking in several areas of the ship.

In the morning, Dawn surprised everyone with a delightful banana and strawberry pancake breakfast made from fresh fruit that she had discovered at a little side-street fruit stand the previous evening. Served with freshly made orange juice and coffee brewed from locally grown coffee beans, the tasty breakfast was a real treat.

Following the meal, everyone gathered their daypacks and headed off to explore the city and local beaches.

Kurt and Madison, Tiona and Charlie, Marcos and Linda, and Larry, all decided to go together, planning to visit Isla de la Piedra, or Stone Island, a long picturesque stretch of beach that is actually a peninsula connected to the mainland by a narrow strip of land at its southern end.

Populated primarily by an indigenous clan of 'islanders' that live off the land and sea, Stone Island was the first stop along the way that truly gave the passengers a glimpse of being in another culture. Cabo San Lucas exhibited vast cultural differences, but the small narrow island is a world unique into itself. While the language is Spanish, the island has its own dialect that is very difficult to understand, or translate. Nearly all of the housing consists of bamboo huts, thatched palm roofs and dirt floors. Along the expansive stretch of white-sand beach, a couple of outdoor palapas (open-air cafes) offer authentic 'islander' food. Pigs, chickens, burros, a few goats, and skinny mangy looking dogs roamed the dirt roads and beaches searching for tidbits of food or fresh vegetation to munch.

The group from the *Explorer* caught the local launch across a shallow bay to Stone Island. Offloading on a short rickety pier, they headed off across the sand to explore. Crossing the sandy terrain to reach the ocean, Kurt and Marcos were surprised to see some impressive waves breaking along the shore. "Darn," Marcos lamented, "I would have brought my surfboard if I'd known there was decent surf."

Kurt glanced around. "Maybe we could rent or borrow a board from someone. Let's ask around." Turning to the girls, he suggested they find a nice spot to soak up some sun while they tried to find a surfboard.

Larry accompanied them to a cluster of nearby huts where several peasant women were hanging laundry on lines stretched between their dwellings. When the men approached, the women turned their eyes downward and shied away. Looking around, Larry noticed a young Mexican boy pushing a beat-up wheelbarrow loaded with coconuts. He approached the young man and greeted him with a broad grin.

At first, the youngster seemed reticent and wary. His dark black eyes peered suspiciously from beneath a set of even darker eyebrows. Larry's first attempts at conversation brought no response; however after several friendly overtures, the young man finally looked directly at him and smiled. Gradually and with considerable effort, the two held a fractured conversation that resulted in exchanging names; but Larry was unable to convey their quest to locate a surfboard. At that point, Kurt set down his small pack and dropped onto the sand, pantomiming a man on his knees paddling, and then he jumped up with knees bent, feet positioned in a surf stance with his hands and arms stretched out as if he were riding a wave. It worked. Grinning and nodding his head, the boy acknowledged the surf demonstration, assumed the same stance and mimicked Kurt's performance.

It took several more gestures and attempts to communicate (which were really quite comical) before Larry succeeded in conveying the idea that they were looking for a surfboard, not just having a chat about surfing. With a nod and a gesture to follow him, Esteban—the young boy—headed off down the beach toward another cluster of thatched roof dwellings.

Behind one of the huts, Esteban greeted another slightly older youth who was busily engaged in shucking brown coconut seeds from their large green outer shells. Wielding a large machete, the second youth was chopping at a coconut shell in wide, arching slashes as the two-foot blade gleamed in the sunlight. He held the shell in his left hand as he swung the huge blade that whacked and slashed just inches from his fingers, one of which was missing at the knuckle. Looking up from his labors, the youth stopped and eyed the strangers.

Esteban spoke to him in their native dialect. After listening for a few moments, the second youth turned to the foreigners and spoke in broken English. "Hola, I am Carlos. So, you surf men?"

Kurt glanced at the others and responded. "Yes, we surf. We are looking for a board to rent or borrow."

Quizzically, the young man cocked his head. "You no have surfboard?"

"That's correct. We're looking for a board to rent or borrow."

Carlos then seemed to make up his mind and turned. "Venga," he gestured, followed by another comment that must have meant 'follow me.'

Walking to the back of a nearby hut, Carlos gestured toward a dusty, crudely patched long board partially buried beneath a pile of discarded coconut shards. It wasn't pretty, but it would probably do.

"You want to use?" Carlos asked.

"Yes." Kurt replied. "We'd like very much to use the board. How much?"

Carlos looked askance at Kurt and the others. "No, I no sell."

"No, not sell." Kurt replied, "To use, to rent. How much to rent?"

Carlos shook his head. "No rent. You use, is okay." He responded, sweeping his arm graciously in a gesture to take it away.

After a few more nods and gestures, Kurt, Larry, and Marcos pulled the big old board from under the pile of coconut remnants and carried it away, indicating they would return it later, which they assumed was understood.

Back on the beach, they saw their things spread out on the sand about a quarter-mile away. The others in the group had already gone into the water. Tiona was topless, her already well-tanned breasts lathered in sunscreen. Linda wore her bright yellow bikini, and her ample figure radiated a polished glow. Madison, having just emerged from the water, displayed a starkly different look, her light skin contrasted vividly with the burnished bodies of Tiona and Linda; but her feminine attributes no less striking or impressive.

Marcos and Kurt removed their shirts and carried the surfboard to the water's edge. Kurt told Marcos to go ahead first. He returned to the sand to sit next to Madison. She handed him a tube of sunscreen and asked him to help coat her skin, informing him that she intended to become more tan so that she could better enjoy the trip. Rubbing the lotion onto every exposed inch of her skin caused a stirring in Kurt's libido, ultimately sending him into the water to deflate his obvious arousal.

Out in the water, Marcos skillfully maneuvered the long board into the approaching face of a wave, propelled himself into the curl, and popped upright as the board glided smoothly across the sweep of the building swell. Shuffling his feet forward, Marcos stood upright, poised in the classical Hawaiian style of surfing, his left foot curled over the tip of the board, 'hanging-five' as the wave rushed along on a smooth and steady race toward the beach. Dropping back into the center of the board as the swell threatened to break, Marcos shifted his weight and forced the board to drop deeper into the trough, where he briefly disappeared in the curl before he and the board popped free and once again lifted on the surface of the wave. At the last moment, Marcos turned abruptly to the right and thrust artfully out of the crashing wave, just seconds before the wall broke into a swirling white mass of turbulence.

Linda sat on the warm sand, watching Marcos surf, and clapped delightedly like a schoolgirl each time Marcos caught a wave. She laughed and giggled at his one fall, calling out to him to be careful.

For about forty-five minutes, Marcos reveled in his favorite pastime, catching about a dozen rides that, while not perfect, were much better than he expected. Normally the surf along the beach at Stone Island is poor at best, protected as it is from prevailing westerly swells by the point at the entrance to Mazatlan Harbor. On this particular day, a south swell had developed, creating the unusually good surf.

Gliding into one final wave, he rode the crest until it broke, then bumped along in the foam as the spent wave rolled lazily toward the beach. Marcos stopped in the shallow surf, and beamed with pleasure. The unexpected opportunity to catch a few quality rides filled him with joy. The others had also gone into the water prior to Marcos heading in to shore. Larry, Kurt, Linda, and Madison sloshed over to where Marcos landed.

"Wow!" Marcos beamed with pleasure, "That was awesome."

"You were terrific." Linda praised him lavishly, "You really know how to surf."

"Thanks," he responded modestly, "I've been surfing since I was ten, but I was a little rusty today. Missed a few opportunities to really shine, but it sure was fun." Turning to Larry and Kurt, he asked if they were going to give it a whirl.

Kurt responded that he wished he had brought his fins, but he was going to give body-surfing a shot even though he recognized that the speed and shape of the waves would be very difficult to body-surf without fins. The waves were in water too deep, and the development of the break was too slow to realistically ride without fins. But he was going to try anyway.

Larry accepted the board from Marcos and began paddling out into the surf, with Kurt swimming alongside. Reaching the break area, Larry continued into deeper water where the swell could best be caught. Kurt lingered closer to the beach, knowing that he would need to kick furiously and be a little lucky to catch the break at the right moment.

Twice Larry missed waves, failing to get the heavy board moving fast enough to lock into the motion of the building crests. On his third try, Larry caught the break, stood and rode a decent wave until it broke over his shoulder and sent him tumbling into the water. His board washed all the way to the sand. On the same wave, Kurt managed to catch the break perfectly. The ride was short, but it did give him a nice drop and tuck-out of the swell before it crashed into a swirling turmoil.

Larry swam back to the beach to recover the board, and then laboriously paddled back out. With the break beginning about two hundred yards from shore, the paddle out to the line of breakers was tiring and difficult.

Once out again, Larry waited a few minutes before trying to catch another. On his next effort, Kurt watched as Larry paddled furiously to get the lift he needed to glide onto the face of the large swell. His timing was off, and Kurt stared helplessly as the board balanced precariously at the top of the break with Larry trying desperately to back-peddle away from the crest. It didn't work; and as the wave broke, Larry and the board fell into 'the hole' on the front of the wave, completely at the mercy of the huge volume of crashing water.

For a long agonizing moment, Kurt scanned the turbulent foam, looking for Larry and the board. After a few seconds, the board popped into the air, spun around, and dropped back into the tumultuous wash where it began to tumble toward shore. There was no sight of Larry. Diving under another approaching wave, Kurt resurfaced and again looked around for Larry. He could not see him anywhere. Waving his arms toward shore, he shouted loudly, "Hey! Do you see Larry?"

Linda, who was the only one watching when Larry fell, ran out into the surf. "I saw him wipeout, but I can't see him anywhere. The board is over there."

Another large wave was beginning to break just beyond Kurt, and he had to swim furiously out to avoid being sucked back up into its break. Diving deeply, he felt the power of the large swell as it rose and crashed into another tumult of swirling sea and foam in the area he had vacated. Popping back to the surface, he spun around, anxiously looking for any sign of Larry. Again without luck, Kurt was about to turn back to yell to Linda to go get more help when he spotted what appeared to be Larry's white and blue swimming trunks about twenty yards to his right.

Without hesitation, he began to swim toward the area. As he swam, Kurt caught a brief glimpse of Larry who appeared to be floating face down in the turbid water. He increased his effort, forcing every ounce of his energy into his attempt to reach Larry's side. Lungs bursting, chest pounding, and muscles taxed to their limit, Kurt strained to reach his brother. With a final pull of his strong swimmer's arms, he reached Larry just before another large wave picked both of them up and tossed them over the top. Grabbing Larry's shorts with one hand, Kurt dug his other arm deeply into the approaching swell in an effort to keep them from going over the top. Kicking and stroking towards deeper water, Kurt felt them both being lifted to the crest; but fortunately they held at the top, rose onto the backside of the breaking crest, and floated clear.

Larry's body was limp. A red stain discolored the water. Wrapping one arm around Larry's chest and rolling onto his back, Kurt began to kick and pull water with his free hand. Another large wave formed, and Kurt could feel the undercurrent pulling them toward the building break. He kicked and pulled as strongly as he could until the moment before the wave rose, and dumped its full force directly onto their defenseless bodies. Kurt grabbed Larry around the waist, took a last gulp of air then tucked both himself and Larry's inert body into a tight roll. Relaxing his body in order to conserve energy, Kurt gave in to the ferocity of the turbulence as the wave tossed them around and around in its inexorable drive toward shore. When the pressing crush of the water pinned them momentarily onto the ocean floor, Kurt recognized an opportunity. Realizing which way was up, Kurt rolled slightly and planted his feet solidly on the sandy bottom and pushed upward with all of his rapidly diminishing strength.

Popping to the surface, Kurt looked around and saw that the wave had pushed them quite a bit closer toward shore. With waning stamina, he once again clutched Larry around the chest and began to kick and paddle toward the beach. As his endurance was about to fail, he suddenly felt another hand grab his. At the same time, a husky voice cried out, "Oh my God, he's bleeding."

Linda was there; her powerful arms nearly yanked Larry from Kurt's grasp as she helped pull him toward the sand. As they entered the shallow water, Madison, Marcos, and Tiona, all of whom had been unaware of the developing drama, arrived on scene and helped carry Larry's limp form from the water.

Carrying him to dry land, they laid him onto the soft sand. "Is he alive?" Marcos asked. "Is he breathing?" questioned Tiona.

Kurt was on his knees alongside, pressing his ear to Larry's chest while trying to listen and watch for signs of life. Suddenly, Larry coughed and spluttered a large mouthful of salt water into the air, covering Kurt in the slimy substance. It was one of the most grateful bursts of disgust that Kurt had ever felt.

They rolled Larry onto his side and let him cough out more salt water. Meanwhile, blood had continued to spread down his neck and back, creating a frightful sight. Realizing that he was at least alive and breathing, Kurt shifted position so that he could inspect Larry's head. A small half-inch gash was visible, along with a steadily growing lump on the left side, near the top of his head. As all head injuries do, it was bleeding a lot. Mixed with the salt water, the thinned blood appeared much more ominous than it actually was.

"Somebody give me a clean rag," Kurt instructed, "Rip up my t-shirt if you need to."

Madison kneeled alongside, and handed Kurt one of her tank tops that she had brought along. "I don't need this. Go ahead and use it."

Kurt thanked her and gingerly cleansed around the wound, peering closely to see if there was evidence of anything more serious. In the meantime, Larry had recovered from his coughing and murmured quietly, "What's going on?"

Kurt was greatly relieved to hear his voice. "Well buddy, you wiped out. Bumped your head on the board, and we had to pull you from the water. How are you feeling?"

He tried to lift himself up, but Kurt held him down. "Not yet, cowboy. You've got a pretty nasty bump on your noggin, and it's bleeding a little. Let me clean it up a bit before you try to get up." Turning to the others, he implored, "Can one of you get some ice out of the cooler?"

Kurt applied a compress of ice wrapped in the fabric that Madison had supplied. Larry tried to sit up, which Kurt somewhat reluctantly agreed to allow. "I could use a cold beer," stated Larry.

Hearing that remark, the others knew that he was probably all right.

After Larry sufficiently recovered, Marcos and Kurt returned the surfboard to the two young 'Islanders' at the coconut shucking huts. They attempted to wave off any 'rent', but Marcos and Kurt persuaded them to accept two dollars American money for the use of the board.

∞

When it became obvious that Larry was okay, and the lump on his head had diminished in size, the group elected to visit one of the small beach palapas for lunch and a few beers.

After lunch they returned to the beach. Tiona, Linda, and Madison attracted quite a bit of attention from the local male population. About a dozen men could be seen hanging around the nearby huts and peering out to where the girls sunbathed and splashed in the surf. Tiona was obviously a center of focus in her topless suit; but Linda in her bright yellow bikini and Madison in her more demure flowered bikini also attracted an abundance of appreciative stares.

After a while, it became evident that the men in the huts were hitting the rum bottles as they became more vocal and moved closer, out from the shade and onto the beach. It seemed like a prudent time to leave. Packing up their things, the group headed back to the loading dock and caught the shuttle boat back to the *Explorer*.

∞

Back on board, the beach-goers took a 'ship shower,' learning to conserve fresh water by minimizing the volume of water flowing from the spigot and turning the water off when lathering with soap. Afterward as they gathered on the foredeck for afternoon cocktails and snacks, Captain Ellis returned to the ship with a well-dressed man in his mid twenties wearing a sport coat and tie. They did not speak to nor acknowledge anyone, and both men disappeared almost immediately into the Captain's cabin.

Speculation was that the other man was a representative of the owners of the vessel, since he looked way too young to be an owner or partner.

Therefore, it was a big surprise to everyone when about an hour later Captain Ellis and the young man came back out on deck and he was introduced as Brian Walters—one of the owners of the ship.

Brian was a tall good-looking man of twenty-six. His family owned an entire fleet of ships in Vancouver, Canada; and his father had made a gift of this ship to him and two older brothers in recognition of a successful contract they had recently negotiated with another shipping company. The three brothers subsequently developed a plan to deliver the *Explorer* to Jamaica where it would be put into service as an inter-island dive excursion yacht. Brian was to oversee the daily operations of the ship.

Captain Ellis introduced Brian to those guests that were gathered on the foredeck. "Brian is here to deliver some of the supplies we were promised for this trip and to assist us in restocking the stores needed to continue on our journey. He will answer questions any of you might have."

Immediately, the questions began to fly. "Did you bring all the items we were promised when we signed up for this trip?" someone asked, followed by a dozen similar questions concerning broken promises and the obvious lack of amenities and/or funds to purchase and replenish supplies.

For nearly an hour, Brian fielded the questions, patiently and honestly. Gradually, it became clear that what existed on board the ship would be the norm, although he did promise that Captain Ellis would have sufficient funds to purchase adequate food supplies and other essentials for the remainder of the trip. As for some of the other 'luxuries' that were originally promised, like more skiffs, wine with meals, scuba gear, fishing rods and reels, and a host of niceties in the ship's limited quarters, they simply were not going to materialize.

He did promise each passenger that they would be offered a free one-week excursion aboard the *Explorer* in either Jamaica or the Cayman Islands when they reached their destination and the business venture was established. When one of the passengers asked for that promise in writing, Brian assured that the offer would be guaranteed in writing.

One couple expressed their concern about arriving in Jamaica on time, particularly in lieu of the delays.

Captain Ellis replied that the trip would likely take a few days longer than originally anticipated, at which point several people voiced their displeasure. "We can't go longer. We only have five weeks. You told us it would be a five-week cruise. Now you're telling us that we won't be there on time. What are we supposed to do? We've already purchased plane tickets to return home from Jamaica." It was not a pretty scene.

Brian, Captain Ellis and Dawn—who had joined the discussion a few minutes previously—promised to help exchange tickets and anything else they could do to resolve some of their issues. Fortunately, most of the passengers had heeded the original advice of Captain Ellis to wait until they reached Jamaica to make their return arrangements.

As for their immediate plans, Captain Ellis and Brian informed everyone that they would spend the following day shopping and getting supplies for the next leg of the trip. According to the Captain if all went as planned, the vessel would depart at around six p.m. the following evening and everyone should be back aboard by four. It was not to be.

At four the following day, Captain Ellis informed everyone that they had encountered a mechanical problem that would necessitate another day in port. When the next night also went by without any departure preparations, four more passengers announced they would be leaving the ship and flying home.

In the meantime, all of the remaining passengers found ways to entertain themselves. Several of the passengers spent the days and nights settled into their favorite local bar, drinking cerveza or rum drinks and eating their meals on board the ship. Most journeyed across the bay to Stone Island to enjoy the surf and sand, although the surf had all but disappeared by the following morning.

On their third night in port, Kurt, Larry, Guillermo, Marcos, and Sam Gilford invented a new and rather bizarre game they aptly named 'kick the rat.' Hundreds of large rats made the wharf area home, coming out at night to forage for food. Often the rats would climb up the anchor or docking lines of the ships tied to the quay. Most of the ships had anti-rat deflectors attached to their anchors and across their hawse fittings to try and keep the creatures from getting aboard. For the most part, the anti-rat contraptions were ineffectual and pretty much every ship had an infestation of the unwanted intruders.

Late that night, the guys discovered that if they tossed scraps of food from the dinner table onto the docks, the rats would immediately and without any fear scurry out of their holes to munch the tidbits. Whether they were simply oblivious of the men standing in the shadows or merely fearless, the rats did not try to run when the men approached.

As a consequence, the men took turns lining up on one of the rats then giving it a boot as far as they could out into the water. It was somewhat like trying to kick field goals; and some of the kicks were truly impressive, with the rats flying airborne into the water as much as fifty or sixty feet. Most swam back to the docks, or out to the nearest anchor line. A few floated face down. Larry claimed the title of best kicker, scoring at least five 'field goals' when his rat flew over all the docking lines and between the two ships tied along the quay.

Another pastime that several of the men found entertaining was to catch a few of the very large cockroaches that scurried about the wharf, then race them against one another. Creating a barrier lane with some pipes that were discarded along the dock, the men made a course where the cockroaches could race; and the men placed bets on which cockroach could run the twelve-foot 'racetrack' the fastest. It was quite entertaining to watch the antics of the men urging on their cockroaches, whooping and hollering when their chosen specimen won.

On the fourth day in port, Captain Ellis announced that they would be departing at noon. Gus, the Chief Engineer, worked with Sam Gilford to complete some sort of 'miracle' mechanical repair on the port engine that was originally diagnosed as irreparable. Had the repair not been made, it was widely assumed that the ship would continue the trip with only one operating engine—which would be a dauntingly unfeasible undertaking.

∞

Underway again, the ship cruised slowly southward, staying relatively close to shore for several hours. A considerable change in the topography along shore became evident. It was much more lush and tropical looking, and the imposing mountain ranges stood out starkly in the background. Around noon, Captain Ellis altered course to a more offshore heading, cutting a more direct line to the next scheduled port of call: Manzanillo.

Late in the afternoon, the silhouette of an island group came into view about twenty miles to seaward of the *Explorer*. Larry, Ron, and Marcos spoke with Dawn and requested a meeting with Captain Ellis. The islands in view were the Islas Marias, a small archipelago consisting of nine islands, the largest and only populated one being Isla Maria which boasts one of Mexico's largest federal prisons.

Located about ninety miles offshore, Isla Maria has a domestic population of about one thousand; and it is said that at least that many prisoners are incarcerated in the federal penitentiary. Of the other islands in the chain, only three could actually be considered islands. The others looked like nothing more than large clusters of exposed rocks.

Larry and Marcos were hoping to convince Captain Ellis to make a stop at the islands. Captain Ellis agreed to make the stop, albeit of short duration.

Anchoring in a small horseshoe-shaped cove at the southeastern end of Isla Maria Cleofas, the southernmost island in the chain, Captain Ellis gave the passengers about three hours to swim and relax. However, he would not allow use of the skiffs for any fishing or diving—a big disappointment for Kurt, Larry, and a few others.

Led by Guillermo, a few of the passengers gathered their snorkeling gear and swam approximately two hundred yards to the nearest point. Guillermo was in excellent shape for a man in his early sixties, exhibiting considerably more endurance and stamina than most of the others. His fluid Australian crawl rapidly outdistanced everyone except Kurt, whose own swimming prowess barely allowed him to keep pace with Guillermo. When they reached the rocky point at the eastern tip of the cove, the two treaded water patiently while they waited for the others to catch up. Once the six of them were together, Guillermo advised all to stay in pairs and remain relatively close to the point and on the inside of the cove. He could see from the swirls and whorls on the surface that a relatively strong current prevailed along the deeper water shelf on the outside of the rocky headland.

Below the surface, the group discovered a wonderful world of tropical beauty. Several varieties of colorful coral formed clusters in between the darker volcanic rocks that shaped the base of the reef. A large mass of silvery sardinas schooled in the shallows, the teeming mass swirling and flowing as if choreographed by some unseen natural force. Large parrotfish, wrasse, and numerous other species of tropical fishes clustered below, darting between the rocks and coral in their endless predatory quest.

About half an hour into the snorkeling excursion, Peter experienced a leg cramp. He clutched his left calf with both hands while he struggled to keep his head above the surface. His snorkeling partner, Marcos, swam to his side to assist. Pulling Peter's mask down around his neck, Marcos advised him to try and pull his fin and foot forward in an effort to stretch the calf muscles. Seeing that Peter was in pain and having a tough time trying to do much of anything, Marcos called out for help.

Guillermo and several of the others heard the call and swam quickly to their location. Guillermo told Marcos to get behind Peter and help keep him afloat, while he moved into position at his feet. Placing Peter's left leg against his stomach, Guillermo then forced Peter's fin and toes toward his shin as steadily as he could, relieving some of the immediate cramping while telling him to relax and breathe deeply. Guillermo held him in that position for several minutes, as the strain gradually dissolved from his features. Once he felt that Peter was sufficiently over the cramping, Guillermo told the others that it was time to head back to the *Explorer*. He asked Peter to remove his left fin and give it to Kurt. He then grasped Peter's swim trunks at the waist and began a slow steady swim back to the boat, encouraging Peter to kick with his right fin to assist their progress. Twice along the way, Peter's leg cramped again, and they stopped and treaded water while Guillermo and the others performed the same cramp-easing maneuver. Kurt and Larry both offered to relieve Guillermo; but he declined the offer, assuring them that he was fine. Just as they reached the boat, Peter suffered another strong cramp, grimacing in pain as he was pulled from the water and onto the boarding platform. Unable to walk, several other passengers assisted to help to pull him up the ladder and onto the deck. It would be a few hours before the pain and cramping eased, and Peter's calf remained sore for the better part of two more days.

When everyone was back aboard and accounted for, the Captain ordered the engines started and the anchor hoisted. Bidding adieu to Isla Maria Cleofas, the vessel was underway again to Manzanillo, approximately two hundred-forty miles south of the Las Islas Marias.

Everything went smoothly for the remainder of the day. The younger women climbed up to the top deck for their 'topless hour,' working diligently to bronze as much of their fair skin as possible. Tiona went a bit further than the others, removing all of her clothing. Even Madison had joined in the tanning sessions, forsaking her long-standing practice of avoiding sun exposure. She now worked diligently at her suntan, which was slowly turning a light golden hue, dotted with an increasing number of freckles.

After dining that evening on a stringy beef stew, Madison convinced Dawn to let her bake a large batch of oatmeal cookies. Some of the cookies she baked with chocolate chips, some with raisins, and one batch she made with 'Mexican Oregano' (marijuana) was served only to a select few.

Those who shared in the special cookies spent the next couple of hours seated together on the foredeck, laughing, watching the oily looking sea surface slide under the hull, and digging into their own private stashes of candy and other snacks to try and satisfy their 'munchies.'

Tiona, who ate four of the cookies, became frisky and flirtatious, expressing her sexual fantasies and cravings to all, but focusing particularly on Kurt. Madison, obviously perturbed, withdrew into her own private world in the shadows of the overhead canopy. Noticing her aloofness, Kurt slid his deck chair across to her side.

"What's up Madison?" Kurt questioned softly. She glanced at him briefly and turned away, an expression of hurt evident in her delicate features.

He reached out and touched her cheek, gently turning her face toward his own. Her eyes brimmed with tears.

"Go ahead," she whispered, "Go with her. It's obvious that you want her as much as she wants you."

Kurt kept his eyes locked on hers. "Madison, you're wrong. I don't want her. I want you. Sure she's fun, and it's flattering to be singled out, but I am not interested in her. Besides, she is with Charlie. She's just had a few too many of your magical cookies, and you've seen how she can be when she gets a little loose."

Madison wiped at her tears and told him, "Yeah, I've seen how she gets when she drinks a lot or smokes a joint or two, and she always seems to go after you."

"Yes," Kurt admitted, "she does tend to flirt with me a lot; but as I told you, I'm not interested in her. I only want you."

"I've seen you looking at her breasts when she is topless," she said dully, "You can't take your eyes off her."

Kurt took a deep breath. "You're right, I know that I stare. But I also stare at yours when you are topless, Men are not accustomed to seeing women topless, and it should be understandable that we enjoy checking your breasts out when we have the opportunity. It doesn't mean that I want her or that I don't want you. It's natural to want to look; and after all, I am a man."

She remained quiet, stiff and sulking as he put one arm around her waist and gently stroked her hair while tenderly massaging her scalp, neck, and temple. Eventually she relaxed, allowing her head to rest against his shoulder. After a while, he suggested they retire to their bunk.

Dispensing with their evening rituals, Madison and Kurt lay side by side, staring silently at the myriad of stars shining brightly in the moonless heavens. Both of them were still under the influence of the 'magic cookies,' although Madison's body was rigid, her countenance stony and inflexible.

Kurt desperately wanted to soften her petulance. He turned onto his side, and leaned on one elbow as he reached across and softly stroked her thick and lustrous hair. His fingertips languidly caressed her scalp. It took an agonizingly long time, but his steadfast ministrations did, finally, elicit a relaxation in her posture; and she turned to look into his eyes. She had that dreamy expression that he always associated with her tacit acceptance of sexual advance.

He lowered himself toward her, tenderly brushing his lips against hers. He brushed her nose with his lips, her eyebrows, her cheeks and her forehead, then returned to her lips. She puckered very slightly, and parted her lips to allow his tongue to enter. His passion was aroused, but his senses were in turmoil. Inwardly, he sensed that she was not in the mood, but outwardly he couldn't—or didn't want to stop. He tried to go slowly and considerately, caressing her smooth curves deliberately, very lightly fingering her soft skin. She didn't try to pull away, but neither did she respond with much enthusiasm.

Abruptly, Madison reached down and grasped his erection, wrapped her slim fingers around the shaft and began sliding her wrist steadily up and down. "Put it in me," she whispered.

Kurt moved between her legs and entered her warmth. Initially, he moved slowly and attentively, attempting to arouse her further with a deliberate and gentle motion. But his own arousal was just too much for him to control, and soon he began vigorously driving harder, forcing a yelp from Madison. "Easy," she cried, "you're hurting me."

He eased his stroking, purposefully suppressing his urges but still sliding in and out in a frenzied rhythm that quickly brought him to a shuddering conclusion.

She hardly moved in response, lying submissively beneath him as he found relief.

Kurt realized that it was a big mistake. He was fully aware that Madison was withdrawn and upset. He lay next to her contemplating the moment. Silently he vowed to be more attentive to her needs—sensitive, compassionate, and understanding.

Chapter Five

Early in the morning, the *Explorer* slowed to about half-speed as it approached the coastal port of Manzanillo, located about midway down the Mexican coast, halfway between the US and Guatemalan borders. Known in the fishing industry as the 'Sailfish Capital of the World', the port boasts an active sports fishing fleet that attracts anglers from all over the world to fish for sailfish, marlin, dorado, and huge tuna.

With the change in engine pitch, many of the passengers awoke to see what had caused the slowdown. Gathering on the foredeck, the early risers gazed out at the rolling hills and rugged mountains surrounding the city.

Dark menacing clouds hung low over the hills. As the sun rose, the skies took on a violent look, brooding and heavy over land but spreading vivid purple/pink striated clouds out over the ocean. Rain seemed imminent.

∞

Originally, the plan had been to skip Manzanillo and continue on to Acapulco; however, failed delivery of several very necessary engine parts while in Mazatlan and a lack of available cash for purchase of food and other essential supplies prompted Captain Ellis and Brian to schedule the stop. In an effort to save on costs, the decision was made to anchor in the outer bay rather than incur the expense of wharfage fees.

Maneuvering into the entrance to the bay, Captain Ellis picked a calm location inside Bahia Santiago, about halfway between the Juluapan and the Santiago Peninsula. He set the anchor in about forty feet of water and put a call out to the Captain of the Port to gain Customs and Immigration clearance. The officials from Manzanillo proved to be very pleasant and accommodating, stamping the papers and clearing everyone to go ashore in less than an hour.

Once cleared, Captain Ellis and Brian informed everyone that they expected to be in port overnight and planned to pull anchor and move on at daybreak. Therefore, they advised all to return to the ship before midnight when the last launch run would be made.

Nearly everyone decided to go ashore to see the sights and to replenish personal items. A flu-type illness spread through the boat a few days earlier, and a few passengers were still suffering, so the local farmacia was a popular place. Some had trouble communicating. Larry informed those who knew no Spanish to simply say 'inferma' (sick) and pantomime coughing and sneezing. He promised that the druggist would understand and prescribe a medication.

Most of the passengers headed off to visit the recently completed Las Hadas Hotel; an imposing structure built a few years previously on the Santiago Peninsula and a landmark attraction for wealthy tourists. Constructed in an Arabian style of architectural design, the Las Hadas had already earned a worldwide reputation as one of the premier destinations in all of Mexico.

For Kurt and Madison, their tight budget sometimes prevented them from joining the others in their various shore excursions; but they figured they could buy just one beer each while they enjoyed the luxurious pool and other amenities that the hotel offered. Madison was understandably quiet following the previous night's fiasco, while Kurt was doing his best to be both charming and nonchalant. His upbeat demeanor was working well for Tiona, who giggled and fawned at his humor—much to Madison's chagrin. Kurt recognized Madison's resentment and moved away from Tiona, curtailing his attempt at entertaining the others.

They spent the afternoon lolling about the pool, sipped cocktails, and munched on platters of chips and salsa while enjoying the local music of strolling mariachi groups. Kurt stayed clear of Tiona, despite her efforts to get close to him whenever possible. At one point when Kurt went for a swim and Madison relaxed on her lounge chair, Tiona surprised him by sliding up underneath him as he swam. Startled by her touch when she clutched at his stomach, Kurt immediately looked toward Madison. Fortunately, she was not watching.

"Tiona," Kurt admonished, "you need to back off. Madison is not happy with all the attention you are giving me. It has to stop."

"Oh, you spoil sport. I'm just having a little fun."

"Maybe so," Kurt replied, "but I'd appreciate it if you would have your fun some other way. Madison is already mad at me, and I really don't want to provoke her any more. Please, when she's around, try to keep your distance." He immediately recognized his mistake.

She looked at him coyly. "Okay," she demurred huskily. "So when she's not around, I'll come looking for you." And with that she turned and swam away.

Around four-thirty, most of them decided that it was time to return to the boat for the evening meal. Marcos and Linda elected to remain at the hotel for dinner—Linda's treat. Each of the others took an outdoor shower before leaving the hotel, in consideration of the water situation.

After taking the skiff back to the boat, the group went their separate ways to change and cleanup. Following an enjoyable plate of chicken tacos, everyone with the exception of Kurt and Guillermo—who had the evening watch—climbed aboard the skiffs and headed off for an evening in town.

Madison went with Larry, Tiona, and Charlie, and seemed to be in a more upbeat mood.

Kurt felt bewildered. It was not in her character to go off without him, nor to be interested in the party atmosphere. She had always clung closely to him, seldom going off on her own. Her personality had always been reserved, somewhat shy, and definitely introverted. With her recent tendency toward self-assertion, Kurt felt that she was losing some of her dependency on him while at the same time becoming more detached emotionally. He didn't like it very much.

The deck watch proved uneventful. At anchor in the bay, there was little to do or see. After sunset, with minimal traffic on the water, Kurt and Guillermo sat on the bridge of the ship and talked quietly together, mostly about fishing. They assisted the deckhands as they made their every-other-hour runs.

On the second run, five passengers, including Tiona, returned to the vessel. Charlie was not with her. Neither was Madison.

Tiona climbed up to the bridge and, looked directly at Kurt. She inquired coyly, "Is this a private party, or could a lonely young lady join you?"

Before Kurt could reply, Guillermo stood and responded eagerly. "Sure, please join us. It would be real nice to have a little female company for a change. Not that Kurt is boring, mind you, but a bit of female companionship is always a welcome event in any man's life."

"Great," Tiona intoned as she slid gracefully into the wheelhouse and planted herself in one of the two captain's chairs. "So what do you boys talk about when you're sitting here guarding the ship?"

"Fishing mostly," commented Guillermo with a twinkle in his eye. "We talk about fishing trips we've been on, funny things we've seen while fishing, and once in a while we talk about the women we've known."

"Oh, I like that!" Tiona gushed, looking quickly to Kurt. "Let's talk about that some more."

When Kurt failed to respond, Guillermo began to share some of his personal affairs, telling her about his two former wives and how each of them left him for other men. After hearing about his former loves for a few minutes, Tiona interjected that 'they both must have been very shallow and superficial because as far as she was concerned he was a real hunk'. Her comment, of course, boosted his ego, and prompted him to tell her about another woman he was currently seeing and had tried to convince to join him on this trip—to no avail.

Tiona responded, "Well, she should have come because she's really missing out on a whole lot of fun, right Kurt?"

Kurt was momentarily lost in his own thoughts, replying after an almost awkwardly long moment. "Yeah, Guillermo, she should have joined you. She is missing a lot." With that, Kurt looked up at the ship's clock and announced, "Our watch is nearly over, and relief should be here shortly."

Soon after, Captain Ellis entered the bridge area to take over the next four-hour watch. Leaving the captain to himself, Kurt, Guillermo, and Tiona headed back to the second deck.

"Can I fix you a drink, boys?" asked Tiona.

"Not for me, thanks," replied Kurt, "I'm going to call it a night."

"Oh come on," Tiona implored, "it's early, and one little drink won't hurt at all."

"Sounds good to me." Guillermo agreed, "I'd love a drink. Come on Kurt, why don't you join us?"

Kurt really liked the idea of a cold drink, but he was reluctant—or more like afraid—to spend too much time in Tiona's company, especially when they were drinking. He excused himself, telling them to enjoy the evening, and went off to his own private deck space.

After preparing his bunk, Kurt pulled out the book he was currently reading and curled up on his cot. One chapter later, the shore skiff returned to the boat. He fully expected Madison to be aboard; but when he looked over the rail, she was not among the few passengers that were seated in the small skiff. Neither were Linda, Larry, Madison, or Charlie.

He returned to his reading, but was having trouble concentrating. After reading the same paragraph three times and having no clue what he had just read, Kurt put the book down and started to reflect on his relationship with Madison. Once again he contemplated the independence that Madison was exhibiting. It was really out of character. Because of Madison's naiveté when they had moved in together, her mother had implored Kurt to always stay with her and to take good care of her. Kurt promised that he would.

His reverie was interrupted by soft footsteps. Tiona, wearing a loose-fitting, full-length cotton wrap, tiptoed over and stood next to him. She looked down and saw a deep furrow on Kurt's forehead. Tiona said quietly, "You look a little troubled, Kurt. Can I help?"

Returning her gaze, Kurt responded, "No, Tiona, I think you're part of the problem not part of the solution."

She stared at him, her yellow eyes searching his handsome features. After a few moments without any reaction, Tiona reached over and pulled on the sash holding her wrap together, the soft cotton fabric opening fully. She was completely naked underneath. Her body radiated golden in the shadowy glow of the muted deck lighting. Her breasts, tanned and oiled, jutted proudly, and the dark V of her pubic hair stood out distinctly in the small lighter triangle of skin that her bikini usually covered.

Kurt gulped, instantly aroused by her lurid appearance, and unable to shift his eyes from her body. She smiled at his masculine response and reached out with her hand, quickly locating his already engorged phallus. "Oh my." she purred, "You are the man."

Initially he was lost in the moment, relishing the sensations coursing through his body and his mind. There is nothing quite like the carnal touch of someone new, and he was ever so close to succumbing to her boldness. But something deeper inside also loomed strongly, his love and devotion to Madison. He reached down and grabbed Tiona by the wrist. Impetuously, he tore her hand from its grasp. "No, Tiona, I'm not ready for this."

Evidently surprised by his reaction, she laughed. "You've got to be kidding! If you're not ready, how do you explain that?" She demanded, pointing down at the rigidity in his shorts.

Kurt's response was quiet, but firm. "Yes, Tiona, I am completely and utterly turned on. You are desirable, intriguing, and alluring. But I am deeply involved with Madison; and regardless of your allure, I won't allow myself to violate our relationship."

She took a deep breath and slowly shook her head. "Okay Kurt Decker, I'll take no for an answer right now, but I want you. I've wanted you from the first day I laid eyes on you on the dock in Ensenada; and if you ever change your mind, or if another opportunity arises, I fully intend to ravish you in a way that you've never been ravished before."

He laughed softly, "I don't doubt that a bit. But for now, I think it would be best if you return to your own sleeping quarters."

She left. It was going on midnight and there would be only one more run of the shore skiff. Kurt's anxiety increased as time passed. He wasn't sure what he might do if Madison was not on the next boat.

When he saw it approaching, it was obviously at its capacity. He hadn't realized there were so many still ashore. Looking over the faces of the six passengers aboard, Madison was not one of them. He was about to go down to the second deck and talk with some of those disembarking when he heard Pablo—who was operating the skiff—holler out that there were four more still ashore and he would be returning shortly.

On the second run, Madison was aboard along with Charlie, Linda, and Larry.

It was a few long minutes before Madison made it up to the second deck. She had obviously been drinking; unsteady on her feet, her cheeks flushed with the glow of heavy alcohol consumption. She never could drink much without getting quickly and noticeably intoxicated.

He watched her, not saying anything.

"What?" she slurred, almost accusingly. "What? Is there a problem if I go out and have a little fun once in a while?"

"No Madison, there's not a problem unless you've got something to tell me." Immediately he regretted the remark.

"What's that supposed to mean? You don't trust me?" She snapped.

Kurt was very aware she was drunk, but he could also see that she was vexed, perhaps even hostile. It was not the right time to try and appease her. "Madison, everything is fine. I'm glad that you had a good time. But it's late, and I think we should just get some sleep."

Standing there swaying slightly, she maintained a look of churlish drunkenness. Kurt felt a sense of sorrow seeing her like that, realizing that she was melancholy and morose despite or perhaps because she was intoxicated, and that her angst was definitely directed at him. She stood rooted in place for a minute, her features eventually softened slightly. "Okay, I'm going to get ready for bed." She said.

After taking care of her needs, she returned and curled into a fetal position next to him, falling quickly asleep. As always whenever she drank too much, she began snoring softly.

∞

The following day began disastrously. Gus, the chief engineer and perhaps the most invaluable person on board, quit. He announced that he was sick and tired of the working conditions and unfulfilled promises. One of them had to do with money and the fact that he had not been paid for two months. His engine room helper, Timothy, went with him. Adding to the turmoil, Phil, an Australian carpenter and deckhand, quit as well. He cited the general working conditions, lack of materials and tools, and failed promises from the owners and Captain Ellis. A somber mood prevailed.

To make matters worse, the promised additional supplies and cash infusion from Canada had not arrived yet. Captain Ellis and Brian called another general meeting to try and allay some of the concerns that were running rampant throughout the ship. Brian informed the passengers that he would be assuming the duties of chief engineer, assuring everyone that he had an engineering degree and was intimately familiar with the *Explorer's* operating machinery. He also promised that supplies and additional funding would arrive soon, although it might not be for another day. That announcement prompted two more passengers to announce they would be leaving the ship, and they did not even attempt to ask for any reimbursement.

Captain Ellis offered several suggestions for those staying aboard, including the use of one of the skiffs for Guillermo and 'Hugo' (Howard Jones, a thirty-five year old former child actor) to take out diving. He also suggested a bus tour of the city, having made arrangements for a discounted price of only seven dollars American for the three-hour tour. Six passengers signed up.

Kurt and Madison elected to stay aboard. Madison was not too chipper, as she was suffering from a heavy hangover. Most of the others chose to go back to the Las Hadas to spend the day.

Kurt helped Guillermo and Hugo load the skiff with their dive-gear and checkout the outboard engine. With everything in order, they headed out to the far headland where diving was reportedly excellent. They promised to return by five o'clock.

By six o'clock, there was still no sign of the skiff with Guillermo and Hugo. Captain Ellis asked Kurt where they had gone. When Kurt pointed out toward the point and explained their plans, he informed the captain that he would be willing to take the other skiff out and search for them when it returned from its next shore trip. Captain Ellis agreed.

Taking Bob Bradley with him, Kurt headed off to the headland about two miles distant as night was rapidly approaching. When they reached the headland where they expected to find the skiff, it was nowhere in sight. They cruised around the point for about a mile, focusing on the beach in case they had gone aground. They saw nothing.

They were just preparing to return to the ship when Kurt spotted a small boat moving slowly toward them from down the coast. Waiting patiently for it to near, Kurt and Bob were relieved to see a panga towing the wayward skiff in its wake. Waving their arms, Kurt and Bob pulled alongside the panga and relieved it of its tow. Bob handed the sun-browned fishermen a ten-dollar bill for their help.

Irate, Guillermo cussed and cursed their fate.

He told Kurt and Bob that they had decided the currents were too strong at the headland, so they headed around the point and down the coast a couple of miles. After trying several locations, they found a small cove that was full of life and proceeded to spear a few fish and grab several lobster. As they started back, they ran out of gas. They attempted to anchor; but they were running too close to the rocks. The skiff became caught in the surf, rolled over and ended upside down.

Guillermo was caught beneath the skiff as it plummeted toward the rocks; but he managed to free himself just in time to avoid a real bashing. He lost a chunk of skin from two of his fingers during the dunking. Hugo managed to swim to a small sandy beach behind the rocks, where the skiff eventually settled. They went back out three or four times in search of their dive gear and other equipment, finding about half. They lost all of the fish and lobster.

After a couple of hours, they managed to flag down the panga and swam a towline out to it. With Guillermo and Hugo pushing from shore and the panga engine wound-up as tightly as it would go, they managed to pull the skiff loose and climb back aboard. Fortunately, the aluminum skiff was not holed, albeit severely dented.

Back at the *Explorer,* Captain Ellis began to berate Guillermo and Hugo for going off too far. Guillermo became furious, lashing back at the captain about the inadequacy of the skiff.

"I thought this son of a bitch motor was supposed to run all day on a tank of gas!" Guillermo screamed.

"You should not have gone so far!" retorted the captain.

"Big deal, man! So What? So we went a few hundred yards further. If this little bastard motor was worth a shit, we wouldn't have had to worry at all!"

"Okay, that's enough!" Brian jumped into the fracas. "It's over. Hopefully it taught all of us a little lesson."

Tempers cooled, and Guillermo and Hugo cleaned up the skiff. They lost some expensive dive gear; but at least they made it back, and the skiff still had the engine attached. Brian helped them remove it from the transom and turn it upside down in a barrel of fresh water (grey water from the galley), keeping it submersed until he could pull it apart and make repairs during the daylight hours.

It was a quiet night aboard. Most of the remaining passengers decided to stay on the boat that evening, playing cards and talking amongst themselves about the days events and their concerns about how long the 'five-week' cruise was taking. Already they had been aboard for over three weeks, and they were only about one-fourth of the way to Jamaica. At this rate, making even Panama within the five-week time allotment was unlikely, which could become a major issue for many of the remaining passengers.

Early the following morning, a few of the promised supplies arrived at the docks. Captain Ellis made arrangements to dock alongside one of the wharfs where they could load the equipment, staples (toilet paper, bags of potatoes, a new ice-machine, and other items) onto the ship. Once loaded, they went back out to anchor while Brian stayed ashore to try and finalize the wire transfer of additional funds. He was gone all day. On his return, he and Captain Ellis went into the Captain's cabin, emerging about ten minutes later to inform all that there was another short delay. They hoped to have everything resolved by early the next morning.

When Brian went ashore the following morning, Captain Ellis denied shore leave for any others, asserting that Brian would not be long in completing his task, at which time they would hoist anchor and depart. It was a hot day, humid and sultry, and the mood aboard the ship darkened as the day wore on. It would be almost nightfall before Brian returned, whereupon he announced he had received part of the promised funding and the remainder would be waiting for them when the ship reached Acapulco, slightly over four hundred miles distant. The Captain decided to get underway and clear the port before dark, with a plan to cruise through the night, and likely for the following three and a half days.

∞

Underway again, the slow lazy roll of the Pacific met the *Explorer* broadside, until the ship was far enough from shore to change to a more southerly course. With the change in course came a change in the ship's motion, the slight lift and fall of the swell soothing and comforting.

Toward dusk, a number of sailfish put on an airborne display, knifing majestically from the deep indigo-colored water, twisting in the fading sunlight to display brief flashes of brilliant silver and iridescent blue before falling back into the briny depths. Several large gray/brown dorsal fins also appeared on the glassy sea surface behind the boat, probably mako sharks lazily swishing their sleek tails in their incessant search for weak or unsuspecting prey or for scraps tossed overboard. It is quite common to have makos follow in a ship's wake, especially slower vessels. Jettisoned table scraps and other food items are easy pickings for the voracious predators.

After dinner, the passengers all gathered on the foredeck to while away the hours.

Guillermo entertained the group with stories about his life in Montana, colorfully describing some of his favorite escapades. After a while, everyone drifted off and went to their deck spots to sleep.

Dawn broke with a crimson glow in the eastern sky, a portent of foul weather. As the vessel churned southward along the Mexican coastline, dark brooding clouds steadily built. By ten a.m., a heavy squall rumbled off the distant shore, bringing gusty winds of about thirty knots, heavy rain, thunder, and lightning. The squall was localized, and the sea surface became a little choppy; but it was not a large enough disturbance to create heavy seas. All of the passengers relished the rain, going out onto the deck to cast their arms upward and let the deluge wash away the sticky sweat and grime from the heat and humidity.

Kurt and Madison helped Pablo rig a canvas rain-catcher that fed into a couple of empty fifty gallon barrels. On the boat, there was never enough fresh water available; and the extra hundred gallons could be used for a number of things, including rinsing dive masks and snorkels, cleaning fishing lures, and merely splashing a little cool fresh water onto the body.

Soon the squall passed, and the heat and humidity returned with a vengeance. Lots of tiny flying fish sparkled as they broke the surface, gliding gracefully for a couple of hundred feet before splashing carelessly back into the water. They were running about fifteen miles offshore, but the coastline was barely visible through the heat vapors wafting off the surface of the peaceful sea.

Kurt and Madison walked up to the bow and leaned on the fore-rail, watching the sharp prow of the ship slice through the deep purple-colored water. Madison wore a short, loose fitting white cotton sundress, her now tanned legs, arms, and shoulders glowing in the sunshine. She looked absolutely ravishing with her lustrous strawberry-blonde hair burnt white-blonde by the past few weeks of tropical sun. It was as if she had transformed from a cute librarian or schoolteacher into a captivating beach goddess. She shifted her weight, the soft curve of her hips jutting provocatively, evoking an animal-like sensuality—as a wild cat might appear in the shadowed duskiness of the jungle.

Kurt was mesmerized, observing her in a vastly different light than he was accustomed to seeing. Suddenly, he was cognizant of the fact that she had a new awareness of her femininity, and he felt slightly disturbed by this new realization. In his mind, it explained some of her recent independence and gave him a possessive desire to refocus on their relationship. Perhaps it was not as strong as he thought. Perhaps he was taking her too much for granted.

CHAPTER SIX

Entering the Bay of Acapulco was a treat for everyone on board. Lush tropical landscapes covered the steep hills that surround the scenic tourist destination. Backed by high mountains in an elongated mushroom-shaped bay, the shoreline of the city is lined with hotels, businesses, restaurants, and bars. With a population in excess of five hundred thousand, Acapulco is Mexico's largest coastal city.

Captain Ellis set the anchor in the northwestern portion of the bay, about three hundred yards from what they soon discovered to be the Acapulco Yacht Club. The Captain called on Channel 16 for port clearance. The Captain of the Port arrived on scene within fifteen minutes, and rapidly cleared everyone for shore leave.

All of the passengers were anxious to get to shore, both to replenish their own supplies—especially alcohol and snacks—but also to find a bar where cold drinks were available. Since the refrigeration went down about forty-eight hours earlier, the demand for cold drinks, even water, had magnified.

Dozens of magnificent yachts lie anchored in the protected waters. At the nearby yacht club basin, many smaller yachts and well-maintained pleasure craft line the docks. Quite obviously, Acapulco is a port with much more affluence than any of the other ports previously visited. Luxurious hotels are visible from the ship, their austere Spanish and Mediterranean structures spreading imperially into the hillsides. Thousands of coconut palms stand tall and erect along the shoreline, swaying gently on their tall trunks, their rounded canopies heavy with coconut seeds. It is truly an impressive destination, ripe for adventure.

∞

As soon as customs and immigration cleared everyone for leave, the two skiffs started taking passengers ashore. Captain Ellis informed all that the ship would be spending two days in Acapulco, with a scheduled departure time of two p.m. two-days hence.

Nearly everyone went to shore. Kurt and Madison stayed aboard for a while, swimming and frolicking in the warm waters of the bay. Madison was using one of the small foam Boogey-boards. After a while, they swam the roughly two hundred yards across to the Acapulco Yacht Club, an elegant resort with two large swimming pools built at the edge of the water, overlooking the bay. They were about to start the long swim back when a rather imposing figure approached them at the edge of the dock.

The tall dark man had an aura of mystery and power surrounding him. Large and burly, he stood well over six-feet tall, and his dark good looks added to his mystique. Kurt and Madison were momentarily wary; but when he spoke, the friendly timber of his voice helped to set them at ease.

"Hola," he greeted them, "I am Santiago. Would you join me for a cocktail?"

They accepted the offer; and after two delightful mixed drinks and some animated conversation, they informed their host that they should return to their boat.

Both of them were relieved and appreciative when Santiago offered to take them back in his dinghy. They climbed into his twelve-foot inflatable skiff and headed back to the boat. Pulling alongside, several of the other passengers, including Larry, Marcos and Linda had just recently arrived in the aluminum skiff. They were standing near the rail watching the inflatable approach. Linda leaned over the rail and called down, "Oh my. It looks like you two found a new friend!"

"Yes. This is Santiago. He gave us a ride back from the yacht club."

Santiago waved, and then turned to Kurt and Madison while pointing over to another rather large boat anchored nearby. "That is my boat, the *El*

Viejo," he told them. "Perhaps you could join me for lunch tomorrow and bring a few of your shipmates?"

His offer would result in a very unexpected turn of events.

∞

Back on board, they found the beginnings of a small party in progress. Several of the passengers had returned from shore with coolers packed with ice, replenishments of beer, rum, vodka, and tequila, and adequate quantities of fruit juice for mixers. Kurt and Madison joined the party.

As the liquid spirits flowed, the individual spirits of the passengers soared. Soon they were swimming, diving from the stern deck, and frolicking in the warm eighty-one degree water. Into the night the partying continued with everyone getting drunker by the minute. Someone found a local radio station playing American music from the sixties, and although it was slightly muffled by static, the beat was enough to get many of the group dancing. As usual, Tiona danced at the forefront, showing her exuberance with great abandon. Madison soon joined in the dancing along with Linda. The three girls put on quite a show for everyone, swinging and swaying together until Captain Ellis came out on deck and requested the party be toned-down so that he and others could get some sleep.

It was nearly midnight, and they all wandered off to their sleeping areas.

Pausing near their sleeping space, Kurt asked Madison if she might like to go for a little moonlight cruise in the bay in one of the skiffs.

"But we're not supposed to take the skiffs out without permission," she responded, referring to one of the Captain's edicts. "He'll hear it start and won't be very happy with us."

"It's okay," reassured Kurt, "I'll paddle us away from the boat so that nobody can hear the engine start."

Intoxicated enough to let her usually conservative inhibitions down, Madison agreed.

Kurt untied the skiff and helped Madison aboard, then paddled about two hundred feet out into the bay, opposite the Captain's quarters. Satisfied that they were out of earshot, Kurt started the engine, and they headed out into the center of the bay. The lights of the city sparkled luminously in the warm tropical air, the reflective shine sending streaks of shimmering radiance across the mirrored surface of the dark calm water.

When they reached the approximate center of the bay, Kurt shut down the engine, and they drifted. Together they absorbed the ambiance of their surroundings. After a few minutes, she glanced coquettishly at him and whispered, "So, what are we going to do, just sit here all night?"

Kurt moved across to her seat, and murmured huskily, "Actually, I had something else in mind."

"Yeah," she responded sweetly, "I figured you did."

For the next little while the two shared each other intimately, reveling in the pleasure of each other's yearning, as well as the excitement and titillation of the moment. The small aluminum skiff was not the most comfortable place for making love; but using the lifejackets for padding, they made it work.

Afterward, they sat quietly side by side, savoring the hedonistic pleasure. Neither bothered to get dressed, instead they relished the naughty feeling of sitting in the middle of Acapulco Bay nude, enjoying the lingering sensations of their lovemaking and guilelessly stimulated by their mutually uncharacteristic exhibitionism.

Madison smiled softly and cuddled against Kurt. She shivered slightly and Kurt wrapped his arms around her.

She touched his chest, and rubbed her fingertips softly over his toned physique. He responded rapidly to her touch. She reached over, turned his face toward hers and whispered. "Stand up."

He grinned, shifted his legs to gain balance and stood before her. In the middle of Acapulco Bay with Madison kneeling before him, Kurt smiled, oblivious to everything except the pleasure.

Madison looked up into his face, and Kurt could tell that she was smiling also.

Afterward, they sat down together on the seat of the skiff. "I'm thirsty," she told him.

"I guess I should have brought along something to drink." He apologized, as he looked around to confirm that there was nothing on board to quench her thirst. "Shall we head back to the boat?"

She looked over at him. "No, not yet, let's just sit here for a while."

They sat together happily, his arms cuddling her, with her head resting against his chest. Surrounding them, the sights and sounds of the City of Acapulco were beginning to diminish as morning drew near. It was close to four a.m., the night owls were heading for home, and the morning work crews were just beginning to stir. It was perhaps the quietest hour of the day in a city that slept only minimally. When the first faint vestiges of dawn broke above the dark mountains to the east, they put their clothes back on and headed back to the ship, before daylight caught them out where they were not supposed to be.

∞

Back on board, Kurt and Madison slept the entire morning, awakening around noon. Most of the others had gone ashore to explore the city and surrounding countryside. It was sultry and humid once again, a thick layer of heavily laden stratus clouds threatening rain. Kurt awakened drenched in sweat despite the fact that he had slept with only a thin sheet. When he rolled off the mat, his movement awakened Madison, and she whispered gutturally, "God, it's hot. What time is it?"

Kurt had stowed his pocket watch right after they departed Ensenada several weeks before. He saw no need to know the time, nor even the date. He looked down at Madison's sleep swollen face, bent down, and kissed her lightly on the nose. "I have no idea, and I could care less. The only thing I know for sure is that you are the loveliest woman in the world, I am hot and sticky, and I'm going to jump into the water and try to cool off."

Madison rolled off her own sleeping mat and responded, "Wait for me a few minutes, and I'll go in with you."

The swim was refreshing although it caused them to miss lunch. They settled for a couple of bananas from Marcos and Linda. It was amazing how flavorful the local fruit taste—completely unlike fruit purchased in grocery stores in California. Every kind of fruit from the bananas to mangos, papayas, kiwi fruit, melons, literally everything they tried was bursting with natural flavor and succulent juices.

In the early afternoon, Kurt and Madison decided to go ashore and do a little exploring on their own. They walked the streets of Acapulco, and marveled at the variety of plants and flowers and the abundance of palm trees adorning the coastal flats.

After spending about four hours ashore, Kurt and Madison returned to the boat and discovered that Brian had hired a ski-boat for the afternoon. Many of the passengers aboard the *Explorer* took advantage of his largesse; taking turns water skiing around the bay. The boat was not powerful enough to pull two skiers at a time, but it served well for towing one. After waiting to take his turn, Kurt slipped on the skis and relished his opportunity to ski.

Later, it was a quiet and peaceful evening aboard the boat, where everyone soaked up the ambiance of the night, and the beautiful glow of the city lights dancing upon the rippled surface of the bay.

∞

The following morning, the tender from the *El Viejo* pulled alongside their boat. A deckhand asked to speak to Kurt. When Kurt reached the rail and looked down, the deckhand called up to him, "Captain Santiago has extended his lunch invitation for you and your friends. May I tell him yes?"

Before Kurt could reply, Tiona, who was standing nearby responded.

"Ooh, it sounds very intriguing," she purred, "A dark and mysterious man inviting all of us aboard his yacht for lunch. Count me in."

After discussing the matter with those standing nearby, Kurt accepted the offer from the deckhand, informing him that there would be six or seven in their group.

"Very good. I will inform the captain!" He shoved off and headed back to the *El Viejo*.

At precisely noon, Kurt, Madison, Larry, Tiona, Marcos, and Linda piled into the skiff and headed across to the *El Viejo*. Charlie confessed to a slight dose of turistas and wasn't up to socializing.

Arriving alongside, they were met at the boarding ladder by Santiago and another conservative looking man in his late forties or early fifties.

The yacht was a little smaller than theirs, about one hundred-ten feet in length overall. On the stern in bold calligraphy was the name, *El Viejo* (the Old One). Like the *Explorer*, it was a classic full-displacement, wooden-hulled design, featuring the rounded sweeping fantail, the sheer prow, and lots of varnished mahogany. Unlike their vessel, all of the varnish, paint, and other cosmetic touches aboard the ship were meticulously maintained and immaculate.

"Welcome!' beamed Santiago, sweeping his arm out in a theatrical manner, "My ship is at your service."

He then proceeded to introduce the other gentleman as one of his partners. His name was Manuel, and although he appeared to be friendly, he spoke little.

Santiago, on the other hand, proved to be a very interesting man. He stood roughly six feet-four and weighed perhaps two hundred thirty pounds—all solid looking. His square jaw bore a perpetual five-o'clock shadow; his dark wavy hair and well-manicured jet-black mustache projected a brooding, almost menacing countenance—that is until his eyes made contact. His eyes, shielded by thick, heavy eyebrows, shined incredibly large and black as polished coal. Oddly, as dark as they were, they twinkled as if illuminated from within. When his eyes made contact, it was almost as if they had a life of their own, full of humor and seemingly aware of everything.

Tiona seemed particularly mesmerized. She extended her hand and stepped forward. "Hi, I'm Tiona. Thank you for inviting us aboard your ship."

Santiago reached out with both of his large bear-like hands, smothering Tiona's hand in a firm grip before pulling it gently to his mouth for a long lingering kiss. "It is my complete pleasure to meet you, Tiona," he told her in his deep resonating voice while gazing into her yellow cat-like eyes.

She stood rooted to the deck, mesmerized by his chivalry, and unable even to breathe. After a few moments, she finally took a deep breath, and that breath broke the spell that encompassed both of them. He released his grip on her hand and slowly lowered her arm back to her side. Turning partway to the others, but keeping his eyes on Tiona, Santiago said, "Please join us on the aft deck."

Turning to one of his deckhands, he ordered, "Miguel, please bring us all one of your fruit specialties, with rum. No, wait just a moment. Are there any of you that do not wish a touch of our special Acapulco rum in your drink?" When there were no negative responses, he politely bade Miguel to go ahead with his request.

Seated in the shade of table umbrellas, Santiago proceeded to tell his guests about himself.

"First, and last, I am a pirate. But also I am an honest businessman. My work is my pleasure, and my pleasure is to enjoy life." He laughed, throatily, "And that, my friends, is what I do." Pausing for emphasis and with a gesture with his muscled arm, he went on, "As you can see, I fly the flag of the pirate; but I also fly the flag of Acapulco and the American flag. It is easier in most countries if the American flag is flying. I carry more than two hundred flags of many cities and countries aboard my ship, and I will fly each one when it is the time to do so. But I will always fly the colors of the pirate. It is the universal symbol used by the original pirates of Spain. Of course, they were marauders as well, and vicious murderers, which I am not. But a pirate is a pirate, and I am a good one!"

He threw back his head and roared a loud and raucous laugh. It was a laugh emanating from the very core of his body, and everyone was caught up in its power and effect. A person could not help but laugh with him.

When asked just what it is that he does in the business world, Santiago responded, "As I have made clear, first and foremost, I am a pirate. But I also make movies."

He paused and looked around, apparently satisfied that he had all their attention.

Santiago continued. "I make children's movies. It is my passion to make films that children can enjoy and that are suitable for young children. They are the most difficult of all productions. Adults, you can sell them anything. They are fooled easily and entertained by everything from naked whores to boat-eating sharks. A child, he does not fool so easily. The child, he knows a shark could not eat the boat, a whale maybe, a shark no. I must make movies that are believable to a child, and can give them glimpses of life that maybe have meaning; but more than anything, something that they can just simply have fun to watch. That is my challenge, and that is what I do well."

The drinks were brought in, and they were impressive. Served in hand-blown tumblers with palm trees etched onto the surface, the twelve-inch tall glasses contained nearly a quart of delightful fruit juices, cuts of lime, pineapple, and oranges as well as rum; and they were served with crushed ice and brightly colored, triple-looped straws. "Please note the color of your straw." Santiago informed the group. "Each is distinctive; so you can tell yours from the others if you should set it down."

After the drinks were served, Santiago continued with his lively dialogue. "Not all of my work, though, is for children. My family has a large cattle ranch in Sonora, Mexico. We have shrimp boats in Guaymas. We have hotels here in Acapulco and restaurants in several cities. We also help our peasant peoples. They sell our cheap products on the streets—shirts, pottery, baskets, and hand-carved figurines. We are a large organization, and we try to help our people. Our country, it is good and beautiful; but the politicos move more to the left all the time; so we are also starting to invest in the United States."

Brazenly, Larry asked, "Are you associated with or part of the Mexican mafia?"

Santiago leaned back and roared his deep, booming laugh.

"Mafia? Of course! We are pirates! We are mafia! We are business! It is all the same! There are only factions—the left, the right, the middle! We like to walk the centerline. It is much easier there and not quite so crooked." He laughed deeply again at his little joke then continued. "It is better for us to stay in the middle, that way one is not as apt to stumble and fall, or at least not fall too far. But then, I am being too serious now, yes? Work is such a small portion of life. Fun and happiness is much more. So, let us be alive. Let us have fun. Let us live!"

With that, he ordered another round of drinks for all, despite the fact that most of the drinks were not even half consumed, and directed his staff to serve lunch. The meal consisted of an array of fruit, platters of thinly sliced meats and cheeses, a shrimp platter, assorted breads and bolillos, and colorful Mexican cookies. Everyone ate ravenously, enjoying the splendid quality and ample quantities of delightful cuisine.

Afterward, he advised Miguel to have his other guests join everyone on the aft deck. He suggested that everyone swim off the boat, informing all that he had twin guest dressing rooms; the ladies with a pink door on the port side of the salon and the men a blue door on the starboard side.

Each of the guests had brought along their swimwear and went in to change. Returning to the aft deck, it was surprising to see about a dozen more people, including several children running around the ship. Many of the guests took turns jumping from a specially designed 'diving board' slipped into a custom created slot on the fantail. It was about eight feet above the water and was a great sport, especially for the youngsters. Between the swimming and diving, everyone sat around with Santiago and his other guests talking and laughing together. A trio of pretty young Mexican ladies in their early twenties was among the other guests, and they had a great time laughing and joking with Larry and Marcos in their fractured Spanish.

Later in the afternoon, Santiago invited his guests on a tour of his boat. Going through the ship, everyone was impressed with the lavish accommodations, custom woodwork, and unique amenities that were built into every room and cabin.

He took the small group into his own private master cabin. The woodwork was impressive, with elaborate hand-carved exotic woods built into the large and expansive room. Everything was curved and smooth with all the tables, counters, drawers, and chairs beautifully carved and seemingly cut from one single tree. An ornate headboard with a king-size bed left plenty of walk-around room. Clearly the room was designed for more than mere privacy, with four hand-crafted sitting areas carved into the outer walls of the room, each strategically positioned to give a view of the sea from one of the shining brass portholes. It was truly a room built for a king.

Seated on the pillowed end of the large and comfortable looking bed, Santiago reached over and slid open a hidden drawer built into the headboard. From the foot-deep drawer he extracted a custom crafted and highly varnished wooden box carved from a reddish-purple exotic wood. Opening the box, Santiago pulled out a velvet-covered bag and zipped it open. A deep pungent aroma immediately filled the room.

"This," he stated unequivocally, 'is the finest 'Acapulco Gold' in all of Mexico." Turning to Larry, he reached over and asked, "Would you care to roll a joint for us to share?"

Larry grinned as he took the outstretched bag, which contained at least a full pound of the most golden-hued marijuana that he had ever seen. "I would be proud to roll a joint. Since there are seven of us, should I go ahead and roll a couple?"

Santiago laughed, "There is no need of that. One is more than enough for all of us." He took the first hit, a slow shallow drag that he inhaled easily, and then passed it along to Tiona. "Please be careful. Do not try to drag too deeply as this blend is probably more potent than anything any of you have ever tried."

Taking the joint and looking into his deeply glowing eyes, Tiona purred huskily, "Oh, I think I've sampled some very high quality grass in my time but thanks for the warning." She took a somewhat deep drag and immediately began coughing.

"Ah!" Santiago guffawed, "So, it is rather potent, yes?"

Seeing Tiona's reaction, the others inhaled much more cautiously; but even so, a couple of the others could not avoid a coughing fit. The joint went around the room twice before Santiago inquired laughingly. "So, does anyone of you feel the need for more?"

His laughter became infectious, and soon the room was filled with tear-raising laughter. The yellowish-green entrails of smoke wafted in the air. Each of them was lost in a heightened state of sensations, floating comfortably in their own world of euphoria. Time seemed to drift. Some light conversation took place, but mostly the guests simply sat in the cabin absorbed in the beauty of the room or lost in their own private thoughts and visions, laughing inexplicably on occasion. After a while, Santiago suggested they return to the deck, and they all followed along as the children of Babylon had followed the piper.

Returning to the deck, Larry commented that it was time to go, as dinner would be served shortly. They all made their farewells and thanked Santiago profusely for his hospitality. Nobody was too surprised when Tiona announced that Santiago had asked her to stay for dinner, and she had accepted.

Climbing back into the skiff, Kurt started the engine. As he headed back toward their boat, Linda asked timidly, "What are we going to tell Charlie?"

"Well," Kurt responded, "maybe we just don't say anything unless he asks; and if he does, I guess we just tell him that Tiona stayed for dinner." The others pondered this response, not making any comment.

On the way back to the ship Kurt altered course to go around a large cargo ship that was apparently moving up the channel. Applying a little power to move around its high bow, Larry called out sharply, "Kurt! Look out! That ship is going to run us over!"

Changing course to swing back toward the stern of the large ship, Kurt completed a full circle and went approximately fifty feet before stopping the skiff and reassessing the situation. After looking closer, he began to laugh.

"What's so funny?" Madison questioned.

"It's at anchor!" Kurt replied, as he laughed and realized that all of them were still feeling the effects of the powerful 'Acapulco Gold' that they had shared on Santiago's yacht.

∞

On board the *El Viejo*, Santiago sent all of his other guests to shore to one of his family's restaurants for dinner on his tab, leaving him alone with Tiona, two crewmen, and his chef. He also made arrangements for his guests to stay ashore in one of his company hotels.

Instructing his crew to set up the upper deck for a candlelight dinner, Santiago proceeded to woo Tiona in elegant fashion. The deck area soon took on a very personal and romantic setting. Subtle lighting added to the ambiance.

Santiago told his crewman to bring up a bottle from his private selection of wine. He explained that the grapes are grown exclusively in the valleys outside of Acapulco, and the wine is considered perhaps the finest wine in all of Mexico, available at only two locations.

They dined on dainty filet mignon, lobster, and a host of succulent sliced fruits and fresh vegetables, although neither ate too heartily. Instead, both chatted animatedly, exhibiting a building sexual tension, and anxious to get beyond the formalities of food and drink. Once their meal was finished, Santiago instructed the crew that he no longer needed their services, and that they could go ashore, He informed them he would call on the radio when needed. Once they were gone, Tiona and Santiago immediately turned to each other and embraced.

Tiona looked flushed, and he sensed her urgency.

"Ah, my dear," he whispered huskily, "You are eager, willing, and wanton. But let us not rush too fast. Instead, let us savor each other and the moment more leisurely. I assure you, it will be to your great pleasure."

With that, he began a very slow and deliberate caressing of her body, rubbing her skin softly through her sheer summer dress, touching her with strong gentle fingers that brushed her lightly.

He could see that she was his for the taking, beyond ready and willing. Yet still he lingered, tantalizing her further with gentle caresses, while somehow managing to hold her at arm's distance.

She stepped back and lifted her thin light dress over her head, exposing her bare skin. She wore no undergarments.

"Ah, delightful!" Santiago laughed lightly. "You are as beautiful as I expected, perhaps even more so."

"Please," she begged him, "stop toying with me and give me what I want."

Smiling enigmatically Santiago continued to hold her with his powerful hands, gazing over her tanned female curves and preventing her from touching any part of him except his hands, wrists and arms. "Alright my little one," he finally agreed, "I will now let you do with me as you wish."

With that, he released her from his grip and in a smooth motion pulled off his own loose-fitting shirt and pants, then stood before her in his own bare skin.

Tiona stared at his incredible masculinity, transfixed by his animalistic torso. He was an absolute male Adonis. His broad shoulders, barrel chest, narrow waist, and powerful legs were covered in thick curly black hair. "Oh my God," she whispered.

She had known a lot of men in her life, many of them full of virility and well endowed. But never had she known anyone even close to Santiago. With dry lips and her heart pounding furiously, Tiona appeared lost. She licked her lips. Her fingers entwined in his curly hair, and she whimpered breathlessly, "Oh, my God. What are you doing to me?"

"I am making pure and perfect love to you, my dear. Are you enjoying yourself?"

"Oh, yes," she purred huskily, "more than you could possibly know."

He grinned, an almost angry-looking smile that seemed to excite her even more as he took her to places she could not have known existed.

∞

Twice more, Santiago brought Tiona to incredible heights. While not as powerful as the first episode, each successive coupling left her trembling. When he told her that he must retire for the night, and would fetch the skiff to take her back to her boat she felt hurt and disappointed. She wanted to stay with him.

She pouted and became quiet. He seemed almost indifferent, furthering her despair.

He went into the cabin and put out a call on the radio. When the skiff drew alongside the *El Viejo*, Santiago leaned across, lifted her chin, and kissed her warmly on the mouth. He told her, "You are special, and I enjoyed the evening very much."

She waited. He said nothing more. After looking into his dark eyes, hoping that something more might be forthcoming, she eventually turned away and climbed down the boarding ladder and into the waiting skiff.

Back aboard, she very quietly entered her cabin and prepared for bed. It was after three a.m., but she sensed that Charlie was awake. She also knew that he would not rise or say anything. After taking care of her needs, she climbed into her bunk. Sleep was a long time coming, partly because she was relishing the incredible feelings that still simmered within her body, and partly because she just didn't understand her abrupt dismissal by Santiago. Eventually, she fell asleep.

In the morning, Tiona awoke sore and stiff; but she also still felt the lingering, pleasurable effects of the previous night's lovemaking. When she climbed stiffly out of her bunk and went to the cabin porthole to look out at the *El Viejo*, tears welled in her eyes. It was gone. Somehow she knew that it would be. She crawled back into her bunk and cried herself back to sleep.

∞

On board the *Explorer*, a couple of changes had taken place. First Mate Leonard had departed the ship, taking another position on one of the large cruise ships that frequented Acapulco Harbor. To take his place, Captain Ellis found an Englishman who professed to have considerable boating background and navigational expertise. His name was Jeffrey Smythe. His strong English accent indicated that he had spent most of his years

Doug Oudin

living in Britain. Larry quickly bestowed the nickname of 'El Jefe' upon Jeffrey Smythe.

The passenger count was down to nineteen, and two cabins were available for anyone wanting more privacy. Not everyone wanted to be considered for the cabins, but those that did dropped their names into a bowl, and two names were drawn. Marcos was one of them; so he and Linda relocated from their deck space into their own cabin.

Captain Ellis also informed everyone that there would be another delay of at least two more days before departing Acapulco. His announcement caused one more couple to leave the ship.

Hearing the news of yet another delay, Kurt and Madison, Marcos and Linda, and Larry elected to do a little exploring outside of the city. Tiona and Charlie had not come out of their cabin.

Catching a bus marked with a destination of Pie de la Cuesta, the group of five rode the bus out of town to the north, along the rugged La Azteca mountain range to a point where the paved road ended. The ride out of town was quite beautiful. As was their custom when traveling aboard the local buses, Larry and Marcos began to loudly sing the Rocky Raccoon song. As usual, their enthusiasm grew contagious, and soon everyone in the bus hooted and hollered encouragement. When the song ended, Larry began loudly reciting one of the Spanish lessons he had memorized in high school. His recitation didn't make much sense, something about meeting some girls in the library and taking seats around one of the tables; but everyone on board thought it was hilarious.

When the bus reached the end of the line at a dirt road, the group from the ship climbed off to a rousing ovation from the other passengers. Waving and hollering 'Adios,' they looked around at the spectacular scenery. On one side of the road, the blue Pacific sparkled. On the opposite side of the road, a lovely lagoon partially covered in lily pads and surrounded by lush tropical plants, trees, and flowers lent a magical ambiance.

They headed off along the narrow strip of land separating the sea and lagoon. Large frogs became startled along the edge of the lagoon, leaping and splashing into the calm water and sending a series of semi-circular wavelets across the placid surface. Several white egrets sat perched on mangrove branches along the shore of the lagoon. Under an overhanging guava tree, were two small hand-carved canoes piled high with coconuts.

Kurt pointed out a four-foot long green iguana sunning itself on one of the limbs of a nearby mahogany tree. It was a primitive scene, raw and surreal, yet exotically beautiful.

About a half-mile into their walk, a brightly painted Volkswagen bus pulled up alongside. A friendly looking man stuck his head out of the window and spoke to them in Spanish.

"Good afternoon. My brother and I saw you walk by our house. We think you look hot. We invite you to our home for refreshments." Larry translated for the others. It was very hot, and they were all thirsty. The man sitting behind the wheel looked quite friendly, his smile infectious. They accepted the invitation.

The driver smiled broadly, climbed out, and slid open the side door. All five piled into the vehicle, and the van drove a few hundred yards back to a side road that led to a small white house they had noticed about a quarter of a mile back on the ocean side of the road. When they arrived at the small cottage, another man a few years older stepped off the porch and greeted them in heavily accented, but understandable English.

"Hola, I am Alfonso, this is my brother Victor. We get few visitors here. Please, be seated and I will bring you each a cold beer."

It was a beautiful place, nestled on a knoll between the lagoon and the ocean with a spectacular view of both. The home was tiny; probably no more than eight hundred square feet, and completely surrounded by a well-maintained white covered porch. All around the property, exotic plants with colorful flowers bloomed. Several brightly colored tropical birds sat perched on the branches of nearby trees, and numerous hummingbirds darted in and out of the flowering blossoms. Situated between the ten-mile long Coyoca Lagoon on one side and the blue Pacific on the other, the property was truly a picturesque paradise. Large Montezuma Pine, Mexican White Oak, and assorted fruit trees shaded the grounds. Flowering Poinciana, abejon, acacias, mimosas, and organ cactus provided color and variety to the peripheral landscape, with flowering hibiscus, thick bougainvillea, fragrant plumeria, bird of paradise, and dozens of other colorful native plants adding to the beauty.

The brothers took great pride in their garden and kept everything trimmed and well manicured. Several large land lizards scurried between the vegetation, while green iguanas clung passively to the lower limbs of trees. Multi-colored parrots and macaws perched regally in the treetops, adding bright colors to the already majestic canopy overhead. Dark little monkeys hung lithely from several branches, occasionally swinging into motion as they climbed from limb to limb.

This was what they had all been waiting to see. This was the tropical paradise that each of them had envisioned when they signed up for the 'five-week' cruise. All around them, the beauty and vivid natural choreography of the tropics captured the imagination. It was a magical setting, and each of the five travelers from the *Explorer* relished the environment.

Victor kept the cold beers coming, and soon everyone was a little drunk. The songs continued with Marcos taking the guitar and banging out a few songs that he knew.

Alfonso then excused himself for a few minutes, returning with a young girl, a bottle of rum, and a large pile of shelled coconuts. They mixed rum and coconut juice for all, pouring the rum directly into small holes cut into the coconut shells, then gave instructions to drink the tasty mixture through reed straws. Alfonso also instructed the young girl (she was perhaps fifteen years old) to go out back and prepare a couple of rabbits. She went behind the house to a large enclosure and rapidly killed two large white rabbits.

While they were being prepared, Marcos, Linda, and Kurt decided they would go for a swim in the ocean. Alfonso advised them to be careful as the surf was rather large and could be very unpredictable due to the underwater topography. Larry and Madison remained behind, chatting with their newfound friends.

They walked across the wide white sand beach where a few isolated clusters of mangrove trees reached the end of the sand and spread out randomly as far as the high tide line. The sand was hot on their feet, so they hurried to the water's edge. The heavy surf pounded against the shore, larger than it had appeared from the porch. Occasional breakers of four to six feet crashed onto the sand. In between the largest waves, moderate three to four foot breakers rolled more leisurely up the steeply sloped beach. Kurt turned to Marcos and Linda and cautioned them, "The surf is pretty heavy, and there's an undercurrent sweeping toward the north. I'm going to give it a try, but you guys might want to stay out."

All three of them were a little drunk and feeling somewhat reckless. Rejecting Kurt's cautionary advice, Marcos and Linda plunged into the frothing water along with Kurt. Marcos stayed near Linda, paddling just out beyond the smaller set of breakers. Kurt deftly caught a couple of short rides, turning out of the wave just before it crashed onto the sand.

After riding a couple of waves, Kurt noticed that Madison, Larry, Victor, and Alfonso had walked out to watch them in the surf. He also noticed that the undercurrent had carried him several hundred yards to the north. Kurt swam out to sea to avoid the undertow, and began swimming back toward Marcos and Linda. Alfonso hollered something that Kurt could not hear. As he continued to wave and yell, Kurt looked to seaward.

Kurt saw what Alfonso was pointing out. A huge rogue wave was building in from seaward. Marcos and Linda were caught in between the shallow breaking sets and the one looming farther out.

"Swim out!" Kurt hollered, waving his arms frantically. "Swim out!"

Marcos and Linda saw him hollering but could not hear his advice. They continued to dog paddle leisurely in the clear blue water, completely unaware of the looming wall of water moving steadily in their direction and growing larger and more menacing as it neared the shallows.

"Get out!" Kurt yelled at the top of his voice, "Swim out!"

An awareness crossed Marcos' face, and he turned to look to seaward. A wall of water at least ten to twelve feet high rushed toward shore. The undertow began sucking them out toward the building mountain of water; and the water they were in became much shallower, pulling them strongly away from the beach and toward the huge cresting wave. Marcos turned to Linda and yelled "Dive down! Dive down deep and swim out! Try to stay as deep as you can."

Fright clouded her eyes and she froze. Marcos grabbed her arm. "Linda! Dive down deep with me. Take a deep breath and try to stay as close to the bottom as possible. Hurry!"

Taking a deep breath, Marcos dove downward, holding firmly to Linda's wrist and tried to kick and swim to the bottom. The power of the swell sucked them upward, pulling tons of water molecules toward the surface where it would soon crash. He knew that if they could not stay near the bottom they would be sucked into the wave as it broke, and there was serious danger if they were caught at or near the apex of the crashing wave.

He felt the sandy bottom with his free hand. Digging his fingers in, he felt something solid. Gripping onto a chunk of something firm, he held as tightly as he could as the mass of water began its inevitable rush toward the beach, its force grew steadily as the water surged toward shore. He could feel the powerful wave pulling upward, trying to rip Linda loose from his grip. He clutched desperately to the sea floor and to her wrist. Straining with all of his might, Marcos frantically tried to hang onto the terrified woman at his side. He could not hold them both.

With a powerful wrench from the churning water, he felt Linda yanked free. His first instinct was to let go of the bottom and try to grab her again, but his common sense told him they both stood a better chance if he could hold on and avoid being sucked into the tumult.

For an agonizingly long moment, Marcos clung to the bottom, reaching down with his other hand to strengthen his hold. He could feel the surge of the powerful swell as it lifted and built. At its peak, the swell measured at least twelve feet.

∞

When Linda felt Marcos' grip break free, she panicked and opened her mouth to let out a scream. Her mouth filled with salt water, and she felt a sickening feeling of hopelessness and despair course through her mind and body. She tried desperately to refocus and avoid swallowing any more water, but she was losing control of her senses. An overwhelming blankness overcame her, and she closed her eyes and felt herself succumb to the ocean's fierce power. It could take her as it would, and she was helpless to cope any longer. At that moment, the huge wave crested and began its break. For a brief moment, Linda was lifted up the front of the crest. She emerged momentarily from the water's fierce clutches and her head and shoulders broke above the sea surface and into the air. She gulped deeply, inhaling the precious oxygen that is so often taken for granted. The dose of fresh air jolted her back into an awareness of her situation, and she opened her eyes to a terrifying sight.

Her body was now poised at the highest point of the swell, and she was gazing down its formidable face. Her eyes bulged widely, and she thought to herself 'Oh, my God.' At that moment, she began to fall, dropping from the crest of the wave into the void created by the immense curl. She was in free fall and felt like a little toy going over a steep waterfall and plummeting into a fast-moving river. Instinctively, she inhaled as deeply as she could, bracing herself for the inevitable.

On shore, the others watched helplessly as they saw Linda's impressive body rise atop the huge swell, hang precipitously at its peak, then begin the plunge. None of the others were strong swimmers, and they knew that it would be foolish for them to venture into the churning water to try and render assistance. They could not see Marcos, and they could just distinguish Kurt about thirty yards to the north, swimming frantically back toward the other two.

Linda struck the outgoing surge with a splash, the impact knocking the wind out of her. For a moment, she thought everything would be all right, that she had survived the worst of the wave's force and would be able to make it back to shore. Then the full force of the wave hit, crushing down on her with the power of a gigantic sledgehammer. It pummeled her underwater where she became briefly stuck on the seabed, her right side slammed fiercely against the ocean floor. Pinned to the bottom, it felt as if the weight of the ocean was crushing the life from her torso. The initial impact was powerful; but the force on her body continued to expand, pushing her harder against the ocean floor until she felt as if she would explode internally.

Then suddenly the pressure eased, and she felt another strange force snatch her from the sand and toss her violently sideways. From all directions, powerful currents began pulling and yanking her to and fro. She began to tumble along the sand, tossed around like a leaf in a river, her body feeling as if it were being tugged and violated from everywhere at once. She had absolutely no control over the situation. The turbulence of the crashing wave tossed her around savagely in the chaotic demise of its fury. Several times her body slammed against the seafloor, peeling skin from her shoulders, hips, and arms. Her swimsuit was ripped from her body as she tumbled. Her head struck the sand hard, and she lost consciousness.

∞

Marcos clung with all his might to the seafloor until he sensed that the wave had passed. He was desperate for air, having held his breath for close to a minute. He released his grip on the rock, or whatever it was that he had managed to grasp beneath the sand, and propelled himself toward the surface. The water was deeper in the aftermath of the huge wave, and it took an agonizingly long time to break out into fresh air. Bursting into the open, he gulped deeply, savoring the sweet life-giving oxygen.

He looked around, hoping desperately that he would see Linda nearby. She was nowhere to be seen.

Frantically, he scanned the water between himself and shore. The churning white surface showed no sign of anyone or anything except white froth and bubbling foam where the spent wave slowly but steadily began to vanish.

At that moment, Kurt reached his side. "Where's Linda?" he asked frantically.

"I don't know. I couldn't hold onto her any longer."

"Shit! Okay, she must have been caught in the break and is somewhere between here and shore. Let's go!"

With that, the two of them began a desperate sixty or seventy-yard search between their position and the shoreline, hoping beyond hope that they would find her still alive.

On shore the others continued the vigil of looking for Linda. "There!" Victor shouted, pointing toward a spot between the waves where he had glimpsed something in the surf. As they rushed toward the spot, the bright red fabric from Linda's bathing suit top tumbled through the lapping wave. Larry waded out and picked it up, looking back at the others with a forlorn expression.

$$\infty$$

Kurt and Marcos continued their searching swim from the deeper water toward shore. About two-thirds of the way in, Kurt's foot briefly brushed against something soft as he stroked powerfully through the eighty-one degree water. At first, he thought he must have touched a fish, but some instinct told him otherwise. He turned around and swam back to the spot. Dog-paddling around the area, his hand brushed something, and he sensed immediately that it was human flesh. Diving down and reaching around blindly, his hands dug into the soft pliant skin of Linda's submerged torso. He wrapped his arms around her and began kicking upward. With a final burst of leg power, he emerged from the depths and pulled her with him to the surface.

"Marcos!" he yelled. "Over here. Help me!"

Immediately, Marcos was at his side. He grabbed one arm and helped Kurt swim toward the beach with Linda, working together to keep her head above the surface. When they reached the shallows, the others ran out waist deep to help pull her onto dry land.

Her body looked badly tattered. Blood oozed from multiple abrasions on her hips, arms, legs, and shoulders. Her skin was a sick pasty blue, the color of a drowning victim after prolonged submersion.

"Oh, my God, she's dead." Madison whispered as she fell to her knees and started to cry.

∞

Stunned briefly, Kurt quickly positioned himself at her left side, felt her neck for a carotid artery pulse, and tilted her head upward trying to detect any breathing against his ear. There was none. Placing his palms below and between her ample breasts, he initiated a vigorous chest thrust. On the second thrust, salt water gushed from her mouth, thick and heavy rushes of water mixed with mucous. There was no sign of life. He turned her onto her side to let more salt water flow from her mouth. Once the flow stopped, he rolled her again onto her back.

He continued to thrust, the volume of water expelled from her throat decreasing each time. On the fourth thrust, Linda jerked and coughed, spewing another volume of seawater and mucous. A series of racking coughs followed, and some coloration began to return.

The others began to cry joyously. She was alive, still choking and coughing; but she was trying to move around, and her eyes opened. They were clouded and seemed to be floating separately in her eye sockets. Kurt reached behind her, grabbed her other arm, and rolled her onto her side. "Don't try to move." He instructed her firmly. "Look at me."

She did not seem to be aware of anything. He tried again. "Linda, look at me. Can you hear me? I need you to look at me!" Having had numerous training sessions in First Aid and CPR, and having once seen a drowning victim, he was well aware that prolonged submersion in water and ingestion of salt water could be extremely dangerous and might result in long-term debilitating health complications.

He tried again. "Linda!" he said more sharply, "Can you hear me? Look at me! I need you to look at me!"

Slowly she turned her head, and her glazed eyes began to blink. Between blinks, her focus began to improve, with both eyes moving together rather than separately. She looked up at Kurt. He waited patiently while her eyes stabilized then asked again, "Can you hear me?"

She nodded. He smiled softly. "Who am I?"

"Kurt." She croaked, rasping and vomiting another small quantity of water and mucus. Her coughing fit was much shorter and less volatile, and she looked back at Kurt with a painful smile creasing her lovely face. She tried to sit up.

A broad smile covered Kurt's face as he turned to the others. "I think she's okay," he told them, "but we need to get her to a hospital as quickly as possible."

"I'll go get our van." Alfonso offered as he quickly leaped up from his knees and headed toward his hacienda.

In the meantime, Madison realized that Linda was lying there stark naked, her magnificent body bruised and bleeding. She asked Larry for his t-shirt, which he quickly handed to her. She draped it over Linda's midsection.

Alfonso brought back a blanket. They carried Linda to the vehicle. She was bruised and peeled raw in a few places; but slowly and surely her mental awareness returned, and there did not seem to be any serious injuries or broken bones.

They never found her bathing suit bottom, although two days later a young boy walking the beach with his mother came across it washed up onto the sand. They left it there, and it disappeared on the next high tide.

∞

When they arrived at the hospital in Acapulco, Alfonso called upon one of his associates in the administrative department to ensure that she receive the best treatment and care possible. After a thorough examination, the doctors treated her scrapes and contusions, and concluded that she appeared to have no internal or mental after effects, but recommended she remain overnight in the hospital in case any lingering issues might manifest. Marcos stayed with her.

Alfonso took the group back to the docks where a call was made to the *Explorer* on VHF radio, requesting a ride back to the boat. Pablo picked everyone up in the skiff. Fond farewells were given to Alfonso, along with a promise to return for another visit, if time permitted.

Back aboard the ship, the group related the experience to Captain Ellis and the other passengers, informing them that Linda and Marcos were expected back aboard the following day. Captain Ellis expressed concern for Linda but also advised them that he hoped to put to sea the following afternoon; so it was imperative that they return before midday. Kurt assured him that he did not foresee any problem with that timeline.

∞

Guillermo, Hugo, and Pablo found a new diversion on shore. On the eastern edge of town, the trio discovered a very clean and friendly whorehouse called La Huerta (The Farm), which Guillermo happily reported has 'the pick of the crop of young Acapulco girls.' Once they found La Huerta, they spent most of their day and evening enjoying all of the pleasures that fifty dollars American could buy.

Charlie had emerged from his cabin. Neither he nor Tiona had come out of their room since her night aboard *El Viejo*. Charlie was noticeably sullen, wishing to stay more or less to himself. After a while, Kurt approached him in private and inquired if everything was okay.

"She's in a real funk," Charlie told him. "I know that something happened aboard the boat with that Santiago fellow, but she won't tell me what it was. She's being very quiet and introspective. I've seen her like this before, and I just need to let her get it out of her system." Kurt listened patiently, aware that Charlie seemed to appreciate the opportunity to talk to someone. He waited until Charlie continued.

"We have a very unusual relationship. I know that she has flings now and then. She keeps me around because it is more comfortable for her to go places with a man on her arm. But when she finds someone interesting, I am expected to fade into the background and let her do her thing. I'm okay with that, for the most part, because she takes care of me. She has money from an inheritance—not a fortune—but enough to live her life the way she wants to and to keep me around for company. I serve as her escort and her bed-partner when she is lonely—which is most of the time. This arrangement usually doesn't bother me; but some day I wish she'd see me for who I am, and how much I really care for her."

He paused, seeming to mull over another thought, then continued, "She's had a really tough life. Her wealthy parents basically deserted her, leaving her in a nanny's care when she was young. As a teenager, she got into drugs, alcohol, and attempted suicide twice. She puts on a good front, but she's really very fragile and insecure. When she gets into one of her dark moods, I worry about her. I'm always concerned she might do something rash."

With noticeable sadness in his voice, Charlie continued, "I love her. I truly do, and I wish she could see how much I truly care. But every time I try to broach the subject, she laughs and dismisses me as if I'm just kidding around. She either doesn't believe me or doesn't want to believe me. But it makes me sad when she gets into one of these moods, and I think that guy the other night really put her into a deep funk."

Kurt nodded and responded quietly, "I know what you mean, Charlie. She might come around; but if she doesn't, you just need to live your own life and do what is best for you. Maybe you stay with her, or maybe you just tell her that you can't continue living under her terms alone. I know that it's a tough place to be. At some point though, you need to think about yourself."

"Yeah, you're right Kurt. Thanks for the advice. I'll keep it in mind. Now, how about a cold beer?"

They went out onto the foredeck and joined the others. All of the remaining passengers except Linda and Marcos were aboard. They all stayed out on deck for a few hours talking about their various adventures ashore and things they had seen. Linda's near drowning left them all pensive and concerned.

∞

In the morning the skies hung heavy with dark tropical clouds blocking the sun. A brief but powerful thunderstorm struck, lashed the blackened skies with flashes of lightning, and sent booming crashes of thunder across the bay. Torrential rain darkened the air even further, restricting visibility to mere feet. Many of the passengers aboard the *Explorer* took the opportunity to go out on deck and take a fresh water shower, allowing the pounding rain to wash them thoroughly. It was very therapeutic.

Following breakfast prepared by the hippies Sally and Peter (who had taken to lending a hand with nearly every meal) and while they were putting leftovers away, Peter inadvertently closed the door to the large walk-in cooler while he was inside. Trapped inside the chilled tomb-like cubicle, Peter began pounding on the door. It took quite a while for someone to hear his muffled cries and let him out. He had a mild case of hypothermia, and both of his hands were sore and numb; but he was otherwise unharmed.

Captain Ellis informed everyone aboard that the *Explorer* would not be ready for departure until at least six p.m. That announcement encouraged a few of the passengers to go ashore.

Larry and Charlie went to the hospital to check on Linda. They met Marcos at the reception desk where he told them that she should be released soon. Within minutes, the doctor cleared her to go and said that he did not believe she had any after effects from the near drowning. However, he did advise her to undergo another checkup at the next opportunity. They all caught a taxi back to the docks. Linda was wrapped in numerous bandages; so it wasn't easy for her to climb in and out of the skiff or onto the ships boarding ladder. She was made as comfortable as possible on one of the deck lounges.

By late afternoon, all of those who had gone ashore returned to the ship. Most of them were happily drunk, feeling chipper and in high spirits.

To no one's surprise, Captain Ellis gave an update to the group and said they would not be departing that evening as expected but he hoped to cast off early the following morning.

By noon the following day, with the sun at full strength and the humidity even stronger, a growing unrest spread throughout the ship. Kurt implored Captain Ellis to allow shore leave, even if it were just for a few hours. His response was out of character. "I said there would be no shore leave!" he shouted, stomping off to his cabin. Dawn, who had been standing nearby came to his defense.

"I apologize for my husband's poor behavior. As you must be aware, all of this delay is very frustrating for him. It is beyond his control. We require more money to continue the trip, and funds are not coming through as promised. Mr. Walters is onshore trying to arrange for a wire transfer of additional cash, and he has assured us that it will be accomplished by early morning. Please bear with us and be patient," she implored.

That episode put a damper on the mood of the evening.

Kurt was on duty from ten to midnight. Because they were not underway, the shift required only one person. He remained on the foredeck where he was soon joined by the new first-mate, Jeffrey Smythe.

Jeffrey Smythe stood five feet six, and weighed perhaps one hundred fifty pounds. From the color and texture of his wrinkled skin, he obviously had spent a lot of time at sea or at least in the sun. His ruddy complexion and scruffy red beard made him appear older than his thirty-three years.

"Hello Mate," Jeffrey Smythe offered, extending his surprisingly small and almost effeminate right hand for Kurt to shake. Kurt purposefully avoided squeezing his hand firmly. For Kurt, it was awkward. He thought a firm handshake was an indication of a strong character, and a soft handshake conveyed a sign of weakness.

"Pleased to meet you, Jeffrey, I'm Kurt Decker."

"Jeff. All my friends just call me Jeff."

"Okay, Jeff, but you might want to get used to the name 'El Jefe.' My brother Larry always comes up with nicknames for people, and he immediately tagged you 'El Jefe.' Hope that doesn't bother you."

"No mate, not at all. After all, El Jefe means 'The Chief' in Spanish, and I kind of like that."

Kurt nodded, acknowledging the comment but thinking to himself, 'for some reason that doesn't surprise me.'

It was not like Kurt to judge people unfairly; but he was already developing a negative opinion of their new first-mate. He seemed to be an arrogant Englishman with a 'small-man's' complex. Realizing his impression might be wrong, Kurt vowed to give the man a chance to prove himself.

∞

At daybreak, Brian and Captain Ellis headed to shore, leaving instructions for everyone to remain aboard until their return. The day broke bright and sunny, and it was hot and sultry even before the sun climbed above the peaks of the surrounding mountains.

An overall sense of disillusionment prevailed aboard the ship. The five-week cruise was now halfway through its fourth week, and there was absolutely no possibility of completing the trip on schedule.

By ten a.m., the temperature had climbed into the low nineties; and combined with high humidity, the atmosphere on the boat was sweltering and extremely uncomfortable. Nearly everyone donned swimsuits and spent more time in the water than out.

Linda was reluctant to join the others. Her body sores were beginning to scab, and multiple purple and blue bruises covered her body as a result of the pounding she took in the surf at Pie de la Cuesta. She was very self-conscious about her appearance; but the heat was so stifling and uncomfortable that she finally gave in and took the plunge, wearing one of Marcos' t-shirts to hide the worst of her body bruises. She and Marcos swam leisurely away from the ship, relishing the soothing comfort of the relatively cool water.

Tiona and Charlie joined the others a while later. It was Tiona's first appearance since her demoralizing episode with Santiago. She averted everyone's sympathetic stares, keeping her normally bright and inquisitive eyes downcast. Charlie attempted to keep things light and airy, acknowledging everyone with a cheerful greeting. Together they stepped to the dive-rail platform on the stern and jumped in, holding hands as they jumped. They swam around for a few minutes before Tiona climbed out, grabbed her towel, and moved quietly away from everyone else toward the bow of the ship.

∞

Watching her, Madison sensed an overwhelming sadness. She recognized the signs of extreme melancholy permeating Tiona's normally cheerful and optimistic persona. She waited until Tiona settled onto one of the deck chairs then walked over and stood next to her, waiting patiently until she looked up.

"Hi. How about a little company?"

Tiona reacted very slowly, and gazed at Madison with a blank stare. Finally she shrugged and quietly responded, "Sure. Why not?"

Madison took the seat next to her and waited, her eyes taking in the surroundings. "It sure is beautiful here, isn't it?"

Tiona seemed surprised by the innocuous question, perhaps expecting something more personal. The young girl sitting next to her appeared comfortable, friendly, and nonjudgmental.

Tiona sighed deeply and said, "Yes, it is very beautiful."

They both sat quietly, taking in the beauty and ambiance of their lush tropical surroundings, the calm blue water of the bay, and the structured architectural development of the City of Acapulco.

After a few minutes, Tiona began to speak in a soft, reflective voice, almost as if she were reciting from a script. "He was magnificent. I've never known a man like that before. Everything about him was manly and powerful. Yet he was also very gentle and considerate. He was completely self-assured, but still seemed humble and understanding. I thought we had found something together." She paused briefly and glanced over at Madison. Madison made a very brief nod, encouraging Tiona to continue.

"You should have seen him with his clothes off! Oh, my God, there cannot be another man on the planet that has the physique and the... um, equipment of that man. He was amazing. And he knew how to use all of it! I've had a lot of experience and known a lot of men in my life, but never anyone like him. Never!" She stopped and was quiet for a few minutes.

Madison let the silence linger. Finally Tiona whispered, "Why did he leave? And why didn't he even say goodbye?"

"Men are men, just like women are women." Madison stated simply. "Neither can understand the other, at least most of the time. He may have a cold and cruel streak. Or he may have been scared. Or maybe he had no reason at all. I try not to second guess what a man might do or say, ever, because when I do, I'm usually wrong. Sometimes they surprise me and respond or react how I want, but most of the time they do, say, or act in a manner that I just don't expect. I find it is easier to take a wait-and-see approach. That way I'm not as apt to get angry, disappointed, or hurt." She paused and looked over at Tiona, saw tears brimming in her eyes, then continued, "Don't be sad, Tiona, be thankful. You experienced something that was special and wonderful. Relish the memory and hope that you might find it again sometime."

"Yeah," she responded pensively, "who knows, maybe he'll be waiting in the next port."

∞

Late that afternoon, Captain Ellis and Brian returned to the ship with good news. They had received the wire transfer of additional funds and were ready to depart.

The skiff was being hoisted onto the upper deck and the anchor hauled. In the rush, one of the spring-lines snagged on a bollard, snapped the line, and tore loose a fastener and two of the ship fenders. Jeffrey Smythe managed to snag the fenders with a long boat hook as the *Explorer* began to make way.

Two new crewman had also boarded the ship prior to departure: Benjamin Franklin (Big Ben), a huge black man standing about six feet six and weighing well over three hundred pounds, who signed on as an engine room helper, and Norm Rombowski (Rom), an engineer from one of the fishing boats in Acapulco that had blown both of its engines, thus making him available. Rom stood even taller than Ben at about six-eight, and he weighed at least three-fifty. Those two would certainly place a little extra burden on the chef.

Underway again, the ship encountered smooth seas. The huge red-orange sun undulated, its shape distorted and color vibrant, as it settled into the broad expanse of the distant silver-blue horizon.

During the night while Larry stood helm watch, one of the emergency bilge lights went on. When he called down to the engine room, Brian, who was on engine-watch, reported a break in a fresh-water pipe and nearly six hundred gallons of fresh water leaked into the bilge. Fortunately, the water tank held twelve hundred gallons total, and there were four fifty-gallon drums of rainwater strapped to the stern railing, so at least there was some water on board. But once again, it meant no fresh-water showers, and very limited use of water until the ship reached the next port.

At the end of his watch, Kurt was surprised and pleased to find Madison waiting up for him. After Kurt took care of his evening grooming, he and Madison cuddled together and enjoyed a leisurely bout of lovemaking under a moonless sky filled with millions of twinkling stars. When he attempted to talk with her about her unexpected desire for intimacy, she hushed him with a kiss and whispered easily, "Let's just enjoy cuddling."

CHAPTER SEVEN

Early in the morning at that mystical time when the sky begins its gradual transformation from dark to light, Guillermo heard a snapping sound from one of the trolling lines. His sleeping space was on the stern, just a few feet from the cleat that held the trolling gear.

He jumped up and peered astern into the steel gray wash of the wake. Guillermo could just make out the telltale flashes of a fish slashing and darting at the end of the line. He hollered, "Hey, anyone awake? We've got a fish."

He grabbed the gloves that were kept near the coils of three-hundred-pound test trolling line, reached out and clutched the quivering line, slowly pulling one hand over the other while coiling the loose line near his feet. After about three or four pulls, Marcos appeared at his side and exclaimed, "Finally! Looks like a tuna!"

Guillermo nodded without commenting, concentrating on his slow methodical retrieve of the trolling line. Twice the fish turned broadside in the wake, and he was forced to relinquish some of the line he had gained; but when it turned back with its head pointing toward the ship, he was able to gain line. After about five minutes, the tuna was in the prop wash under the fantail. Marcos, lying on his belly with a long handmade gaff gripped tightly in his right hand, reached out and stuck it in the belly. He lifted it upward and passed it off to Guillermo, who in turn swung a shimmering twenty-pound yellowfin tuna over the rail and onto the deck.

Much hooting and hollering ensued, and everyone gathered around the tuna as it slapped against the deck, blood flying. As soon as the slapping reduced to a quiver, Guillermo pulled out his hip-knife and slashed open the belly of the tuna, letting it bleed out. He then rinsed it in a bucket of salt water, rinsed the blood from the deck, and took the fish into the galley where he filleted it in two quick smooth motions.

A short while later, with everyone seated around the galley table eating banana pancakes, a horrible screeching noise resounded through the ship, and almost immediately it lost speed. Most of the men scampered below decks to see what had happened.

One of the lifters on the port engine had snapped and lodged in a rocker arm. In turn, it jammed a piston, grinding the engine to a halt. It would take hours to repair, if there were enough parts available.

After assessing the situation and explaining to Rombowski and Big Ben what they would need in order to try and affect repairs, Brian instructed them to engage the starboard engine and get underway on the single screw.

∞

Speed reduced to about four knots, and a building southerly swell had the ship rocking steeply back and forth in a deep trough. It was hot and muggy and people were getting seasick. Abruptly, another loud grinding noise rumbled through the decks of the ship, and suddenly everything became eerily quiet. Both engines were down.

Adrift in a continually growing southerly swell, the ship rolled sluggishly from side to side, at times listing nearly twenty degrees. After discovering the latest problem, a failed oil pump on the starboard engine, Captain Ellis came out of his cabin and ordered the anchor dropped as a sea drogue in order to turn the ship into the swell. Once the anchor was deployed, the bow swung into the seas and helped alleviate some of the discomfort of lolling in the steep troughs.

With the bow pointed into the swell, the passengers lowered the boarding platform and began jumping or diving into the purple depths of the sea. They were about one hundred sixty-five miles south of Acapulco and west of Punta Maldona, Mexico, adrift in the vast Pacific where predatory sharks roamed. At all times, one of the passengers took turns on the upper deck watching for the telltale fin.

In the engine room, Rom, Brian, Big Ben, Larry, Guillermo, and Pablo worked together to unbolt and remove the failed pump. Fortunately that was one of the spare parts the ship carried aboard. Even so, it was a hot and miserable job. The temperature outside held in the mid-nineties; but in the engine room, without the fan working, the temperatures pegged the thermometer at one hundred twenty degrees. The men took turns splashing fresh water from a one-gallon container over themselves in an effort to keep from succumbing to heat exhaustion or worse. Every fifteen minutes or so, each of them had to leave the sweltering engine room to go topside and lower their body temperatures. Most did that by joining the others in the sea. It took approximately two hours to make the repair; but finally the starboard engine roared back to life, and the ship was once again underway, cruising sedately at about four knots.

The remainder of the afternoon passed slowly, the reduced speed just enough to generate a slight movement of air across the decks. A beautiful sunset culminated with several passengers claiming to see the 'green flash' of the setting sun. There was little revelry aboard that evening, and everyone adjourned early, trying to sleep despite the sweltering heat.

During the night, the southerly swell lay down, and the rolling of the ship lessened. By daybreak, the seas calmed completely, and the ocean turned flat and glassy.

At around nine a.m., Captain Ellis called down to the engine room to shut down once again to 'perform a little work' on the engine. The ship was about sixty miles offshore in the Gulf of Tehauntepec, a notorious stretch of coastline that mariners usually approach with trepidation.

Tehauntepec has the reputation of being the worst and most treacherous stretch of water along the Mexican coast. Sandwiched between the Sierra Giganta Mountains on both sides of a wide, shallow valley, the low, flat plains of Tehauntepec are prone to powerful offshore winds that can develop unexpectedly and often gust above fifty knots. Most sailors tend to stay close to shore when transiting the Gulf to avoid the closely spaced swells that the winds often generate farther offshore. It's considered a rare crossing when the fierce Chubasco winds named 'Tehauntepeckers' do not affect boats transiting the Gulf.

However as luck would have it, the passage across the Gulf for the passengers and crew could not have been easier. The seas were more flat than on any previous stretch of ocean, even though the ship was some sixty miles from land—a normally foolish course to follow.

∞

Kurt was now fully aware that cruising in offshore waters in the tropics is a truly unbelievable experience. The ocean is incredibly clear and beautiful, and the colors incomparable. Depending on the time of day and the direction a person is looking, the ocean radiates a myriad of shades and panoramic beauty. Perhaps the most striking is the deep purple-blue hue that is prevalent midday when the sun is overhead. At that time, when one is standing on the top deck, the ocean seems to have a depth and clarity that defies comprehension. In the early morning hours and in the evening, more vivid tints of blues, grays, greens, and purples come and go. At night, incandescent florescence and phosphorescence pulsate from the wake and the prop-wash of the ship as it slides across the surface. Dolphins appear periodically, sometimes staying with the ship for long periods of time. Always they swim just ahead of the bow, riding the wake, leading the ship, darting off, and then gliding back into position. They spout from their blowholes, make squealing noises, turn on their sides, and stare up at the humans leaning over the rail, their large silvery black eyes gazing deeply into the eyes of the onlookers. And they smile. Always they smile. They most certainly are the happiest creatures on the planet.

Sea turtles were also becoming more prevalent. At least a dozen green sea turtles were spotted one day, made more visible by the omnipresent tern standing lightly and gracefully atop their rounded shells.

At times, hundreds of tiny flying fish ripple the surface as they spread their small silvery wings and soared airborne, gliding on the gentle breezes that flit across the calm Pacific. Those small flying fish, like the larger ones that are prevalent in higher latitudes, frantically whip their tails on the surface as they try desperately to take flight. Once clear of the water, their thin delicate wings spread to their full width in order to create the lift needed to carry them through the air. At night, some of them invariably become disoriented and fly right into the path of the oncoming ship. Some crash into the hull and become food for the predators of the oceans. Others are high enough in the air to slam into the various superstructures of the boat, then flop and thrash their final death throes on the deck of the ship. Those fish were taken to a special container in the freezer compartment and saved for bait.

As the ship plodded its path slowly across the placid sea, the swell again began to build. Its direction, almost due south, remained enough on the bow to help keep the ride comfortable. For a while, it looked like the ship would be encountering some foul weather. The barometer began to fall, a dark wall of clouds formed to the east, and the east wind freshened. But the squall passed to the east, and the winds abated.

Night fell quickly, engulfing the ship in a darkness illuminated only by the myriad of a million stars shimmering overhead. Most of the passengers stayed on the foredeck, lying back on the lounge chairs and contemplating the heavens. Some small talk developed; but for most, it was an evening for sitting around quietly enjoying the serenity and wonder of the heavens.

∞

By daybreak, the *Explorer* was nearing the southernmost reaches of the Mexican mainland, approaching Guatemala. At approximately fourteen degrees north latitude, the climate was now totally tropical. On the distant horizon, building thunderheads loomed, their ever-changing shapes looking like primordial creatures lured from the shimmering depths of the vast Pacific.

Madison and Kurt rose early and went to the bow, where they leaned against the starboard gunwale and contemplated the fascinating panorama.

Madison reached over and gripped his hand. "It's so beautiful. Every day is different, yet every day is so much like the one before. There's something about the ocean that permeates everything. It's in my thoughts and my feelings. I feel like the ocean has found its way into me, almost as if I have become part of the ocean or it has become part of me. I can't explain the sensation, but I feel as if I've discovered a part of me that never existed." She paused and looked into Kurt's eyes, squeezing his hand tightly. "Thank you, Kurt. Thank you for bringing me here. I know that we are moving and this particular moment in time is transitory. But this journey we are taking, this experience we are sharing, is something that I knew was here. I knew this existed. I feel so alive, so privileged to be here at this moment, at this spot on the ocean. With you." She paused, looked up into his face and felt that he understood her emotions, sentiments, and ideology. And at the same time, she recognized that it was not new to him as it was to her.

She knew he was already there, and had already experienced and lived with the revelations that she now felt. As a result, she understood him better. Looking into his eyes, she recalled several instances when he had tried to share this 'sea connection' with her, but she had never been able to make such a connection. His life and his travels had given him the opportunity to reach and become 'a man of the sea.' Now she felt those same influences, those same links, the same bonds. It made her happy.

They sat quietly together, listening to the rush of the sea rolling slowly and methodically along the sides of the ship, its full displacement hull knifing stealthily through the aquamarine water. They watched with fascination as the sun lit the eastern sky with a startlingly luminescent glow, the high, streaky cirrus clouds and the silver tops of the bulbous cumulonimbus clouds illuminated brilliantly as the first rays of the sun created a colorful prism of purples, reds and pinks in the early morning sky.

Kurt reached over and pulled Madison in front of him, wrapped his arms around her waist, and leaned her back against his chest. She rested her head under his chin and felt complete and utter contentment.

A rather high-pitched distinctively British greeting broke their reverie. "Ahoy, Mates, I hope I'm not intruding."

Before Kurt had a chance to respond, Madison rapidly sat upright and replied, "Oh, good morning Jeffrey. You're not intruding at all. We were just sitting here enjoying the sunrise. It is very beautiful, isn't it?"

"Quite," he answered a little too shrilly. "It is lovely."

∞

Kurt's entire countenance darkened. He resented the intrusion. He knew that Smythe had seen them from a distance before he decided to interrupt, and it irked Kurt that this smarmy Englishman either did not have enough courtesy or common sense to recognize that he and Madison were sharing a special moment.

He stood upright and said he was going to see if the coffee was ready, leaving Jeffrey Smythe and Madison together.

∞

"Well," Smythe intoned in his best British accent, "he seems a bit surly this lovely morning."

Madison turned and looked at him. She had met very few 'Brits' before, and she truly loved the melodious cadence of his accent. She found it intriguing and musical. "Oh, he's fine," she said, dismissing Kurt's apparent rudeness. "He just likes his coffee as soon as he is awake."

"Yeah, I guess most American blokes are that way. We Brits are more in tune with our afternoon tea respites. We could care less about coffee."

They stood together on the foredeck, making small talk until Kurt returned holding two cups of steaming coffee.

"The pot's full if you want any," he informed Smythe.

"No, thanks mate, I'm not much of a coffee drinker. I prefer tea."

Kurt turned and looked directly into his eyes, tempted to respond but instead merely smiled.

He wasn't quite sure what it was, but Kurt realized that despite his efforts to be nonjudgmental, he didn't like Jeffrey Smythe. He had a certain air of arrogance which, combined with his properly British accent, got under Kurt's skin. To make matters worse, it bothered Kurt that Madison seemed a little entranced. She told him soon after their first meeting that she found Jeffrey's accent fascinating. He couldn't see anything else she might find appealing in the man. Kurt considered him physically unattractive, skuzzy and effeminate. His teeth were crooked, his face pockmarked, his chin and nose pointed, his red beard scraggly, and his torso thin and frail—in Kurt's eyes the antithesis of a handsome virile man.

Jeffrey Smythe began telling Madison about life in the British Isles. Kurt stood and listened casually, smiling occasionally when Smythe made a comment or observation that Madison seemed to find amusing. Kurt was doing his best to remain polite and to conceal his disapproval. But the longer they talked, the less Smythe included him in any of the conversation. He talked to Madison as if Kurt wasn't there.

When finally a brief pause occurred in Smythe's monologue, Kurt reached over and lightly gripped Madison's arm. She flinched from his touch. Recovering from the brusque reaction, he asked casually, "Hey, would you like to go get some breakfast?"

She turned to Smythe, "Sure, how about you, Jeffrey, will you join us?"

"I would love to."

Kurt reached out for Madison's hand, but she pulled it away, reaching instead to fling a loose tress of hair from her forehead. She smoothed the front of her thin dress and began walking toward the galley, Jeffrey Smythe followed closely by her side. Kurt seethed inwardly but was determined to not let it show.

Breakfast was, for Kurt, an uncomfortable blur. He didn't pay attention to anything that was served, eating without any pleasure.

Jeffrey and Madison maintained an animated conversation about his life in Britain, his travels in the Mediterranean and Caspian Sea, and his current adventure in Mexico and Central America. She seemed to hang on every word, laughing lightly at several comments that Kurt considered completely inane.

Others joined them at the table, and all of them seemed to take great pleasure in Smythe's dialogue about his sea-going adventures, his descriptions of exotic ports, and his opinions on everything from European politics to the obvious poverty in most parts of Mexico and Central America. Finally after about forty-five minutes, Captain Ellis entered the room and asked Smythe to join him on the bridge.

After they left, Madison turned to Kurt and smiled broadly, "Isn't he fascinating? He's done and seen so many things. I just love listening to his stories."

Trying to hide his true feelings, Kurt smiled and responded, "Yes, he seems to have led a very interesting life."

∞

Near midday, the cranking noise from the second engine reverberated through the decks of the ship, eventually turning into a low rumbling vibration as the port engine came to life. Working tirelessly with Rom and Big Ben, Brian had managed to locate all the parts needed to make repairs, and she was running again on two engines. The hull speed increased to nearly eight knots as full cruising speed was reached.

The seas were calm with very little swell or wind. As night settled, the cloud layer persisted, blocking out any stars or moonlight. Kurt and Larry shared a watch. Kurt talked with Larry about his perceptions of Jeffrey Smythe. Larry agreed that he didn't think too highly of Smythe either and suggested that Madison's apparent infatuation arose solely from not encountering many foreigners in her lifetime, and that it was perfectly natural to become intrigued by something new and different. He told Kurt not to worry, that the newness would wear off soon enough and that she was completely and thoroughly devoted.

Kurt wasn't so sure.

CHAPTER EIGHT

Kurt arose around daybreak to check the trolling lines. As he walked along the port side of the ship, he heard an odd guttural growl coming from near one of the picnic tables. When he got closer, he saw two huge forms locked together on the aft deck. At first he wasn't sure what to make of the sight. His initial thought was that they were embracing. But as he stepped closer, he could hear heavy angry breathing.

He moved around to the backside of the table and got a better look at the strange sight. Rom was lying on his side, his thick arms wrapped tightly around Big Ben's head, squeezing tightly in a firm hammerlock. Ben's eyes bulged, his large black face turning purple.

Rom's voice rumbled deeply, "You black son of a bitch! I'll break your fucking neck you bastard! Take a hammer to me will you? You black bastard, I'll kill you!" Rom roared.

"Take it easy, Rom! Easy!" Someone called out. It was Captain Ellis.

Big Ben uttered an anguished cry, "Aarrgh." Followed by what might have been "Help me!"

Captain Ellis reached them and again said, "Take it easy, Rom!" Rom seemed to lighten his grip.

Ben twisted and lurched sideways and tried to break free from the death grip that Rom held him in. His attempt to escape caused them both to roll over against the table, push it about four feet and slam it against Captain Ellis' leg. The impact of the table opened a two-inch gash in his right shin.

"Go get more help!" Captain Ellis ordered, "Get the rest of the crew!"

Marcos and Guillermo were now also at the scene, and they attempted to calm the situation. "Rom let him go!" Guillermo pleaded. He seemed concerned that Ben was nearing unconsciousness. "You're going to kill him!"

"You're damn right I'm going to kill him! The fucking black bastard attacked me with a hammer!"

"Rom, you can't kill him! You'll go to prison. Let him go!" Guillermo pleaded.

With a final wrenching twist, Rom loosened his grip on Big Ben's neck and whispered ferociously, "Okay you lazy black bastard get up! But if you try anything else, I will kill you! Now get up, and get your lazy black ass into your cabin and pack your bags. You're getting the hell off this ship as soon as it reaches port!"

Nobody ever quite figured out what caused the fight. Rom insisted that Ben had attacked him with a hammer for no apparent reason. Ben didn't try to defend himself. He merely maintained a sullen silence. Whatever the cause of the fracas, Captain Ellis sided with Rom and agreed that Ben would leave the ship as soon as it made the next port.

Fortunately, neither man was seriously injured in the fight, but Captain Ellis' leg required a few rather crude stitches by Dawn, who had once served as an emergency room nurse.

All of this took place about an hour from the next port, San Jose, Guatemala.

∞

The port of San Jose, Guatemala, isn't really a port at all. It is merely a long pier jutting out into the Pacific. The pier is more than seven hundred yards long and extends beyond the ocean swells that break relentlessly on a long expanse of beautiful white sand beach. A railway that runs down the center of the pier during daylight hours is in constant use, moving freight, produce, and supplies from ships to shore.

When the ship slowed her engines and prepared to drop anchor, a slow-moving south swell was sending six to eight foot breakers onto the beach. Those breakers rolled ponderously under the planking of the pier and wrapped around the tall pilings that supported the massive deck beams. At the end of the pier a large crane worked constantly, as it lifted and lowered cargo from the decks of ships that moored, Med-style, alongside the impressive structure.

Anchoring outside of the congested pier area, the passengers and crew watched in fascination as the freight and cargo was moved back and forth. Along the shore, people and a few vehicles could be seen bustling near the base of the pier.

Where the aquamarine waves tumbled onto the bright white sand, a few people splashed and played in the surf. At the point where sand ended, lush vegetation interspersed with tall swaying palms provided a scenic backdrop. Several single-story warehouse structures surrounded the base of the pier. Numerous palm-thatched huts nestled into the surrounding thick foliage, lent an exotic tropical appearance to the shoreline. In the distance, the outlines of the twin volcanic peaks of Volcan Fuega and Acatenango rose majestically into the skyline. The scene was truly picturesque, the lovely landscape augmented by the shimmering beauty of the waves breaking upon the pristine shoreline.

Everyone stayed aboard the boat for about three hours, during which time a trio of officials from the immigration department came aboard to check paperwork and receive payment of ten Quetzals (the currency of the country) for the privilege of going ashore.

Getting onto the pier proved to be a very unusual experience. Seven of the passengers, including Kurt and Madison, Marcos, Linda, Larry, Guillermo, and Bob Bradley, squeezed into the aluminum skiff with Pablo at the helm. He maneuvered the skiff to the side of the pier where a large pallet encased in netting was lowered by crane until it neared the sea surface. Then timing the swell carefully, each of the skiff occupants grabbed hold of the netting and one by one carefully climbed out of the skiff into an opening in the netting, then onto the pallet. Once they were all huddled on the pallet and clinging to the netting, the crane operator hoisted them from the water's edge and onto the pier.

This process was duplicated twice more until everyone except a skeleton crew was offloaded safely.

On shore, there were many soldiers carrying rifles. This was quite disconcerting to everyone at first; but before long, it became apparent that the soldiers were very friendly and did not appear to pose any problems. Even so, it was not all that comfortable to be around so many young—and many of them appeared very young—soldiers bearing military rifles.

Captain Ellis had given everyone shore leave until midnight. At that time, he intended to pull the anchor and depart; so he cautioned everyone to be back aboard on time or be left behind.

Larry acted as interpreter. It was quite challenging as there are numerous dialects and several variations of Spanish used in Guatemala. There is a huge indigenous Indian influence, and their language appeared to be a mix of Spanish and Central American Indian. Fortunately, one of the dockworkers spoke a loose combination of Castilian Spanish and English. Eventually, Larry was able to determine there was bus service about a block away that could take everyone into Guatemala City for the day, returning around ten p.m.

Guatemala City is about sixty miles from the small port of San Jose. Ten of the passengers climbed aboard a brightly painted bus with several locals on board. Some of those locals were women with huge baskets piled high with fruits and vegetables. They carried their baskets balanced atop their heads, not bothering to use their hands to balance the heavy-looking loads. The men sauntered casually alongside, not carrying a thing. It was obvious that they expected the women to carry the burden.

As the bus drove over the pothole-filled road, it made several stops, picking up more peasant people bearing loads of produce, breads, chickens, and even a couple of pigs. They all piled into the bus, some of them tossing bags of items and sometimes small animals in cages onto a rack on the top of the bus. Sometimes the driver climbed a ladder at the back of the bus to help with the 'luggage'; other times he would let the passengers load the goods themselves. Several times the driver had to stop on the road to let range cattle cross. Once, it was a herd of goats.

At one point the bus broke down when one of its radiator hoses popped a small hole. The driver found a thick rubbery-looking plant on the side of a hill and deftly wrapped it around the leaking hose, sealed the leak, and then refilled the radiator. The entire fix took less than fifteen minutes. There was also a brief stop for an incredibly heavy thunderstorm that hit with such ferocity that the driver was unable to continue. In addition, there was a rather high mountain that needed to be climbed, and it seemed doubtful that the bus could make the ascent.

But by having most of the men climb out and walk alongside during the slow grind up the most severe grade, the heavily loaded bus smoked and trudged its way to the top. It reminded Kurt of the story, 'The Little Train That Could.'

∞

Lush vegetation in all shades of green brightened the countryside. Vines covered many of the trees and plants that grew wild nearly everywhere. From the mountainous slopes, the views of distant valleys were breathtaking. Cocoa bean and tobacco plantations were interspersed in the native foliage, along with farms growing various types of fruits and/or vegetables. Numerous rivers and smaller tributaries ran through the region, with sloughs and swamplands spreading their watery tendrils.

Reaching the heart of Guatemala City was a shock for all of the passengers from the *Explorer*. The town was in shambles. A few months previously a devastating earthquake hit Guatemala, destroyed buildings, and killed more than twenty thousand throughout Guatemala City and in nearby Antigua.

Everywhere they looked entire blocks of buildings lay in rubble. Dotting the sidewalks and spilling over into the streets, ramshackle clapboard dwellings were haphazardly constructed from the debris from the quake. Where once stood five and six story buildings, huge piles of concrete and brick rubble covered massive areas, their ruins marking what had once been a thriving business center.

Hundreds of the residents in the city bore physical reminders of the chaos and devastation, some were still wrapped in bandages, others used sticks and tree limbs as canes to help support their broken or missing body parts. Families gathered austerely together under canopies made from cardboard, and in lean-tos built from any number of scraps of lumber and other materials pulled out of the rubble.

Oddly enough in some parts of the town, there was no apparent damage. Shops and buildings bustled with activity and commerce continued as normal, while across the street, or a block away, everything lay in ruin. But regardless of the chaos, the peasant people looked happy. They smiled at the Americans as they walked past. They greeted them with shy, but friendly "Hola's". It was truly remarkable how stoically they bore the after effects of the disastrous quake. Their overall attitudes and demeanors conveyed a deep sense of peacefulness and satisfaction with life. It was as if they bore the burden of devastation as a natural part of their existence.

Staying together as they walked through the streets of the city, the Americans sensed a general attitude of quiet acceptance from the people who lined the doorways of partially crumbled buildings, or lived in hastily constructed little shacks and what might be considered dwellings in the alleys and small parks that survived the carnage of the earthquake.

When they found a bustling shopping plaza, they purchased items to take back aboard. Beautiful hand-knitted shirts that would cost ten times more in the States, they bought from the shops and street vendors for next to nothing. Hammocks, hand-woven hats, and lovely handcrafted jewelry could be purchased for unbelievably low prices. Every one of the passengers spent freely, partly because everything was so incredibly cheap, and partly because they felt compelled to do what they could to help the obviously hard working people of Guatemala try to recover from the destructive quake.

In one shop, Madison became careless and forgot her small recently purchased handbag that held their traveler's checks. Her forgetfulness caused a very hectic evening for Kurt and Madison as they retraced their steps in an effort to recover the lost handbag. The biggest problem was that they were not sure which shop they had been in when she left her bag. As they ran from shop to shop, they discovered that several had closed. Luckily at one of the closed shops where they had bought a couple of Guatemalan shirts, the shopkeeper saw them from his nearby residence. Seeing their frantic dismay, he reopened his shop to check for her missing handbag. Sure enough, they found it lying on the counter near the register. Thanking him profusely, especially when he declined their offer of a tip for his help, they started the long journey back to the ship, realizing that they had less than four hours to get back on board and they were nowhere near the primary bus line.

When they made it to the last bus of the night just moments before its scheduled departure time, they were greatly relieved. It was a dark night, the skies heavy with a dense cloud cover that wrapped everything in a shroud of eerily quiet blackness.

They arrived back at the ship at eleven forty-five p.m., just fifteen minutes before their ship was scheduled to depart. Not surprisingly, they were told there was another delay, and the ship would not sail before sometime the following morning.

The delay that caused the late departure was unclear. Captain Ellis remained rather surly and reclusive, staying alone in his cabin during the entire stay in San Jose. Dawn delivered food to his room.

Brian and Rombowski worked through the night and into the morning on the mechanical problem. In the sweltering heat, everyone waited anxiously for the roar of the engines to signal that they could get underway. Tensions continued to build as the day wore on; and by nightfall, there was a general sense of despair and frustration coursing throughout the ship. Captain Ellis remained in his cabin, and Brian appeared only briefly when he crawled out of the engine room to cool off. Larry and Guillermo did their best to cheer things up, initiating a poker game to try and keep everyone busy and distracted. Unable to use the galley stove because of the mechanical issues, dinner that night was a hastily thrown together salad with the remnants of the barbecued tuna tossed in.

∞

Around eleven the following morning, the starboard engine rumbled to life, the anchor was hauled, and the *Explorer* was once again underway. Rom, with assistance from Brian, managed to repair the damages to the port engine, and it also fired off about an hour later. Rom was not completely satisfied with the work and advised Captain Ellis to operate at no more than fifty percent horsepower. Even so, running at half-power on two engines allowed much better progress than running on one. They settled into a cruising speed of about six knots.

The southerly swell abated during the night; and except for a light offshore breeze rippling the surface, the seas remained mild.

Once again the ice machine conked out, and both Rom and Steve Bilko (who was brought aboard in Guatemala to replace Big Ben) tried diligently to bring it back on line. After about six hours of hot and sweaty frustration, Bilko announced that they could not finish the repairs until they reached land and were able to purchase parts.

The fresh water tanks were once again tainted, slightly permeated with diesel fuel from an accidental transferring problem while the ship was at anchor off San Jose. The water was usable, but just didn't taste, or smell good.

Many of the remaining passengers aboard continued to gripe and complain about the conditions and the lack of amenities aboard, although the core group of Kurt and Madison, Marcos and Linda, Larry, Tiona and Charlie, Bob Bradley and Guillermo took it all in stride. During one of the impromptu general meetings aboard the ship, Guillermo tried to downplay the 'problems'.

"This is an experience that could never be replicated," announced Guillermo. "We're all living a dream of a lifetime, visiting exotic places, seeing things from a unique perspective, sharing things that few people ever have a chance to share. So what if there are a few inconveniences? This is a trip that is remarkable, and incomparable! I really think all of you should quit your bitching and start enjoying this adventure."

"He's right!" Marcos asserted. "We've all seen and shared some wonderful experiences and places. It might not be the most comfortable and lavish way to travel, but it is certainly something none of us will ever forget. I know that not all of you have been as lucky as me. I mean, after all, there are not too many women in the world as beautiful as Linda, and probably none with her other attributes."

Linda turned bright crimson and punched him on the arm. "Marcos, don't say things like that," she implored, although it was quite obvious that she was pleased with his adoration.

∞

As the vessel cruised along the coast of Central America, the serenity and beauty of the peaceful Pacific seemed to mesmerize everyone on board. A south swell rolled the ship a little more than in recent days; but the swells were widely spaced, and a very light breeze from offshore helped to keep the seas flat and calm.

The passage between Guatemala and El Salvador remained basically calm and uneventful, with the exception of an episode in the early morning hours on the second day at sea.

It was not quite daybreak when Guillermo awakened to the distinctive sound of a change in the engine pitch. Listening for a few minutes, he determined that the noise that he heard was nothing more than an adjustment to the throttle controls, resulting in a reduction of the rpms. He found himself hoping that the slowing of the engines was merely a practical adjustment and not another mechanical problem.

He rubbed the sleep from his eyes, crawled out of his 'bunk' and ambled back to the head. Moving to the stern of the ship, he immediately recognized the characteristic tautness and erratic motion of the starboard trolling line, indicating that a fish had been hooked. Looking astern, the faint glow of daylight was not yet strong enough to see with any clarity, but it was obvious that something was splashing at the end of the trolling line. Guillermo reached into the gear bucket and put on the fishing gloves. As he began pulling line over the rail, pausing every few feet to coil the line, his eyes adjusted to the misty gloaming of daybreak, and he recognized the distinctive coloration of a medium-sized dorado (mahi-mahi) 'pancaking' on the surface in the ship's wake. As he continued to pull the fish slowly toward the boat, he realized that the fish must have been dragging for some time since it made no attempt to jump or dive below the surface but merely flapped along on its side like a flapjack as he pulled it to the boat.

After pulling the fish about halfway to the stern, Guillermo observed another motion a few feet behind the fish. Something was following it. Thinking that it was probably a large shark, he turned his head around and called out, "Hey, anybody awake that can give me a hand?"

Bob Bradley jumped from his berth and responded immediately. Reaching the stern, Bob asked, "So what's going on?"

Guillermo told him, "I'm pulling in a nice dorado; but look behind it, there appears to be something following it."

Bob squinted into the gray mist of morning. Sure enough, he clearly saw the dorado and another larger, darker shape following closely.

"I am trying to pull the fish in quickly so that we don't lose it to the predator. Will you coil the line so that I can try to get it to the boat before that thing grabs it?"

"Got it!" Bob responded, coiling the line as Guillermo pulled the fish closer.

A few others arrived on scene. Fascinated, the others watched as Guillermo steadily pulled the flapping dorado toward the boat. About forty feet out, the long dark shadow behind the splashing fish rose to the surface, revealing a high dorsal fin and a beautifully illuminated set of 'broad shoulders' that lit up brightly in the churning foam of the ship's wake.

"Holy shit!" Guillermo shouted, "It's a marlin!"

Sure enough, the huge fish was now half exposed, its magnificent coloration glowing vividly as it stalked what was likely intended to be its first morning meal.

Guillermo paused momentarily, so fascinated by the sight of the huge marlin that he stopped hauling in the line.

"Guillermo, pull! Pull fast, or it's going to grab the fish!" Bob shouted.

Jolted from his entrancement, Guillermo gave a quick yank on the line, pulling it forward just as the huge marlin opened its gaping triangular jaws to engulf its prey. Its lower jaw brushed the dorado's tail.

Enthralled, everyone on deck watched the spectacle of a huge blue marlin silently stalking the dorado. It was very exciting, the marlin intent on feeding, and the anglers determined to pull the fish into the boat before the gigantic marlin ripped it off the hook. The marlin was so enormous that the good-sized dorado looked like nothing more than a 'small mouthful' by comparison.

Guillermo pulled faster, determined to get the fish to the boat before it was swallowed by the marlin. He pulled steadily as the huge marlin loomed purposeful and resolute in the boat wake. Finally a mere ten feet from the stern, the marlin made one last futile lunge for the dorado. It seemed to pause briefly to look up into the eyes of the people on deck before it rose nearly clear of the water, and revealed its entire bulk in all of its majestic glory. Then it rolled to its side and plunged into the depths.

Guillermo hauled the dorado over the rail and onto the deck. When put on the scale, it weighed twenty-two pounds.

"How big do you think that thing was?' Bob Bradley asked nobody in particular.

"I don't really know," Guillermo responded. "I've seen several large marlin caught over the years, including one that was nearly five hundred pounds; but I've never seen anything even close to that size. If I had to guess, I'd say it was well over one thousand pounds, maybe more."

As the adrenaline wore off, the gathering slowly dispersed to take care of their morning rituals and prepare for breakfast. At least there would be fresh dorado for dinner.

CHAPTER NINE

During the night, Captain Ellis slowed the ship to about two knots so that he could enter the port of Acajutla, El Salvador, in daylight. Puerto Acajutla lies on the western shore of El Salvador about thirteen degrees north of the equator. Small in geographical size and nestled between Guatemala, Nicaragua, and Honduras to the east, El Salvador is the most densely populated country in Central America. The capital, San Salvador, is about seventy miles inland.

The small port of Acajutla proved to be busy, with numerous small freighters continually loading and offloading freight, cargo, and mainly pallets of coffee seed and sugar cane bushels. Built in 1961 and expanded in 1970, it serves as the primary port of El Salvador.

Encompassing the port is a large, flat valley surrounded by distant dark-green hills.

Its people, much like those of Guatemala, are a mix of Spanish and Inca/Mayan ancestry. As a whole, they are short in stature with predominantly dark skin, dark hair, dark eyes, flat noses, and wide foreheads. The travelers aboard the boat who worked on improving their Spanish (Larry, Marcos, and Kurt) got along famously with the local population, finding them warm and friendly. Most of the other passengers found the El Salvadorans to be cold and distant and felt they projected an air of resentment or hostility.

After checking through Customs, which was surprisingly quick and easy, the passengers were all allowed off the ship to explore at their leisure.

Captain Ellis announced a day and a half layover, planning to haul anchor and depart at four p.m. the following afternoon.

In El Salvador, like in Guatemala, squadrons of military police, heavily laden with small arms and belts of ammunition were often seen roaming the streets on foot and in vehicles. Rumors of civil unrest circulated through the countryside, and the first inkling of a military coup was garnering headlines in the local newspapers. In fact, 1976 was destined to become the start of a long period of social and military strife in the country.

Once ashore, Kurt and Larry quickly ascertained that there was a regular bus service between Acajutla and San Salvador (the Capital City) that departed every four hours, beginning at seven a.m. and ending at eleven p.m. Most of the guests aboard the Explorer elected to catch the eleven a.m. bus into the Capital.

Compared to the bus rides in Mexico and Guatemala, the bus trip to San Salvador was less of an eye-opener than the earlier rides. As usual, Larry, Marcos, and Kurt mingled and interacted with the peasants, engaging them in conversations with fractured Spanish, singing songs, and passing around bottles of home-grown liquor that always somehow materialized when the singing and laughter began.

The scenery was spectacular. Thick wild vegetation alternated with coffee plant and sugar cane fields, then rows of balsam trees—a primary export of El Salvador that is used in syrups, perfumes, and as a base for certain liquid medicines. Swamplands steamed between the planted fields. As the bus wound its way into the interior, it skirted numerous low hills covered with verdant foliage.

Along the way, the bus made many stops. Most stops were in remote areas where there was no real indication of any habitation; but invariably, several small dark bodies would step out from the thick foliage. The driver stopped in the center of the road while they loaded their goods, produce, animals, and children. Soon the bus was standing room only, and as usual, the native men stayed seated while the women stood.

As the bus chugged along, the road became steeper and narrower, winding its way high into the mountainous terrain. The vegetation changed as the bus climbed, with the hills sporting an abundance of coco palms, banana trees, mangos and papayas, and other tropical plants and flowers. Farther up, manzanita and orange trees gave way to jacaranda and pine. It was hot and humid. Heavy black clouds appeared overhead, and the sound of booming thunder shook the bus as intense tropical rains pounded the metal rooftop. Twice the driver stopped for a few minutes because he could not see through the deluge.

After a squall passed, the sun reappeared, and the pavement and nearby vegetation exuded copious steamy vapors. The vapor lingered until the moisture from the downpour evaporated. The humidity increased rapidly with each passing rainsquall, and the bus interior soon reeked unpleasantly of human bodies in varying forms of cleanliness.

Upon arrival in San Salvador, the American visitors were very relieved to depart the bus, even though it was also hot and humid.

The group split up and went different directions, the women wanted to shop and the men interested in absorbing the nuances of the city and its people. Madison, Tiona, Linda, and Marcos went off in one direction in search of native clothing and other items. Larry, Kurt, and Charlie walked around town in search of a bar to get a cold beer. Their plan was to meet later at the local post office.

Somewhere along the way, their signals crossed, and the connection was not made.

It was not too difficult for the men to begin tracking the others. Their inquiries on the streets elicited an immediate response as soon as they described Linda, Madison, and Tiona. Three voluptuous American women—one standing a good foot taller than most of the local men, one with long golden hair unlike anything most had ever seen, and one wearing a short tight-fitting skirt with a tiny bright yellow tank-top—stood out like the proverbial sore thumb. Their trail was easy to follow.

Half an hour after beginning their search, the men located Marcos and the other women. It was especially interesting to see the reaction the El Salvadorian men had to Linda. Her statuesque size and shape were particularly impressive to the native men, whose average size was about five feet-four, and weight maybe one hundred twenty pounds. To see and be near a gorgeous woman that stood nearly six feet was enthralling for many of the native men. They literally could not take their eyes off her.

The children were fascinated with Madison. Her long and lustrous golden hair completely captivated the young children, especially the girls who were accustomed to the omnipresent black hair of native El Salvadorans.

Tiona also garnered the attention of the men, partly because of her scanty short dress and blouse but even more by her saucy mannerisms.

Continuing on their exploration of the city, the group found a McDonalds hamburger shop located in one of the newer shopping areas. After nearly six weeks of shipboard food, a greasy American-style hamburger with fries and a vanilla milkshake was beyond delicious! All of them ate their food ravenously; relishing a meal they would normally consider junk food.

The stop for a meal at McDonalds resulted in a change of plans for the group of seven. Since they lingered over the meal, they missed the bus bound for Acajutla. As there was no special rush to get back to the ship— they had most of the following day to get back—the group decided that it might be fun to get a hotel room.

After getting directions, the group walked about four blocks to a small hotel recommended by one of the locals. More than likely it belonged to a relative of the person that made the recommendation.

Upon arrival, they were told only two rooms were available. The proprietor assured them that it would not be a problem since he had extra mattresses for the large room, which could sleep up to six. The other room with one double bed was setup for two.

Tiona stepped forward with an immediate solution to the pending dilemma. "Let's just flip a coin. Odd-girl out gets the single room."

The others agreed to the suggestion.

Each of the girls pulled out a coin, tossed it into the air, and Tiona won the flip. She and Charlie had the single room for themselves, and the others would share the larger quarters.

So Linda and Marcos, Madison and Kurt, and Larry, helped move the spare mattresses into the larger room. It soon became obvious that beds in El Salvador were designed for the 'typical' El Salvadoran physique, not the larger Americans. Each of the beds, including the double that was centered in the large room, was slightly less than six-feet in length. One of the mattresses appeared to be designed for a child and was perhaps five-feet long. Larry agreed to take that one, hoping to use one of the extra cushions to support his feet.

Once they had settled on sleeping arrangements and put their few overnight items away, Linda, Marcos, and Larry decided to head down the street to a local bar for a cold beer. Kurt and Madison elected to stay behind.

Locking the door for privacy, Madison and Kurt wasted little time in taking advantage of being left alone in the hotel room. Madison seemed anxious to be alone with Kurt.

"How about a quick shower?' She asked as she grabbed his hand and led him toward the bathroom.

"Great idea!" Kurt replied.

Madison was completely naked by the time she reached the edge of the small concrete enclosure. Kurt gazed at her supple body, immediately aroused by her voluptuous curves. He shed his own clothes and stepped over the low threshold of the door-less stall where Madison had already begun to adjust the water temperature. Warm was about all there was, but that proved to be absolutely perfect.

As Madison turned, Kurt reached out with his hands to touch her smooth lush body. It felt wondrously silky and slick from the mix of fresh water, sunscreen and sweat that covered her skin. He pulled her close and reveled in the sensation of her body against his. They kissed.

The sexual energy was electric. Her eyes turned a glassy milky blue. His eyes shined a fiery green, radiating brightly.

Her eyes clouded, tears of pleasure formed under the lids. "Now," she whispered. "Take me now, please."

He lifted her against the shower wall, and they became lost in the pleasure.

Gradually, they each grew aware of where they were and what had happened.

Kurt recovered first. His arms and legs felt rubbery; and for a moment, he was afraid he was going to drop her.

"Wow," he murmured, gradually lifting her from his loins and lowering her to her feet. "That was incredible!"

"Yes," she breathed softly, "it certainly was."

When they regained their senses, they each took another long and languid turn under the shower, rinsing then turning the hot water knob completely off. For several minutes, they let the cold water run over their bodies, tempering the sweat and heat that lingered.

Recovered, they moved onto the bed and lay together entwined. They touched each other tenderly. Their lips brushed, and their passion rose. The heat from their bodies soaked the sheets. Afterward they laughed, softly and happily, relishing the joy of the gift they had just shared.

Eventually they moved back into the shower and rinsed again. This time when they dried each other, it was with a different purpose, solely to remove the water from their sensitive skin.

∞

They dressed and sat side by side on the small couch that was the only other piece of furniture in the room. They engaged in small talk.

When the others returned, they could sense the lingering after effects of the afternoon.

"Are we interrupting something here?" Linda asked, a twinkling of understanding in her eyes.

Madison glanced at Kurt, "Not at all. We're just sitting here remembering a few of the fun things we've been able to enjoy on this trip."

"Mmm. Yes, I can see that your memories are pleasurable." Linda commented.

Madison blushed and quickly changed the subject. "So how about dinner? I'm famished. Does anyone have any ideas?"

"Actually, the proprietor said they would be happy to prepare a meal for us if we'd like," Larry offered. "I'd be willing to bet it would be good, and cheap."

He was right. The woman who ran the establishment and took care of the kitchen served a delicious dish of rice and beans mixed with chicken that was ladled over a mound of freshly baked tortillas broken into small pieces. They all drank a few beers and sat around chatting with the proprietor and his wife—Salvador and Isabel. They both spoke a small amount of broken English. Although their accent was difficult to follow, Larry, Marcos, and Kurt managed to carry on a conversation in mixed Spanish and English.

In the morning, Isabel fixed a plate of eggs, beans and cheese, and warm homemade tortillas.

The entire stay, including the meals, cost twelve U.S. dollars per person.

∞

For the most part, the bus ride back to the port was uneventful, and the bus surprisingly empty. The driver explained that most of the populace waited until later in the day to ride the bus, preferring to work early in the day before the temperatures climbed, then do their traveling later.

They arrived back on board at eleven, well ahead of the noon deadline. Predictably, another delay soon became evident. For some inexplicable reason, all of the battery power was out of commission. Bilko managed to fire up the generators, and the batteries were recharged by two p.m. Captain Ellis ordered the lines hauled aboard, and the vessel was underway.

Because the *Explorer* was way behind schedule—nearly three weeks—the Captain decided to bypass Honduras and Nicaragua and proceed straight to Costa Rica.

The plan was to steam along for approximately eighty hours until they reached the port of Puntarenas, Costa Rica. Unfortunately during the night, a lightning storm caused another failure in the generator system, and the ship was forced to heave-to early the next morning.

Rom, Bilko, Sam Gilford and Brian went to work trying to repair the system. The ship was adrift about sixty miles offshore in calm crystal-blue water.

While fixing the generator problem, the engineer discovered a diesel leak had dumped nearly three hundred gallons of diesel fuel into the bilge. There was no way the ship would make it to Puntarenas with the amount of fuel remaining. The Captain decided to turn toward land and see if they could take on fuel in the tiny Nicaraguan port of Punta Corinto. It was either that or alter course and backtrack northward about thirty miles to the Gulf of Fonseca, the only section of Honduras that borders the Pacific Coast.

Upon arrival in Puerto Corinto, Captain Ellis discovered that the fueling station was closed. He had a decision to make. Should he head back up the coast thirty miles or wait until the following day to fuel? It was a matter of time, and he was well aware that time was his biggest problem.

The port itself was also rundown. Several large buildings sorely in need of paint and repairs lined the wharf. Quite obviously, the city was poor and struggling; and judging from the military presence, the politics of the country was likely in turmoil.

A full cadre of shabbily dressed military personnel lined the adjacent wharf. They looked equally innocent and threatening. They appeared ragtag, and disheveled, but their M-16 carbines looked very real and sinister. Captain Ellis maneuvered the ship alongside and waited for the authorities.

Surrounding the port, imposing forested mountains loomed. A thin trail of smoke curled above one impressive peak, obviously volcanic in nature. An occasional low rumble could be felt and heard from the east, and the volcano would belch a billowing cloud of gray-black smoke. It appeared that the volcano was ready to erupt.

When the port authorities came aboard, the demeanor of most of the twelve boarders was shy and unassuming, almost as if they were guilty or ashamed of being aboard. However, one individual, obviously their leader, was quite the opposite.

The diminutive but impressively ornamented Nicaraguan leader greeted them in booming, heavily accented English. "Hello! I am Capitan Velasquez. I am your official greeter! I am here to welcome you to Nicaragua, except I am sadly not possible to let you ashore. You are our guests, but must remain on this ship. So, welcome to Puerto Corinto! Who of you is the Capitan?"

Captain Ellis stepped forward and held out his hand in greeting. "Good afternoon, I am Captain Ellis."

"Ah! Captain Ellis, I am please to meet you. Could you show me all of your papers, and tell me, for what reason do you stop in our port?"

"We are in need of fuel. I spoke with someone on the radio and was informed that there is fuel available, but that it cannot be pumped until tomorrow. Is that true? Is there no possibility to take on fuel this afternoon?"

"No, forgivamente, but fuel cannot be pumped because the wife of the fuel man is making a baby. He will be back tomorrow."

"I see," said Captain Ellis, "and I assume that no one else can run the pumps?"

"Ah, Gracious de Dios, No! Only Senor Montezuma can operate the pumps. It is his duty!"

Captain Ellis rubbed his hands through his hair, demonstrating his frustration. "Okay, excuse me for a moment while I gather our papers." With that, he turned and walked off to his quarters where all of the ships documents were kept.

Meanwhile on the wharf, quite a crowd had gathered to look at the unusual spectacle the *Explorer* made. Few private vessels make stops in this small mostly commercial port, and the few that do rarely have the cast of characters that comprised the ship's passenger list.

At one point when Linda went to a deck cooler to pull out a cold drink, the crowd of native onlookers standing on the wharf actually let out a cheer when she bent over to get the drink. Her ample posterior obviously made a big impression.

After making a concerted officious inspection of the ship's papers, Captain Velasquez handed the paperwork back to Captain Ellis and pronounced. "Excellente! Your papers are in good order and proper." He turned to one of the other soldiers and instructed him to stamp all of the Passports.

"Unfortunately," Captain Velasquez intoned with a tone of seriousness to his voice, "I cannot allow you to go ashore. Our Country is undergoing some minor difficulties with a small band of renegade rebels, and our government has restricted tourism. You and your passengers must remain aboard your vessel. However, tomorrow we will be here to help with fueling, and we are hoping you will be pleased to enjoy your stay." With that, he turned abruptly to his men and instructed them in Spanish to return to their posts.

That evening turned stifling hot and muggy, and the mosquitoes were out in full force. The water in the small port was brackish; fresh water from the Rio Nicaragua mixed with salt water from the ocean. As a consequence, the mosquitoes were prolific.

For the passengers, it was a double whammy. The stifling humidity and heat inside the cabins and lounge room were unbearable. Outside on deck, the mosquitoes so ubiquitous it was impossible to slap them away. As a group, the passengers decided the lesser of the two evils was to remain inside, either in their own cabin or on cots in the main lounge and dining hall.

Cots and mats were moved into place, and a concerted effort ensued to seek and destroy as many of the mosquitoes already in the room as possible. After killing all they could, nearly everyone pulled lightweight sheets over their bodies to ward off the remaining pests. Even with that, it was difficult to sleep due to the pervasive sound of mosquitoes humming as they sought tender flesh. It was a tough night for all except the mosquitoes.

At dawn, everyone rose early, anxious to put back to sea. With the sun up over the surrounding mountaintops, the mosquitoes began to disappear.

Shortly after eight a.m., Captain Velasquez arrived at the wharf with a huge man, announcing in his booming voice, "Good morning my friends, this is Enrique Montezuma, he is our fueling expert, extraordinaire. He will help you to fuel and accompany you to his fueling dock."

Enrique Montezuma was not the typical Nicaraguan. He stood nearly six feet-four and weighed in excess of four hundred pounds. His features were round and smooth—his head so immense that it made all of his other features seem tiny and out of proportion. He had tiny looking ears, a small pug nose, and a mouth that looked like it should be on a child. His eyes were small, beady, and wide set. Except for the small mouth, his appearance immediately brought to mind the appearance of a hippopotamus. His demeanor was, however, quite jovial.

"Welcome to Puerto Corinto," he offered in heavily accented but understandable English. "I am sorry that I was not here and could not assist you yesterday. I was with my wife, who blessed me with another fine son. I now have seven sons, but not a daughter. Soon enough we will try again as my wife is determined to have a little hija. But for now if I may come aboard, I will accompany you to the fueling station and you may be on your way."

Senor Montezuma was surprisingly spry and agile for his size, although the small gangway bent and creaked precariously under his weight. It held, and dock lines were dropped. It was only about a two-hundred yard move to the fueling station, where a single fuel hose ran down from a tiny little booth built onto the side of one of the nearby warehouses.

It took nearly two hours to take on the fuel because of the small gas motor that ran the pump and the tiny half-inch diameter size of the fueling line. The ship took on four hundred gallons of diesel, and it was hard to imagine how long it might take for one of the larger ships to take on a few thousand gallons. Finished, Senor Montezuma happily took payment in U.S. dollars and bade the ship and its passengers a pleasant farewell. The ship was again underway.

∞

As the ship departed the port of Corinto and headed out the Rio Nicaragua, a loud rumbling noise overshadowed the steady throbbing of the engines. A billowing dark gray cloud of smoke burst from the distant volcano. No visible signs of lava emerged, but it seemed as if the top of the mountain was about ready to blow. One of the port authorities had told Kurt that the volcano roared and spit smoke and fire periodically, but they weren't concerned. Kurt wasn't so sure.

Away from the harbor, it was interesting to see the distinct difference between the commercialism of the port and the rustic beauty of the surrounding village. Thatched huts and palm-covered cabanas dotted the hillsides. Lines of clothes drying in the sunshine added a distinctly peasant touch to the scenery. Thick vegetation covered everything that was not obviously manmade. It was an idyllic scene.

Throughout the afternoon, they chugged along the scenic coastline, inching inexorably away from shore into deeper waters. By evening, land was barely visible.

With the sun beginning to settle toward the distant horizon, the sky began to dramatically change. A panorama of clouds had formed—striated cirrus, truncated stratus, developing nimbus. Accented against the deep sapphire blue skies, the clouds began absorbing the rainbow colors of the setting sun. A myriad of vivid colors emerged. Violet shades formed on the high clouds with dark crimson hues nearer the horizon. An extraordinary prism of colors illuminated the sky.

On watch, Kurt stood at the wheel transfixed, awed by the incredible display of nature. Ahead of the ship, the undulating surface of the sea absorbed the rainbow colors of the sky, turning the glistening surface into

147

a surreal stratum of brilliance. Where the sea met the sky, colors danced about like the interior of a kaleidoscope. As the sunset unfolded, he felt as if the wondrous scene was pulling him toward it, infusing him with its magic. It was as if he was floating in the sky, wafting from cloud to cloud, and at the same time hovering in or on the sea. He was lost in the panoramic incandescence of the heavenly sunset. He was so mesmerized that he forgot that Charlie was on the bridge with him.

"Kurt, are you okay?"

The voice pulled him out of the trance that he was in. He glanced over at Charlie. "I'm sorry, Charlie, what did you say?"

"You were making a funny sound, kind of a humming noise, and you seemed to be in a trance."

"Sorry Charlie, I guess I was. I don't think I've ever seen anything quite so breathtaking, as awe-inspiring as this sunset."

"Yeah, it truly is incredible," agreed Charlie.

They stood together for another half-hour as darkness finally enveloped them—the skies gradually turning blood red before fading to blackness.

∞

When Marcos and Larry relieved them at eight-o'clock, Kurt was anxious to find Madison and share the wonder that he had witnessed. As he rounded the corner of the makeshift shower stalls across from their 'living space,' Kurt halted momentarily in the shadows when he heard Madison's light-hearted laughter.

Kurt's brows furrowed when he saw Madison sitting on one of the lounge chairs with Jeffrey Smythe seated close-by. Smythe was talking animatedly in a voice loud enough that Kurt could hear what he said.

"Mother was always very prim and proper," he intoned in his melodious British accent. "She always expected me to do everything correctly, from my manners, to my studies. She would always tell me, 'Jeffrey, there is a right way and a wrong way. You must always do things the right way'. I didn't have much of a chance to do anything boyish as she always expected me to stay around our cottage. I didn't have a lot of friends."

Kurt watched Madison tilt her head and respond, "Oh, I find that hard to believe. You are so nice and personable; I would think that you had many friends."

"Well, once I was away from home, I began to cultivate friendships better. But when I was growing up, I just did not have much of an opportunity."

A brief pause followed, and Kurt was ready to join them when Smythe continued.

"Father was much different. His world was his work. He toiled in the steel mills, working primarily the evening shift; so I did not see him too much. He slept late, and I was at academy early. When I returned home, I would go directly into the study to complete my class instructions; and he often left before I finished. On the weekends, he was rarely at home, preferring to spend his days with his co-workers at the neighborhood pub, or quite frequently attending rugby matches. He played rugby when he was younger and hoped to become a professional rugby player, but a severe knee injury ended his hopes and left him with a permanent limp."

Madison listened to Smythe's reflections, leaning forward in obvious attentiveness.

Smythe continued. "The one thing that father did that I have always rejoiced in was the day he took me to the River Thames for an afternoon of sailing with one of his peers. On that day, I developed a love for sailing and vowed that I would someday make sailing, or at least the sea, a part of my life. After I graduated from academy, I informed mother and father that I would be moving away and going to the coast. They were unhappy with my decision, and they still hold misgivings about my lifestyle. But from the day I left home, my life began to change. I moved directly to Portsmouth, got a part-time job helping out on the docks. Eventually I secured a position as a Boson assistant on a Britain-to-France transport ferry. From there, I worked my way around various ports and ships along the southwest shore, studied for and secured my Captain's License, and wound up on board a luxury schooner that took me to Acapulco. However, I was at odds with the captain—a cocky bastard with a real Captain Bligh attitude—and was just hanging around waiting for a new gig when the *Explorer* came along."

"Your life sounds fascinating," Madison gushed. "You've seen and done so much. Tell me more about your travels."

"Well, I...."

His dialogue was interrupted by another voice. "Kurt!" Tiona exclaimed as she rounded the corner from behind the shower stalls. "What are you doing standing here in the shadows?"

Kurt grimaced, and tried to find a response that did not sound too lame. "Oh, I'm just getting off from my bridge watch."

"But you're leaning here against the wall as if you have nowhere else to go," Tiona observed innocently.

"Not at all, I'm just heading for the bunk," Kurt responded casually as he stepped from the shadows and moved toward Madison and Jeffrey Smythe.

"Hi guys, what's up?" Kurt attempted to sound as friendly and innocent as possible, although he realized that they were undoubtedly aware that he had been standing there listening to their conversation.

Madison did not say anything, and Kurt felt the acrimony in her glare. "Well, I best be on my way. It was nice chatting with you." Smythe stood, smiled smugly toward Kurt, turned and nodded sweetly at Madison, and walked toward the upper gangway.

Tiona looked from Kurt to Madison, then back at Kurt. Never one to mince words, she stated, "I see there's a degree of tension in the air here. Is there anything I can do to help?"

Kurt smiled enigmatically at Tiona. "No. But thanks, Tiona, everything's fine."

He turned to look at Madison, but she averted her eyes. Obviously, she was not pleased. He turned to Tiona. "So, what's up with you?"

"Oh, I was just walking around the deck, enjoying the evening. After that incredible sunset, I just felt like staying out on deck for a while."

Kurt had forgotten about the sunset, although its mention brought back a fleeting memory of its glory. He looked again toward Madison, but she seemed curled up into a shell; so he thought it best to hold off. He was hoping that Tiona would continue on her way, but she stood nearby, as if waiting for him to say more.

"So, is Charlie around? We stood watch together and he saw the sunset with me."

Tiona replied, "No, he went back to the cabin to read. I don't feel like going back into that little cave just yet. Do you mind if I join you two for a while?"

Kurt was anxious to talk with Madison alone, to attempt to clear the air about his apparent eavesdropping, but he did not want to seem rude.

"Not at all," Kurt offered, pointing to the deck chair formerly occupied by Jeffrey Smythe. "Please have a seat."

Tiona sat on the edge of the chair, and Madison moved almost imperceptibly deeper into her lounge seat. Obviously, she was not interested in joining the conversation.

"That really was quite the sunset, wasn't it?" Kurt commented. "I couldn't believe the colors. It seemed to illuminate the entire sky. And it just got better and better, although at the very end the deep dark red just before dark settled in took on an ominous look and feel."

"Oh, I thought that last few minutes was the most beautiful of all!" Tiona mused. "It was like it had a life of its own. It somehow reminded me of a symphony orchestra reaching the final crescendo of a powerful concert. It grew and built into a magical performance, then the curtain crashed down in a final denouement."

Kurt chuckled at her analogy. She was right. The sunset did have the quality of a symphony. Looking at it from that perspective, he reflected on the colorful metaphor. A brief recollection of several of Beethoven and Bach's masterful compositions flitted through his mind, and he could almost hear the sounds merging with the ethereal specter that graced the tropical skies an hour before. "That's quite poetic, Tiona. I wish I had thought of it in those terms while I was watching earlier. I might have heard the music."

Madison had turned her head away. Kurt was hoping that this discussion might be enough to draw her into the conversation; but obviously, she was still not inclined to participate.

Tiona also could see Madison's withdrawal, and she looked sympathetically toward Kurt. She reached up and placed two of her fingers to her lips, pushed upward as if forcing a smile, and winked. When he responded with a forlorn tilt of his head accompanied by a shrug, she seemed to realize her intrusion. She hopped to her feet and stated merrily, "Okay, I think I'll go up to the bow and watch the stars for a while."

Madison did not react at all. Kurt looked back at Tiona, shrugged again, and turned his palms upwards as if to say, 'Not much I can do.'

When Tiona was gone, Kurt sat down on the chair, hoping that Madison would speak to him. After a few minutes, it became obvious that she had no intention of initiating any conversation. Kurt breathed deeply, his mind running through a myriad of things to say that might be appropriate. After going through several ideas, racking his brain on where he should start, he decided to simply ask, "So, what's wrong?"

She acted as if she didn't hear him. He waited patiently. It was a long pause before she finally turned and accused him, "You were spying on me!"

Her reaction caught him off-guard, and he became defensive. "No, I wasn't spying," he replied, knowing all the while that she was right. He had been spying. He didn't like Jeffrey Smythe, and he didn't like the fact that Madison seemed to enjoy his company so much.

"You were! Tiona caught you hiding in the shadows watching and listening to our conversation." Her voice was trembling, on the verge of hysteria. "Why were you spying on us? And how long were you standing there watching and listening?"

Kurt took a deep breath, looked down at his feet, and admitted his mistake. "Yes, you are right. I was watching and listening to your conversation. But I wasn't spying. I just don't like that creep, and you seem to think he's something special." He took another deep breath and continued, "I don't like the way he looks at you, and he always seems to seek you out whenever I'm not around. He's obviously enamored of you."

"No, he's not enamored. And he's not a creep. He's just being friendly. He's a nice person, and I resent the fact that I can't just talk with someone I like without you becoming jealous."

Kurt thought for a few long moments before responding. "Yes, you're right. I am jealous. I love you Madison, and I guess I just want you all for myself. I resent it when someone like him weasels his way into your confidence, and I think he's more interested in you than you realize."

"No. You're wrong. He's not coming on to me. He's just friendly. Besides, his feelings about me, whatever they may be, are not what matters. I'm not interested in him and that's what matters. If I want to have someone as a friend, I think you should trust me."

He knew that she was right. He needed to trust her, or their relationship would spiral rapidly downhill. If there was a mutual infatuation between Madison and Smythe, he had to let it run its course or she would resent him for interfering with her personal needs and wants. Life was simply that way, complicated, but simple.

He moved closer, and knelt before her on the wooden deck. "You're right. I apologize. I won't try to dictate or interfere with your choice of friends. But don't be upset if I don't go out of my way to befriend him. I still think he's a creep."

She looked into his eyes for a long while, her own big blue eyes unblinking and thoughtful. Kurt stayed where he was, unflinching, although his knees were becoming uncomfortable on the hard wooden deck. As he looked at her face, he realized how much she meant to him. Her angelic heart-shaped face etched a perpetual vision of loveliness into his mind. He could feel his own heart thumping heavily, sending a message throughout his body to tread lightly so that she would not drift away.

She reached out and placed her delicate hand on his cheek. "Okay," she said. "Now why don't we take a little walk and enjoy the stars?"

They stood up, clasped hands, and walked toward the aft deck. Tiona had stated that she was going to the bow, so they moved to the stern. On the aft deck, the overhead canopy obscured much of the sky; but as they looked back into the *Explorer's* wake, the stars lit the surface and the night sky with a twinkling array of tiny lights, almost Christmas-like. The stars sparkled like tiny fireflies above the silvery wake of the ship, dancing along the horizon as the ship rose and fell on the minimal swell. They stood together silently, leaning against the rail, and thinking their own private thoughts.

Later they lay down beside each other, and silently continued their individual musings. After a while, Madison raised herself onto her side, leaned over, and kissed Kurt firmly on the mouth. Her kiss was like nectar to his lips. When she led him slowly and quietly to the next level, it was a huge relief for Kurt.

CHAPTER TEN

Kurt woke to shouts of excitement from the stern of the ship. Jeffrey Smythe was standing at the fantail pulling on one of the trolling lines with Guillermo alongside shouting encouragement. As Kurt approached, Smythe let out a sharp cry of pain and released the line he was holding. "Bloody damn!" he cursed, "I've cut open the palm of my hand."

Kurt looked down at Jeffrey Smythe's upturned palm and saw a thin streak of bright red blood oozing from the pad of his hand all the way across his middle and index finger. The dorado at the end of the heavy trolling line had made a run, and the taught line had cut his palm as neat and cleanly as the sharp blade of a knife might have done.

"I'll get the gloves." Kurt hollered, while reaching out to the basket that held gloves and assorted trolling gear.

Slowly and carefully, Kurt recovered line, coiling it at his feet. With care to keep the line from snagging on anything, Kurt worked the fish closer to the boat, twice giving back line as it dove deep. Several more times the majestic fish leapt from the depths, each time displaying varying shades of gold, silver, blue, green, and a combination of all—changing colors and patterns with each leap.

When Kurt had the fish under the fantail, Guillermo reached down with the long handled gaff and stuck the hook into its belly. Deftly he hauled the fish up and over the rail.

Sadly, as the dorado died, its colors diminished rapidly, ultimately becoming nothing more than a greenish/gray dead fish lying on a similarly gray deck, its drying blood turning a dull brown.

Kurt and Guillermo cleaned the fish right away to preserve its quality.

By late morning, the fishing slowed, and overall interest in the trolling lines waned. Soon, however, another display materialized when a huge pod of dolphin—numbering in the thousands—began to leap and frolic around the boat. Nobody ever tired of watching the dolphin, regardless of how frequently they showed up.

A short while later, after the dolphin pod had disappeared, Kurt who was standing on the foredeck saw a large green sea turtle. He ran back to the lounge area where Madison, Linda, and Tiona were reading and relaxing. The girls rushed to the bow, but the turtle was no longer in sight. It was incredibly hot in the afternoon sun despite the light breeze created by the forward motion of the ship. They were heading back to the shade of the deck canopy when Kurt called out, "There's another."

Returning to the bow, they looked out and saw the mottled green hump of the sea turtle floating above the surface about fifty yards to port, its tiny oval-shaped head poking into the air. "Oh look," Linda cried out, "It's really cute."

"There's another," Kurt exclaimed, pointing to an area off the port bow, "and another."

For the next hour, the bow of the ship was heavy with passengers as they witnessed the spectacle of hundreds of green sea turtles swimming leisurely upon the glassy calm surface of the Pacific. Each of the turtles was heading in the same direction, their slow moving flippers propelling them southward along the Costa Rican coastline. At times it appeared that the ship was destined to run over at least one, if not more, of the ponderous creatures; but as the prow of the ship neared, the turtles flipped up their small pointed tails and dove surprisingly quickly below the surface. Eventually the turtle herd was behind them, and the excitement of the morning and early afternoon waned. Nearly everyone went down for a nap.

That evening, while they all sat around the foredeck, Guillermo once again took the stage and told some of his travel stories.

Guillermo was quite a character. His stories were always told with a high degree of animated gesturing and facial expressions. His voice rose and fell as his dialogue unfolded, often placing the emphasis on the final word of each sentence.

He went on for nearly an hour, regaling the other passengers with his perspective of life in Thailand, relating a hunting experience in Montana where he shot a rogue black bear, telling a sordid story about a former girlfriend whose father served as the local sheriff and threatened to lock him up forever if he didn't stop dating his daughter, and a final story about his experiences trapped in a snowstorm on the coast of New Brunswick. All of his stories were told as if they had just occurred yesterday.

After Guillermo was finished, the passengers gradually drifted off to their sleeping quarters. Kurt and Madison along with Marcos and Linda moved to the bow where they stood together talking and watching the coal black water slide silkily under the keel. Several times they reacted with a start when a large fish darted away from the boat, streaming away in a vivid streak of phosphorescence. The brooding water rippled away from the bow as if it had a life of its own, while farther out the sparkle from a million stars lent an almost spectral image to the night. It was a moving experience, one of those moments in time when the immensity of the sea, the grandeur of the heavens, and the wonder of the universe all combine to make humanity seem very small.

Kurt and Larry stood the early morning watch together; the 'awakening watch' (four to six a.m.) when night fades into daylight. Seated at the helm watching the morning unfold, the two brothers shared their thoughts about the journey they were experiencing and reflecting on its uniqueness.

As the sun began to light up the morning sky, the Costa Rican coastline came into view about thirty miles to port. Eager with anticipation of a promised layover at Isla Cocos, both Kurt and Larry were surprised to see the mainland coastline so close. Captain Ellis had promised a few days earlier that the *Explorer* would visit Cocos *before* making port in Costa Rica. Isla Cocos lies about three hundred miles west of Costa Rica, so seeing the coastline near was not at all what they expected.

"Maybe we're off course," Larry commented.

Kurt looked at him, "Yeah, maybe. Or maybe we're not going to Cocos after all. Smythe and Charlie are scheduled for the next watch in about ten minutes. Hopefully, Smythe will let us know what's happening."

For the next few minutes both men became quiet, absorbed in the incomparable beauty of sunrise unfolding over the Costa Rican coastline. Few clouds were visible in the early morning, but the skies nonetheless blossomed in a rich apricot-hued canopy that stretched from horizon to horizon. The rising sun turned the ocean surface into what appeared to be a glistening sheet of tinted chrome, reflecting the downy cream-colored sky like a mirror. There was no visible distinction between sea and sky; They blended into one, as would a mix of succulent tropical fruit poured from a blender.

Jeffrey Smythe and Charlie entered the wheelhouse just as the burning orb of the sun poked above the distant treetops, striking the vessel as if it was being lit-up by a multi-watt spotlight.

Squinting in the brightness, Jeffrey Smythe offered a pleasant 'Good morning' and asked how the watch had gone.

"Everything is in order," Kurt informed him rather stiffly. "However, we expected to find ourselves considerably farther offshore. It was our understanding that our next stop would be at Cocos Island."

"Ah, yes," said Smythe somewhat smugly. "That was the original plan. However, last night Captain Ellis and I spoke about the already considerable amount of time we are behind schedule and decided that it would be much more prudent to forsake the layover at Cocos and proceed directly to Puntarenas."

Kurt and Larry were extremely disappointed that they would not be visiting the fabled Isla Cocos, where the diving and snorkeling were reportedly some of the finest in the world. They knew others on board would be equally disappointed. Adjourning to the salon, they drank coffee and waited while the late-sleeping passengers slowly gathered for breakfast. Dawn, Sally, and Peter had prepared a large bowl of porridge mixed with several large papayas that had turned nearly over-ripe. The mix was surprisingly tasty.

As the sun rose in the east, the Costa Rican coastline became more distinct. The *Explorer* was cruising just south of Cape Velas, near the northern end of the Nicoya Peninsula. The verdant landscapes of Costa

Rica climbed steadily to distant mountain peaks. Brilliant white sand beaches broken occasionally by small rocky headlands gave the coastline a beautiful contrasting tropical appearance. On the beaches, the breaking surf left a fine line of white mist floating in the early morning air.

CHAPTER ELEVEN

By early afternoon, the *Explorer* rounded the tip of the Nicoya Peninsula and headed into the wide Golfo de Nicoya. On the opposite side of the peninsula, the coastal town of Puntarenas came into view.

Navigating into the shallow bay, Captain Ellis watched his depth sounder carefully to avoid going aground. As he maneuvered closer to the port, he could see several medium-sized commercial ships lining the somewhat dilapidated wharf. Deeper into the bay, a few miles north of Puerto Caldera, an anchorage area came into view that harbored about a dozen ships of varying shapes and sizes. He positioned the ship between two rust-streaked commercial fishing boats and dropped the anchor in the middle of the murky bay, about one fourth of a mile from shore. Due to the shallow nature of the Gulf of Nicoya and the incessant flow of runoff from local rivers and tributaries, the water in the bay is constantly murky with very poor visibility.

Immediately after settling on anchor, two small canoe-type craft paddled out from a nearby embayment, partially hidden behind a series of thick mangroves, and approached the ship.

"Hola, amigos!" Chirped several friendly voices ringing out all at once, followed by a steady stream of Costa Rican Spanish that nobody could follow.

"No Comprendo," Kurt, standing at the starboard rail responded, "Do you speak English?"

"No Engles, Amigo."

Kurt threw his arms wide, palms up, as if to say 'Well then, I guess we're at a standstill.'

Captain Ellis came out to the rail and asked Kurt or Larry to inquire about the Captain of the Port. Larry called down, "Por favor. Donde esta El Capitan de la Puerto?"

Nodding knowingly, a man aboard one of the canoes pointed toward a gray building at the base of the distant wharf. Captain Ellis nodded his head, then instructed the deckhands to launch a skiff for going ashore.

Customs was a breeze. Not only did the Captain of the Port speak fluent English, his attitude, as well as the demeanor of his staff, proved to be extremely friendly and hospitable.

Puntarenas, located at approximately nine degrees north, eighty-four degrees west, is the largest physical province of Costa Rica with a regional population of nearly seventy thousand people. The port was developed around 1840 and looked somewhat rundown, with much of the wharf area and surrounding buildings in serious need of updating and repair.

After hearing from Captain Ellis that the *Explorer* would be in Puntarenas for at least two or three days, the passengers were all granted shore leave with instructions to check-in within forty-eight hours. It was late afternoon, and there would be time for some shopping and sightseeing before dark. Phillip and Brian shuttled all the remaining passengers to shore.

Everyone wanted to go to the nearest bar and get a drink. At the head of the wharf, directly across from the offices of the Captain of the Port, a picturesque thatched-hut bar/restaurant aptly named The Wharf offered cold beer, tacos, and friendly 'Ticas'.

The passengers headed toward a group of tables bunched together under a palm-leafed canopy. They proceeded to pull the tables together and seated themselves. Two strikingly beautiful young ladies dressed in mini-skirts and tight-fitting tank tops, sauntered up to take their orders.

Guillermo and Sam Gilford wasted little time in praising their beauty. "Well, I can't believe our good fortune!" Guillermo exclaimed. "You two young ladies are the most beautiful girls we have seen in months!" He turned to the girls from his ship, "Present-company excluded, of course!"

Sam concurred with his statement. "Wow! You are pure visions of loveliness! How did we get so lucky as to find girls as beautiful as you for our waitresses?"

To Sam and Guillermo's surprise, the two young ladies fully understood their comments and both blushed deeply, dropping their eyes coyly as they pulled out their order forms and asked for their requests in accented but clear and concise English.

"Beer!" Guillermo chimed in, "Ice cold beer!"

"Okay, we have Imperial, Pilsen, and Bavaria," one of the girls informed them. She was a beautiful young woman with rich light chocolate colored skin burnished by the sun, long jet black hair, and strikingly deep sapphire-colored eyes surrounded by thick black lashes and similarly dark untrimmed eyebrows. "Which choice would you like?"

"Imperial for everyone!" Guillermo proclaimed.

She nodded and began to count heads; but before she had completed her count, several of the other passengers commented that they would prefer mixed drinks. The patio area was alive with anticipation and the energy level running high. It took a while for the two girls to sort out the orders; but after a few minutes of confused, light-hearted banter, and laughter, the girls took the drink order inside to the bartender.

"Can you believe how beautiful those girls are?" Asked Guillermo of nobody in particular. "They're gorgeous!"

The passengers aboard the vessel had heard about the women of Costa Rica, widely recognized as being among the most beautiful women in the world. If these two were any indication, there was a lot of truth to the rumors.

The two girls waiting tables at The Wharf were striking examples of the beauty of the 'Tica' women. While the first exuded the dark exotic allure and sensuality of a harlot, the other possessed the vestal charm and appeal of a schoolgirl. She was more petite but vibrantly wholesome. Her skin radiated a light olive texture, her curly hair amber/blonde. Her facial features were extraordinary, with high cheekbones, fathomless green eyes, full rosy lips, a thinly pointed chin, and a line of almond-colored freckles splashed across her nose and cheeks. None of the men from the *Explorer* could take their eyes away from either of them.

As the afternoon wore on, the two girls—Mercedes and Aldonia—served a steady flow of cold beer and rum-laced tropical drinks to the thirsty Americans. As the drinks flowed, so did the lifted spirits of the passengers. After three full days at sea, and not being allowed ashore in Nicaragua, they were all very eager to kick-up their heels and let their hair down.

As the sun lowered behind the distant hills of the Nicoya Peninsula, the skies to the east grew heavy and dark. Rapidly the clouds spread across the bay and engulfed the entire coastline. Within minutes thunder rumbled all around them, and brief streaks of lightning flashed nearby. A few large drops of rain thumped on the overhead palm fronds.

The air seemed to thicken, and an eerie quiet settled over the group. Every one of the passengers looked around, seeming to sense that something was about to happen.

It happened with a tremendous burst of thunder and lightning, a resounding boom that crashed overhead in a cacophony of sound that caused everyone to cringe. At the same time, a torrent of rain poured from the clouds, a deluge of water that seemed to have been unleashed from a huge overhead spigot. The volume of water falling from the sky became so intense, so extreme, that it caused the overhead palm fronds to sag, then a gush of water burst through the leaves.

Startled by the copious volume of water that was unleashed, the passengers from the *Explorer* were at the mercy of the storm, within seconds all were soaked to the skin. But they were also slightly drunk, and someone began to laugh. Soon they were all laughing, turning their heads upward to let the water cascade onto their upturned faces.

Aldonia and Mercedes ran out from the asylum of the restaurant and hollered above the discord that there was shelter inside, but the group was not interested. They were rejoicing in the majesty of the deluge.

Tiona reached out and grabbed Linda and Madison by the arm, dragging them into the nearby street. "Let's dance!" Tiona encouraged them. "Charlie, turn up the music." she ordered, yelling above the din of the raging torrent.

Linda and Madison were laughing and going along with Tiona's antics. The unpaved street turned into a muddy mess, and the girls were splattered with mud within minutes. Their light cotton clothing stuck to their skin almost as if painted on, and their braless breasts flopped around wildly, much to the delight of the men watching.

But then as abruptly as it had started, the rain stopped. The girls stopped dancing and looked up, as if asking what had happened. After a few moments, they joined together, hugging and laughing as they stood in the middle of the muddy road, soaking wet and covered in mud.

They returned to the tables. Tiona put her top back on with a little help from a very appreciative Guillermo. Mercedes and Aldonia brought more drinks, and the group continued to party. After a while, Bob Bradley and Hugo offered to order some food for everyone, requesting several platters of assorted Bocas (snacks), which included the customary Gallo Pinto (a native dish of rice and beans), tortillas smothered in a zesty meat and cheese mix, and hand-rolled tamales stuffed with beans and meat. It was a delightful meal and helped to soak up some of the copious amounts of alcohol being consumed.

Around dark, dozens of Costa Ricans began to arrive, taking seats at nearby tables and obviously intrigued by the drunken Americans. The 'end of the month' Carnival was happening in Puntarenas, a customary tradition wherein Costa Rican natives from the Capital City of San Jose and other nearby towns get away for a weekend of fun and frivolity at the seashore.

As usual, Larry wasted no time in engaging the new visitors in conversation. When he drank, he tended to try and speak solely in Spanish, even when many of the new partygoers spoke adequate English. His voice raised an octave or two, and his gesticulating increased proportionally to the amount of alcohol in his bloodstream. He was loud and extremely animated.

Quite a few Ticas also began to arrive; and soon the music blared even louder, and people were again dancing, including of course the Americans. The dancing soon spread into the streets, and a larger crowd began to gather. Tiona, Linda, and Madison danced together, and the men soon joined them. The lively unabashed gaiety rapidly spread to everyone, and the Tica girls, along with a few rhythmic males, began trying to teach the women the sensuous moves of the Salsa dance. Tiona picked up the moves quickly, although her dancing remained a mix of American and Latino, with more than enough sensuality to make up for her lack of finesse. Linda and Madison were less adept at the Salsa moves, but their energy plus their voluptuous figures more than made up for their inability to perform the moves that make the Salsa one of the most provocative dances.

Marcos began drinking the local booze Guaro, a sugar cane based liquor that is very powerful. He was highly intoxicated, and his effort to join the dancing frenzy turned somewhat awkward. He was quite a sight dressed in a brightly colored poncho that he bought in Guatemala; along with a pair of loose-fitting cotton pants made from flour bags and rolled up to his knees. He also wore a green freshly woven hat that he had purchased from a street vendor. He danced in the street with all the others, flailing his arms and kicking his legs wildly in an effort to be part of the gaiety. But nobody wanted to be near him. He looked like a wild man, his long reddish blonde hair curled out from under the green hat, his photo-gray glasses slightly askew and reflecting the rays from a nearby street lamp, his thick red chest hair glistened with sweat, and his rolled-up trousers revealed his hairy legs and size thirteen feet. Sadly, his state of drunkenness was such that he was making a fool of himself and embarrassing Linda. She found Kurt, who did not seem as drunk as most of the others, and asked if he could do something.

Kurt tried to dissuade Marcos from dancing, but Marcos would not listen. Slurring his words nearly incomprehensively, Marcos attempted to tell Kurt that he was just having fun and just wanted to dance. Kurt made a few efforts to take hold of Marcos arm and lead him away, but Marcos jerked away and at one point took a looping swing at Kurt. His movements were so sluggish that Kurt was easily able to sidestep the punch. That caused Marcos to lose his balance, and he toppled into the street that was still sloppy and muddy from the earlier downpour. He landed on the dirt with a splat, rolled onto his side, and puked.

After several minutes of heavy retching, Marcos seemed spent. Kurt managed to help him to his feet and half carried him to one of the nearby tables.

By that time, Linda and the other girls were mortified by his behavior. They were not nearly as drunk as most of the other Americans, and all three decided it was time to return to the ship. Kurt tried to coax Marcos to leave also, but Marcos was determined to stay and 'have a good time.'

Kurt told the girls to go on back to the boat without him and that he would stay and try and convince Marcos to go back with him soon.

After a few minutes sitting at the table with his head lying across his arm, Marcos suddenly sat upright and blurted out that he needed another drink. Kurt did his best to dissuade him, but Marcos insisted and soon another round of Guaro appeared on the table. Marcos slugged it down in short order, slammed the empty glass down on the table and ordered another. Kurt again tried to discourage him, telling the waitress not to bring the drink. Marcos waived off Kurt's efforts and told the waitress— who was now a new one, to bring another round. Not sure what to do, Kurt looked around for Larry.

He was seated at the far side of the patio area. Kurt left Marcos at the table and walked over to his brother Larry, who was seated with a group of local men and girls.

"Larry, I need some help with Marcos. He's really drunk and continues to order more drinks. The poor waitress doesn't know what to do, so she keeps bringing more. To make it worse, he's drinking Guaro, whatever that is, and it's making him kind of crazy."

Larry laughed, "Oh, don't worry about Marcos. He gets like that once in a while. He knows what he's doing, and he'll be okay."

Kurt was not convinced, and he had sobered up a lot, but did not feel great. "Larry, I don't want to leave him here like he is, but I want to go back to the ship. The girls left a while ago. It's getting late, but I'm worried about Marcos."

"Go on back to the boat. I'll be here, and I'll watch out for Marcos."

Kurt thought that Larry appeared to be sober enough; and after all, he was Marcos' roommate, and he was the one who brought Marcos on this trip. It seemed as if it should be okay to leave Marcos in his care.

Guillermo, Bob Bradley, and Jeffrey Smythe were still there, seated at a nearby table with three Tica ladies. Kurt walked over and told them he was leaving and asked if they could help keep an eye on Marcos. They all agreed they would. One of the Tica ladies eyed Kurt up and down and invited him to join them. Kurt graciously declined the offer and bid them goodnight.

Back on board the ship the three girls, Tiona, Linda, and Madison, sat in the lounge talking. All three of them looked as if they'd had a rough night. None of them wore a lot of makeup, and the little that they did wear was smeared from the rain and the wild dancing. Their hair looked matted and unkempt.

He approached them and told them that Marcos seemed to be okay and that Larry and the others still at the bar would look after him and help keep him out of trouble. Kurt could see that the girls were involved in some sort of 'girl talk.' He excused himself and went to bed.

∞

In the morning Linda learned that Marcos was in jail.

Guillermo told Kurt that after he left, the party amplified with the arrival of a new group of locals that had been partying at another nearby bar. Soon the party spread again to the streets; and before long, the police arrived and arrested about ten of the revelers, including Marcos.

Kurt and Madison escorted Linda to the nearby Police Station where they found Marcos seated on the floor in a large concrete room surrounded by about a dozen others. After speaking with the local *Policia*, Marcos was released with a firm warning to stay away from the Guaro. He paid a thirty-five dollar fine to the police, gathered his belongings, and promised to behave.

The following day was a fuzzy blur for almost everyone. The antics and the alcohol from the previous afternoon and evening had taken its toll. Heads pounded, lethargy was the norm, and there was a lot of napping.

∞

Linda and Marcos were having trouble in their relationship. Linda's parents, who had refrained from interfering with their daughter's courtship with Marcos, were extremely upset over the episode that sent Marcos to jail. They had counseled her on the propensity of men inclined toward heavy drinking habits to have a similar disposition toward spousal abuse and other social dysfunctions. A heated argument ensued.

Linda became defensive. "You're wrong about Marcos!" she cried. "He is gentle and understanding and is always a gentleman. His one incident of indiscretion does not make him a dangerous drunkard." Still in the back of her mind, some doubt about his character had manifested.

"You might be wrong about him." Her father stated. "You do not seem to see his true character, and we feel you should return with us to the States."

"No!" Linda cried out. "You are wrong! He is a good man."

"Well, we are leaving." Her father said, "and we want you to leave with us."

Stunned, Linda looked from her father to her mother, who stood solidly at the side of her husband, nodding in agreement.

Tears formed in Linda's eyes as she contemplated this unexpected turn of events. Her parents meant everything to her, and she had never defied them, but she desperately wanted to continue the cruise, and despite her recent misgivings, she believed in Marcos.

After a long and awkward silence, Linda whispered. "I am not leaving."

Her parents stood silently, unmoving for several minutes, and then her father spoke. "Alright, Linda, you have made your choice, but we are leaving."

They gathered their bags, hugged briefly, and left the ship.

∞

When Linda told him, Marcos downplayed their departure. They were seated on the upper deck, looking out over the bay. "It's probably for the better." He told her. "They didn't seem to be having much fun anyway, and now you don't have to worry about what you do, or what they think."

Linda glared at him and said, "How can you be so callous? They are my parents, and you made a fool of yourself!"

"It was nothing," he assured her. "I just let my hair down a little, and the Guaro was much stronger than I thought it would be." He looked sullen and seemed to resent her concerns and accusations. She did not relent.

"But you were thrown into jail! Doesn't that tell you something? Like maybe you went too far?"

"Let it go." He responded with finality. He stood and walked away, leaving her sitting alone.

She glared after him, doubt clouding her dark thoughtful eyes. Maybe he wasn't the man she thought him to be after all. She sat there for a few minutes, pondering this unexpected and confusing turn of events.

∞

Early the following morning, Captain Ellis informed everyone that there would be another delay while they waited for a wire transfer of funds from Canada. He extended the shore leave by twenty-four hours.

With a full day ahead, many of the passengers decided to take a trip into the capital city of San Jose. Linda remained on board to sort out her thoughts.

There was regular bus service between Puntarenas and San Jose, departing on the hour between six a.m. and midnight. Most of the passengers gathered for the nine a.m. departure.

Surprisingly the bus was modern, a newer model designed for rider comfort. Individual seats with adequate legroom made the bus quite comfortable. It was also relatively empty, with less than half of the seats occupied. As a consequence, nearly all of the passengers from the *Explorer* fell asleep during most of the two and a half hour, eighty-mile ride from Puntarenas to San Jose.

When they arrived, there was a major downpour in progress. Heavy unrelenting rain fell; and from the look of the skies, it was not going to stop anytime soon.

A chill wind blew down from the surrounding mountain ranges, and the ambient air temperature hovered in the low sixties. None of the passengers had thought much about encountering cool temperatures, and all were dressed for the customary heat and high humidity. T-shirts and shorts were the attire for the men, with tank tops or lightweight summer blouses and shorts for the women. Stepping into a cool blustery wind with incessant rain was not at all in their plans. Within minutes, all were drenched, shivering, and wished they had planned better.

Marcos and Larry needed to go to one of the local banks. Marcos had apparently lost two or three checks during his drunken escapade two nights previously. Larry needed to transfer funds from his bank in California.

Most of the others decided to do a little shopping. Kurt, Madison, Tiona, Charlie, and Bob Bradley headed for the central market district in the downtown area. A few others decided to find a local bar where they could relax and get out of the rain. All agreed to meet at the bus stop for the four p.m. departure.

∞

Unfortunately, the return trip was not quite as comfortable as the ride into San Jose. The bus was an older style, with a cab-over engine, much like the older model school busses used years previously in the U.S. It was painted a pastel blue with off-white puffy clouds and a dull yellow sun above the rear window. As it accelerated, a steady stream of black smoke spewed from the exhaust. At the wheel was an intense looking young man who drove recklessly. Despite the obvious years on the rickety old bus, the driver pushed it hard. He kept his foot mashed to the floorboard on steep inclines and slammed the brakes radically whenever he had to slow or stop. His driving made it difficult to enjoy the scenic beauty along the route.

Cocoa and coffee plantations covered much of the terrain, but there were also areas of thick tropical jungle. In places, small farms dotted the hillsides and green valleys. Large floppy-eared Brahmin cattle roamed lazily over rich grasslands, munching heartily on the thick grass. In several of the fields, one or two Guanacaste trees, a very large and beautifully proportioned tree that Kurt and Larry nicknamed 'the perfect tree,' spread their luxuriant foliage. Not all of the Guanacaste trees were 'perfectly' shaped, but those that were exhibit a huge, umbrella-shaped canopy that spread shade nearly thirty yards across. Herds of light gray Brahmin cattle clustered together in the shade of the majestic trees, munching the tender leaves until they formed a perfectly trimmed canopy that provided shelter from the intense tropical sun.

One of the riders aboard the bus spoke fluent English, and he initiated a conversation with the Americans.

They learned that Diego Varralas managed a large coffee plantation in the hills of Alajuela, a sprawling provincial area to the north of San Jose, not far from the majestic Arenal Volcanic Park region.

"It is so beautiful here in Costa Rica." Tiona commented.

"Yes," he agreed. "It is beautiful. But it is not lush as it once was. When I was a boy, those distant hills and valleys were a thick tropical jungle full of hardwood trees, colorful birds, monkeys, and other mammals. Then 'progress' arrived, and deforestation became the name of the game. In the late 1930s and 40s, corporate America began to invest hundreds of thousands of dollars into the local economy, buying up land and clearing it for cattle grazing. This took place primarily in the northern province of Guanacaste, where the 'perfect trees' that you have labeled were once thick and abundant. At the same time, investors began purchasing land for coffee plantations, clearing the jungles of all growth. Many of the trees were merely burned, but the exotic hardwoods, such as the teak, mahogany, and cedar, were milled and shipped to the United States and various European countries. Also while they were clearing the forests, they trapped and shipped thousands of beautiful native birds and monkeys out of the country. Macaws, Toucans, parakeets and white-faced monkeys earned a high price for the local peasants, much more than they ever earned tilling their fields. Yes, today the countryside is still beautiful, but it is nothing like it was when I was a boy."

Tiona looked at his darkly handsome face for a long time. A tear formed and trickled down her cheek. "That's so sad. Here I thought we were looking at a natural paradise that was virtually untouched by progress. The picture that you describe makes this beauty seem almost drab and colorless by comparison. Is the deforestation still continuing?"

Diego smiled wanly, "Yes, it is still occurring, but there are steps being taken to slow the process. Our government has designated several National Parks and promises that there will be more. At the same time, some of the lumber interests are beginning to replant a few of the choice hardwoods, particularly the teak and the mahogany. As a trade-off for harvesting more wood, the lumber interests must replant twenty percent of their harvest in protected areas. In time, this will help restore some of the beauty and diversity of the land."

Kurt asked Diego about the rain forests that they had heard so much about and whether they too were being destroyed.

"Yes. Some of them are. But there is also some protection in place and more promised." He pointed to the east to a high mountain range smothered in clouds that seemed to encircle the entire valley. "That area is the Monteverde Rain Forest Reserve. It is now a fully protected region. Along the coast, south of the Nicoya Peninsula, is the small but beautiful Manuel Antonio National Park, and further south is the recently created Corcovado National Park that covers almost the entire Osa Peninsula. There is also talk about turning the Arenal Volcano region into a National Park, as well as several other pristine areas of our country."

Tiona tilted her head and appraised him closely. "Diego," she said, "you sound very passionate about the natural beauty of your country; yet, you also seem to take great pride in your position as manager of a large coffee plantation. From what I understand, the plantation that you manage was once a forest. Is that correct?"

Diego nodded knowingly. "Yes, my dear. I am somewhat of a contradiction. I do make a good living working a plantation that was once a beautiful forest. It was stripped and cleared in order to plant coffee. But that was when I was a boy. It is true that I have benefited personally from the changes that have taken place in my country in the past fifty years, but I also take great pride in keeping abreast of current political measures that are being taken to slow the deforestation and to protect areas that remain natural, as well as to try and reestablish some of the damaged areas. I am on the board of advisors of a large group that serves to provide information and recommendations to both our local and national government to slow deforestation and to establish protected regions from future destructive 'progress'."

Unfortunately, the conversation with Diego was cut short when he had to disembark in a small town about halfway to Puntarenas. He explained that there was a town hall meeting that evening that concerned the very subject that was being discussed; the clearing of another natural valley for a proposed plantation. He commented as he left the bus that approval for the plantation was not likely.

The remainder of the ride was uneventful, except for the white-knuckled driving of the bus driver. On several occasions he had to swerve radically back into his own lane when attempting to pass a slower vehicle on the narrow two-lane highway. Larry attempted to explain to the driver that nobody was in a hurry, but his effort to encourage a slowdown was ignored.

Everyone arrived safely back at the docks.

Disconcertingly, the passengers learned that Rom had decided that he had had enough of the *Explorer* and packed his bag and left the ship. Tired of the working conditions, the lack of parts, supplies and materials, and most of all the fact that he had not been paid, the Chief Engineer told Captain Ellis and Brian that they could take the 'Ship of Fools' and shove it up their respective assholes. His departure left the mechanical operation of the ship in the less qualified hands of Brian and Bilko. Together, they would have to try and maintain the constantly failing machinery.

∞

The Explorer weighed anchor early the next morning.

For the first hour, the murky waters of the Gulf of Nicoya churned cocoa brown in the ship's wake. There was not much point in setting trolling lines until blue water was reached.

While Linda and Marcos worked on their strained relationship, Tiona became involved in an episode with Guillermo.

Guillermo, despite his sixty-three years of age, was in great physical shape and retained the vitality of a man much younger. His sexual appetite and interest in women remained strong. Tiona shared a mutual flirtation with Guillermo.

Charlie was accustomed to her flirtations and did not seem too troubled by Guillermo's philandering, due to the fact that he was nearly twice Tiona's age. He tolerated her flirtatious bantering as innocent friendship.

On that particular morning, Charlie did not feel well, and he informed Tiona that he intended to remain in their cabin, to read and try to recuperate from a bout of fever and associated stomach discomfort, leaving Tiona alone to seek her own diversions for the day. She focused her attentions on Guillermo (or Bill, as she called him).

She approached Bill after breakfast and asked him if he'd like to share another cup of coffee laced with a splash of rum. He agreed, but her 'splash' turned out to be about half rum and half coffee. After their second cup, the two were feeling the effects of the liquor, and her behavior turned coquettish.

"So, tell me Bill, what is it that you have that the ladies find so appealing?" Before he could respond, she continued, "I know that you have had a lady friend in nearly every port we have visited. The ladies seem to be attracted to you like bees to honey. What's your secret?"

He looked at her with a gleam in his eye and replied in a husky voice. "I like women. They can usually tell that I like them. And when a man shows a woman that he likes her, she tends to respond in a positive manner."

She looked at him, slowly crossed her long brown legs and leaned forward. Her short white cotton skirt slid up her thigh and her light-blue blouse stretched taught over her full bosom. Her auburn hair hung loosely over her shoulders, and she wore little makeup. "So do you like me?" she asked throatily.

"You know I do. I've liked you since the day you walked onto this boat."

She thought for a moment then asked, "Would you like to go for a little walk with me?"

"Sure," he chuckled, "but we certainly can't go very far."

"Oh," she purred, "You'd be surprised."

Standing and looking around to see whether they were being watched—which they were not—Tiona turned and led him down the starboard side of the ship to a small doorway located near the dining salon where a 'secret love nest' had been discovered and used on occasion by a few.

Slipping into the doorway, Tiona pulled him inside. She latched the door and flicked on the dim light.

"Okay, Bill. Show me how much you like me," she whispered.

He lifted her onto the table, and whispered his intentions as he brought her to readiness.

She giggled, spread her legs invitingly, and he entered her warmth. Together they relished the guilty pleasure of spontaneous sex.

As their sensory gratifications diminished, they disengaged and rearranged their clothing. Tiona reached out and cupped her hands around his face and pulled him toward her, kissing him lightly on the mouth. "Thank you Bill. I needed that. But please, put it out of your mind. This was a onetime thing. I already feel guilty about doing this, and I don't want Charlie to find out. Please just forget this ever happened and let's just be friends, okay?"

He gave a slight crooked smile and reassured her. "Thank you Tiona. You let me fulfill a fantasy that I've had since the first day I saw you. You're quite the woman, and Charlie is a lucky man to have you. This will be our own personal secret and it's one that I will remember with great fondness."

She smiled sincerely as she made a final adjustment to her skirt and cracked open the door, peering out to see if anyone was nearby. Nobody seemed to be around; so she opened the door and stepped out into the bright tropical sunlight. As she closed the door behind them, Charlie walked around the corner of the cabin. He froze, seeing them standing there together, flushed and slightly disheveled. He could see the expressions of culpability and guilt on their faces, and he knew immediately what had just taken place. On several occasions, he and Tiona had shared their own pleasures in that little room. He turned and walked away.

Tiona and Bill Carlson stood frozen in place, remorse and shame palpable.

"Oh no," Tiona stated flatly. "He knows. He knows. I have to go." She couldn't look at Bill. She turned away from him and walked heavily across the deck and turned around the corner where Charlie had gone.

∞

Guillermo stood motionless for a few minutes, a pained expression spread across his wrinkled features. A feeling of doleful regret engulfed him. He felt as though he had just lost something from his life, as if a precious gift had been tendered then taken away. He wanted to run after Tiona, find Charlie, and apologize. Try to explain to them how sorry he was for...for what? Being caught? They did something wrong. They let themselves stray from the path of right and wrong simply to gratify their own personal urges and temporal desires. He recognized that their little tryst had lost all of its glory. The brief sense of gratification that he had relished was now tarnished, and he would not be able to have the pleasure of remembering the interlude with any sense of fulfillment or satisfaction. It would become a forgettable mistake, at best, depending upon how Charlie reacted.

∞

When Tiona reached Charlie, he was preparing to close the door to their cabin. He turned and looked at her coldly. "Not now," he stated flatly. "Don't. Just don't." He told her as he turned away and closed the door.

She started to rush forward and beg his forgiveness, to plead with him to let her explain. But she stopped short of knocking, realizing that there was no explaining to do. There was nothing she could say that would excuse or diminish the sadness of the moment. She stood looking at the closed door, the pathetic misery of her sorrow spreading across her face. She turned and walked to the stern of the ship. She leaned against the rail, feeling wretched.

This was not the first time that Charlie had known that she had been with another man, but it was the first time that he had caught her in the act, and it left her feeling vile. She crossed her arms over her chest, squeezing herself tightly. Tears of despair welled-up in her blank unseeing eyes, flowed down her cheeks, and dripped from her chin. A dull grayness enveloped her.

Standing alone at the stern of the ship, Tiona felt ashamed, dirty and worthless. Staring through blurred vision, she stepped up onto the fantail, reached up to grasp the upper deck support, and pulled herself upright onto the rail cap. She looked down into the foaming froth behind the boat.

Then she jumped.

She hit the water with a thud and was immediately pulled under by the churning wash from the large propeller blades. She tumbled, spinning round and round as the turbulent mass of water from the props sucked her deeper and closer to the massive bronze blades. Her eyes were open, and she caught brief glimpses of the splotchy red bottom of the hull and keel, of the encrusted barnacles, and the pretty bubbles bursting as they formed then spun away from the relentlessly turning blades. One of the blades sliced the water just inches from her face, its smooth surface glistening in the diffused lighting beneath the boat. Sucked into the vortex of the rotating blades, it seemed only a matter of time until they would slice her wretched body into chunks of shark food.

It did not happen. Miraculously, even though drawn inexorably toward the churning blades, her body was thrown outward away from the hull, and she rose briefly to the surface. Her head popped out of the water, and she involuntarily gasped for air. Her mind had deceived her into thinking she was already gone, that she had met her demise in the propeller blades. But now she was aware that she was still there. She didn't care.

For a moment, she thought of yelling for help, then she remembered what had happened and why she was floating in the water nearly twenty miles from the Costa Rican shore in shark-infested waters. It didn't matter to her. She had survived the initial attempt to end things. Now it was only a matter of time. She resigned herself to the inevitable, leaned her head back, and floated silently on the calm surface, her eyes closed and her mind going blank, waiting for the sharks to find her.

Abruptly she felt a strong tug on her lower body. She looked down half expecting to see only part of her still intact. But she was whole. There was nothing visibly wrong. Except that her skirt was gone, and the lower half of her body was now completely naked. How appropriate she thought as she looked back and saw the transom of the ship fading into the distance. She leaned back again and floated, calmly, stoically waiting for the inevitable.

∞

On board the *Explorer*, Kurt sat on one of the deck lounges talking with Madison about their time in Costa Rica. They both agreed that it was a beautiful country and that the people were exceptionally friendly and very handsome. He was about to comment on Linda and Marcos problems when, out of the corner of his eye, he saw a flash in the ship's wake.

"I think something just hit one of the lures," he told her. "I'm going to go check."

He ran back to the stern. Sure enough, something had tripped the shock-cord on the starboard line. Looking outward, he could see something just below the surface—out where the lure trailed. At the same time, he saw an odd-looking shape bobbing farther out, perhaps one fourth mile astern. He made a brief quizzical noise to himself, a questioning hum—as if to acknowledge that he had no idea what he might have seen in the distance—and began to pull in the starboard line.

Whatever it was on the end of the line was somewhat heavy, but it was not putting up much resistance. As Kurt pulled it steadily toward the stern, he could see that whatever was snagged on the hook was not a fish. When he pulled it aboard, he realized that it was some type of clothing or rag. It was a little heavy, soaked as it was with saltwater, and Kurt was surprised that it looked clean and fresh. Obviously, it had not been in the water for any length of time.

He called out to Madison, "Hey doll, come back here, I want to show you something."

When Madison reached his side, he had unhooked the piece of cloth from the trolling lure and was holding up what was obviously a woman's skirt.

Kurt laughed lightly and said, "Check this out. Guess it must have blown off one of the decks and got snagged in the trolling line."

Madison's brow furrowed. "That's Tiona's skirt. I recognize it. Where is she?"

"I have no idea," Kurt responded. "I guess she's probably in her cabin with Charlie."

While they pondered this turn of events, Guillermo walked back toward them, an odd expression molding his features as if he were deep in thought or troubled by something. He turned to walk away from them when he too recognized the skirt.

"Where did you get that?" He asked Kurt.

"Can you believe I caught it on the trolling line? Who'd ever think you would snag something like this way out here. I guess it must have blown off the upper deck."

Guillermo looked behind the boat, his troubled features growing darker. "When did this happen?" He questioned Kurt uneasily.

"Just now," Kurt informed him. "I saw something in the wake of the boat, and when I got down here, this skirt was snagged on one of the hooks."

"Oh, Christ!" Guillermo groaned. "Kurt, throw something over to mark this spot. We've got to turn around. I think Tiona went overboard." He raced forward to the wheelhouse and barked orders to turn the ship around.

Kurt looked around and pulled a cushion from one of the deck chairs and tossed it over the side. "Watch that cushion." He instructed Madison. "Don't take your eyes off of it."

It was not easy to turn the ship on a reciprocal course. Brian was at the helm at the time, and he began a slow but steady turn of the ship.

At the same time, Brian ordered Guillermo to alert Paul and Phillip to check Tiona's cabin and search the ship to try and locate her.

Brian performed a Williamson turn, a port-turn maneuver that would put them onto a reciprocal heading. It was a ponderously slow process, taking nearly half a mile to complete. As the turn was being made, Madison, whose long-distance vision was not good, lost sight of the cushion. When Kurt ran back to get a visual on the cushion, she told him that she could not see it any more.

"Damn!" Kurt blurted. "Where was it the last place you saw it?"

"Over there in that direction," she told him, pointing toward their port bow.

Kurt scanned the water where she was pointing, hoping that his eyesight might pick up the shape or color of the cushion. After a moment of intense scrutiny, he caught sight of the cushion a few degrees to port. Keeping one eye on the cushion, Kurt moved to a position forward of the wheelhouse and pointed in the direction where he had seen the object. Brian was very close to completing his turn, and the cushion was by then almost dead ahead. At about the same time, Paul and Phillip returned to the bridge and informed Brian that they had checked her room and completed the search of the ship and Tiona could not be found.

Brian ordered, "I want everyone up on the bow keeping a watch for anything unusual. If anyone sees something, tell them to point in that direction."

Kurt called out for others to join him on the bow. Within moments, more than a dozen eyes were focused on the water ahead, searching for anything bobbing on the surface.

When they reached the cushion, Brian slowed to a near stop, maintaining only minimal, forward propulsion. "Anything?" He called out.

"Nothing yet," Kurt responded, maintaining a vigilant watch over the glassy sea.

Brian maintained his course, moving forward at less than one knot.

"There! Over there!" Kurt yelled, pointing a degree or two to starboard.

About one hundred fifty yards away, something floated on the surface; but from their angle, with the sun reflecting on the surface of the sea, it was not clear what Kurt had seen. As the ship moved closer, Kurt called out loudly, "It's her! It's Tiona!"

Nobody could tell whether she was moving, or alive.

Brian pulled the engines out of gear and let the ship glide forward without power. As they got closer, he turned the helm sharply to port, allowing the ship to slow its momentum further and to drift broadside to the body that floated face-up in the purple-blue water. "Launch one of the skiffs!" He ordered, not directing his order to anyone in particular. Several people bolted into action.

Kurt stripped off his shirt, stepped to the rail, and dove from the side of the ship. Surfacing, he began a purposeful stroke toward the body that floated motionless about thirty yards away. When he got there, his first thought was that she was dead. She appeared lifeless, her upturned face expressionless and her body inert. Approaching her, he called out, "Tiona. Tiona, are you alright?"

She did not respond. He reached out and touched her, expecting to feel the cool clamminess of death on her skin. But when he touched her, her entire body jerked, reacting to his touch. She flinched spasmodically, and her face turned to the side, her open mouth inhaling a mouthful of saltwater. She coughed, and her prone body stiffened, losing its buoyancy so that her head popped upright and her torso dropped perpendicular to the surface.

"Tiona!" Kurt exclaimed. "You're alright!"

She turned and looked at him, an expression of intense dismay distorting her features. "No! You're not supposed to be here. I… I…." She began to sob. "Don't! Leave me alone! I want to be left here. I'm…. I'm… Oh, God. Why is this happening now?"

Kurt was confused. She was okay, but here she was sobbing uncontrollably and ranting insanely. It didn't make any sense.

"But Tiona," Kurt reassured her. "You're okay. I'm here and the ship is right here with me. We're going to get you back aboard, and you're going to be fine."

She looked at him with a glazed expression, as if she were in some other place or world. "You don't understand," she murmured, "I don't want to go back. I want to stay here. I want to die."

Kurt wasn't sure what to say or do; but fortunately, the skiff came alongside about that time. Phillip, Paul, and Guillermo reached out and caught her by the wrist and lifted her awkwardly over the rail of the small aluminum skiff. Then they helped Kurt climb aboard. Guillermo removed his shirt and spread it across her waist to cover her nakedness.

They all sat there quietly for a few moments, each thinking their own private thoughts. The others had caught part of the conversation that Kurt held with Tiona, but only Guillermo knew what had happened. He avoided looking directly at her.

∞

Back on board, a towel wrapped around her waist, Tiona slumped down onto a bench and asked to be left alone. Kurt asked where Charlie was, and someone said that he had been there a few moments ago but had disappeared. More perplexed than ever, Kurt suggested that Madison and Linda stay with Tiona and implored everyone else to give them some privacy. They dispersed.

Kurt went to Charlie's cabin and knocked. Charlie's voice rang out clearly and with finality. "Not now. I do not want company. Leave me be!"

Recognizing the tone of resignation in his Charlie's voice, Kurt turned and slowly walked away.

Alone with Madison and Linda, Tiona remained unresponsive to their attentiveness. They had helped her put on a pair of white shorts and a dry halter-top. She stayed withdrawn and showed no reaction to the gentle questions and comments tendered by her friends. Seated on one of the deck lounges with her knees drawn up to her chest, Tiona stared, vacant eyed.

After their initial attempts to talk with Tiona got no response, Madison and Linda sat with her quietly. They were clueless about Tiona's indiscretion and therefore had no idea what was troubling her so deeply. They waited.

Eventually, several minutes later, Tiona spoke.

"I wish they would have left me there."

Following a long pause, Madison asked quietly, "Why Tiona? Why would you wish that?"

She turned and looked directly at Madison. Her eyes filled with tears, and she blurted, "I'm not worth saving. I'm a slut. I don't deserve to live."

Madison stood and moved to her side. She sat down and wrapped her arm around Tiona's shoulder, and held her tightly. Tiona began to sob, deep wracking sobs that went on and on for several minutes. Gradually, her weeping slowed, and she curled into a near fetal position on the lounge. Madison sat quietly, hugging Tiona.

Linda moved closer and kneeled before Tiona. She reached out and stroked Tiona's shoulders and head. "Tiona," she asked tenderly, "can you tell us what happened?"

Tiona remained quiet for a long time, but then blurted, "I screwed Bill. Charlie wasn't feeling well, and I got drunk and took Bill into the 'love nest' and screwed him. I don't know why I did it. Charlie caught us. He knows what we did. I feel so dirty and vile. I'm nothing but a slut."

"No," Linda tried to soothe her. "You're not a slut. You just made a mistake, and now you need to try and deal with it. You are our friend. You have a lot of friends here on the boat. Everyone likes you. You need to just find a way to come to grips with this whole thing and put it behind you."

Tiona looked up at Linda and gave her a forlorn smile. "Oh sure, everyone likes me, especially the men."

"No," said Madison. "We are your friends. We all make mistakes. We all do things that we regret and wish that we could take back, or undo. But it happened. Now you need to come to grips, talk to Charlie. We're here to help."

Tiona went quiet again. Madison and Linda sat with her, offering the occasional words of comfort and support that true friends try to give to a friend in need.

∞

Meanwhile, Kurt and Larry heard from Guillermo what had happened. Guillermo was obviously upset, mainly because he liked Charlie and Tiona, and knew that his act had caused such grief.

"Christ!" Guillermo said. "She nearly killed herself. That was a really dumb thing that I did." He turned and looked at both Kurt and Larry and stated, "I'm such an asshole! How the hell can I ever make up for this?"

Kurt thought for a minute and said, "You can't. You really messed up. Just leave them alone and let them try to get past this mess."

"Yeah," Guillermo grunted morosely. "Like maybe they can pretend it just didn't happen."

"No, it won't just go away," Kurt agreed, "but when the time is right, at least let them know that that you regret what happened. From there, the two of them will have to move forward the best they can. It won't be easy and maybe they'll never really get over it. But you should at least let them know that you're sorry and maybe, just maybe, they will find a way to put it to rest."

At that point, Guillermo said he needed to be alone. Kurt and Larry looked at each other, unsure whether they might need to keep an eye on him so that he didn't do anything rash. Guillermo sensed their apprehension and assured them, "Don't worry about me. I'm too heartless to do anything foolish. I just need a little time alone."

Kurt and Larry went back toward the stern to see how Tiona was doing; but as they approached, Linda gave them a hand signal that clearly indicated they were not needed. They turned and went back to the second deck.

For the rest of the afternoon, the gloom aboard the vessel was palpable. Cruising along the beautiful Osa Peninsula should have been a pleasure for all; but on that particular day, there was little joy.

Toward evening, while Madison stayed with Tiona, Linda went to the galley and brought back some food. At first, Tiona would not touch anything, but eventually she agreed to eat a few bites. As the sun set in the west—another of those incredible tropical sunsets that usually had everyone pulling out their cameras and expressing their pure joy and wonder—the mood aboard the *Explorer* remained somber.

Just before darkness fell, Charlie walked onto the back deck and asked Tiona if they could talk. She left with him and went into their cabin.

"Do you think we have to worry about her?" Linda asked Madison.

As they walked away, she answered, "No. I don't think so. Charlie is a good man."

With that, they went to their respective quarters and joined their men. For all, it was an early night with little talk and less joy.

CHAPTER TWELVE

Kurt awoke to the sounds of silence. Listening, he realized the ship was once again shut down. He rose from his mat, used the head, and went down below to see what the problem was and whether he could help.

The *Explorer* drifted off the coast of Costa Rica in the Gulf of Dulce, approximately fifteen miles north of the Panamanian border. All power was out, and Kurt learned that there had been an electrical problem with the main generator. Below decks, a pungent electrical odor filled the air, the burnt rubber smell indicating some type of a short in the system. Bilko and Brian were busy trying to track down the source of the malfunction. In addition, Kurt learned that a 'grinding noise' had occurred in the port engine during the night, and it too was out of commission.

On deck, stillness filled the air, and the seas reflected a smooth glassy shimmer of indigo. Above, a blanket of high strata-cirrus clouds, broken occasionally by small patches of pale blue, filled the skies. In the distance, looming above the mountainous green panorama of southern Costa Rica and northern Panama, dark gray cumulus clouds smothered the mountaintops.

After drifting for about an hour and a half, the rumble of the diesel generator indicated that some mechanical progress had been made. Soon the starboard engine coughed to life. Unfortunately, the port engine continued to emit the grinding sound when engaged, and so that engine stayed out of service, at least temporarily. Jeffrey Smythe took the helm under single-engine propulsion, and the ship again chugged ponderously underway.

∞

Captain Ellis seemed on the verge of a breakdown. His character continued to change, as it shifted from being friendly and interactive with the passengers to being surly and distant. He spent a lot more time in his cabin, and rarely went on deck. Dawn and Brian served as liaisons with the crew and the passengers, doing their best to maintain a friendly and positive attitude. Nobody knew what caused the transformation in Captain Ellis. Everyone knew that he was very upset over the suicide attempt made by Tiona and that he held Guillermo in strong contempt for his involvement. There was talk that Captain Ellis and Dawn were having troubles, especially after a loud shouting match that many overheard when Dawn confronted him about being elusive and unapproachable. Their shouting match lasted for several minutes and resulted in Dawn sleeping on the second deck alone for the first time on the trip. Rumors were also whispered of drug use, and that he was strung-out because his supply had diminished.

Charlie and Tiona seemed to be working on a resolution to their problem. Both of them spent a lot of time together, sometimes sitting quietly on the top deck where everyone gave them plenty of space. They both avoided making much contact with others, and everyone respected their efforts for privacy.

Marcos and Linda seemed to have resolved their differences and once again displayed their new-lovers vibes.

That afternoon the ship passed the line of demarcation that separates Costa Rica from Panama. Everyone hoped for a layover at the Pearl Islands (Islas Las Perlas), but it would not take place. Again Captain Ellis sent word through Brian that the ship was too far behind schedule and that pleasure stops were not going to happen, another disappointment for the passengers.

Cruising along the coastline of Panama, the *Explorer* remained close to shore, seldom venturing more than two miles from the coast.

On the shoreline, a steady swath of white indicated the breaking surf, a relentless battering of the rocky shore that periodically sent white walls of water crashing against shoreline cliffs. Above the surf line, dense foliage met the water in most areas; but occasional small sandy beaches dotted with palms revealed secret little coves and inlets, often at the bottom 'v' of upland canyons. Waterfalls could also be seen, disappearing into the thick jungle growth. Farther up the canyons, the lush hillsides disappeared into the omnipresent gray shroud of clouds that smothered the higher reaches of the mountainous terrain.

Late in the afternoon, about half the passengers gathered on the foredeck to enjoy the sunset and discuss some of the rumors currently flying about the boat.

One rumor revealed that food stores were becoming scarce. Sally and Madison confirmed that rumor. Still, they reassured everyone, as long as fish continued to be caught, there should not be any real issue with primary meals. Breakfast and lunch were another matter. All of the eggs were gone, there was no bread left, no fruit, nothing fresh, although there was a decent supply of oatmeal and some pancake batter.

Another rumor circulated that the ship was nearly out of fuel. That problem disconcerted everyone, and Kurt and Larry, who had been below decks talking with Brian earlier in the day, verified the rumor. Brian informed them that they should have just enough fuel to reach Panama, presuming there were no extraordinary events during the next twenty-four hours, after which the ship should reach the next port of call: Panama City, Panama.

The last and most disturbing rumor hinted that everyone would be kicked off the ship when it reached Panama.

That possibility posed a real downer for all. Most of the remaining passengers were extremely anxious to see and reach the final destination of Jamaica. There wasn't much anyone could do about the rumor of getting kicked off the ship, other than wait it out and hope the cruise continued.

∞

Kurt and Jeffrey Smythe shared the ten to midnight duties that evening, an important watch that would require a significant change of course when the *Explorer* cleared the outcropping of the Azuero Peninsula, approximately one hundred fifty miles from the entrance to the Panama Canal. Complicating the course change, the ship would continue on an inshore heading in order to save as much fuel as possible. With two distinct headlands to round, Punta Mariato and Punta Mala, at the head of the Gulf of Panama, the helm watch would require close attention to avoid any potential hazards in the area—of which there were several.

Kurt did not relish spending watches in the company of Smythe, although he did recognize and appreciate his knowledge and experience in navigation.

Smythe remained diligent in adhering to their heading, frequently checking their course on the charts and religiously determining their exact position according to his dead-reckoning techniques. He advised Kurt to keep a good lookout, including the positioning of lights on land and on ships underway in the vicinity. During the past couple of days as they neared Panama, shipping activities had shown a significant increase, with numerous ships spotted throughout the day and night.

During the watch, one time slot became particularly tense when Kurt could not see or identify the lights from Punta Mala, a navigational beacon that should have been visible from their location. In many areas of the Mexican and Central American Coast, aids to navigation often proved unreliable, although Smythe was quite surprised that the lights near the Canal would not be working properly, particularly due to the large number of ships that transit the region.

A noticeable shift in wind and sea conditions also developed. For most of the cruise down the Mexican and Central American coast, their vessel had been blessed with minimal following seas, an idyllic cruising condition.

Now rounding the headland and turning more eastward toward Panama City, a brisk north wind cooled the air and brought about a change in the ship's motion. Where they had lolled lazily for days in the push of a following sea with only an occasional beam trough, the ship now began to plunge and rock into a beam sea, and one that built steadily. At midnight when Brian and Bob Bradley stepped onto the bridge to assume watch duties, the splash of seawater began to drench the foredeck and even the windowpanes of the bridge station.

With a partial waxing moon, visibility was fair; but the salt-spray that drenched the windows limited their ability to keep a vigilant eye on their surroundings. When they turned the helm watch over, Smythe slowed the cruising speed from its current five knots to three knots, both to conserve fuel and to ensure that their arrival into the heavily congested Bay of Panama would be made during daylight hours. Smythe stated that he would be gone only for a short while to freshen-up and that he would remain on duty until they were safely secured at anchor.

∞

Morning arrived with a gray drab-looking sky and a continuation of the northerly wind and chop. Several passengers had become seasick. Dawn informed the few passengers at breakfast that all stores of coffee were depleted and she had only tea to wash down the pancakes that she and Sally were preparing.

An ebbing tide slowed the movement of the ship considerably. It was almost like traveling upriver—the tidal current so strong that the ship made only minimal way. Low green islands dotted the Bay of Panama, all covered in thick shrubs and dense trees. The bay looked murky, a sludgy color mottled with splotches of bubbly ooze, most likely generated from the fast moving currents of the outgoing tide.

Hundreds of brown pelicans and frigate birds soared overhead or perched atop the nearby rocky points and trees of the nearby islands. A well-defined path of navigational buoys marked the entrance to the canal, occupied by several ships. Nearly all the ships entering or exiting the canal were fully laden with fuel or other cargo. Many of the ships carried the insignia of Esso, Gulf, or Standard Oil on their hulls and smokestacks.

After setting the anchor between two small islands located about one mile from the entrance to the Canal, Bilko shut down the power and informed everyone on board that the fuel situation was so dire that he could not run even the small generator until fuel was taken on. If it sucked air, he would need to bleed the entire system, a dirty and tiring task that he wanted to avoid.

Captain Ellis refused to come out of his cabin; so Brian and Dawn went ashore on a Customs launch to try and clear Customs and see what arrangements could be made for refueling and re-provisioning.

Brian spent most of the day attempting to receive a wire transfer from his backers in Canada. Meanwhile, Dawn went to Balboa—the U.S. Sector of the city—to purchase what meager food supplies she could with cash (approximately two hundred U.S. dollars) that she and Brian pulled from their own personal resources. Fortunately, at the Commissary in the U.S. Sector, a friendly officer helped her gain admission. She was given the same discounts available to military personnel, so she managed to purchase a fair supply of essential food items. She also purchased a large bag of locally grown coffee.

Clearance was granted; however, the local authorities refused to give permission to launch the *Explorer's* skiffs. The only option for getting onshore was to hire one of the local launches at a rate of twelve U.S. dollars per person—an outrageous amount for the less than quarter mile run. All of the passengers were furious, but nothing could be done about the price. Everyone elected to stay aboard.

A short while after learning of the exorbitant shoreboat fees, the passengers received another frustrating piece of information: swimming from the ship was not allowed. At first, their reaction turned to outrage. But when they learned the reason for the swimming ban was the presence of numerous man-eating tiger sharks in the murky waters, their angst eased.

With food supplies almost gone, the ship's fresh water supplies nearly exhausted, and while wilting in the heat and high humidity, the passengers overall mood turned glum if not downright surly. Larry and Kurt attempted to keep spirits elevated by pointing out they were anchored within a mile of the entrance to the Panama Canal aboard a 'luxury yacht' and were blessed with several gorgeous women for company; at which point Guillermo blurted, "Well, perhaps you could share them,' before realizing his faux pas. His tryst with Tiona was still fresh in everyone's mind and so his comment to share the women did not go over well. He muttered a guttural apology and turned to stare out to sea.

∞

The Bay of Panama bustled with activity. Ships of all sizes, shapes, and colors maneuvered throughout the murky waters. Many of the freighters and tankers moved out of the Canal and headed directly to sea, but a few settled on anchor and sent crewmen ashore for various purposes. Dozens of smaller escort boats and local fishing and commercial boats also plied the nearby waters, servicing the large ships and transporting food and other supplies from shore to the anchored vessels.

From their anchorage, they could see the sprawling town of Panama City silhouetted on the southern skyline. To the north, a series of low verdant hills obscured their view; but from what they could see, it appeared considerably less populated. Connecting the two areas, the *Bridge of the Americas,* the high expansion bridge that connects all of the Central American countries, spanned the harbor.

With very little food onboard and restrictions on going ashore, the passengers retired for the night in a foul mood.

∞

Early the next morning, a meticulously maintained launch pulled alongside, and three uniformed American officers requested permission to come aboard. Captain Ellis, looking haggard and disheveled, emerged from his cabin to inquire what the officials wanted. They informed him that they had received a two-page complaint through an unidentified source that claimed unsafe conditions and equipment aboard the *Explorer.*

The officers then ordered Captain Ellis, Brian, and Bilko to escort them throughout the ship on an inspection of the engine room, safety equipment, sanitation facilities, galley, and bilges. They also ordered the Captain to start the main engines and generators. When Captain Ellis explained the low-fuel situation, the officials agreed that the startup of the engine and generators could be brief. Brian informed them that they were encountering problems with the port engine and it was currently out of commission. The officers, somewhat reluctantly, agreed to the starting of only the starboard engine.

Fortunately, the starboard engine and generator started without any problems. The supply of life jackets, the life rafts, and the bilge passed inspection.

One of the officers engaged Madison and Linda in innocent conversation during the inspection. He strongly advised against going into the heart of Panama City where, according to his counseling, 'unsavory elements roamed the streets in great numbers.' He suggested they stick to the Balboa area where the American contingency maintained a safe and inviolable living and business sector.

Gaining clearance (including permission to launch the skiffs), Brian made the announcement that funds should be transferred by that afternoon and that the ship would transit the Canal as soon as the funding arrived and fuel and supplies could be purchased. They launched the skiffs, and everyone except the watch-crew of three went ashore.

Onshore, the difference between the American Sector and the native district became astonishingly obvious. Panama City, as well as its surrounding villages, exhibits the haphazard features of most Mexican and Central American communities. Thatch palm huts, clapboard shacks, and a mixture of cement and mortar buildings form an amalgam of living and business accommodations that appear to have no rhyme or reason.

Diametrically opposite, the U.S. Sector displays a modern upscale community of immaculately maintained homes and buildings with manicured lawns, sidewalks, and meticulously crafted landscapes.

The difference between the two sectors looked stark and dramatic.

Kurt, Madison, Marcos and Linda, Tiona and Charlie, Guillermo, and Bob Bradley all traveled together by taxi to visit the U.S. Commissary. When informed that only military personnel and Canal employees and their families were allowed access to the Commissary, the girls befriended a couple of Americans in uniform and went inside with them to purchase two cases of beer and a boxful of snacks to take back to the ship.

Those two servicemen joined the group for lunch at a nearby café where 'the best burgers in Central America' were served. During lunch, which all enjoyed, the soldiers told the group about a lovely town named Chorrelo about twelve miles to the northwest.

Upon returning to the ship, the group learned that the anticipated funds were once again delayed and that it would be at least another full day before the Canal journey could begin.

Sam Gilford could not stay any longer. He had allotted only five weeks, and they had already exceeded that time frame. He bid all a fond farewell and left for the Panama Airport.

∞

Stuck in Panama for at least another day, Kurt and Madison, Marcos and Linda, Tiona and Charlie, and Larry all decided to take a trip to the town of Chorrelo.

Finding a taxi driver who offered to take them all for ten U.S. dollars, the group piled in and began the journey. Across the Pan-American Highway Bridge and a few minutes outside of the city, the Panamanian countryside turned lush and thinly populated. Towering trees broke out above the thick jungle canopy along the highway, leaving the road cast in shadow. Vines covered everything, seemingly on a quest to smother all other plant life. Plants of all sizes and shapes grew ubiquitous, their strong branches and thirsty leaves gathering energy from the frequent tropical rains to feed their roots and nourish their prolific growth.

About fifteen minutes into the ride, the taxi driver turned off onto a narrow dirt road marked with a handwritten sign nailed onto a rickety post with the word Chorrelo. He followed that road about a mile to a point where the road ended at a medium-sized river.

Chorrelo proved to be not really a town, but a tiny village of thatched huts clustered on the banks of the Chorrelo River. When the taxi driver dropped the group off in front of an open-air café with a small supply store attached, it was like being dropped into another world. A few scrawny chickens and pigs roamed the dirt road. The chickens pecked under fallen leaves for grubs or ants, and the pigs rooted in nearby bushes for any sustenance they could dig up.

According to the soldiers at the Commissary, there was a spectacular waterfall only a short distance from the little village. The group began walking up the riverbank, following a well-worn path that meandered through the jungle growth.

The sounds of the waterfall could be heard well before they saw it. Upon arrival, the beauty and splendor of the falls and the semi-clear pond at its base nearly took their breath away.

Falling twenty feet, the waterfall spread nearly a dozen feet wide and dumped tens of thousands of gallons of water into a pond formed by the constant deluge of water. Moss and lichen covered the surrounding rock walls. On the west side of the waterfall, a narrow path led to a smooth outcropping where one could conceivably dive from the top of the falls and into the pond.

In order to reach the pond, a swim of about ten yards across the river was necessary.

Kurt and Larry stripped down to their trunks and dove into the water to check things out ahead of the others. Reaching the other side, they climbed out onto the bank and surveyed the area. They dove from the bank and went as deep as they could Neither could locate the bottom; so they determined that diving off the ledge should be safe. They concealed their bags and things under an elephant ear plant. They climbed the slippery steps to the top of the falls, and reached the natural platform visible from the opposite side of the river. Larry was the first to go, jumping feet-first into the clear water of the pool.

Soon they were all happily cavorting, taking turns jumping and diving from the ledge into the tranquil waters.

Kurt noticed a rope swing that hung from a tall overhead branch, but had caught on another nearby bough. Freeing the rope from the limb, he proceeded to climb the opposite bank to another perch and swung out through the waterfall and dropped into the pond. The others soon followed.

For about three hours, the group played and frolicked at the falls, exhausting themselves in their effort to enjoy the lovely place. Eventually, they realized that they must return to the ship. They reluctantly swam back to the opposite bank where they had left their belongings.

Looking around, they realized they had neglected to make arrangements with the taxi driver to take them back.

Larry turned to Kurt and said, "Let's go see if anyone here has a phone, or might know how to contact a taxi." They walked toward the little café that appeared to be closed.

"Hola. Hola," Kurt and Larry called out. Nobody answered. They walked around back. Seeing no one, they went back to the other side of the small enclosure to what appeared to be a small store. The doors were locked, with no indication of anyone around.

They returned to the others and suggested they had better walk back to the main highway.

The air turned muggy and hot, and the cooling pleasure of the pond faded quickly. The sky darkened, and the air grew heavy. About half way into their one-mile trek back to the Pan American Highway, the skies opened up, and a drenching rain pounded down. Within minutes, all were soaked, but at least felt refreshed.

They reached the highway without any problems, although they were all saturated and splattered with mud. Only a few vehicles passed, and the presence of seven wet Americans standing alongside the road must have been quite a sight.

After about twenty minutes, while it continued to rain, a bus traveling in the right direction appeared. They waved it down and fortuitously, the bus stopped. There were quite a few people on the bus with only two seats available. Tiona and Linda took the seats while the others stood.

Larry explained in Spanish where they were going, and the bus driver told him it would be forty cents each for the ride. Larry gave him a five-dollar bill and declined the change. The driver seemed very pleased. Returning to the *Explorer,* the group enthusiastically told the others about their trip to Chorrelo. For each of them, it was an experience that they would always cherish.

∞

Early the following morning, Jeffrey Smythe introduced a new passenger, Bob Lancaster, who Larry immediately nicknamed 'Sanford.' Sanford had become stranded in Panama after delivering a truck from California that one of the big global freight lines used to move cargo from the Canal Zone to other cities in Panama and nearby Nicaragua. Brian signed Sanford on for the remainder of the cruise. Sanford paid one hundred fifty dollars for the passage through the Canal and on to Jamaica.

Sanford's pleasant smile, regardless of his mood or temperament, served him well in his ability to make friends and ingratiate himself with others. He also seemed pleased with his new nickname. Nobody quite understood why Larry decided to start calling him Sanford, but the name stuck and seemed to fit.

After delivering the truck to Panama, Sanford decided to stick around for a while to see the sights, and he hoped to find a boat on which he could transit the Canal. On his second day in Panama, Sanford found a woman he liked. He had a fetish for large women; not the regal statuesque beauties such as Linda, but rather the fleshy rotund women that a lot of men find unappealing. To Sanford, robust women were delightful, and he relished the opportunity to lose himself in their warm rolls of flesh. Much to his pleasure, he found such a woman working at a currency exchange booth near the Canal. When he made it clear that he was interested in her, the woman quickly and decisively took him into her fold, and he reveled in the warmth of her very large and very comforting bosom.

On the day that Sanford signed on board the *Explorer,* he told her that he was going out for a while. However, she covertly watched him pack his belongings into his single backpack and place it outside the door of her small apartment. Sanford was unaware that this woman, Sabrina, had followed him to the port and was waiting surreptitiously for him in the shadows of a nearby building. She sat there for most of the day.

Following dinner, Kurt and Madison along with Marcos and Larry invited Sanford to join them for drinks at the local yacht club situated in an old wooden building about two hundred yards from the anchorage. He readily accepted the invitation, and they all hopped into the shore skiff for a ride to the docks.

Upon arrival at the wharf, the five of them disembarked and headed toward the pub. As they passed the building where Sabrina patiently waited, she rushed over to Sanford and planted a wet kiss on his cheek. He jumped away as if he were being attacked. "Sabrina, what are you doing here?"

"Oh, Mi Amor, I knew you would come back for me," Sabrina gushed.

Sanford stood staring at the woman, not knowing what to say or how to react. As he continued to stare, Sabrina again moved to his side and wrapped her large brown arm around his waist. "Mi Amor," she whispered, "I am so happy."

Sabrina spoke clear and concise English with only a slight Panamanian accent, the result of having lived for eleven years in an American convent located on the outskirts of the city. From age twelve until age twenty-three, she lived and studied with the seven nuns who taught at the convent. At the age of twenty-three she got into trouble with one of the local boys. The sisters gave her the ultimatum of either taking her vows as a nun or leaving the convent. She chose the latter, and moved into Panama City where her mastery of the English language gave her multiple opportunities for work. She chose a job as a cashier at one of the few currency exchange offices located near the apex of the cruise-ship terminal, a position that paid rather well and also gave her the opportunity to mingle with American tourists and visitors. That was where she met Sanford.

Obviously rattled by the unexpected appearance of Sabrina, Sanford excused himself to the others, and explained that he had some 'unfinished business to attend to.' He put his arm around Sabrina's broad shoulder and slowly walked away with her, after telling Kurt and Larry that he would see them back at the ship.

Not sure what to make of this latest development, the others shrugged off the incident and headed to the nearby yacht club.

Chapter Thirteen

The Balboa Yacht Club in Panama attracts an eclectic mix of visitors, primarily yachtsmen passing through the canal on their own personal sailing odysseys. Some of them are pursuing lifelong dreams of traveling the high seas, some seek adventure in exotic lands, and others sail away in order to escape from the pitfalls of society. Whatever the reason that brings them to Panama, nearly all are just passing through and rarely stay for any length of time.

After ordering beers at the bar, the four passengers from the *Explorer* took a table in the back of the room. Seated at a nearby table was an ancient looking man with a scraggly white beard. Deep wrinkles covered every visible part of his anatomy, including his shining bald head. An incredible set of thick bushy white eyebrows sprouted wildly from his tanned forehead. He nursed a beer, and beneath his great eyebrows, his rheumy blue eyes shined bloodshot but bright.

"Ah," he raised his beer in a salute. "Americans. Welcome to Panama."

Each of them smiled at the grizzled old character and raised their own glasses in return.

The old gentleman turned his chair around so that he faced the quartet. "So, my friends," he asked in a deeply guttural voice, "what brings you to Panama?"

Kurt responded, "We're on a yacht on its way to Jamaica. We were expecting an immediate transit of the Canal; however, we have encountered delays."

"Ah!" He exclaimed, chuckling, "of course you have encountered delays. That is a very frequent dilemma for many of the adventurers who pass through this godforsaken place. If I were to guess, your delays are either due to lack of funds or mechanical problems?"

"Well, as a matter of fact," Kurt replied, "you're absolutely correct. We are aboard a rather large yacht, having paid passage to help get the boat delivered to Jamaica, but the Captain has encountered continual financial troubles along the way. Both engines have caused us trouble throughout our voyage. As a consequence, we have had numerous delays since we left San Diego several weeks ago."

The old man nodded his head knowingly; a smirk creased his craggy features. He was quiet for a minute, and he closed his eyes and lowered his head to his chest. For a moment, they wondered if he had fallen asleep or was having a problem. Kurt started to walk over to see if he was okay, but his eyes opened again and he began to talk.

"I guess you're kind of wondering about me? What is an old coot nearing the end of his years doing hanging around a yacht club?" He paused and raised his bushy eyebrows while looking, in turn, directly into the eyes of each of the four people sitting at the nearby table.

"Well, let me tell you a story. My name is Walter Davis, my friends call me Walt, but lately they've taken to calling me Pops. I'm eighty-six years old. I've been living here in Panama since I was sixteen. I came here to help build the Canal in 1906; two years after the Americans took over the project from France. I helped build the Canal. Nearly lost my life twice in the process, but I made it; and after it was done, I had nowhere else to go. So here I am sitting at the same table I sit at nearly every night."

He looked at the four again, apparently trying to ascertain whether they were listening or not. Satisfied that he had their attention, he continued.

"Feel free to interrupt. But if you want to hear it, I'm going to tell you nice folks the story of the building of the Panama Canal."

Fascinated by the fact that the old fellow was eighty-six years old and yet seemed as lucid as someone much younger, Kurt and Larry ordered another round of beers—including one for the old man—and asked him to please continue. His speech was slow and deliberate, but his voice rang strong and clear. He elucidated each word and emphasized each of the most profound statements, adding character and mystique to the discourse.

"I came here with my father. He was an engineer, and they hired him to help with the design of the Canal after the U.S. took it over from France. As I said, I was sixteen, strong and healthy as a bull, and willing to do just about anything. They paid real good wages, especially to the Americans; and my father had a position of authority, so he earned even more.

'In the beginning, the U.S. had to redesign the Canal. France started the project way back in 1880. The Frogs spent nearly twenty years trying to dig a canal at sea level. They thought they could cut through the mountains and open a passage that ships could transit directly from one ocean to the other. They weren't too smart, though, because digging out the entire fifty-mile mountainous stretch of the proposed canal was just not possible. It was doomed to failure. They spent millions of dollars and lost more than twenty-thousand lives trying to dig across the country and, ultimately, had to give the entire project up." He paused to sip his beer, and then continued.

"By the time the US took over in 1904, a lot of the work was done, but the mountains were not about to be moved. That's when the American engineers—including my father—sent a newly designed plan to the U.S. government that proposed constructing locks to help raise and lower the ships from one side of the country to the other. The U.S. agreed to pay France forty million U.S. dollars and Panama ten million dollars for the rights to build and operate the Canal.

'As I mentioned a moment ago, the French lost many lives along the way. Malaria and yellow fever killed most. By the time the U.S. took over, scientists and medical researchers had found a way to lessen the deaths attributed to the fever and malaria; but nearly five thousand others, including Americans, died before the Canal was finished, as did my father.

'I was a victim too. I contracted yellow fever, and was on death's doorstep. I also caught malaria, and it almost killed me again. But I guess I was just too ornery, and I survived both. It laid me up for a while, as you can imagine; but once I had kicked the fever both times, there was not much else that could hold me down. I went back to work on the Canal and stayed with it until it was officially opened in 1914. After that, I found myself a sweet little Panamanian lady and got married. I was hoping to have kids with her; but the diseases must have done something to my procreative abilities, and she never got pregnant. She died two years ago. She was only eighty-one years old."

He had finished his beer, and Larry bought another round.

Several times during Walt's fascinating story about the building of the Canal, he became sidetracked with personal anecdotes about people and other things that happened during the construction years. His discourse kept everyone thoroughly and completely captivated.

"Anyway, as I was saying, the building of the Canal has been called *'one of the supreme human achievements of all time',* and let me tell you, that profound statement barely encompasses the truth of the matter.

'When the U.S. took over and began to engineer the lock concept, there were several key areas that would require some of the most creative engineering ever attempted. Beginning on the Caribbean side, at Colon, the engineers had to devise a way to develop a series of locks at the Culebra Cut—which would later be renamed the Galliard Cut in honor of one of its principal engineers—that would lift ships as much as one hundred-sixty feet above sea level. That's where I spent most of my time working on the Canal, although I did transfer to the Pacific side to help complete the Mira Flores Locks near the end of the construction phase. That's also where my father contracted malaria and lost his life.

'Millions of tons of soil were removed in an effort to lower the rise over the continental divide and to clear the path for the locks to be built. I worked with the heavy machinery, running all sorts of equipment and helped modify machinery to make the job easier. It took us nearly eight years from the time I started working to finish the Culebra Cut. When it was done the waters of the Chagres River flooded a huge man-made basin that formed Lake Gatun. That Lake is now one of the two lakes that help form the passageway of the Canal. You'll go through it when you get clearance to make the passage."

Walt paused at that point, finished and accepted another beer. He peered out from under his incongruously thick eyebrows as if to ensure that he was holding the attention of his listeners. Each of them was absorbed in every word of his narrative, envisioning the Herculean task that he was describing.

He continued. "After completing the Culebra or Galliard Locks, I moved across the Isthmus to help complete the Mira Flores Locks. Those locks were a challenge also, but not nearly as big a challenge as the first set of locks. When they were finished in 1914, twelve sets of locks had been built. The final height of the Canal above sea level was lowered to around twenty-six meters (eighty-five feet). The first ship to cross the Canal was one of the French construction boats, a crane-carrying vessel named the *Alexandre La Valley*. I made the passage aboard that boat along with about twenty other engineers and Canal workers. I'm proud to be one of the few remaining individuals on earth that not only helped build the Canal, but was on board the first vessel to cross from one ocean to the other."

Walt seemed to slump slightly at that point, obviously slightly intoxicated, but also probably weary from his lengthy history lesson.

"That's a remarkable and fascinating story, Walt." Kurt commented. "How many people do you estimate worked on the project in total?'

Walt didn't hesitate long before answering, "Probably more than seventy-five thousand in all. As I explained, roughly twenty-five thousand lost their lives during the construction—most of them Frenchmen. Many of the laborers were either from the East Indies, or inhabitants of other nearby islands. Fortunately for them, most residents of the tropics are immune to the diseases that took the lives of so many white men. Not many Panamanians actually worked on the Canal. They are basically lazy and don't like to work that hard."

"What did you do when you were finished building the Canal?" Madison asked.

"Oh, I continued to work for the Canal Authority, mainly trouble-shooting when slides or other things went wrong during the first few years after the Canal opened. After that, when I got married, I worked here in Panama City at the Mira Flores Locks, either running the 'mules' or helping out when problems developed. I stopped working about ten years ago."

"Ten years ago?" Madison asked, "So you worked until you were seventy-six years old?"

"Yep. I would have kept going for a few more years, but my old bones were making it hard for me to jump off and on the docks or the equipment as easily as when I was a little younger. Besides, I wanted to spend more time with my little wife, make love during the day, and rest up for more at night." He laughed a deep cackling laugh that rumbled through the room.

"Yep, we were crazy in love, and we kept the fires burning right up until the day she died. In fact, our last bout of lovemaking occurred just four hours before she laid her head down and never woke up."

The few other people that had been at the club were long gone, and the bartender came over to the table and interrupted.

"Hey Walt," he interjected, "do you suppose they've heard enough of your story for one night? I'd kind of like to go home to my own little lady."

Walt lifted his thick eyebrows and grinned. "Sure thing, Paco, it's never a good thing to keep the little woman waiting too long."

With that, each of the passengers shook hands with Walt, and thanked him for the fascinating history lesson. Madison gave him a kiss on the cheek, which caused him to comment, "You're a sweet one. If I was a few years younger I'd like to try and give that man of yours a run for his money."

Madison laughed, "Yes, Walt. I'll bet you would, and you'd probably give it a pretty good run." He cackled, and bobbed his head up and down.

They asked him if he would like an escort home, but Walt just laughed, and informed them that he walked the four blocks from there to his house every night.

Kurt asked if he'd be back the next evening, commenting that he would love to hear more of his stories. Walt told him, "Of course I'll be here. And if you're not here, I guess I'll have to tell my stories to someone else."

With that, they bid goodnight to Walt and returned to the ship.

∞

Early the next morning, Dawn informed everyone that funds had been transferred and transit of the Canal would be scheduled for one p.m. Brian and Jeffrey Smythe delegated duties to nearly everyone in order to accomplish all of the tasks that needed to be completed prior to entering the Canal.

The first step was to take the vessel dockside for fuel. From there, the ladies and a couple of the men were dispatched to the Commissary and other stores to purchase food and supplies. Pablo and Phillip were put in charge of refilling the water tanks, while Jeffrey, Kurt, Larry, and Guillermo assisted with relocating and fueling. Sally and Peter accompanied Dawn, Madison, Linda, and Guillermo on the shopping expedition. Charlie and Tiona went to the local *farmacia* to restock some of the depleted medical supplies on board, as well as to fill a couple of prescriptions for other passengers. A lot needed to be done in a very short time.

Despite their efforts, Bilko and Brian could not make repairs to the port engine. Docking would need to be accomplished on one engine only.

Fortunately, both Brian and Jeffrey Smythe were skilled boat operators. They managed to navigate close enough to the docks to attach and secure lines.

It took about an hour to take on the fifteen hundred gallons of diesel fuel needed to reach Jamaica. After fueling, the ship moved about four hundred yards ahead to another docking area to wait for everyone to return.

Directly ahead of the *Explorer,* a Korean commercial fishing vessel with the name *Tiburon #1* hand-printed on the side of the rusting hull lay tied alongside the wharf. Kurt and Larry approached the boat to see what type of fishing they did. None of the crewmen spoke a word of English; but following a series of hand gestures and pantomimes, one of the crewmen went below and returned with a solidly frozen fifty-pound tuna and a dorado nearly as large. Kurt and Larry 'traded' that gift for a bottle of rum that had been purchased at the U.S. Commissary, two t-shirts, and cold beers for each of the seven crewmen that were visible on deck. As another token of their appreciation, the Korean fisherman then gave both Kurt and Larry one of their twelve-inch diameter hand-knotted and hand-blown glass fishing buoys.

About an hour later, a thunderous crash reverberated throughout the ship. Rushing onto the upper deck, those passengers and crew that remained on board were dismayed to see that the heavy twelve-foot long wooden boarding ramp that was positioned across the expanse from the top deck to the wharf planking had crashed onto the port rail as a result of a falling tide. It had crushed one of the rails on the second deck and became lodged askew between the wharf and the side of the ship, teetering toward going into the water.

Kurt and Larry reacted quickly, and tied a couple of dock lines around the ramp and secured it to the rails on the upper deck. They then persuaded one of the dockworkers operating a forklift to help hoist it back up to the upper level.

The cause of the incident was the extreme nature of the tides. When they first secured to the wharf, the tide was full; and the bridge between the ship and the wharf nearly level. As the tides began to drop, the *Explorer* settled rapidly with the falling tide—which in Panama can be as much as twenty feet, or more. Nobody noticed the rapid tidal drop. Consequently, the ramp canted farther and farther downward until it slid off the wharf and crashed onto the deck.

Captain Ellis should have been aware of the potential for the incident to happen; but he was again holed-up in his cabin, not performing the true duties of a Captain. First mate Jeffrey Smythe took the blame for not anticipating the extreme drop in tide; but he was below decks working with Bilko to make a final engine room check before heading into the Canal. Nobody else noticed the situation developing. Fortunately, the damages to the ramp and rail were not too severe, and all could be repaired when underway.

When the ladies returned from their shopping excursion, the food and supplies were loaded using one of the forklifts and a couple of pallets tied with lowering lines. All of the perishables were quickly transferred to the refrigeration units, and the dry goods moved into the galley holds.

By eleven thirty, all of the tasks were accomplished; and Brian confirmed with the Canal authorities that the *Explorer* was ready to transit the Canal.

∞

At twelve-thirty, after completing all of the ship duties, Brian and Jeffrey Smythe fired-up the starboard engine and waited for the radio call that would tell them they were ready to proceed to the entrance of the Canal. Brian had negotiated a self-powered passage, saving approximately five hundred dollars in tug fees by convincing the port authority that he could maneuver and navigate the Canal without the aid of a tug— despite the fact that she was running on one engine only. However, it was necessary to take on a pilot—a requirement for all vessels transiting the

Canal. Total cost of the transit was set at four hundred eighty dollars U.S. with additional charges pending should a tug be needed along the way.

The Canal Pilot, along with an assistant, had boarded at the fuel dock, and they were becoming familiar with the ship before it began the transit. Brian or Jeffrey Smythe would serve at the helm, but the Pilot or his aide would accompany Brian or Smythe at all times, instructing them as needed.

Several other ships waited their turn to enter the Canal. Two very large tankers and one container ship floated nearby held in position by powerful tugboats lashed alongside. The Pilot aboard the *Explorer* spoke passable English, and he explained that the two tankers would move into the Canal first, followed by a fishing vessel, then their ship.

The time had come to pass through the Panama Canal.

CHAPTER FOURTEEN

All of the passengers stood on deck eager to undergo the long anticipated transit of the Canal. Just prior to casting off, a loud shout came from the dock. "Wait! I'm back! I'm going with you!"

It was Sanford running across the rough wooden planks of the wharf.

He arrived with literally no time to spare. Kurt and Larry were untying the spring-lines as he approached. They held them secure for a moment, allowing Sanford to climb down the pier decking and get aboard. They tossed off the lines, and the *Explorer* moved slowly away into the bay. At that moment another wail arose from the wharf, this one coming from a very large, very loud woman on the dock. "No! You cannot leave me!" Sabrina cried, her voice carrying loud and clear across the water. "You cannot leave me!" She shouted again.

Jeffrey Smythe, standing at the helm with Brian, looked imploringly down to Sanford, and tossed his hands up into the air as if to ask 'What now?'

"Go!" Sanford said as he waved his arms, "Just go. I told her I was leaving. Just keep going."

Not sure what to think or do about the situation, the passengers aboard the ship stood quietly and watched the large brown-skinned woman wave her arms and call out plaintively. Sabrina's cries faded as the ship continued on its way. Eventually her voice could no longer be heard, but her sagging form remained visible until the vessel passed a small island that hid her from their vision.

∞

When the ship cruised slowly into the back portion of the Bay, the first lock, Mira Flores, came into view only a short distance inland. Following the Pilot's advice, and adhering to the navigational aids, Brian and Jeffrey Smythe worked together to pass messages between the engine room and the bridge, ensuring that the engine was engaged and disengaged in a timely and effective manner. The last thing they wanted to have happen was mechanical problem that would require the assistance of a tug.

For the passengers, the entire scene was fascinating. From the bow of the ship, they gazed upon the entrance to the Canal in awe.

The bay teamed with boating activity. Besides the ships transiting the Canal, dozens of brightly painted commercial skiffs and small boats buzzed around the placid water, running at what appeared to be full throttle to reach whatever destination they sought. The low undulating hills surrounding the Isthmus of Panama created a picture-postcard scene. Scattered homes dotted the verdant green hills. In the distance, the densely populated downtown center of Panama City could be seen rising above the lush terrain.

Nearing the locks, they could see that massive amounts of concrete and steel formed huge enclosures where ships of varying sizes and configurations assembled, some waiting to enter the long chamber of the lock, others slowly exiting the bay under their own power. Odd-looking little locomotive-type machines moved along each side of the concrete abutment. These were the 'mules' that serve to pull ships along the walls of the one thousand-foot long canal.

As the *Explorer* entered the first tract of the Mira Flores Lock, the heavy steel gates swung closed and almost immediately a huge surge of water began to swirl and fill the basin. Millions of gallons of water poured into the lock; and within ten minutes, their vessel and the other boats in the lock rose twenty-five feet.

Once the optimum water level filled the chamber, linemen working on shore heaved 'monkey-fists' (heaving lines woven into a round ball and attached with ropes) to attach long steel cables onto the bow and stern cleats on the vessel. Those steel cables attached to the 'mules'—the electric-powered locomotives that pull the ships through the locks until the ships can exit under their own power, or their attached tug's power.

All of the linemen were quite obviously having a great time working with this ship. Tiona, Linda, Madison, and Sally were out on the foredeck watching the action as the ship progressed through the lock.

Tiona pranced about the decks in her short yellow skirt, swinging her hips, and making herself as visible as possible to the delight of the linemen and other canal workers. The sight of her tanned skin and voluptuous curves held their rapt attention. The other girls appeared much less animated, but their mere presence and physical beauty garnered nearly as many stares as did Tiona.

Once the ship reached the end of the lock, the mules disengaged; and the *Explorer* followed the other three vessels out of the lock and into the next phase of the passage.

Shortly after the ship powered through a narrow man-made gorge and entered the second set of locks in the Mira Flores system, the darkening skies unleashed a torrent of heavy rain accompanied by thunder and lightning. That tropical squall sent the girls back under the deck coverings. Even though the rain was warm, the winds blowing with the rainfall were enough to chill their scantily clad bodies.

After clearing the second lock in the Mira Flores chamber, the *Explorer* motored across the narrow Mira Flores Lake. The skies remained leaden and heavy, but the rain held back. Visibility diminished due to the vapor left from the rain, a vapor that spread across the three-quarter mile wide lake in the form of low-hanging clouds and convection fog. Along both sides of the lake, a thick verdant growth covered everything, although the copious foliage nearly disappeared in the mist. Several small densely forested islands popped out of the foggy shroud near the shoreline, adding mystery to the primordial scene. The lake turned glassy calm, and swirls of fog and mist spun around the stern with the passage of the boat. It seemed an unearthly sight, and Larry commented that he 'expected some sea monster or dinosaur to emerge from the whirling shadows.'

Shortly before entering the next set of locks, the Pedro Miguel chamber, the clouds thinned out, and within minutes, the broiling tropical sun emerged. Mists and vapor continued to hang on the surface of the lake, but when the ship entered the lock, visibility improved. Humidity rose; and in the late afternoon shadows, the mosquitoes began to attack.

Everyone coated their bodies with insect repellent and silently rejoiced that they had taken their obligatory malaria shots.

After going through the San Miguel locks, they entered the narrow Galliard Cut, the man-made canal that winds its way through one of the narrow gorges carved out during the construction of the Canal.

Many years after the completion of the canal, jungle growth regained its foothold along the banks of the cut, smothering the nearby banks with trees, vines, bamboo, and other greenery. Occasionally, sheer black granite walls jutted from the murky waters; passages blasted out and cut during construction.

From the heart of the jungle growth, the sweet melodic sounds of tropical birds filled the air with natural music. Often the brilliant colors of parrots, macaws, toucans, and other birds flying or perched within the thick tropical foliage brightened the scenery.

Exiting the Galliard Cut and entering the huge expanse of Lake Gatun, the scenery once again changed. Numerous small islands dotted the lake surface, some covered completely with jungle growth, others displaying a scattering of native dwellings—bamboo sided shacks and palm-thatched huts.

Soon the afternoon shadows engulfed the ship and surrounding landscapes as evening neared. Approaching the small town of Gamboa, the Canal pilot suggested that the ship seek a location to anchor for the night. The main channel of the Canal is well lit with navigational buoys; but because of floating trees, logs and other debris, he highly recommended running during daylight hours only. With dusk nearing, Brian and Jeffrey Smythe heeded the advice.

Following directions from the pilot, Jeffrey Smythe eased the ship into a secluded bay encircled by three small islands. Watching the depth carefully, Smythe instructed Phillip and Pablo to drop anchor in about twenty feet of water, leaving adequate room to swing if the wind changed direction. He also discussed tides with the pilot, who politely informed him that tides were not a factor since they were in a lake. Smythe admitted to being a bit of a fool for that obvious blunder.

With help from Sally and Linda, Dawn barbecued the dorado that Kurt and Larry got from the Korean fishing boat. While cooking, they fought off mosquitoes that swarmed around their heads and bodies. Even though they slathered on insect repellent, the ubiquitous pests succeeded in leaving small red welts on nearly every inch of their exposed limbs. All of the other passengers were holed up inside the main salon, with doors closed and incense burning in several canisters to ward off the pervasive insects. Despite the nuisance of the mosquitoes, the dinner was delightful; and the overall mood aboard the *Explorer* improved.

∞

At first light, the rumble of the starboard engine reverberated through the ship. Shortly thereafter, the rattle of the anchor chain tumbling into the anchor locker signaled that the ship would soon be underway.

Kurt arose and headed for the bridge. Jeffrey Smythe and the pilot perused their charts and made radio contact with the Canal authorities. All was in order. After the pins were secured on the anchor windlass, the vessel entered the main channel of Lake Gatun.

Madison, who had remained in her bunk when Kurt got up, did not expect to hear Tiona's voice at her side.

"Madison," Tiona whispered, "are you awake?"

Raising herself onto one elbow, Madison looked at Tiona with concern furrowing her brow, thinking that something must be wrong. "Hi, Tiona, is everything alright?"

"Oh, yes, everything is fine. I just wanted to talk with you about something that has come up."

Madison rubbed the sleep from her eyes and rose to a sitting position. "Sure Tiona. What's up?"

Tiona seemed nervous, unsure of herself. "Well, Charlie has once again asked me to marry him, and I'm trying to decide if I should tell him yes."

"Wow! That's quite a surprise," Madison replied candidly, "After all you two have been through in the past couple of weeks, I certainly didn't expect this."

"I know. I don't know what to think. I'm just not sure of anything right now." Tiona admitted.

"Go with your heart," Madison responded sincerely. "It's not what you think, but what you feel that matters."

Tiona sat silently for several minutes before sharing her thoughts with Madison. "I just don't know. I want to make Charlie happy. He's so good to me. He makes me laugh, and he makes me happy; but I just can't get Santiago out of my thoughts. The way he made me feel, and his lovemaking were just so incredible."

She sat quietly for a few moments, her eyes clouded.

"I just don't know," she admitted to Madison. "I just can't seem to make the commitment. I've never been good at making decisions, and most of the ones I have made have been wrong"

"Then wait. Charlie will understand." Madison reached out and clutched Tiona's hand. "Time is always the best answer for uncertainty. When the time is right, you will know it and make the right decision."

Tiona looked deeply into Madison's eyes and nodded. "You're right. Thank you. It's nice to have a friend that I can talk with. I've never really had many female friends, and I'm grateful that you have accepted me."

"Yes. I understand you completely," Madison confided. "I can relate. For most of my own life, I have had very few close friends either, and I want to thank you for letting me be here for you."

Tiona started to respond when Kurt walked up.

"Am I interrupting something?"

Tiona and Madison exchanged a slow look, then Tiona answered, "No Kurt, we were just having a pleasant little chat—one girl friend to another."

As the *Explorer* cruised over the flat calm waters of Lake Gatun, all of the passengers and most of the crew stood on deck gazing at the tropical surroundings and watching the steady procession of ships heading in both directions.

With the ship underway, Kurt and Larry helped Brian make repairs to the gangway and mid-deck rail that was damaged at the quay in Panama. Kurt cut and shaped a section of two-by-six that had been pulled from the water while the ship was at anchor in Balboa, and then Larry and Brian drilled holes and inserted bolts to make the repair solid. The task was completed within an hour.

Most of the passengers napped, but Kurt, Madison, and Larry stayed on deck enjoying the surrounding scenery. It was certainly a lush panorama, but seemed somewhat surreal. Misty vapors still clung to small surrounding islands while heavy gray clouds encapsulated the distant mountains. Farther away, bulbous cumulonimbus thunderheads loomed. Navigational buoys marked the deep-water passage of the lake, and an occasional ship passed port to port on its journey through the Canal.

By early afternoon, their ship reached the gateway to the Gatun Locks. A backlog of ships traversing the locks in both directions lay congested at the lock's entrance. The pilot suggested to Jeffrey Smythe that he drop anchor while they waited their turn to enter the lock system.

Soon after setting anchor another deluge of intense tropical rain burst upon the scene. The pounding rain drummed an incessant roar for nearly an hour. It stopped as abruptly as it had started, its demise arrived with a sudden quiet that was almost as disturbing as the initial clamor.

Around four p.m., the linemen were ready, and the ship weighed anchor. A thick gooey mud covered the anchor and chain, its noxious odor fouling the late afternoon air. Phillip and Pedro tossed numerous buckets of saltwater onto the ground tackle to try and wash away the foul-smelling ooze.

Oddly enough, dropping down in the lock system was slower than rising. Kurt asked the pilot why the locks took more time to empty than to fill, and his brief response did little to answer the question. "Your ship is a yacht," he said. "We move the water slower in order to not damage your ship." That was all he would say about the matter.

Exiting Gatun Lock, they entered the salty waters of Limon Bay in the Caribbean Sea. On land, the rundown cities of Cristobal and Colon border the Caribbean waters; areas that nearly everyone recommended be avoided. Political and social unrest had plagued both cities for several decades under the corrupt military dictatorships of Omar Torrijos and Manuel Noriega. The ship anchored about one quarter mile from shore and radioed for a shore taxi to pick-up the pilot and his assistants.

The passage through the Panama Canal was complete.

Brian, somewhat concerned about the rumors of pirate activities on the eastern seaboard of Panama, setup a night deck-watch while they spent the night at anchor waiting the dawn. The deck-watch was done in similar shifts to the helm-watches, with two-man teams assuming two-hour shifts. The night proved uneventful. At first light the crew hauled anchor, and Brian set a course for Jamaica.

Chapter Fifteen

Almost immediately upon setting off into the Caribbean Sea, a distinctly different motion affected the passage of the *Explorer*. Suddenly, the bow ploughed into the sea and swell, and the ship took on an entirely different pattern of movement. Rather than the gentle glide of the hull over the surface, the vessel plunged into low wind chop and bucked and rode up and over the larger ground swells.

Several passengers quickly became seasick, not more than an hour into the next passage—a nearly six hundred-mile excursion that was plotted to take about four days—if everything went smoothly with no stops along the way.

Kurt and Brian worked the first wheel-watch together. Navigating became a totally different experience. Both men had to hang onto something at all times to avoid being tossed to the deck as the ship plunged and bucked on the ever-present Caribbean swell. Brian had passed over these waters before aboard a passenger liner that, due to its immense size, was virtually unaffected by the seas. "It's a different animal, hey Kurt?" Brian observed

"Yep. It sure is different. I think that nearly all of the remaining passengers are seasick. Do you think this is a temporary condition, or are we likely to encounter this kind of sea for a while?"

"It's here to stay," Brian responded. "The prevailing wind and seas in this section of the Caribbean are like this for about nine months of the year. It's a steady condition that only desists for a short span of time during the late fall, or when hurricanes and tropical depressions form. And WE DO NOT WANT THAT!"

It turned out that Brian was right. For the next twenty-four hours, the vessel pitched and rocked in seas ranging from four to eight feet, abating only slightly during the hours of darkness. Suddenly, the one hundred forty-seven foot ship seemed a lot smaller. Kurt and Larry were forced to cover multiple back-to-back wheel watches, since nearly everyone else on board was immobilized by seasickness. The only other passenger unaffected was Sanford. Jeffrey Smythe quickly took Sanford under his wing and instructed him on the nuances of standing helm watch, helping to ease the pressure.

On the second night of the passage, Kurt shared the wheelhouse with Sanford. They exchanged stories of their recent travels, Kurt filling him in on the adventures aboard the *Explorer*, and Sanford relating some of his own adventures in Central America. The two men enjoyed each other's company and soon became fast friends.

In the meantime, Captain Ellis continued to become more and more abhorrent. Rarely did he even come out of his cabin; but when he did, his demeanor and attitude reeked of ill-tempered rancor. Nobody knew what had turned him so negative or bitter, but the latest rumor insinuated that Dawn was having an affair with Brian. Dawn and Brian were obviously friendly, although nobody admitted to witnessing anything between them other than cordiality. On the other hand when they went to their respective cabins (which were isolated from the remainder of the ship), the two were often absent from the decks at the same times. Whatever the cause of his erratic behavior, the appearance of 'Captain Ahab' always caused discord among the remaining passengers and crewmen.

On the second night of the long and arduous passage from Panama to Jamaica, Captain Ellis entered the wheelhouse during one of Kurt and Larry's late night watches. His sudden appearance caught both men by surprise.

After an awkward moment of silence, Kurt offered a friendly, "Good evening, Captain Ellis."

"What's so damned good about it?" He slurred almost indecipherably, then lost his balance on a large swell and lurched into the wheelhouse wall before crashing onto the deck.

Kurt jumped from his helm seat and rushed to the Captain's side. The Captain lay in a heap, moaning lightly. Kurt reached down and touched his shoulder, not wanting to move him in case there was something seriously wrong.

Captain Ellis moaned again and tried to sit up. A trickle of blood ran down his cheek from above his left temple.

"Captain Ellis, are you alright?" Kurt asked, as he kept a restraining hand on the Captain's shoulder.

"I'm fine. Just move out of my way and let me up."

"You're bleeding," Kurt told him. "Will you just stay still for a minute while we check you out?" He turned to Larry and suggested he get some help.

"That's not necessary. I'm fine." Captain Ellis brushed Kurt's hand away and awkwardly turned and pulled himself onto his feet, keeping one hand connected to the wheelhouse wall. "I just got a little nick on my head when I lost my balance."

Kurt looked at him closely. He appeared to be okay, but his voice sounded different, as if he were either drunk or drugged. He tried to look into the Captain's eyes, but Captain Ellis avoided eye contact.

"I came up to see how our progress is going. How far do you estimate we are from Jamaica?"

"About three hundred miles. We should be there in two days."

"Good. I need to get off this damnable ship." With that comment, Captain Ellis worked his way out of the helm station, carefully keeping one hand on the closest wall or doorway in order to maintain his balance. Even with an effort to keep upright, his mobility seemed impaired and awkward; and both Kurt and Larry commented on the Captain's appearance as soon as he departed.

"He's an odd fellow," Larry observed. "What do you suppose is eating at him?"

"My guess is that he's just not suited to be a true captain—that and the rumor that his wife is screwing Brian. But he certainly is not the same man that he was when we first boarded this ship." Kurt said.

Before Larry could comment again, the cabin door opened, and Brian entered. Brian greeted them cordially, "Good evening gentlemen. Nice night."

Obviously, it was not a very nice night, with the wind blowing steadily out of the north and the seas running between six and eight feet. It was hard to tell if Brian was being sarcastic, or if he truly was enjoying the evening.

"I couldn't sleep," Brian stated. "I have the watch in about thirty minutes anyway and thought that perhaps the two of you might want a little early relief."

Kurt and Larry glanced at each other before Kurt responded. "We've always held a two-man helm watch. It doesn't seem quite right to leave you here alone."

"Oh, it's not a problem. Guillermo is going to work the watch with me. In fact, he's already up and told me he would be here within ten minutes, or so."

Brian paused briefly, and then spoke to them again in a more serious tone. "We are also going to have to change plans and make an unscheduled stop at San Andres Island. There is a problem with the fuel pump on the starboard engine; and we do not have a spare. We're going to stop and try to find another pump, or if not, at least have this one serviced. You guys can go ahead and get a couple of hours sleep before we reach San Andres. We might need a hand upon arrival. I don't think too many of the others are in any condition to be of much help."

"Yeah, just about everyone aboard is sick. We'll listen for the engines to slow, and then return to lend a hand docking, or anchoring, whichever we are going to do."

"Great," Brian responded. "I'm not sure whether we'll tie alongside the commercial docks or anchor in the bay when we arrive. Depends on how busy the harbor is. But I appreciate your offer to help. We'll see you in a few hours. I'm estimating that we are about four hours from San Andres."

∞

Shortly after dawn, the sound of reduced power awakened Kurt from a deep sleep. Standing stiffly, he walked to the starboard rail and looked around. Ahead he could see the outline of a lovely tropical island dotted with palms and other vegetation.

Less than one half mile ahead, the color of the water changed dramatically. The rich purple-blue of the open sea faded, replaced with a pale turquoise that illuminated the surface in a magical glow. As the *Explorer* drew nearer to shore, the hues and tints of the shimmering waters became more opaque, transformed into a light aquamarine that took on an amazing clarity. It was almost like looking into a swimming pool. The water turned so crystalline clear that the sea floor appeared to be dangerously shallow, when in fact it was more than thirty feet deep. Where reefs and drop-offs existed, the underwater topography blended with the varying shades of aquamarine and topaz to create a mosaic pattern of lighter and darker blues—a bright cobalt where white sand lies underneath, a richer azure where coral reefs jut toward the surface. The shimmering ultramarine waters spread a liquid glow that gives the Island its well-deserved nickname, 'Columbia's Seven-colored Sea.'

On shore, a brilliant white sand beach encircled the bay. Palm-thatched huts, pastel colored houses and white mortar buildings surrounded by palms and fruit trees dotted the low island landscape.

Jeffrey Smythe carefully maneuvered the ship alongside a concrete break-wall with heavy timbers hanging down to provide a buffered surface for mooring alongside. Kurt and Guillermo attached a series of large inflated fenders and secured the ship to the quay.

Within a few minutes, two official looking men dressed in military uniforms approached the ship. Their dark skin contrasted vividly with their bright beaming smiles.

"Hallo, welcome to San Andres!" they intoned together.

Brian served as spokesman for the ship, and greeted the two men pleasantly. "Hello. Thank you for the welcome. We are here for a brief stop on our way to Jamaica and are hoping to go ashore for some needed supplies and mechanical service and perhaps a little social recreation."

The taller and elder of the two men responded in his heavy Caribbean accent. "Ah, that could be a slight difficulty. Today it is Sunday, and our Customs inspectors they do not work today. It could be that you will need to wait until tomorrow for clearance to go ashore."

"Oh, that is too bad." Brian responded. "Our passengers are all American, and they had hoped to be able to go ashore where they could enjoy some of your local establishments, and spend some time and money in some of your restaurants, stores, and bars. Is there any way that you could give us temporary clearance to go ashore today, and we will check-in and clear with Customs first thing tomorrow?"

That question caused the two men to pause and contemplate the situation. Americans are widely recognized as free-spenders, and the island community would certainly benefit from an infusion of cash from these new visitors. As the two men contemplated whether they could make an exception and allow the passengers ashore, Tiona and Linda walked out onto the starboard deck and smiled at the two officials. Their appearance, dressed as they were in similar short white skirts and low-cut flowered blouses, seemed to help the officials make a decision.

"Perhaps we could grant you permission to go ashore, provided that you do not stray too far from this area. It would not seem to hurt anything to allow you to go ashore to the nearby shops and casino, although you will find that many of them are closed because it is Sunday."

"That would be great," Brian agreed. "We will instruct everyone to stay nearby. Thank you for your help and kindness. Is there anything we should know before we go ashore?"

Grinning broadly, the spokesman for the two replied, "Only that we are a friendly island and enjoy our lives to the fullest. We will be pleased to share our lovely island with you and your crew. We might suggest that you visit our beautiful Johnny Cay," he said, pointing to a small atoll situated a short distance from where they stood. "It is the most spectacular natural aquarium on our planet."

Indeed, San Andres appeared to be a beautiful and enchanting, tropical island. Because of its remoteness, situated as it is nearly three hundred miles from the nearest mainland shore, it is 'off the beaten path' and gets fewer visitors than many of the more popular Caribbean islands.

Upon receiving permission to leave the boat, the passengers couldn't wait! They were already beginning to recover from the seasickness that plagued most of them since leaving Panama, and setting foot on solid ground was something they all looked forward to with great enthusiasm.

Most elected to go ashore; but Kurt, Larry, Sanford, and Guillermo opted to take the aluminum skiff out to Johnny Cay for some underwater exploration.

The half-mile run from the dock to the small islet known as Johnny Cay took only a few minutes. Once there, it quickly became evident that the underwater domain at this isolated little island would prove to be exceptional. Looking down into the crystal clear water at the submerged coral reef and abundant fish life became an eye-opening experience. The shoreline of the tiny atoll glowed. Hundreds of coconut palms rose into the clear Caribbean sky, their rounded tops swaying in the prevailing trade winds. A broad expanse of brilliant white sand illuminated the transparent waters even more.

Dropping the small anchor into a patch of submerged sand, the four men donned their snorkeling gear and went over the side of the skiff to explore 'nature's most spectacular aquarium.'

It was like entering another world. Immersed in the warm eighty-two degree water, the four men encountered what Sanford would later describe as 'an immediate and vivid illusion of incalculable beauty'. This particular coral reef captured their imagination like nothing they had encountered before. Huge multi-hued brain coral interspersed with vibrant coral fans spread across the underwater panorama as far as the eye could see. Between and above the spectacular coral outcroppings, swarms of colorful tropical fishes wafted languidly or darted from the shadows, always in search of unsuspecting prey or tidbits of food. On the outer edges of the underwater garden, the sleek grey shadows of several reef sharks glided spectrally through the water.

As Kurt swam, his gaze fell on a large conch shell. He dove down about fifteen feet and plucked it from the sandy bottom. Turning it over, he discovered that it was empty, abandoned by its host or discarded by some fisherman after removing the delectable conch meat from the shell. Kurt took the ten-inch shell back to the skiff, enthralled by his discovery. The shell's lustrous opalescence glowed brightly in the warm tropical sunshine.

The men stayed in the water for nearly two hours, their hands and feet turning to 'prunes' from the prolonged submersion. They were all reluctant to leave. However, they realized two things: one, they were getting tired despite their captivation, and two, the others might become worried and would probably like to share in the incredible underwater experience. Reluctantly, they climbed back into the skiff and headed back to the ship.

Not too surprisingly, only a skeleton crew remained aboard. Everyone else had gone ashore to explore the small island and enjoy the sights.

Guillermo had plucked a couple of smaller conch shells from the seafloor, and both of those shells still contained the animal inside. Applying a trick that he had learned in Panama to the task of removing the animal from the shell, Guillermo inserted a hook into the meat and hung it from a piece of fishing line tied to a rail. Within fifteen minutes, the sound of the shell falling to the deck signaled that the shell and meat had separated. He sliced the meat, tenderized it with a wooden maul, and quick-fried the conch for lunch. It was delicious.

Several hours later the others returned from their excursion to shore. They had found a small pub nearby that served ice-cold Red Stripe beer for twenty cents per bottle. Four or five beers later—each—and they were noticeably intoxicated.

Ample replenishment of liquor stocks had also been purchased onshore, and Charlie purchased a bagful of high-grade locally grown marijuana from one of the taxi drivers. He shared his bounty with everyone willing to partake. The evening aboard the *Explorer* turned boisterous.

The following morning Brian and Dawn, accompanied by an agent from the City of San Andres, went to the Customs House and quickly and easily cleared everyone to 'legally' go ashore. Upon their return, everyone except Captain Ellis and two crewmen disembarked to explore the island paradise.

Sanford rented a funny little car. The car looked somewhat square shaped like a Jeep, but not nearly as solid. Its tires were narrow, about the width of a motorcycle tire, with spoke wheels. It had no top, and did not seem to have any springs or shock absorbers. They managed to crowd seven into the little vehicle, squeezing together cozily.

Sanford, Kurt, Madison, Marcos, Linda, Larry, and Tiona piled into the little car for an exploration of the island. The middle seat in front was a wooden box braced between bucket seats. Kurt agreed to sit there with Marcos and Sanford on each side and Larry and the three girls together in back. Heading out along the narrow road encircling the Island, they were most impressed by the beauty of the surrounding waters. Shimmering in the warm tropical sunshine, the sapphire blue waters shined crystalline clear. Coral heads were visible from the road, along with the occasional flash of large parrotfish and shoals of brightly colored reef fishes. None of them had ever seen anything quite like it, nor could they get enough.

On land, the scattered huts and homes of the locals were painted in a variety of happy pastel colors; and most sported lovely green lawns, beautiful flowerbeds, and fruit trees heavily laden with fruit. Mangos, papayas, bananas, and countless other fruit hung from the trees; like a tropical Garden of Eden.

They drove slowly to enjoy and not miss any of the sights. The locals waved and smiled, some called out singsong hellos, all laughed and seemed to thoroughly enjoy life. Several times Sanford stopped the car to engage someone in a brief conversation. Often people on the road made friendly comments about the three beautiful girls riding together in the back seat, some even whistled and whooped at the sight.

When they reached 'El Centro' or downtown San Andres, the group parked and walked around. They found a small café where they enjoyed conch fritters and a cold beer.

Near the east end of the island, an old grizzled black man wearing cutoff jeans and a ragged t-shirt stood outside of a fence attempting to coax a donkey through the gate. Despite his coaxing, the donkey would not budge. Sanford stopped the car, leaned out, and asked the old guy if he needed help.

"Oh, no, it is this way sometimes with animals. They do not think as we do. When he decides the time is right, he will move." He grinned and asked in his strong Caribbean accent, "Do you need help?"

Everyone laughed. Sanford replied, "No. We are fine. We're just out for a drive around your beautiful island and saw you struggling with your donkey."

Linda needed to go to the bathroom. Sanford looked over at the small plum-colored house sporting a roof covered with palm fronds that sat tucked underneath two towering avocado trees. "Is that your house?" he asked.

The old guy nodded his head. "Yes. I am the man who made this house. I make my own house, my own food, my own decisions. Time for me is only a position of the sun. It needs no more attention than that."

He spoke very deliberately. His dark black eyes covered with a gray film, stared directly at each of them in turn. "I am Pepa. My home is for you. I am living here for sixty-six years. This is my island, and it is your island. We are one. We are the people of the land."

"Well, Pepa," Sanford asked, with his hand on Linda's shoulder. "Do you have a bathroom that this young lady might use?"

"No. Bathrooms are in hotels. I have an outhouse. It is out behind that mango tree." He told them, pointing at a large tree at the back of the yard.

While Linda used the toilet—which turned out to be a seat over the top of a dugout basin that flowed downhill into another larger hole—the others were invited into Pepa's house. His house was a veritable embodiment of the sea. Everywhere, inside and out, there were things from the ocean. Copious amounts of shells, coral, sea fans, glass balls, driftwood, and whalebones adorned the entire house, porch, and yard. The house consisted of two small rooms separated by a hanging wall made from shells and assorted flotsam.

On a rustic coffee table made from bamboo were a copy of High Times magazine and a brown paper bag.

"This," said Pepa, picking up the copy of *High Times*, "is a book for the mind. In it is the essence of spiritualism. In this bag is the herb of the mind. It is my medicine, and it is for healing and for pleasure. I am happy to share my medicine with you if you would like."

Sanford looked at the others and shrugged. Marcos nodded, and Tiona said, "Sure."

Pepa rolled a large 'spliff' in a sheet of thin brown paper that he cut from a roll. He leaned against a rail made from tree limbs and lit the spliff. The sweet pungent aroma filled the air, and each took a turn inhaling from the expertly rolled joint.

Pepa began to talk. "When I was young, on this island there was no law. There was no need for it. The people ruled themselves and made their own laws. All of those laws were about being good people, living together in harmony. There was no jail. There was no need for a jail. And life was very good. Now, things have changed. There is law, and there is control of our lives. We cannot live as we choose. We must live for others. It is not good this way. I have dined and smoked ganja with the President of

Columbia. I have smoked with the Presidents of Peru, Venezuela, and Argentina. I attended the first meeting of sorcerers and witchcraft."

He paused, becoming pensive. It was apparent that he was revisiting the past, recalling other times when his life was different. He was an interesting character, an individualist, and an artist. His house served as a testament to his individuality and to his lifestyle.

Abruptly, Pepa emerged from his reverie and turned to Tiona, telling her, "You will return tonight, and we will have a party. Bring all of your friends. I will have good food and ganja. You bring drinks." With that, he turned and walked back out into his yard, focusing his energies on digging in his garden.

Tiona and the others sat around the porch for a few more minutes watching Pepa as he shoveled. They discussed his offer and decided that they would think about it and make a decision later. They all walked out to the car and said goodbyes to Pepa. He smiled and waved but said no more.

As they continued around the island, the population density lowered at the southern end. There were fewer dwellings, and the terrain turned more rugged. Along the shore, black and rust-colored cliffs bore the evidence of volcanic formations. The shores dropped rapidly to great depths. The few homes that dotted the countryside looked small and simple, much like Pepa's. All of the people worked in gardens or tended fruit trees. No other vehicle traffic could be seen. People either walked or rode horses. The native women walked along the dirt roadside with bananas and other fruits piled atop their heads. Often those piles rose three or four feet above the top of their heads. Some of the men could be seen chopping coconuts and slicing banana clusters from the banana palms, then passed them along to the women to carry. When the funny little car carrying the Americans passed by, the locals stopped what they were doing, smiled broadly, and waved. Life appeared very simple.

When they returned to the ship, some of the others had just come back from Johnny Cay and began telling everyone about the beauty and loveliness of the tiny island. This group had also discovered another nearby reef called 'The Aquarium' that harbored another vast array of tropical fishes and incredible tropical reef formations.

Later Kurt, Madison, Marcos, Linda, and Larry decided to wander out toward Pepa's and see if there actually was a party in the making. Several of the passengers had already gone ahead—some riding in Sanford's rented car, others walking the approximate one-mile distance.

When they arrived at Pepa's, the party was in full swing. Pepa, as promised, had several tables laden with food, piles of bananas and other fruit, a huge pan filled with slow roasted pork, bread-cakes, and a large kettle of boiled beans and rice. Unexpectedly when Kurt and the others arrived, two young native girls asked them for a donation.

"Oh," Kurt responded. "Pepa is charging for the party?"

"Yes," replied one of the girls, "Pepa always charges only ten dollars for his parties."

"Did the others pay?"

"Yes, although a few did not want to pay; so they are not here."

Kurt asked her to wait just a minute. He caught Guillermo's attention where he stood not too far away from the entrance gate. He waved him over.

"Hey, Guillermo," Kurt greeted him. "Did all of you have to pay a fee to get in the gate?"

"Yeah, we did. Surprised us a little, we did not know we were expected to pay. But when Pepa showed us the spread of food and the bags full of high quality weed, we all agreed that it was probably a fair price. They even have a three-piece calypso band that is taking a break right now, but they are very good."

Kurt and Madison stepped aside and spoke quietly between themselves, agreeing that they could not afford the twenty-dollars it would take to get them in the gate. They told Marcos and Linda that they were going to walk around. Larry also opted out, deciding that his budget could not afford the fee. The three of them wandered around the island for a while, then returned to the ship.

∞

When they awoke in the morning, another surprise was in store. Five soldiers from the Columbian military stood at attention, near the boarding ladder holding semi-automatic rifles. Two other official looking men dressed in less obvious military attire stood on the main deck talking animatedly with Brian and Jeffrey Smythe. Quite obviously, there was some tension in the air. The soldiers were preparing to search the ship, having received a tip from an unidentified informant that contraband drugs were being smuggled aboard the *Explorer*.

Brian and Jeffrey Smythe loudly denied the accusation, but it soon became obvious they were losing the battle. Kurt remembered that Larry had some 'stash' hidden somewhere in his possessions. He whispered to Madison that he was going to warn Larry. He slipped back to the aft deck. Once there, he told Larry what was going down, and Larry quickly grabbed his cache of marijuana and took it to where they stored the fishing gear. He was hoping that the bucket full of fishing tackle would dissuade the searchers from looking too closely at that item.

After a few minutes, the officials on board called three of the soldiers onto the boat and ordered them to begin a thorough and complete inspection.

The soldiers spent nearly three hours searching the ship from stem to stern but found nothing except a few marijuana seeds and a tiny bit of light powder in one of the drawers in the cook's cabin. They did not search the fish bucket. It didn't matter. One of the officials informed Brian and Jeffrey Smythe that the ship was in violation of contraband and was under suspicion of smuggling drugs illegally into a Columbian port. They arrested the cook and Captain Ellis (who had finally come out of his cabin during the search), and placed the entire ship under arrest. They took the cook and Captain Ellis away, and advised everyone else to stay aboard. Two of the soldiers stood guard at the gangway, rifles held rigidly.

About three hours later, Captain Ellis returned with the cook and informed everyone to prepare to get underway.

The passengers soon learned that the Columbian officials, after protracted but futile efforts to extract 'fines' from Captain Ellis and the cook, had contacted their leaders in Columbia. Since they were unable to 'convince' the Americans to pay cash fines, the officials decided to let the ship depart rather than have to feed and watch over the *Explorer* and its crew for at least three weeks until the chief magistrate from Columbia could arrive in San Andres to prosecute. They urged the crew to cast off and depart the island immediately and admonished them not to stop in Providencia.

Brian fired-off the starboard engine and lines were cast. A few feet from the dock, the engine stalled, and the ship was adrift. Kurt and Jeffrey Smythe, who had tended the dock lines, each managed to lasso one of the bollards on the wharf and re-tie the vessel to the dock. After working on the engine for about twenty minutes, Brian got it started, and once again the ship headed out. The soldiers stood on the quay watching the ship head out.

This time the ship made it about halfway out of the bay before the engine failed. The anchor was dropped, and Brian and Bilko went about trying to get the ship running. As dark approached, they decided to remain at anchor for the night.

The Columbian authorities visited the ship in a small tender, and demanded to know why they had stopped and anchored. When the engine failure was explained, the leader informed them that they would watch them carefully throughout the night and that if anyone attempted to get off the ship and go to shore they would be shot. Nobody intended on leaving the ship anyway; and early the following morning, the engine started. After the engine was tested sufficiently, the anchor was hauled, and the ship headed back to sea.

∞

Much like the run from Panama to San Andres, the seas became rough as soon as they cleared the lee of the island. The northeast trade winds blew steady at twenty knots with prevailing seas unrelenting at about six feet. Rolling in the trough, many of the passengers became sick once again.

During the night, the wind increased to twenty-five knots, and the swell rose to about eight feet. When Kurt went into the wheelhouse for his four a.m. helm watch, the ship pitched and rocked severely. Madison was one of the few passengers not afflicted with seasickness, and she decided to get up and work the watch with Kurt, giving green-faced Bob Bradley the opportunity to forego his shift and crawl into his bunk. Within minutes, it began to rain heavily, and visibility became so poor that the bow could not be seen. Plunging into the bleak and dreary night, Kurt hoped that nothing materialized in their path.

Madison seemed surprisingly at-ease and comfortable despite the stormy weather and rough seas. She chatted animatedly with Kurt about the events of the day and how fortunate they were to be allowed to leave San Andres rather than have to face a Columbian military tribunal.

At one point during their watch, Madison turned to Kurt and commented, "I love this! Even now when we can't see a thing, and the boat is bucking and pitching all over the place. It is invigorating and exciting!"

Kurt responded, "Yes, it is. But when it's stormy and rough like this, there is also a part of me that feels apprehensive. It's not the time or the place to have something go wrong, especially with the limited resources we have aboard."

"Oh, Kurt, don't be a worry-wart. Nothing is going to go wrong, and this is really an amazing experience."

Not wanting to cast any aspersions on her obvious enthusiasm, Kurt downplayed his concerns. "You're right, Madison. Everything is and will continue to be fine."

When daylight broke, the rain began to ease, and the wind and swell diminished somewhat. Dark gray clouds scudded across the surface of the sea.

Larry and Jeffrey Smythe relieved Kurt and Madison at six, and they went to their bunk area for a few hours of sleep.

When they awoke, they ate some leftover scrambled eggs and cold toast, and then went up to the wheelhouse to find out where they were and what was planned next.

Brian and Jeffrey Smythe stood at the helm, poring over charts and making calculations. The sextant was lying on the tabletop, waiting to be put to use. "So, what's up, Brian?" Kurt asked.

"We're trying to get an accurate position. According to the charts, the Serranilla Bank should be within sight. And right now there is nothing."

"So, what might the Serranilla Bank look like?" Kurt inquired.

"It's not much to see, just a large underwater reef about twenty-five miles in length. But it does have several sandbars that are often exposed, as well as a small atoll or two with a few palm trees. According to the Coast Pilot, it should also have a small building where a tiny Columbian outpost is supposed to be in service. The reef should also reflect a brighter sea surface due to its shallow depths; therefore, we should see a bright glow on the water or in the sky. Of course, this damnable cloud cover is not helping."

Kurt informed Brian that he would go up the mast to the lookout station and see if he could spot anything from there. He climbed up the wooden stakes to a makeshift crows-nest. The ship pitched and bucked violently, and occasionally the bow plunged into a swell. One slip and serious injury could occur. He climbed the rungs slowly and reached the platform without difficulty.

Once in the crows-nest approximately fifteen feet above the top deck, it didn't take Kurt long to spot the lighter coloration of the water a few miles off the port bow. He hollered down to Brian, who altered course about ten degrees and headed for the bank.

The ship had not gone a mile before a sputtering sound coughed up from the engine room, and the engine died. Almost immediately, the ship turned broadside in the seas and began rolling back and forth, noticeably listing to starboard.

How odd it was that nobody seemed to care.

A few weeks ago there would have been an immediate and widespread uproar from the passengers if the ship's engine had failed out in the middle of nowhere—to say nothing of their being subjected to the rolling swells that pitched and rocked the boat at close to thirty-degree angles. But now, most seemed indifferent to the situation, and everybody simply clutched onto something to keep from being tossed around.

To help minimize the broadside rolling, Jeffrey Smythe asked Kurt and Larry to help him rig an empty barrel with holes on both ends and drop it from the bow for a makeshift sea anchor. They attached the barrel with a length of three-fourths inch manila line and played out approximately one hundred feet. Almost immediately, the ship came up into the wind, and her bow settled into the swell. The ship continued to pitch and rock, but the broadside roll lessened.

In the engine room, the crew discovered that one of the return valves on the fuel feed line had collapsed and allowed the fuel to flow into the starboard tank, which was not opened to the port engine. As a result, the ship had run out of fuel. Brian and Bilko worked together in the sweltering heat of the engine room to repair the fuel line, then painstakingly bled the diesel lines. Within about forty minutes, the *Explorer* was once again running. They pulled the sea anchor, disconnected the barrel, and headed for the Serranilla Bank.

As the ship neared the reef, several shapes came into view. At first it looked like a large rock with an adjacent lighthouse situated on the northern end of the reef; but as the ship drew closer, it became evident that the 'rock' was actually the bow section of a wrecked ship, and the 'lighthouse' was the mast of another. Obviously, the Serranilla Bank could be a dangerous place.

Jeffrey Smythe said that according to stories he had heard while talking with some locals on San Andres Island there were hundreds of known wrecks on the reef and quite possibly many more. Situated in the middle of the Caribbean Sea, roughly halfway between Nicaragua and Jamaica, the reef lies directly in the path of several travel routes to and from Panama, Florida, and the West Indies. Jutting as it does from great ocean depths, it is no great wonder that it is the graveyard of many ships.

Ironically as their ship approached the southern end of the reef, a sailboat about forty-feet in length lay on her side on a white sandbar. On shore, about six or eight people could be seen waving, at least a few of them wearing uniforms.

At the helm, Smythe maneuvered around the southern tip of the reef into the lee of the small atoll, and the crew dropped anchor in about fifty feet of water. A dark gray outboard-powered inflatable dinghy shoved off from the sandbar and made its approach. Four soldiers, each carrying a large carbine, sat on the pontoons.

They greeted the visitors in a friendly fashion. "Hola, amigos! Buenos Dias. Do you have any cold beer?"

Captain Ellis appeared on deck and spoke to nobody in particular. "To hell with them! We will not give any beer to a group of desperate renegade banditos."

Those standing on deck were taken aback by his outburst. After a moment, Marcos called out. "Yes. We have cold beer, but not a lot. Come alongside and we will share one with each of you."

Beaming broadly, the four soldiers reached the side of the ship, and Marcos went into his own cache of drinks and brought out four Red Stripes. He passed one down to each of the men and said, "Sorry we cannot give you more, but we have only a few left. Are you stuck here on that little island?"

The lead soldier laughed and turned to the others, relating to them in Spanish what Marcos had said.

He turned back to Marcos and replied, "No, we are not stuck on this little island, although you could possibly say that. We are stationed here. We are from the Columbian Army, and we are here to protect our rights to this useless little speck of land. We are here for five weeks—as long as any man can stand—then four more soldiers will arrive to replace us." He pointed back to the other three people standing on the little beach next to the grounded sailboat. "Those sailors ran aground on the reef last night. They will wait until high tide tonight and try to sail off the sand. They were lucky to run onto the sand, rather than the rocks. We will be there to help them. Please enjoy your stay, and you are welcome to come ashore if you would like, although we cannot offer you any hospitalities. Our supplies are limited, and we have already had to ration our food and drink supplies in order to make them last." With that, the four soldiers climbed into their little skiff and headed back toward shore.

With the ship now anchored in calm water, several of the passengers appeared on deck, obviously very relieved to be recovering from seasickness. A couple of them, including Linda and Marcos, swung the boarding ladder out into position and jumped over the side for a late afternoon swim. At the stern of the ship, Marcos called out to Larry, who stood near the rail. "Hey Larry, the trolling line is caught on the starboard propeller."

Looking back at the aft deck, Larry realized that they had forgotten to haul in the trolling lines when they settled into the anchorage. He called back to Marcos and asked him if he could get it un-fouled.

After he dove beneath the boat and assessed the situation, Marcos resurfaced and told Larry that he needed a pair of pliers to dislodge the hook from the shaft log.

Larry returned with pliers and passed them down to Marcos. After three efforts, Marcos re-surfaced and told Larry that he had cleared the prop but dropped the pliers in the process. Guillermo stood nearby watching the situation unfold, and told Marcos not to worry that he would dive down and recover the pliers.

Everyone looked at him like he was nuts. The depth measured about fifty-feet where they were anchored, and abundant coral, rocks, and other impediments covered the bottom. Even if he could dive that deeply, it seemed unlikely that he could find the pair of pliers in the underwater clutter, particularly since in the late afternoon the visibility was rapidly diminishing.

Guillermo donned his mask and fins, stepped off the boarding platform into the water, took a deep breath, and dove down.

From the decks, several necks craned outward to watch Guillermo descend. In the fading daylight, he could not be seen clearly; but his shape and shadow remained visible as he continued downward. After what seemed like an incredibly long time, those standing on the deck began to grow concerned as Guillermo stayed near the bottom. Kurt opened his mouth to shout out an alarm when he saw that Guillermo had begun ascending toward the surface. He moved agonizingly slowly, and all of them wondered how anybody could hold their breath for that long.

Finally, nearly two minutes after he had gone down, Guillermo popped to the surface. "Hey," he called out, "give me a hand." He kicked toward the boarding ladder while holding onto something large and yellow in color. When Guillermo reached the platform, clutched in his grip he held a gigantic yellow lobster!

"Don't just stand there gawking!" Guillermo admonished. "Grab this thing so I can get back aboard."

Kurt leaned over and grabbed the lobster with both hands, careful to avoid the kicking and slashing legs. He could not get both hands fully around the body of the huge crustacean, but he managed to haul it up the ladder and lay it down on the deck. Everyone gathered around and stared. Nobody had ever seen a lobster that large or that color. They were not sure if it was an aberration, sick, or if lobster in these waters were merely a different color.

Guillermo climbed up the boarding ladder and approached the group. "Here's your pliers." They all looked at him in wonder. Not only had he recovered the pliers, but he also brought up a huge lobster that, when weighed and measured, checked-in at forty-nine inches long and seventeen pounds!

Guillermo explained that lobster, in some tropical waters, absorb the coloration of their surroundings and there was nothing wrong. Dawn took it into the galley and boiled it in a large kettle. The only problem in cooking a lobster that big is that the outer portion cooks rapidly while the inner meat remains raw. When she took it out the first time, split the tail open, and discovered the insides to be uncooked, she put it back into the pot. The next time she took it out, it was overcooked and mushy. Everyone ate it anyway.

By the time they finished with the lobster and a tray full of makeshift pizza slices, night had settled completely. With no moon overhead, a million stars illuminated the sky. The stars were so bright, bold, and abundant that they stretched from horizon to horizon and seemed close enough to almost reach out and grab. The trade winds whistled across the bow, cooled the air and made the night very comfortable. About half of the passengers sat out on the foredeck of the ship, passed around a few joints and reveled in the beauty of the night.

∞

At first light, the growl of the starboard engine rumbled through the hull. Kurt and Larry went forward to help hoist the anchor. The sailboat they saw the previous afternoon bobbed at anchor about two hundred yards away. It was one of the few lucky ones to go aground on the reef and be successfully refloated. The crew from the sailboat waved farewell. Kurt clipped the anchor stay into place, and the *Explorer* made a full turn to port and headed out to sea.

Kurt and Larry looked back at the tiny atoll where the small shack that housed the soldiers faded into the distance. "It sure would have been nice to spend some more time there." Kurt commented wistfully. "Judging from the lobster that Guillermo pulled up, I'll bet the snorkeling and diving would have been terrific."

"No doubt." Larry replied. "Out here in the middle of nowhere, I'll bet not many people have the chance to swim or dive in these waters. It sure would have been nice." He sighed pensively, and they went together into the galley for coffee.

When they were clear of the bank, the seas again began to build, becoming even rougher than before. The swell built to about eight to ten feet, and the wind increased to around twenty-two knots. Larry went to the stern and set the trolling lines, although he didn't expect much to happen. Other than one small tuna hooked shortly after they had departed Panama, they had seen nothing to indicate any fish in these waters. There were no porpoise, whales, nor turtles, and few birds. About the only thing they saw on a regular basis were small flying fish. There were lots of those, skipping out of the water and flitting into the air where the winds tossed them around before they dipped back into the briny depths.

More of the passengers had become accustomed to the rough seas. Only Charlie, Peter, Sally, and the new cook—Walter—were confined to their bunks with perpetual seasickness. The sun popped out and the passengers played card games, worked on their tans, or stood on the foredeck where the bow plunged into the dark green water and sent cooling spray flying up and over the rail. It turned into somewhat of a game to try and guess which waves would send spray flying and how much. Every once in a while, a rogue swell reared-up; and the bow plunged so deeply into the swell that blue-green water boiled over the rail and drenched the passengers with a rush of water that occasionally knocked them off their feet.

As the afternoon wore on, the seas abated slightly. The seas remained lumpy; but the wind dropped to its customary fifteen to twenty knots, and the swells settled to about four to six feet.

A certain amount of wistful anticipation filled the air as the passengers realized that the end of the journey neared. They should reach Jamaica in about thirty hours. Several of the passengers sat around on the foredeck and reminisced about their adventures and recalled some of the fun and excitement that all had shared since leaving Ensenada Harbor nearly two months ago. They also discussed what might happen next for the *Explorer,* and for Captain Ellis and Dawn.

∞

Morning dawned wet and cool. A thick oppressive blanket of misty fog enveloped the ship. Visibility reduced to perhaps one-fourth mile, and the seas held at six to eight feet with larger swells mixed in. A steady twenty-five knots of wind caused nearly everyone to pull out sweatshirts, jackets, and even foul weather gear.

Food supplies had dwindled again. For breakfast, pancakes without syrup did little for the taste buds, but Sally mixed together a bowl full of sugar and five-spice seasoning that helped make the dry pancakes palatable.

After breakfast, Sanford and Larry invented a 'new game' for everyone to play. They called it the 'Giant Hop.' To do the Giant Hop, all you had to do was stand near the bow of the ship and hop in the air, timing the hop with the lift of the ocean swell. When timed right, a small hop turned into a six to eight foot leap as the hopper went airborne when the bow plunged downward. A well-timed hop left the person momentarily suspended in mid-air. The playful diversion went fine for about half an hour until Marcos mistimed his landing and sprained an ankle. The game ended.

Navigation took on another more challenging dimension. Shortly after leaving the Serranilla Bank, the gyrocompass failed. The gyrocompass is a large circular device that interacts with the ship's autopilot to keep the ship on course. When the gyrocompass failed, it became necessary to steer the ship by hand. Brian worked with Bilko on a repair, but without any success. As a consequence, the helm watches became much more challenging and physically demanding as each operator had to actually steer the ship rather than simply watch the heading and gauges. Brian and Jeffrey Smythe also had to constantly check the dead-reckoning position of the ship to be certain that the correct course and heading were being maintained.

Throughout the afternoon, the oppressive marine layer prevailed. At times, the mist turned to light rain, and the heavy seas continued.

In the galley, two of the three overhead working lights went out, and there were no more spare bulbs on board. Bulbs had been sacrificed from several other locations already. As nightfall approached, Dawn and Sally prepared the evening meal with limited lighting.

While mixing a kettle full of baked beans and pork chunks, Dawn snagged one of the potholders on the kettle handle and dumped the kettle full of boiling beans onto her left arm. She suffered second-degree burns from the accident, and there wasn't much in the First Aid kit to help her. They cooled her burn with fresh water, and then wrapped it in a clean t-shirt that was kept cool with periodic splashes of cold water. Under the circumstances, it was the best that could be done. Sally salvaged as much of the meat/bean dish as possible by scooping the bulk of the dish off the galley decking.

Coinciding with her burn, the spilled beans caused a short circuit in one of the burners on the stove—an electrical stove that already had one of the three burners out of commission. The short circuit left the ship with only one burner for preparing meals. That in itself did not pose too much of a problem since there wasn't much food to cook anyway, and Jamaica was only about seventy miles (twelve hours) distant, assuming things went smoothly.

At midnight, Kurt and Larry shared another helm watch. Kurt took the helm for the first portion of the shift. Having to physically steer the boat made the watch much more intense and exhausting. An inky blackness filled the air, and visibility remained very limited. Fighting the wheel to keep on course, Kurt jerked reflexively when a large dark object flashed ahead, before it disappeared in the next swell. He turned the helm to starboard hoping that whatever he had seen would slide to port. When the ship rode up on the next swell, he cursed as a large palm tree rose up into the air directly ahead of the port bow. The palm tree tilted, and briefly appeared to be growing out of a reef or atoll. Kurt inhaled deeply as he envisioned the ship impaling itself on a jagged coral reef. He held his breath and waited for impact.

A thump reverberated through the hull of the ship when the bow collided with the tree. But that was all—a thunking sound and a slight shudder in the decking.

He soon realized that the palm was merely a drifting tree that must have broken away from some distant shore or atoll and just happened to pop upright in the heavy seas. He felt greatly relieved. He relayed the incident to Brian and Guillermo when they took over the helm watch at two a.m., and suggested that they try and keep a good lookout for other objects that might be floating in the dark waters. He went to his bunk and found Madison awake and waiting for him.

"Hi. I didn't expect to find you awake."

"I couldn't sleep very well; and besides, this will probably be our last night at sea, and I thought we might want to celebrate together."

Kurt grinned. "What do you have in mind?"

She pulled back the light cotton blanket that she used for sleeping, and exposed her naked body.

Kurt gulped. Her exquisitely shaped curves always did that to him. She looked divine. His eyes devoured her, wandering from her smooth tanned legs, up and over her wide, feminine hips, across her smooth flat stomach, then lingered on her full milky white breasts before settling on her heart-shaped face.

"Is there something wrong?" She asked quietly.

"Oh. No. I just want to look at you. You are so gorgeous. I just can't get enough of you. I want to stare at you forever."

"Well, that's sweet, but I'd really like you to kiss me and make love with me."

He smiled broadly. "Yes. I'd like that too."

He removed his t-shirt, and in one easy motion pulled his shorts down over his hips and kicked them off with one foot. Naked, he lowered himself and locked his lips with hers.

He rolled onto his side, and she rolled with him. He leaned back and looked again upon her lovely figure. "You are so beautiful. My God, I just cannot take my eyes off of you."

She giggled. "Okay. Keep looking if you want, but I want you inside of me."

He entered her warmth. They both emitted a low sensuous moan.

They moved together eagerly, their strong young bodies relishing the pleasure. Sweat formed on their skin, adding luster to the glow emanating from their bodies.

Afterward, they slept deeply and peacefully.

∞

In the morning, Kurt and Madison awakened to a cry from the foredeck. "Land Ho!" In the distance, the greenish-blue hills of Jamaica rose from the sea.

With the cry of 'Land Ho,' all the passengers who were not seasick rushed to the foredeck. Dimly visible under the misty marine layer loomed the silhouetted coast of Jamaica. Transfixed, and with thoughts running rampant about having finally reached their destination, the passengers fought to keep their balance on the pitching decks. Heavy seas of eight to ten feet tossed the *Explorer* around like a cork bobbing in a tumbling washing machine. At one point, a very large swell lifted the bow skyward, and then plunged it into the trough—and ensuing face—of another huge wave. A massive wall of water broke over the rails and swept across the deck, with the accompanying spray reaching all the way to the upper deck, more than ten feet above the rails. The wave knocked several passengers down, and tossed a couple of them back against the main cabin bulkhead. The drenching resulted in a few bruises, but no significant injuries.

Fifteen minutes and about one mile later, the seas diminished to less than half, as the ship came into partial shelter of the Island. Another hour of steaming and the seas dropped to nothing more than a light chop as the vessel entered the full lee of the island. The passengers holed-up in their bunks slowly emerged onto the decks to take in the sights of the Jamaican coastline.

In the distance, the varied panoramas of the Jamaican hillsides danced in the sunshine. Rolling hills covered with planted fields led up toward bluish green mountains, dense with tall trees. On the coastline, long white sand beaches stretched expansively between dark jagged cliffs that dropped sharply into the bright blue sea. Small clusters of homes peeked out of the dense foliage, and large, plantation style buildings sat atop several cleared areas.

Another three hours and the densely populated harbor of Montego Bay appeared, its verdant hillsides dotted with homes, and its harbor surrounded by commercial structures.

The 'five-week cruise' was over—two months later and three weeks behind schedule. The fourteen remaining passengers were understandably subdued and pensive. For some, it was a time of sorrow, for others a time of great relief; but for all, it was time to gather their wits and prepare for what they thought would be the closing chapter of their unique and memorable odyssey aboard the *Explorer*.

CHAPTER SIXTEEN

After contacting the local port authority via VHF Channel Sixteen, and receiving directions to a berthing site, Jeffrey Smythe maneuvered the ship cautiously into a u-shaped concrete-walled embayment and awaited further instructions. A small tugboat arrived with two large ebony-skinned Jamaicans on board. In a lilted English accent tainted by the inflections peculiar to Jamaican speech, the men advised the crew to prepare lines for a starboard side docking. Jeffrey Smythe was advised by the port authorities to moor on the back, or inner wall of the u-shaped abutment. Kurt, Larry, and Phillip tended the mooring lines while the small tug swung around to position its bow against the portside quarter of the ship. Turning its tire-wrapped bow to push the vessel toward the dock, the small tug propelled the ship sideways until lines could be secured to the dock bollards. Lying broadside against the back wall of the concrete quay, the *Explorer* had reached her final destination, Jamaica.

Soon after, things became very weird.

∞

Jamaican port authorities arrived on scene almost immediately. Captain Ellis emerged from his self-induced seclusion and introduced himself to the officials. His appearance seemed dramatically improved. Gone was the vacant-eyed, disheveled phantom of a man they had grown accustomed to seeing in recent days. In his place stood the confident, resolute captain that the passengers had encountered at the beginning of the cruise.

Holding the ship's paperwork in anticipation of clearing customs quickly, Captain Ellis was effusive and cooperative, answering their questions and providing information eagerly and efficiently. He explained the reasons for their delayed arrival—the Jamaicans had been informed of their anticipated arrival and expected them nearly a month earlier—and apologized for arriving late. His explanations and cooperation served their purpose, and the ship was cleared for shore access in less than an hour.

The officials departed, and then it happened.

Captain Ellis called for an 'all-hands' meeting, and everyone assembled in the main salon. Without any preliminaries, Captain Ellis announced, "You are all cleared to go. I expect everyone to be off the ship within an hour."

Somewhat stunned, all of the passengers stood there waiting for something further—perhaps a 'thank you,' or 'hope you enjoyed the trip,' anything except silence.

Finally after a long, awkward pause, Guillermo spoke up, "That's it? After all we've gone through and without any consideration for the fact that we all need to make travel arrangements back to the States, you're kicking us off the ship?"

"That's exactly right. I contracted to take you to Jamaica. Well, we are here, now pack your bags and get off of my ship."

"What the hell is wrong with you?" Guillermo blurted. "We've all put up with your foul moods, the poor conditions on this ship, and your failure to get us here on schedule. Now you're telling us to get off the ship without giving us the time to make plans to get home. This is an outrage!"

"I really don't care. I want all of you off this ship before four p.m., or I'll have you arrested for trespassing, or whatever it takes."

With that, Captain Ellis turned on his heels and walked purposefully back to his cabin.

Several of the passengers just shrugged and walked away to begin packing. Others stood around talking about the situation.

After a few minutes, Dawn approached Kurt and Madison and asked them to step aside. Walking with them onto the aft deck, Dawn asked them if they would be willing to stay on to help with things aboard the ship until they could sort things out with the owners and determine what might happen now that they had reached their destination.

After pondering the question for a moment, Kurt asked, "Why us?"

"Because my husband has appreciated your help and cooperation during the cruise, and we need someone to stay aboard to help watch things when we are ashore and while we try and figure out our own plans."

"Well, can you give us a few minutes to talk about this? Also, we are with Larry and Marcos, and we need to find out what their plans are, what they want to do, and how that might affect our decision."

"Sure," Dawn responded. "I'll get back with you in a little while."

Marcos and Linda had already made their decision—they were catching the first available flight back to Los Angeles. Larry wasn't sure, but he thought it might be nice to spend a little time in Jamaica, see the sights and explore the country.

Kurt and Madison spoke with Dawn and asked if they, along with Larry, could discuss the matter with Captain Ellis, informing her that they were not at all pleased with how he had treating everyone.

In the meantime, several passengers had already packed and were prepared to depart the ship. It was a difficult and emotional time. Sally and Peter, Emily, and Bob Bradley were among the first to depart. An exchange of addresses and phone numbers took place, along with hugs, tearful farewells, and a promise to make contact as soon as everyone was settled back into their 'real lives' once again.

Having to bid farewell to Marcos and Linda was even more difficult. Both Marcos and Linda had endeared themselves to everyone, and the moment turned very emotional. Larry spoke privately with Marcos for a few minutes, explaining that he might stay on for a while longer and asked Marcos if he would 'hold down the fort' at home until such time that he returned.' Marcos assured him that he would.

Shortly thereafter, a heated and uncomfortable meeting between Brian and the crew resulted in all of the crewmen, with the exception of Jeffrey Smythe, making plans to depart. Brian promised each of the others that he would do his best to ensure that they received pay for their work, although he admitted it would likely take some time. He gave each of them a handwritten promissory note for the amount they were due, along with contact information for the company's main office in Vancouver. He also took down each of their forwarding addresses so that he could mail their checks. Saying goodbye was not easy. They had all become friends and had shared many unique and wonderful experiences.

Tiona and Charlie announced that they were going to stay in Jamaica for a while. Sanford said that he might hangout for a while also.

Kurt, Madison, and Larry met with Captain Ellis, Dawn, and Brian shortly after lunch. Captain Ellis responded negatively when they asked that Larry be allowed to stay as well. Captain Ellis expressed concern about having to feed another person. After a few minutes of querying back and forth, the Captain agreed that Larry could also stay aboard, at least until they knew what might become of the ship and its future plans. All agreed to meet later in the afternoon, after the remainder of the passengers were gone, to discuss the details of their agreement.

∞

Although none of the passengers had much luggage, it took some time for everyone to pack their things and depart the ship. The last of the passengers departed around four p.m.

Kurt, Madison, and Larry sat together on the foredeck talking after everyone was gone. They were going to miss their shipmates deeply. During their two-months together, they had become very close. For the voyage to end so abruptly and contentiously was not what they envisioned. They each assumed that the ship's arrival in Jamaica would open another door to exploration, wonder, and excitement. Instead, it resulted in a harsh and unfriendly dismissal of their fellow travelers, one that would likely taint the entire memory of the trip for those that were unceremoniously kicked off the ship.

Dawn had gone ashore and, with her last few dollars, purchased enough food for the next couple of days.

Around five o'clock, Captain Ellis, Brian, and Jeffrey Smythe joined Kurt, Madison, and Larry on the foredeck. Plans were discussed. The ship had lost its contract for the Cayman Island dive package. There was no money available, and dockage alone cost sixty dollars per day. Brian informed them that he intended to catch a flight out the following morning to Vancouver to meet with his father and other owners of the company. He then pulled out his own wallet and gave Captain Ellis five hundred dollars to help pay the dockage and cover basic expenses during his absence, assuring them that he would return as soon as possible.

In the meantime, they agreed that it would suffice to leave one person on board at all times as a watchman. The others could come and go at their own leisure; giving them the opportunity to go off and explore the island. This was particularly agreeable to Kurt, Madison, and Larry.

The meeting broke up, and Kurt, Madison, and Larry talked about going ashore to check things out. Their own cash was low, but they still wanted to get out and see some sights.

They had just finished dinner when voices rang out on the docks. Eight of the passengers and crewmen, including Marcos and Linda, Sally and Peter, Hugo, Sanford, Bob Bradley, and Guillermo, were standing on the dock calling out to have someone lower the ramp so they could come aboard.

Overhearing the ruckus, Captain Ellis arrived on scene and barked in a sour note, "Come back to visit?"

"Well, no," Bob Bradley spoke for the group. "We could not book a flight out today, and the hotels are too expensive. So we came back to sleep on the ship."

"Oh, you did? Well I run a ship, not a goddamn hotel! Go find some other place to sleep," Captain Ellis retorted.

"But we don't have any other options. What do you expect us to do, sleep on the ground?"

"Sure, go ahead. I really don't give a damn."

At that point, Dawn pulled him aside and spoke briefly to him in a vehement whisper. He looked at her, then back at the others, and shrugged. He turned to them and muttered his approval, agreeing to allow them aboard to sleep—on the decks only—not in the cabins. He also informed them that they could not eat aboard and that they must be off the ship early in the morning. When they agreed to those terms, Kurt and Larry lowered the ramp, and the forlorn group stepped aboard.

The atmosphere turned uncomfortable. Kurt explained that he, Madison, and Larry were going to stay aboard as rotating watchmen. He told them that they were not sure how long the arrangement might last, but it would at least give them the opportunity to do some exploring and eventually make their own arrangements to return to the States. There was no animosity displayed from the other eight passengers. They all understood that the three of them were merely taking advantage of an opportunity—regardless of the reasons. No one stayed up late.

Early the following morning, the stranded group once again made their farewells and departed. After they left, Kurt, Madison, and Larry went ashore to checkout Montego Bay. Captain Ellis and Dawn also went ashore, leaving Jeffrey Smythe to care for the ship.

∞

Montego Bay proved to be a bustling town, noisy, crowded, and expensive—compared to other places visited on the trip. Street vendors lined the sidewalks, hawking everything from clothing to jewelry to ganja. At one of the outdoor restaurants not far from the harbor, a distinctly British gentleman advised everyone to be careful while walking around the streets. He warned that it was often dangerous—especially after dark and especially if you encountered a group of radical Rastafarians.

Jamaica in 1976 simmered in state of social turmoil. The People's Nationalist Party and the Jamaican Labor Party were embroiled in a political battle to assume control of the troubled country. For years, Jamaica had prospered, or at least remained somewhat stable, under British rule. However since the mid 1950s, a concerted effort led by non-British leaders tried to break away from the 'Mother Country.' After years of seeking independence, Jamaica finally gained independence in 1962 and settled in under the control of the Nationalist Party. As the economy faltered, partly because of a failing bauxite industry, the Labor Party became more active, and radical factions emerged. Michael Manley became Prime Minister, and opposition leaders began to spread their pervasive tentacles into all areas of the society.

The worst political climate existed in Kingston, on the opposite side of the Island; but social unrest festered in nearly all cities, including Montego Bay. The safest and most tourist-friendly place on the Island was said to be Negril, a sparsely populated region on the southwestern end of the Island about fifty miles from 'Mo Bay'—as Montego Bay was often called by its inhabitants.

After hearing stories about Negril, Kurt, Madison, and Larry decided that they wanted to see it for themselves. Returning to the ship, they conferred with Captain Ellis and Jeffrey Smythe; and the Captain agreed that they could have three days to visit Negril. They packed things up and prepared to leave the following morning.

Following a light breakfast of fruit and bread-cake, Kurt, Madison, and Larry left the ship to head off and find transportation to Negril. Having been pointed in the direction of the bus stop, the trio was pleasantly surprised when Tiona and Charlie pulled up in a rented car.

Tiona leaned out the window and called, "Hey there, kiddos, where you heading?"

"Tiona! Charlie! It's great to see you two," Madison reacted as if it had been a very long time since they last saw one another.

She rushed over to the car, leaned in, and gave Tiona a hug. "Gosh. We're looking for the bus that goes to Negril. We heard it's really the place to go; so we're going to head out there for a couple of days to check it out."

"Great!" Tiona exclaimed. "We're about to do the same thing. Hop in, and you can all go with us."

Happy to see Tiona and Charlie, and even more pleased to know that they were also going to Negril, the trio hopped into the back of the small rented Chevrolet Comet, and they all headed off.

They drove leisurely, stopping occasionally to take pictures, or get a closer look at some of the spectacular terrain and scenery. At one particularly lovely canyon where two small streams converged, they stopped and took a pleasant hike up the gorgeous waterscapes that formed the streambeds. The scenery filled them with awe. The crystal clear water of the streams flowed down from the mountains, and spread gracefully across the smooth gray boulders that formed several small waterfalls. They swam in the refreshing pools, and the few natives they encountered seemed to appreciate their American visitors.

Following their brief swim, the group continued on to Negril.

A vast expanse of white-sand beach stretched for several miles along one strip of the road, the evidence of a major construction project disrupting the tranquil beauty. That construction was destined to become the first of numerous luxury resorts that would eventually transform the entire coastal stretch of Jamaica's 'seven-mile beach' and ultimately the entire north coast of Jamaica.

Their arrival in the little village located on the southern end of the island immediately conjured-up images of a jungle paradise. The road had become a narrow one-lane dirt road. Thick jungle foliage spread up from the jagged volcanic shoreline.

The 'town' of Negril consisted of only a few buildings clustered together in a small clearing. Two small buildings served as the town center; a small grocery store, a bar, a fruit stand, and a curio shop with a postal office formed the core of the tiny community.

One of the locals informed them that inexpensive cabins could be found at a couple of small private properties along the road leading southwestward.

Madison and Kurt picked up a few basic food items to prepare a meal while Larry wandered off and found one of the local ganja dealers who sold him a quarter-pound bag of the high-grade pot for fifteen dollars and a bagful of 'magic mushrooms' for another five-dollar bill.

As they wound their way along the narrow dirt road, the group discovered a For Rent sign nailed to a palm tree with a cluster of small cottages tucked back from the road. A tiny wooden sign affixed to a majestic banyan tree identified the location as 'Awee-ma-Way' Village. A beaming heavy-set Jamaican woman sat idly on the porch of a nearby house, Madison and Tiona negotiated rental of two small cottages located side by side for seven dollars per day for each of the units. Both cottages had two tiny rooms, one a combined kitchen/living room, the other a bedroom with two single beds. At the back of the cottages, an outhouse and an outdoor shower stood side by side. It wasn't much; but for the price and with the surrounding beauty of the jungle, it seemed perfect.

While Madison and Tiona prepared a meal of sautéed vegetables and rice, the men walked around the property smoking and passing around a large spliff. When Madison called out that dinner was ready, the men wandered in to join them. Surreptitiously, Larry dumped a handful of 'magic mushrooms' in the sautéed vegetable dish, stirring it into the mix without being noticed, even though Kurt and Madison and Tiona and Charlie had all declined to partake in consumption of the psychedelic mushrooms.

After eating the meal, it didn't take long before the mushrooms took effect.

Soon an unsettling queasiness affected them all. Madison was the first to react to and comment on the discomfort.

"I'm not feeling very good," she commented. "My stomach is turning flip-flops."

"Mine too," Tiona announced. Soon all of the others felt the internal tumult.

"It's the mushrooms," Larry announced. "I put some of them into the vegetables."

"Why did you do that?" Kurt responded angrily. "We told you we did not want to eat psychedelic mushrooms."

"I know," Larry responded, "but they really won't hurt you, and I think everyone will enjoy the high that you get. The stomach discomfort only lasts for a while. Then I really think you will like the effects."

Everyone was quiet as they mulled over the situation. Madison excused herself, commenting, "I think I am going to throw up." She went outside. Kurt followed her to make sure she was okay. Out in the fresh air, the disquiet in their bowels eased considerably; and they began to look around. The surrounding jungle began to pulsate, seeming to throb in a rhythmic beat of natural sounds and vibrations. Humming insects and other unidentified noises created a cacophony of drumming that permeated the senses.

Colors became more vivid. The surrounding jungle glowed. The leaves and shadows of the trees cast a palette of colors from dark green to rich purple. The flowering shrubs and plants came to life even in the darkness. Bright white and yellow flowers lit up like ethereal visions in the faint light of the stars and a waning moon. Above the treetops, the night sky took on an iridescent hue, the lingering indigo of twilight blending with the inky background of nightfall.

After a while, Kurt and Madison realized that the others were also outside absorbing the fascination of the night. It was a sensory visual and auditory experience; and once the disquiet of the nausea had passed, the more pleasurable effects of the mushrooms took over. They all stayed outdoors for several hours, laughing, and running around like young children on a campout. Enthralled by the surrounding jungle and the affects of the hallucinogen they had unintentionally consumed, the group had a wonderful time.

They remained out until nearly daybreak, listening, watching, feeling, and absorbing the pulse and the life of the surrounding jungle. Everything seemed vivid, alive, and naturally intense. The plants and trees seemed to be breathing. The ground seemed to give off the warmth and feeling of a living organism. Even the air seemed filled with a measure of purity and life-enhancing sustenance. The night turned magical, despite the fact that Larry had doctored their food without their knowledge, and all five of them enjoyed the effects.

Eventually, they all retired to their respective beds. Sleep did not come easily at all. Brief flashes of color and intrusive sounds coursed through their senses, even with their eyes closed. Most of the effects of the mushrooms had worn off, but the lingering subtleties of the hallucinogen flickered in and out of their consciousness.

For the next two days, the group of five explored and experienced the natural beauty and ambiance of Negril. They discovered the underwater magnificence of unspoiled tropical reefs teeming with fish and resplendent with rich coral forests. They hiked the narrow trails that had been carved out by the local natives through the jungles on the southern end of Jamaica. They dined on seafood delicacies and the sweet bread rolls that native women sold on the streets for ten-cents each. They sat on the shoreline watching spectacular sunsets and listening to the sounds of the sea crashing against the volcanic cliffs. Life was simple and wonderful.

On their second day, Kurt and Larry decided to swim out beyond the sheltered waters of the small bay where they normally snorkeled to check out another reef that they had heard about from some of the locals. That reef, located south of the point that provided protection for the small cove, required an open-ocean swim of about one-fourth mile to reach its boundaries. The swim would take them into exposed deeper waters that they knew were prone to shark habitation. As a precaution, they each took along implements that they hoped would be adequate deterrents if they encountered any predatory denizens of the deep.

Kurt made himself a hip sheath in which he strapped a two-foot long metal rod sharpened at the tip. Larry carried the small pole spear they used for gigging lobster. They hoped these tools would not be needed.

Swimming side by side, the intrepid snorkelers headed out around noon, promising to return by one p.m. Madison kept an eye on them from shore, sitting atop one of the ledges overlooking the ocean.

Once they were beyond the last point of the small cove, the sea floor dropped off, disappearing into the briny depths. The prevailing trade winds blew unusually light that day—one of the factors that prompted them to choose that particular day for their adventure. Even so, the sea-surface turned slightly choppy, slowing their progress toward the reef. They felt disconcerted to be in deeper waters without any visible sea floor. The water was clear, but the fathomless depths reflected a violet tint that faded into oblivion.

Occasionally, the two swimmers stopped to look around and get a bearing on land to insure they weren't swimming in the wrong direction. They had a pretty good sense of where they were heading, having discussed the location of the reef with their Jamaican friends. Still, they were about to give up and abort their outing when Kurt stopped and pointed toward his right. Submerged in the distance, a mound of colorful coral appeared majestically out of the shimmering blue depths. Turning to look at each other and smiling through their masks, Kurt and Larry turned and headed toward the outcropping.

Upon reaching their destination, the underwater sights made them gasp as they looked around. Huge shoals of brightly colored tropical fishes swarmed around the magnificent coral heads that rose from the depths.

As the two men floated over the reef, the spectacle grew even more amazing. The struggle of life on a coral reef occurred before their eyes as they watched reef dwellers gnaw and peck at the coral outcroppings, dislodging small chunks of matter that attracted other feeders and dwellers. Those movements prompted quick darting attacks from other fish intent upon their struggle for survival. Always, the strong and healthy survived, while the weak and small fell prey to bigger and more aggressive creatures.

Crossing over a gap in the coral outcroppings, Larry pointed downward to a white sand floor where three six-foot long requiem sharks lay resting on the bottom. When Kurt saw what Larry pointed out, they changed direction so as not to rile them.

Near one blue-veined fan coral, Kurt discovered a nesting area of colorful sea horses. Those tiny animals, most appearing to be no more than three inches tall, bobbed up and down with the current, clinging closely to the waving fan. The sea horse colors changed subtly as they dipped into the shade of the fan or rose into the diffused light from the penetrating sun. He reached out and grasped one of the little critters, holding it gently in his fingers so that he could look closer at its protruding eyes, round puckered lips, and ribbed carapace. It was a fascinating animal, and he could not wait to share the experience of seeing a 'herd' of seahorses with Madison.

After spending nearly an hour enjoying the splendor of the reef, the two men decided it was time to head back to shore. The brothers began the long slow swim back to land. They hadn't gone more than fifty yards when Larry grabbed hold of Kurt's arm and pointed toward his right. Three large white-tip reef sharks circled slowly, their thick grayish bodies swaying slowly near the surface.

Kurt and Larry drew closer together, but continued to head toward shore. Keeping a wary eye out on the sharks, both felt their hearts pounding and knew they each felt the same trepidation.

At one point, the largest of the three sharks made a darting pass beneath Kurt and Larry, briefly disappearing behind them as it passed below. Both men spun partly around in the water, frantically trying to keep that creature in view while still keeping a wary eye out on the other two sharks. That action slowed their progress momentarily until they saw the stalking animal swim back into position with the other two. Larry tapped Kurt on the arm, and rotated his hands in an overhand circle, indicating that they should try and speed-up their progress toward shore. Larry nodded agreement and quickened his pace and stroke, while he remained aware of the need to stay close to his brother.

After what seemed double the time it took to swim to the reef, the two snorkelers realized they were nearing shore. Off to their right, the sharks still swam nearby, their dorsal fins protruding from the glimmering surface of the sea.

Finally, after about twenty minutes of gut-wrenching swimming, they reached the point of land that led into the small cove where they had started. Turning into the sheltered waters, they took one last look around and realized that their finned 'friends' had disappeared. Each of them expelled a sigh of relief as they reached the small rock shelf where they had started. Exhausted, they collapsed onto the ground.

"Holy shit!" Larry exclaimed. "That was scary!"

Kurt merely looked at his brother, relieved, and humbled by the experience.

CHAPTER SEVENTEEN

As with everything in life, there comes a time when the next step must be taken. After three days in Negril, they all returned to Montego Bay.

Tiona and Charlie dropped the other three off at the docks and informed them they would be departing in the morning—flying back to San Diego to get married. Congratulations were made, along with promises to stay in touch. The girls cried. The men hugged one another affectionately.

∞

Larry opted to stay in town for a while.

Kurt and Madison boarded the *Explorer* and sat around talking with Jeffrey Smythe about their excursion to Negril. A large white cruise ship appeared at the entrance of the bay. While they talked, the cruise ship slowly and ponderously maneuvered into position to back into the u-shaped wharf where their ship lay tied alongside the back wall.

Realizing that the side walls of the embayment were obviously setup for a two-ship cruise terminal, Kurt, Madison and Jeffrey Smythe watched in fascination as the huge ship spun itself slowly around for a portside landing on the adjacent quay. It's immense size soon blotted out all vistas on that side of the bay and the towering shape of the large ocean liner loomed rather ominously above the decks of the now comparatively tiny *Explorer*.

As it backed down toward the back wall, both Jeffrey Smythe and Kurt thought it was backing faster than it should, all things considered. It was moving at a clip where they both thought it would have a difficult time stopping before it reached the retaining wall. Smythe commented, "Blimey, it seems to be backing at a ridiculously rapid pace!"

At that moment, a heavy plume of black smoke erupted from the smokestack of the large ship, and a shuddering rumble could be heard—perhaps even felt—on board their vessel. The ship had transferred its propulsion from reverse into forward in an effort to stop its momentum. Now in forward gear, its huge propellers were suddenly throwing a river of water abaft its stern. A swirling boil of water erupted from below its transom, whirling and gurgling against the back wall where the *Explorer* was tied. As the prop-wash churned, a surge built, and a river of current began to put a significant strain on the docking lines of the *Explorer*. Jeffrey Smythe, Kurt and Madison watched in morbid fascination as their ship began to tilt to port, its dock lines stretched and groaned as the thrust of water continued to roar against the retaining wall.

"Bloody Christ!" Jeffrey Smythe bellowed, "The bloody bastard's going to snap our dock lines or sink the bloody ship!"

Indeed, the *Explorer* was now listing precariously to port, her one-inch thick docking lines taught as bowstrings and whining loudly with the force of the strain. Still the prop-wash roared from beneath the hull of the huge ocean liner, and black smoke continued to billow from her stacks. Things were beginning to slide on the severely canted decks. Tables, deck chairs, everything that was not battened down or attached to something was sliding or tumbling across the deck.

Suddenly a sharp, ear-piercing snap occurred, followed by the dull thud of a broken spring-line thumping against the wall of the dining salon. A window broke, spilling broken shards of glass across the precariously tilted deck.

"Get down! Hang on, we're going over!" Jeffrey Smythe screamed out over the clamor.

Kurt reached out and grabbed Madison's arm, pulling her toward him as he slid off the deck chair where he watched the spectacle unfold. "Hold onto me!" Kurt cried out to Madison. "Try to move with me!" He instructed her as he tried desperately to pull himself and her up the tilted deck toward the nearby starboard rail. The ship listed so radically that it was impossible to get secure footing, and he was alarmed that they would soon tumble down the deck and crash into the port side, which was now at water level.

Just as it seemed inevitable that the vessel would roll, the stern line snapped. With a sharp cracking sound, the frayed end of the line shot back, and slammed into the galley wall.

No longer tethered to the quay with a stern line or the mid-ship spring-line, the ship began to level slightly as its stern swung outward, away from the concrete abutment. That swinging motion also caused the bow to crunch into the seawall. At the same time, the transom of the cruise ship thumped against the eight-foot tall rubber bastions built into the berth. With its momentum stopped, the helmsman disengaged the engines from forward and the turbulence in the bay began to settle.

Kurt had managed to gain a handhold on the starboard rail, and he and Madison clung together in obvious relief. Jeffrey Smythe had secured a hold on one of the upper deck supports and was beginning to relax his grip as the *Explorer* settled back to a level position.

Smythe looked forward and realized that without a spring and stern line, the bow of the ship was in jeopardy of again striking the concrete abutment. "Kurt, help me get another line attached at the stern."

Kurt worked with Smythe to re-secure the stern, tying the broken ends of the two snapped lines together with a bowline. Kurt then hopped over the rail onto the dock and ran it out and around one of the dock bollards. It was a temporary fix, but at least it prevented the bow from swinging into the dock and causing more damage.

The entire incident had occurred in just two or three minutes. Now that it was over, they all took a deep cleansing breath and looked around to see what damages had occurred. Other than the snapped lines, the only other visible damage was the broken window and a small hole punched into the galley wall from the end of the snapped spring line. Going to the stern to inspect the rail area, Smythe noticed that the aluminum skiff was gone, its painter dangled from a stern cleat with a section of the foredeck of the skiff still attached. Obviously, the skiff was on the bottom of the bay.

One of the crewmen aboard the cruise ship hollered down from above, "Is everyone all right?"

"Yes," Smythe responded, "but we've had some damages and will need to speak with your captain."

"Of course. It will be arranged."

Smythe then climbed up onto the dock and went forward to inspect the bow. Other than some scraped paint, there did not appear to be any issues. Smythe, Kurt, and Madison walked around the ship to look for other damages. A jar of mustard and a container of pancake batter had spilled onto the galley floor, tools were scattered around the engine room, and nearly all of the unattached deck and cabin furnishings were out of place, but no other significant problems were detected.

Settling back to await the arrival of the captain of the cruise ship, Smythe turned to Kurt and Madison and asked, "Anyone else feel they need a beer?"

"We'd love one if you have an extra." Kurt responded. At which point, Smythe went into the galley and brought out three cold Red Stripes.

They sat around and discussed the incident, rehashing the good fortune that had kept the ship from rolling over or anyone being injured. They marveled at the incredible power that the ocean liner generated when her engines went into forward and the ensuing amount of water turbulence that resulted. They all agreed they were very lucky.

A short while later, a well-dressed official, resplendent in a starched white uniform with epaulets on each shoulder, accompanied by two other lesser officers arrived at the dock and requested to come aboard.

The officer in charge introduced himself as the First Officer and informed Smythe that he represented the captain and would give him a report of the damages. Smythe pointed out the broken window, the snapped lines, and the bow section of the aluminum skiff that now dangled from its dock line. The First Officer took notes and agreed to return later in the afternoon when Captain Ellis was back on board. His list included: the broken window, two forty-five foot lengths of braided dock line, one fourteen-foot Valco aluminum skiff with a ten horsepower Johnson outboard motor, and the wall damage.

As darkness neared, Captain Ellis and Dawn returned to the ship, obviously intoxicated.

Jeffrey Smythe wasted no time in relating the incident that had occurred when the cruise ship docked. A dark scowl spread rapidly across the captain's face, and he started to berate Jeffrey Smythe for allowing the situation to develop. Smythe interrupted his tirade before it had a chance to get ugly.

"Wait, Captain. I believe you need to realize and acknowledge that we had absolutely no control over the situation. The ship spun around in the harbor and backed into position without any interaction on our part. We were helpless to do or say anything. Also, you should be made aware that we have made arrangements for full reimbursement for all the damages, and I will presume that remuneration will likely be more than the actual value of the damages."

"Who's going to pay the damages?" Captain Ellis demanded.

"The ship's captain has taken full responsibility. His First Officer has taken a list of the damages to the captain, and we expect his response soon."

That information seemed to mollify Captain Ellis, and he found a place to sit. Although he still appeared sullen, he sat quietly staring out at the lights of Montego Bay. Dawn pulled a chair over and sat quietly at his side.

It wasn't long before they heard footsteps approaching again on the dock. The First Officer and his two associates asked permission to come aboard.

"Please do," Jeffrey Smythe responded, stepping up to meet them at the boarding ladder.

"Excuse me, but I neglected to get your name," Smythe said to the First Officer.

"It's Hans. Hans Eversen."

"Yes, Hans. Thank you." Turning to Captain Ellis, Smythe introduced the two, acknowledging Dawn, Kurt and Madison, and Larry at the same time.

"So, what has your captain instructed?" Captain Ellis demanded.

"He has directed me to offer you forty-five hundred American dollars to compensate you for the unfortunate accident and loss of equipment. Do you find that acceptable?"

Captain Ellis eyed him coldly, calculating what replacement costs might be for the skiff and engine, new dock lines, and a new window. He realized that the offer was way more than the real value of the skiff and engine—after all, they were far from new. He contemplated for several minutes as the others watched him.

"Please tell your captain that I appreciate his offer but it is far short of the true value of the lost boat and engine and what it will cost to repair the damages and replace the lines. I believe the costs could run closer to ten thousand dollars."

"I see," Hans Everson replied. "I will take that information back to my captain. May we get back to you on this matter in the morning?"

'That would be satisfactory. Thank you." Captain Ellis responded. He pulled Dawn to her feet and walked away toward their cabin.

Jeffrey Smythe escorted Eversen and his two associates to the dock and bid them goodnight. When he returned, he commented, "That took a lot of nerve. The old skiff and engine could not be worth more than a grand at most. And the other items could not add-up to more than another thousand, even if a full-fledged carpenter made the window installation and repaired the crunch in the wall. It appears that our good captain is attempting to somewhat swindle the cruise ship. Ah, well, I guess that's his business. We'll see what happens."

∞

Early the following morning, the First Officer from the cruise ship arrived at the boarding ladder with two divers clad in full wetsuits. He announced that they intended to search the immediate area for the lost dinghy and engine and try to ascertain whether they were salvageable. Jeffrey Smythe could not come up with any reason to dissuade them from their effort; so they began a search.

After about twenty minutes, the divers resurfaced and announced that the bottom was so murky and full of sediment that it was virtually impossible to see or find anything. They aborted the effort.

Dawn returned to her cabin and reported the botched dive search to Captain Ellis. He remained there waiting for the next development.

A short while later, the First Officer returned with another gentleman, who identified himself as the Second Captain, Roger Dunleavy. They asked to meet with Captain Ellis. It was half an hour before Captain Ellis emerged from his cabin. In the interim, Kurt, Madison, Larry, and

Jeffrey Smythe conversed with Captain Dunleavy, about life aboard a luxury cruise ship. The conversation was enlightening and interesting, and resulted in a tour and dinner aboard the ship later that evening.

When Captain Ellis finally joined the group, Captain Dunleavy made a counter-offer of sixty-five hundred dollars. Captain Ellis reiterated the ten thousand dollar quote that had been tendered the previous day. Eventually, Ellis and Dunleavy agreed that the cruise line would pay seventy-five hundred dollars for the damages. They shook hands, and Dunleavy said that a check would be hand delivered later in the day and funds would be deposited in the local Bank of Jamaica so that it could be cashed without delay.

Later in the afternoon after the check was dropped off, Captain Ellis sent everyone ashore to perform certain tasks that he deemed necessary. Kurt, Madison, and Larry were sent off to find and make arrangements for a carpenter to repair the windows and cabin wall. Jeffrey Smythe was sent ashore to locate and get an estimate for a new skiff. Captain Ellis informed all of them that he would stay aboard with Dawn until they had completed their tasks, and then he would go to the bank and cash the check.

About two hours later, Kurt, Madison, and Larry returned to the ship to find it deserted. That was odd. Both Captain Ellis and Dawn were gone. They waited another half-hour until Jeffrey Smythe returned. When he did, Smythe went to the Captain's cabin and discovered what he expected. All their personal belongings were gone, and the cabin was empty. There was an envelope on the bunk with one thousand dollars cash inside—no note.

Obviously, Captain Ellis and Dawn had cashed the check and absconded with the remainder of the money.

Nobody could really blame them. They had not been paid for over two months, and there was nothing but uncertainty about the future of the *Explorer*. However, the Captain had negotiated the amount himself; and he did leave a small amount for operating funds.

Jeffrey Smythe took the money and put six hundred of it into a 'ship's fund' to pay for dockage fees, and fuel. He told the others that he expected Brian to return soon with additional funding and a plan for the immediate future. He then distributed one hundred dollars each to Madison, Kurt, and Larry. He kept one hundred for himself.

They sat around discussing this latest turn of events. It was bizarre that none of them had any vested interest in the ship; yet they were the only ones left on board to watch over the vessel.

Kurt, Madison, and Larry expressed a desire to return to Negril for another week or so—or at least until something transpired that would set them on a new path. Jeffrey agreed to remain aboard and stand watch during their absence.

∞

For the next two weeks, Kurt, Madison, and Larry once again enjoyed the beauty and tranquility of Negril. No word came from the *Explorer,* and they assumed that Smythe was content to watch the ship.

They secured one of the small bungalows at Awee-ma-way Village, with two beds, for the rate of seven dollars per night, which split between them was about what their budgets could afford. They caught fish and lobster, ate fresh fruits and vegetables that they picked from the many wild fruit trees and plants thriving in the nearby hills, and enjoyed the delightful bread-cakes.

To their big surprise, they met up with Sanford on the third day of their stay. He had gone to the opposite side of Jamaica for a couple of days, near Kingston, but soon began feeling bad vibes there. The social atmosphere in Kingston Town was heavily charged with anti-white sentiment, even away from the downtown area. He did not venture out at night and stayed mostly indoors while he contemplated what to do next.

When one of the friendly locals told Sanford about Negril, he boarded a bus, made the journey back over the mountains, and found his way to Negril. Once there, he connected with one of the local ladies and soon found himself staying at her little cottage just a few-hundred yards from where the trio were staying. The woman was his ideal type—large, friendly, and loving. She engulfed him with her munificence, smothering him with food and affection.

Her name was Sirene. At five feet-four and two hundred-thirty pounds, she suited his taste in women perfectly.

∞

Sirene had relocated to Negril a few months previously, having left the security and comfort of her family home in Kingston when the social climate began to deteriorate. Four of her friends had been gunned-down outside of her home by a band of marauding radicals, and both of her sisters were raped. She might have suffered the same fate had she not weighed nearly three hundred pounds at the time. For several weeks after the traumatic incident, she tried to persuade her parents to leave as well; but their home was their sanctuary, and they were not about to leave it because of a renegade band of radicals.

In her early teens, Sirene recognized that she was very adept at weaving palm-leaf hats, which for several years she sold to various stores in downtown Kingston. She saved all of the money she made selling the hats, and her personal wealth amounted to several thousand dollars. When she told her parents she was leaving for Negril, they gave her their blessing and assured her that her home would always be there whenever she wanted to return.

Sirene had only been in Negril about a month when she met Sanford. It surprised her that a good-looking white man would be interested in a heavy black-skinned Jamaican woman; but from the moment he introduced himself to her, he was friendly, courteous, and charming. She soon found herself laughing and enjoying his company immensely. It seemed a natural transition to take him back to her cottage.

When she met his friends from the *Explorer*, Kurt, Madison, and Larry, they too showed her considerable humor and friendliness; and they all enjoyed a couple of joyous weeks together in Negril.

Sirene and Madison enjoyed walking together through the densely forested terrain, chatting happily and appreciating each other's company. They also loved the wild fruits and vegetables they picked along the way; mangos, papaya, bananas, breadfruit and avocados were plentiful. They also discovered a tree loaded with otaheite (pronounced ota-eaty) apples, a firm tropical fruit that looks something like a red bell pepper but has a sweet and tasty white meat with a flavor something like an apple/pear combo.

Being roughly the same age, the two young women particularly enjoyed sharing the details of the very different lifestyles each had known and lived. The two made an 'odd couple' walking the streets and pathways of Negril—one a strikingly lovely American with an amazing head of thick blonde hair, the other a heavy-set Jamaican native with short-cropped black curly hair who walked barefoot. They created a sensation wherever they went.

∞

Both Kurt and Larry really enjoyed Sanford's company. He was a great storyteller and also a good listener. They spent many hours sitting around in the jungle-like atmosphere surrounding their cottage, or at the beautiful little cove where they swam and snorkeled, and talked and laughed about their pasts and shared their opinions on everything from sports to politics and, of course, women. Larry particularly liked to badger Sanford about his taste in women; but Sanford defended himself admirably, extolling the benefits of large women—like minimal competition for their favors—and described in great detail some of his finest moments in their boudoirs. Thankfully, Madison and Sirene were not around to hear his colorful recitals because they probably would have beaten him up, or at least never said a word to him again.

The days were glorious and peaceful, and they did a lot of exploring in the surrounding jungle. They met and shared good times and stories with several of the local natives, fascinated by their simple and idyllic lifestyles. They all shared many tokes of locally grown ganja, and Larry and Sanford partook quite regularly in the magic mushrooms that were so plentiful in the area (which they had learned to identify and gather out in the pastures where the cattle grazed). Kurt and Madison avoided the mushrooms, finding them too mind-altering for their tastes.

In the evenings, the friends often sat around on the porch of one of their tiny cottages, relishing the predictable tropical downpours that drenched the Island nearly every day. Those rains frequently brought brief gusty winds and occasional thunder and lightning. The storms hit quickly and with a vengeance, but dissipated rapidly. In their aftermath, a heavy pulsing quiet seemed to fill the air, creating a primordial atmosphere as the mists and vapors of the rains evaporated in the still and humid jungle.

∞

One night while Kurt, Madison and Larry sat idly on the porch, a raucous throbbing beat began to reverberate in the still night air. Looking around for the source of the clamor, they noticed a sporadic flickering of lights dancing erratically through the trees. Thumping in a melodic cadence, the beat pulsed through the jungle, growing in volume as the glow of light took on a fiery hue. Soon they could see a large group of people trudging along the jungle paths, carrying torches and pounding on drums while uttering a low guttural chant that carried eerily on the sultry night air.

Larry, who had consumed a few magic mushrooms earlier in the evening, seemed mesmerized. In order to get a better look at the activity, he walked out to the edge of the road and climbed up onto a limb of a large overhanging breadfruit tree. Perched on the limb, Larry watched in hallucinogenic fascination as the teeming mass of humanity approached.

There were nearly thirty individuals in the band, all obviously Jamaicans and all dressed in white flowing robes or muumuus. Some carried burning torches that cast a spectral glow in the dark jungle air. Others in the group pounded a steady rhythm upon bongo-style drums as they followed behind the torchbearers.

When they saw the throng of black-skinned natives brandishing torches and pounding on drums emerge from the shadows of the jungle, Kurt and the others tensed with dread and uncertainty. Not knowing what the mob was doing, they all gripped the arms of the lounge chairs tightly.

Spread out in a fan-like pattern, the chanting horde moved relentlessly toward the group of bewildered Americans. The Jamaicans covered a widening swath as the trees thinned out and they neared the grassy pastureland that housed the Awee-Ma-Way cottages.

When the ranting natives burst out into the open, the Americans watched wide-eyed as two of the big black men broke free from the formation and rushed forward brandishing what appeared to be a pitchfork-type instrument. One of the men reached out and scooped up a huge crab, lifted it into the air, and then lowered it dramatically into a large brown sack that the other man held. As he dropped the crab into the bag, a cheer rose from the others in the group, obviously extolling the success of the capture. Twice more the men raced forward and repeated the maneuver, capturing two more bluish/brown crabs in their contraption. Apparently satisfied that they had found all the crabs in the immediate area, the chanting assemblage moved away into the night in search of more—much to the relief of Kurt, Madison, and Larry.

Near the end of their second week at the cottage, Kurt, Larry, and Madison received a message through the Post Office in Negril that it was imperative that they return to the ship. They informed Sanford and Sirene that they needed to return to Montego Bay, and tearful farewells were made. Sanford informed them that he planned to stay for at least another week, in the event they might return again. If not, he promised to contact them when he could, after he returned to the States. Madison and Sirene exchanged addresses, with Madison pleading with Sirene to visit her in Hermosa Beach. Their goodbyes complete, Kurt, Madison, and Larry walked back to the main road and hitchhiked back to Montego Bay.

∞

Back at the ship, they found a burly man seated on the main deck talking with Jeffrey Smythe. Smythe introduced the man. "This is Cody. Cody Corcoran. He is one of the owners of the company."

Kurt appraised the man. He looked large and powerful, with the physique of a wrestler or football player. His muscled arms were heavily tattooed where they disappeared into his tight-fitting t-shirt. His unkempt blonde hair was turning to gray and quite curly. It spilled over his ears and was tied up in a small ponytail that dangled onto his nearly neck-less shoulders. His narrowly spaced eyes, gave him a porcine appearance as he peered from his heavily browed eye sockets.

Kurt thought he looked rather sinister.

He spoke slowly, his voice rumbled deeply in his chest, and informed them, "Jeffrey will be leaving the ship soon. He has found another vessel that he will deliver to Florida. He plans to depart within the next two to three days. I have crewmen from Canada arriving on Friday. You three must find other accommodations as soon as they arrive."

Having said that, Cody stood abruptly and walked away slowly and heavily, and disappeared into the Captain's cabin.

Kurt, Madison, and Larry looked at each other. "Well, I guess we'd better figure out what we do now," Larry commented.

Before the others had a chance to comment, Jeffrey Smythe spoke, "I could use help. I have arranged to deliver a forty-seven foot steel-hulled sailboat from here to Fort Lauderdale. The owner offered to pay me fifteen hundred dollars to deliver the boat, and I would be willing to take all three of you aboard to assist. I cannot pay you much since the fee must cover expenses. I might be able to give each of you a small amount once the delivery is made, but I cannot say right now how much that might be."

His offer led to a lively discussion between Kurt, Madison, and Larry. None of them had done much sailing, with the exception of two short day-sails that Kurt had made. They discussed the time that it might take to get to Florida with Jeffrey Smythe. He stated that there were a couple of options to consider.

Smythe explained that the owner of the sailboat expressed no concern about the amount of time it might take to get the boat back to Florida—he would in fact prefer it did not arrive for at least two to three weeks so that he could make slip arrangements. He explained further that there were indeed two options for getting the boat to Florida. Option one was to sail the boat around the western end of the Cayman Islands, up the Gulf Stream and directly to Fort Lauderdale. He estimated that trip would take perhaps four or five days, depending on wind and current. The other option was to sail around Cuba into the southern Bahamas, then slowly sail through the Bahamas to Florida. That trip could take anywhere from two to six weeks, depending on the emphasis they put on travel time.

Kurt, Madison, and Larry discussed this new twist to their adventure. They were already so far beyond their original five-week schedule that all three decided that another few weeks did not really matter that much, as long as they could receive room and board.

They agreed to go with Jeffrey Smythe and take the long way to Florida through the Bahamas. There was no deadline set. All agreed that they would just go with the flow.

Beginning that afternoon and for the following two days, the trio worked with Jeffrey Smythe to provision and prepare the sailboat for the journey.

Chapter Eighteen

The sailing sloop *Cozy* exhibited overall neglect. The absolute worst thing for a boat is to sit in disuse. Everything on a boat works best when it is kept operating and in regular use, particularly the mechanical and electrical systems. Lack of use causes things to rust, freeze-up, and become unwieldy and brittle. All of those things were evident in the *Cozy*.

On the bright side, she had good lines, the sails and rigging appeared solid and in good condition, and the engine—although rusted on the outside—started on cue. While Jeffrey Smythe checked and readied the rigging gear and gave the old two-cylinder Ford Lehman diesel a thorough going-over, Madison, Kurt, and Larry worked on the dirty and similarly neglected interior. With a bucket of soapy water and scrub brushes, the *Cozy* soon began to look ship-shape—if not Bristol.

The marina where the sailboat was moored was less than two short blocks from the *Explorer's* dock, so it was very convenient to go from one boat to the other. All four of them stayed with Cody aboard the *Explorer* until the morning they were ready to depart.

The night before departure, they all went to a local pub with Cody. They reminisced about their adventures aboard the ship, and all of the fun times they had shared. After dining, they picked up a quart of rum and some fruit mix and returned to the *Explorer* for cocktails.

Back on board, Cody went about mixing pineapple/coconut/mango rum punch, emphasis on the rum. It wasn't long before all of them were rip-roaring smashed.

Cody did not talk much, other than to briefly inform them that he was planning to deliver the *Explorer* to Florida as soon as his new crew arrived.

Jeffrey Smythe seemed particularly exuberant, and his joking and story-telling soon had the others laughing heartily—all except Kurt.

Kurt was troubled because it seemed obvious to him that Jeffrey Smythe was performing primarily for Madison; and she seemed to be relishing the attention. His mood darkened, and he developed an alcohol headache. Even though he felt surly, he was not inclined to leave. He did his best to dismiss his growing jealousy, but the more he watched the interaction between the two, the more he became convinced that a connection had developed between Madison and Jeffrey Smythe that he simply did not like. Finally shortly before daylight, the rum bottle was empty, and the party broke up.

When Kurt and Madison went to their sleeping quarters, they prepared for sleep without any personal intimacy. That disappointed Kurt. He had envisioned their final night aboard the *Explorer* as a night for romance, a final culmination of their adventure and an opportunity to seal the memories with a passionate round of lovemaking. It was not to be. They fell asleep with nothing more than a brief peck on the lips.

∞

The following day did not go quite as planned. They intended to head to the *Cozy* early in the morning, make a quick final check of the boat, and set sail for Port Antonio, located near the eastern end of the island about one hundred-twenty miles away. However they all suffered from intense hangovers and it was nearly noon before they pulled themselves together enough to cast off.

Jeffrey Smythe calculated that under sail it would take them approximately eighteen to twenty hours to make Port Antonio, depending on the usually reliable northeast trade winds that prevail along the Jamaican coast. They dropped their mooring lines at approximately noon and set sail out of Montego Bay.

Cozy was aptly named. She was built in the mid-fifties at a yard just outside of New Orleans that specializes in steel-hulled sailboats. Designed for sailing, with a low profile and narrow beam, her berths were roomy and spacious, with adequate headroom for both Kurt and Larry. There were four berths; so Kurt and Madison were given the master's quarters in the stern section, and Smythe and Larry took the two side berths. The forward berth served to store their minimal belongings and extra supplies.

Because they would be sailing through the night, Jeffrey Smythe set a four-hour watch schedule. Smythe would serve watch with Madison and Kurt with Larry. That arrangement did not sit well with Kurt, but he recognized the logic of the watch assignments. Neither Madison nor Larry had any sailing experience at all; therefore, watch duties needed to be setup with one 'experienced' crewman on each watch.

It soon became evident that Jeffrey Smythe knew his way around a sailboat.

After they dropped lines and motored out of the entrance to the bay, Smythe immediately began a crash-course in sailing instruction. He initiated his training course by verbally describing the purpose and location of the rigging, wenches, and sheets—the lines (ropes) used for adjusting the sails. He then went about explaining the general points of setting sails and tending the rigging. After explaining the basic steps of hoisting and trimming sails, Smythe climbed out onto the deck with Kurt and Larry and talked them through raising the main halyard and the jib. As with most boats constructed in the 1950's, the rigging was basic and solid. The bronze wenches and deck hardware were all in good condition, and the rigging all looked ship-shape.

After cranking up the mainsail and jib, the three men returned to the cockpit area where Smythe demonstrated how to trim the sheets and adjust course to maximize hull speed. Due to the angle of the prevailing winds and their desired course, it was a fine line between maintaining a solid close-reach and spilling the wind, which would slow their forward progress and—if they were not careful—could cause a broach. Smythe showed them how to tighten or loosen the sheets in order to adjust the trim. It was a fascinating learning experience, and each of them took turns at the helm and on the wenches. Within a couple of hours, Jeffrey Smythe seemed comfortable with their individual abilities to hold course and adjust the sails as needed. Since they were all relatively fresh and would have most of the afternoon to practice, Smythe posted Kurt and Larry on the first helm watch; and he and Madison would take second watch. That way, Smythe could keep a good eye on Kurt and Larry's technique and capabilities during daylight hours.

Sailing became a new experience for all except Smythe. The movement through the water, the heeling angle of the hull and deck, and the diminutive size of the *Cozy* as compared to the *Explorer,* were radically different. As a consequence, Kurt became seasick in less than two hours. His head-pounding hangover likely contributed to his overall condition.

Kurt felt it coming on as queasiness in his abdomen. Soon he had a dull pounding ache in the back of his neck and head, and he began to feel the uncomfortable swallowing reflex that always precedes the heaves.

He felt frustrated when he recognize what was happening—he hadn't been seasick since he went fishing in a small skiff with his father at age fourteen.

When he began to retch, Kurt moved to the stern on the starboard downwind side of the boat so as not to spew vomit on the decks, or the others. It angered him that he was sick. After all, he had spent much more time at sea than the others—except Smythe—and he believed that getting seasick was a sign of weakness.

Fortunately for Kurt, vomiting until the dry-heaves ended seemed to cure him. He felt weak, and his head pounded; but soon he was back in the cockpit tending to the helm to give Larry a break. Madison brought him some bread to munch on and water to drink, persuading him that it would help. She was right. After he swallowed about a quart of water and ate a half-loaf of Jamaican bread-cake, Kurt felt better. Madison tended to him with care and consideration, quite obviously concerned and showing compassion.

∞

For Madison, Larry, and Jeffrey Smythe, sailing along the scenic Jamaican coastline was a true pleasure. They held a course running about eight-miles offshore where the prevailing trade winds were not affected by the land contours or sea-floor irregularities. As the afternoon wore on, the shadows of the Blue Mountains darkened into a deep indigo, in sharp contrast to the verdant fields of sugarcane and tobacco that covered the lower plains. There was no other boat traffic, and the only sounds were the whistling of the wind in the rigging and the sloshing of the waves against the hull. Eventually, once Kurt had overcome the worst of his seasickness, he too began to appreciate the scenery if not the boat's motion.

Madison went below to prepare a light meal, and Smythe went with her. When they were out of earshot, Kurt turned to Larry and vented his uneasiness about Madison and Smythe.

"I really don't like those two being together on watches all the time. I don't trust him."

"Oh, don't worry." Larry responded. "She's just enjoying herself. She has obviously taken to sailing and is having fun. There's nothing between her and Smythe. I mean, after all, look at him. He's not exactly the prize specimen of a man."

"No, maybe not, but she sure seems to find him amusing." Kurt commented as Madison's lilting laughter wafted out of the galley.

"Trust me, Kurt," Larry reassured him. "There's nothing for you to worry about."

Soon after they had finished eating the sandwiches, Jeffrey Smythe announced that he and Madison would take over the watch. It was nearing nightfall, and he suggested that Larry and Kurt catch a few hours of sleep because the midnight watch would be upon them sooner than they might expect.

Kurt and Larry went below; but for Kurt, sleep was impossible. He was tired, and he still wasn't feeling good and his mind kept running around the fact that he was in his bunk and Madison sat in the cockpit with Jeffrey Smythe. He tried to let go of the nagging doubts. Eventually he drifted off into a troubled light sleep.

Midnight did arrive much sooner than he expected, and Kurt had a tough time crawling out of his bunk. He brushed his teeth, which helped a lot, and went out to receive instructions from Smythe.

They had made a slight course alteration, and it became easier to maintain steerage on their new heading. Smythe explained that they were veering slightly farther out to sea on the new course, and there was no longer any sign of land. "Hold a course of eighty-five degrees. That should allow us to put considerable distance under the keel and make a good approach into Port Royal in the morning." He stood and went below.

Madison remained sitting in the cockpit. She seemed to be particularly exhilarated. A contented smile lit up her lovely features, her hair turned curly from the moisture in the air, and her eyes shone with excitement. She turned to Kurt and commented, "Oh, Kurt, it is so perfect out here. I love the feel of the wind, the sounds of the ocean, and the beauty and tranquility of it all."

Kurt smiled back at her, pushing his inner feelings of jealousy aside. He stepped into the cockpit and sat next to her, laying his hand on the soft cotton of her gray sweatpants. "Yes, it is beautiful," he commented softly. "There is nothing like being at sea."

She leaned into him, and rested her head on his shoulder.

The night was dark with only a sliver of a waning moon and a million stars overhead. Kurt and Madison sat together quietly, enjoying the comfort and pleasure of sharing a few peaceful moments together. After cuddling a while, Madison went below to get some rest.

During the next few hours, Kurt and Larry talked about the significant differences between cruising on the *Explorer* and sailing on the *Cozy*. They chatted animatedly, becoming accustomed to the heel and roll of the boat over the swells and finding it increasingly easy to hold course. It came as a surprise when Jeffrey Smythe popped out of the cabin and announced that he was there to take over the four a.m. watch.

Kurt shared the fact that there was basically nothing to report. The watch was uneventful and everything was in order.

Madison emerged from the cabin also, looking sleepy but bright-eyed. She had bundled-up in her sweat pants and sweater, with an extra sweatshirt of Kurt's hanging loosely around her shoulders. Kurt thought she looked sweet and vulnerable, and wished he could stay out on deck with her. He spoke with her briefly, inquired innocuously about how she slept and if she needed anything. She responded distractedly to him, seemingly anxious to get to the cockpit and assume 'her duties' at the helm. Kurt kissed her lightly on the cheek before she turned away and took a seat next to Jeffrey Smythe.

Kurt slept well that night, although he awakened a little early. When the sun lit the morning sky, Kurt climbed wearily out of his bunk and went up on deck.

He emerged from the cabin to find Madison leaning against Jeffrey Smythe with her head nestled against his left arm and chest. Smythe held the wheel with his right hand. For a brief moment Smythe released the wheel, tipped his head toward Madison and put his index finger to his lips to indicate quiet.

Inwardly Kurt seethed. Outwardly he gave a slight smile.

Kurt's presence woke Madison, and she lifted her head dreamily to look up at him. She blinked sleepily for a moment then sat upright. "Oh. I must have dozed off. Good morning."

She turned and looked at Smythe. "I'm sorry, Jeff. I neglected my duties. I didn't realize how tired I was."

"No problem. The night was calm, and everything is under control. When you drifted off to sleep, I simply could not see any reason not to let you rest." Smythe told her.

"But I am supposed to be on watch to help and to keep you awake. It won't happen again," she said.

"Trust me," Smythe responded. "If there was anything amiss, or if you were needed for anything, I certainly would have aroused you."

Kurt wasn't quite sure how he felt about the situation. At first, he was troubled at the sight of Madison cuddled up against Smythe. After thinking over the situation, he realized that she had likely fallen asleep out of boredom, and he found that oddly reassuring. He determined to let the episode go.

The commotion on deck also awakened Larry, who emerged from down below and joined them in the cockpit.

"Hey. What's going on?" He asked casually.

"Oh, not much," Kurt informed him. "We're just sitting here enjoying the morning."

∞

It was a beautiful morning. The trade winds blew steady at about fifteen knots, and the swells averaged around three feet. The distant coastline of Jamaica transformed from black to blue, and a few low clouds scudded across the azure sky. *Cozy* sailed along smartly on a starboard tack at around eight knots, her sleek hull sliding almost silently across the deep blue Caribbean Sea. According to Smythe's dead-reckoning calculations, Port Antonio was not more than two-hours distant.

Madison and Kurt went below and prepared a simple breakfast. Kurt asked how her watch was. Madison replied casually that it was completely uneventful but she felt very embarrassed about falling asleep. Kurt assured her that he did not believe any harm was done and the extra sleep probably did her some good. They took the food into the cockpit and ate heartily. Kurt felt much better.

On arrival a couple of hours later, Port Antonio looked very similar to Montego Bay, although not as large or busy. It was also not nearly as clean and tidy as Montego Bay, at least near the waterfront. Most of the buildings looked dirty and needed a fresh coat of paint. A noticeable British flavor influenced the architecture, mixed-in with the traditional thatched-hut and palm-frond structures of the islands.

Cozy and its crew rounded the shores of Navy Island, a small picturesque island in the center of the entrance to Port Antonio. They dropped anchor in the center of the cove. Because they were flying the Jamaican flag and had a letter of delivery from Montego Bay, entering through Customs was not necessary, although upon arrival a small tender with two port officials pulled alongside and made a brief inspection of their papers. Satisfied that all was in order, they bid the crew a good day and departed.

Port Antonio is recognized as a port of layover for ships and boats transiting to and from the Bahamas. Because it is the nearest point of land to Cuba, there is also a heavy visitation pattern and Cuban influence in its citizenry. It also serves as the primary port for the export of coconuts and bananas as well as tobacco grown in the hills of Jamaica.

Kurt, Larry, and Madison went ashore and visited a cafe while Jeffrey Smythe went in search of a fuel pump that had begun acting up. While drinking coffee with a group of locals, the trio learned a bit of history about the port. Due to its proximity to Cuba, many of the inhabitants speak Spanish as well as English, with a twist of Jamaican slang tossed into the mix. It made it interesting, if not difficult, to follow the conversation of the natives.

After coffee and sweet rolls, the trio returned to the *Cozy*. Jeffrey Smythe worked in the engine room installing a new fuel pump, the pungent smell of diesel fuel permeating the air in the hot engine compartment. He was shirtless and sweaty, and his pasty-white skin had odd patches of red across the shoulders, either a birthmark or some sort of rash. It was the first time any of them had seen him shirtless, and Kurt smiled inwardly when he saw Madison's surprised reaction to Jeffrey's scrawny unclothed upper torso. She actually grimaced.

"Need any help?" Kurt asked.

"Nope, I'm almost done. Just one more bolt to tighten down, and I'll give her a test."

Smythe emerged from the engine compartment, and wiped the sweat from his face and shoulders. "Spilled a bit of diesel fuel," he said, "I even splashed a bit on my arms and stomach. It kind of burns the skin. Excuse me while I take a quick plunge and rinse off."

That afternoon, Jeffrey Smythe perused a set of old Caribbean charts, and plotted a course that would take them around the eastern end of Cuba and through the often treacherous Windward Passage between Cuba and Haiti—which shares the island of Hispaniola with the Dominican Republic.

After settling on a route, he shared his thoughts with his shipmates. "We have a somewhat uncertain journey ahead of us for the next couple of days. I've looked closely at the weather forecasts, and there appears to be a high-pressure ridge that may bring very little wind for the next twenty-four hours. After that, a low-pressure system may be developing that might affect our next passage. Right now, it appears the system will remain to the south, passing over the southern regions of the Bahamas; but its effects could impact our projected travels. If we head out as planned, we could encounter some difficult sailing. On the other hand if we wait too much longer, we are in danger of encountering yet another larger low-pressure system that is currently brewing off the coast of Africa that could develop into a hurricane. What are your thoughts?"

Kurt caught a glimpse of dread in Madison's eyes, and he remembered that she had expressed concerns about hurricanes earlier in the trip. He did not want her to fret over potential perils of their voyage. He looked at Larry, who merely shrugged as if to say 'Whatever! I'll go along with anything.'

Kurt turned back to Jeffrey Smythe. "What is your suggestion? We are not as familiar with weather in this region as you are, and we don't want to put ourselves into jeopardy."

Smythe looked at each appraisingly, and lingered for a moment on Madison. "I say we go for it. It's likely the weather disturbance that is closest will remain to the south. If we can clear the Windward Passage and reach Great Inagua Island, we will be much closer to the Banks where there are several 'hurricane holes' where boaters can hole-up from foul weather. On the other hand, the longer we wait, the greater the potential for storm development. I vote for departing tomorrow."

Kurt looked at Madison and Larry, who both shrugged, and turned back to Smythe. "Okay, we're with you. What time do you want to leave in the morning?"

"I suggest we depart at first light. If we depart early, we might pick up an offshore breeze as the land warms. That could help us reach the Windward Passage before nightfall, even if we need to motor all the way. I'm estimating about forty-eight hours to make the roughly three hundred-twenty mile passage to Great Inagua, depending on wind and current. If all goes well, we would arrive at the island in the early morning and would have good light for locating the entrance to Mathew Town, the only port on the island."

They looked at each other and nodded. They would depart at first light.

Duties were split up to prepare for departure. Kurt and Madison went out to pick up additional food items, ice, and other supplies needed for the next few days. Jeffrey Smythe remained on board tidying up the ship and stowing away loose items. After a light meal that Madison prepared with Kurt, they all went out to have a drink. Jeffrey Smythe informed the others that he would buy drinks, and several hours later all four were feeling 'in the chips.'

They were drinking in a small pub near the waterfront where they'd made friends with a group of local residents. Included in the group were several comely young Jamaican women. For the most part, those girls sat quietly and listened to the animated conversations.

After about four drinks, Kurt suggested to Madison that they head back to the boat. He hoped that they might find a short time alone. She informed him that she was having a really good time; but if he wanted to leave, she would meet him back on the boat a little later. Against his judgment, he headed the few-hundred yards back to the *Cozy*.

Back on board, Kurt sat on the foredeck gazing at the stars for a while. A little later, he went below and prepared for bed. When he finished, he went up to the cockpit to look back toward the pub. He did not like leaving Madison there with Jeffrey Smythe, even though Larry was with her.

Kurt froze in his tracks as he stepped up to the cockpit. On the bench seat sat one of the young Jamaican girls from the pub. She smiled at his surprised expression.

She spoke to him in her musical Jamaican voice, the British accent trilling on the still tropical air. "I do not like seeing you wandering off to be alone. I think that maybe you would like some company?"

He was dumbstruck. She was a lovely young lady. Her dark ebony skin glowed in the soft lights from the distant waterfront, and her long black hair reflected the shine from the stars overhead. She wore a plain white cotton blouse, buttoned along the front, and a short flowered skirt that ended several inches above her knees. She sat with her bare feet, and long, silky smooth legs extended out and crossed casually, she was a vision of beauty and sexuality. Kurt swallowed, unable to speak.

She uttered a low guttural laugh. Her slim fingers reached out and nimbly unbuttoned her blouse. Kurt watched transfixed. She spread the blouse open and exposed her full burnished breasts, purposefully jutting them forward to enhance their fullness and suppleness. Their smooth roundness glowed, and the tender buds of her dark purple nipples protruded vibrantly from their center.

"Do you like these?" She asked suggestively.

Unable to respond, Kurt continued to stand there dumbly, fascinated by her comeliness and audacity. She reached out and took his hand, pulling him toward her. As he stumbled against her, she took both of his hands and placed them over her breasts.

Her breasts felt warm, firm, and delightfully pliable. He felt an instantaneous arousal in his loins, a dry lump formed in his throat. He stifled a moan as he looked down at the erotic dark loveliness that was being offered. He was about to succumb when he sensed movement in the nearby shadows of the wharf. He turned to look but saw nothing.

That brief distraction brought him out of his trance, and he immediately thought of Madison.

He looked back at the lovely young lady seated before him, his hands still cupped over her exquisite breasts. He released them, stepped back, and coughed self-consciously. "I'm sorry, I shouldn't be doing this. The girl in the pub is my girlfriend. She should be coming back here soon, and I... I don't think I should be doing this."

The young lady smiled up at him, but she cocked her head sideways in a shrug of indifference that seemed to say, 'Well it's your loss.' She buttoned her blouse, swung her feet to the deck, and looked up into Kurt's eyes. "You're a good man. Your girlfriend is a lucky woman." With that, she turned and stepped onto the dock; and with one lingering look back at Kurt, walked away.

Kurt stood watching her go, his arousal still evident. He wished Madison were there with him. He sat on the cockpit seat and gradually felt his body relax. He felt comfortably intoxicated, partly from the alcohol and partly from the tantalizing sexual encounter. He wished again that Madison would return. He wondered whether he should go back to the pub and ask her again to return to the *Cozy* with him. He could not make up his mind and, eventually, dozed off on the seat.

∞

Madison left the pub shortly after Kurt. Larry and Jeffrey Smythe were engrossed in animated conversations with the locals—Larry fascinated with one of the young Jamaican women. Smythe was involved in a philosophical discussion with one of the tall black bartenders about island politics and the Rastafarian movement.

Madison felt good, slightly inebriated, and looked forward to spending at least a short while alone with Kurt—long enough, she hoped, to share an interlude of physical closeness. Her limbs tingled in anticipation, and she hurried her steps.

As she rounded the edge of the last building that lined the wharf, she paused briefly in the shadows to see if Kurt was on deck. What she saw caused her jaw to drop, and her hand flew to her lips to stifle a gasp. Kurt stood before one of the beautiful black-skinned girls that had been in the pub. His hands held her bare breasts. She could see the stark white teeth of the buxom young woman, glowing in the darkness as she looked up at Kurt. Madison stepped back behind the wall of the building, tears brimming in her eyes. She shook her head as if to clear it of the image she had just witnessed, then peeked around the corner one more time, hoping that maybe her eyes had played a trick upon her. Nothing had changed. Kurt still stood before the young girl, looking somewhat awkward, but his two hands still cupped the full, ripe breasts of the young Jamaican girl. Madison turned and fled.

She ran for about two blocks, blinded by the tears that flowed freely down her flushed, burning cheeks. Tiring, she wandered aimlessly for a while until two tall and dark Jamaican men stepped out of the shadows and blocked her path.

Her reaction was immediate, "Just get away from me. I want to be alone." Her voice carried the tone of her anguish, and her demeanor reflected the depths of her misery.

The night was deathly quiet. In the darkness, the whites of the eyes of the two large Jamaicans glowed like beacons in their dark shadowed faces. After a prolonged pause, one of them spoke deeply. "You in trouble, little lady?"

"No! I just want to be left alone."

They stood in her way, blocking her passage on the narrow, dirt path. One of them spoke to her in a deep heavily accented voice. "Look here, little lady, it is not so safe for a young white woman to be walking these streets alone at night. Where you going?"

Madison did not answer. She merely stood stoically before them, a forlorn expression on her brow.

At that moment, another man approached from the direction that Madison had come from. He paused near the three figures, then commented while casting a suspicious glare at the other two Jamaican men, "Hey! You are the lady from the boat on the wharf. What you doing out here?"

When Madison did not answer, one of the other two men responded in a strong Jamaican dialect. "She out alone. We find her walking alone. She crying. She very sad. We do not know where she come from."

Eyeing the other two appraisingly, the man from the pub talked to the other two for a few moments in their unique language. He informed them that he knew where she was from and that he was going to take her back. They accepted his assertiveness, and watched as he walked away with Madison.

Upon her return to the boat, Kurt sat in the cockpit, sleeping lightly. He awoke immediately when he sensed a presence on the dock. Rubbing the sleep from his eyes, Kurt greeted Madison with a cheerful 'Hi.' while gazing distrustfully at the tall Jamaican figure by her side. Madison ignored his greeting, muttered a short comment of thanks to her escort, and went below.

The stranger turned to Kurt. "You need to take better care of your woman. She was wandering the street. She could have gotten into big trouble."

Kurt glanced back toward the cabin, reflecting on her obviously unhappy disposition.

"Thank you for taking care of her. I thought she was still in the pub with my two friends."

The big man stood solemnly before Kurt, and stated firmly once again; "You need to take care of your woman." He then turned and ambled away.

∞

Kurt went below, anxious to find out what had happened. Madison was in the head with the door closed. She remained in there for an inordinate amount of time before emerging. Without looking at Kurt, she slipped immediately into the master bunk that they shared.

Kurt sat on the edge of the bunk. "Madison, what's wrong?" She did not respond. "What happened?" Again, she did not respond. "Madison, why did that man bring you back here and tell me that you were walking the streets?"

"I'm just tired. I have a headache, and I don't want to talk." She curled up and pulled the sheet over her entire body and turned away.

Kurt sat on the edge of the bunk for a long time, hoping that she might respond. After a while, he gave up and crawled in beside her. She did not move, and he made no effort to reach out for her, although he longed to wrap his arms around her. His mind raced, wondering what had happened, whether she had seen him with the young Jamaican girl. What had caused her to roam the streets of a strange and reportedly dangerous city and had anything bad or disturbing occurred?

After a while, he dozed fitfully, waking several times during the night; each time hoping that she might react to his subtle efforts to cuddle. Although she did not react, he could sense a shield of rigidity around her, and her normal purring snore was not in evidence. Sometime later he heard Jeffrey Smythe return and climb into his berth, followed a short time later by Larry.

∞

Before daybreak, Jeffrey Smythe was up and making last minute preparations to get underway. Kurt responded almost immediately to the commotion, sliding out of his bunk to help Smythe get things ready for departure. Larry could be heard snoring loudly in his berth. Madison remained curled under her sheet, and appeared to be in the exact position that she had remained in throughout the night.

Smythe instructed Kurt on how he planned to depart, directing him to cast off the bow lines first, keeping the stern line attached to the bollard so that the *Cozy* could pivot away from the dock smoothly. Kurt did as he was told. After letting the diesel warm-up for a few minutes, they were underway.

Leaving Port Antonio was uneventful. A low-hanging mist hung over the nearby hillsides and spread out a couple of miles to sea. The air was still, and quite obviously the city had not yet come to life. Only a few dim lights were visible on shore as they slowly made their way out of the port, cleared Navy Island, and encountered the glassiness of the abnormally calm Caribbean Sea.

Kurt went below to brew a pot of coffee, and glanced toward his bunk hoping to see movement from Madison. There was none. He remained below as the kettle brewed; and when it was done, poured two cups and went up on deck where Jeffrey Smythe sat at the helm. He handed him a cup of the strong smelling rich Jamaican coffee, and Smythe uttered a guttural, "Thanks." Kurt took a seat on the opposite berth and sipped his coffee. Neither spoke as the sun lightened the morning sky, turning the soft gray into a flaming orange. As the sun rose, the orange glow turned crimson, and Kurt recalled the ominous lore of the sea: 'Red sky in morning, sailors take warning.' When the sun burst above the skyline, the sky instantly shed its fiery hue, and turned cobalt blue within minutes. An eerie stillness blanketed the glistening sea, nothing more than a slight undulation visible on an otherwise mirrored surface. In the quiet, the throb of the two-cylinder diesel pulsated with an almost musical rhythm on the warm tropical air.

Finished with his coffee, Kurt asked Jeffrey Smythe, "Want another cup?"

"Sure."

Kurt went below and poured two more cups. He glanced toward Madison to see if anything had changed. She looked as she had before. Larry continued to snore.

Kurt took the steaming coffee back on deck and handed a cup over to Smythe, who did not react at all. Kurt sat back on the cockpit seat and sipped on his second cup. When it was empty, he set the cup down and sat staring out at sea. Smythe had nothing to say, and for more than an hour the *Cozy* putted slowly across the glassy ocean.

Finally, after making about ten miles from port, Kurt heard movement down below. He stood and went down the companionway.

"Good morning." He offered cheerfully. Madison turned and looked directly into his eyes.

"Good morning. I'm sorry I slept so late. I'm afraid I am a little hung-over."

Kurt searched her eyes and features for any sort of underlying antagonism, rancor, or resentment. He could not detect anything unusual. "Did you sleep well? I was a little concerned last night when you returned to the boat. You seemed quite upset."

"Oh, I'm sorry. I just had too much to drink, and I think I got foolish and went off for a walk by myself. A nice man found me out wandering and escorted me back to the boat. I was not feeling well at all, and I think I may have thrown up. I hope I didn't upset you?"

"Well," Kurt confessed, "I was concerned and worried. When you didn't come back to the boat right away, I was planning to go back to the pub and walk you home, but I dozed off. Next thing I know, you were on the docks with that Jamaican fellow, and you seemed quite disturbed."

"Again, I'm sorry. I just drank too much."

Kurt began to feel relieved that she had apparently not seen his interaction with the young Jamaican girl. Even though he felt that he was innocent of any wrongdoing, it still would have been a difficult thing to explain. Madison seemed in relatively good spirits and appeared to hold no resentment of any kind. He moved to her side and wrapped his arms around her. She stiffened slightly, but then turned to him and hugged him back, nestled her head into his chest and clung to him for a long moment. When she relaxed her embrace, she stepped back and looked deeply into his bright hazel eyes. He stared back into hers, thinking to himself that he could discern a veil in her sparkling blue gaze. But that cloudiness disappeared rapidly, and her eyes shined vividly, reflecting the azure tints from the early morning sky. She held his hand as they walked together up the steps and into the bright morning sunlight.

"Good morning, Jeffrey." Madison greeted him cheerfully. "I'm sorry that I was not up and about to help us get underway."

"Top of the morning to you, Miss Madison. It was not a problem at all. Kurt and I managed to cast off without any difficulties." He paused, and looked from one to the other. "If you wouldn't mind, I could use a little relief at the helm."

"I'll take it." Madison offered quickly and moved out into the cockpit as she slid in next to Jeffrey Smythe.

"Thanks, Madison. Keep her on a heading of forty-five degrees for now. We want to avoid getting too close to Cuba but still cut the route as short as possible. I will make a course adjustment in a couple of hours."

Jeffrey Smythe went below, and Madison and Kurt settled in next to each other behind the helm. *Cozy* ran smoothly under power at around six knots. Not a breath of wind stirred, and the seas remained oily calm with only a minimal swell undulating gently beneath the keel. With a thirty-five-gallon fuel tank and a range of about one hundred forty miles, it was imperative that they find some wind—the existing fuel would carry them only about half of the distance to Great Inagua Island.

The air grew hot and humid. Except for the movement of the boat through the water, an odd stillness almost palpitated. The sun burned down from the heavens with a vengeance, beating down on the deck and cabin top. The only relief from the scorching sun came from the small bimini top that covered the aft portion of the cockpit. Kurt and Madison moved backward onto the aft rail cap in order to find at least some shade. Sweat ran down their cheeks and dripped from their chins and noses. They had both stripped down to their swimming suits, but their bodies soaked in perspiration. Kurt periodically hauled a bucket of seawater aboard to splash over their skin in an effort to keep cool. Even though the seawater was a tepid eighty-four degrees, it did provide a little cooling effect, particularly with the flow of air created from the moving vessel.

Larry came out on deck a short while later, and complained about the heat and humidity. "God it's hot!" He exclaimed. "Where's the wind when you need it?"

Jeffrey Smythe stayed below. When he returned to the deck, he informed the others that he had been listening to radio reports about the weather; and that at least for now, it appeared they would not be impacted by the developing low-pressure system forming in the southeast.

For three more hours, the *Cozy* chugged along under power, putting another twenty miles under the keel. The vague outline of the coast of Cuba materialized in the distance.

Suddenly a hissing sound came from inside the cabin, and a wispy cloud of mist poured from the companionway. "Damn!" Smythe bellowed. "We've got an engine problem! Shut her down," he ordered Madison. Stunned by the sudden turn of events, Madison froze momentarily, seemingly unsure of what to do. Kurt leapt forward, reached down, and pulled the kill-switch. The engine coughed, then died altogether. A hush fell over the boat.

Jeffrey Smythe was already down the companionway and pulled up the engine cover. He looked in dismay at the cloud of white steam engulfing the engine. He waved his hands and arms ineffectually in an effort to disperse some of the mist. Slowly the cloudiness evaporated, and he was able to look down into the engine compartment. Immediately he discerned the problem: there was a ruptured salt-water intake hose. He closed the petcock valve. Having gone through the boat thoroughly, he was aware that there was no spare intake hose on board. He realized that if they were going to use the engine again, he would need to jury-rig a fix for the ruptured line. He went back out on deck and explained the problem to the others.

"The engine needs to cool down before I can attempt repairs," he informed them. "In the meantime, let's pray for a little wind."

Idly they sat and drifted. Without the movement of the boat over the water, the heat and humidity became much worse. Kurt sat huddled under the canopy of the bimini alongside Madison, remembering lines from the Rhyme of the Ancient Mariner, *'Day after day, we stuck, no breath, no motion—as idled as a painted ship upon a painted ocean.'*

Kurt looked over the side of the boat, surprised to see a slight flow of water moving tiny specks of flotsam over the oily surface. Peering down at the waterline, he saw that there was a similar movement of water ebbing along the hull. He pointed this out to Jeffrey Smythe.

"Yes," Smythe responded. "We are caught in a rather powerful current moving up from the southeast. It is pushing us at about two knots in the direction of Cuba. Until I can make repairs, or until the wind freshens, we will continue to drift toward the coast of Cuba. Let's hope that something changes soon, because we do not want to run afoul of the Cuban Navy."

Smythe went below to try and figure out something to use to make repairs to the intake hose. Kurt followed him down into the cabin, intent on helping in any way possible. After scouring the interior, Smythe seemed at a loss for anything that might resolve their problem. He checked out other hoses on board to see if he might be able to exchange one, but the sizes were not compatible. Kurt suggested they cut an aluminum can, wrap it around the hose, and tape the ends closed as a temporary fix. Smythe agreed that could suffice as a short-term temporary repair; but it was not something they could depend upon for long because the rupture was close to the manifold and the heat from the engine would eventually destroy the tape. For the same reason, using a foul-weather coat or any other rubber-based material would not work. Together they cut a can and readied the duct tape to make the short-term fix. They continued to look for another option, but eventually gave up and went back out on deck.

It got hotter and more humid as the morning wore on. There was not a breath of air, and the coast of Cuba loomed closer and closer as the Cozy drifted on the current. The dark green topography of the country's tropical terrain became visible.

As the *Cozy* drifted aimlessly on the flat Caribbean Sea, the four occupants sat quietly, saving energy and tried to keep under at least some form of shade. It was an effort to stand up and walk the few short steps to the cabin entrance and go below for water. Fortunately, fresh water was not a worry—the boat's water tank held eighty gallons, and they had filled it prior to departure, plus they carried two extra ten-gallon water bottles as a backup. Even so, they did not want to use fresh water for cooling off, although they would allot a gallon or so for a rinse-off at the end of the day.

The sea surface remained greasy calm, unruffled by even a zephyr, except for a slowly building widely spaced swell, noticeable only because of the eerie calm.

∞

After several hours of drifting, the crew of the *Cozy* realized they were likely within the twelve-mile 'zone of influence' of Cuban waters, and continued to drift closer as the day wore on. They ate a light lunch of fruit and sweet bread, but even that was tough to swallow in the stifling heat and humidity. A short while later, Jeffrey Smythe murmured a muffled, "Oh, shit." The others looked over at him and peered out over the port side in the direction he was staring. In the distance, perhaps three or four miles out and about three points abaft the port beam, a large dark gray ship appeared on the horizon, its high bows casting a low white wake as it ploughed through the mirrored water. Fascinated, the four travelers watched silently as the large gray ship grew in size as it moved inexorably closer. Soon it became evident that the vessel was a navy ship of some sort, its narrow beam and high conning towers rising stately above its long low decks. When it came to within about a half mile of the *Cozy*, it slowed and even seemed to stop. Reaching for the binoculars, Smythe announced, "It appears to be a Cuban naval ship."

In turn, each member of the *Cozy* held the binoculars and inspected the Cuban vessel. On its foredeck, three large guns pointed menacingly forward, the center gun larger than the two side-mounts. On the second deck, four more gun placements on turrets were visible. Several figures in uniform could be seen scurrying across the decks; and on the bridge, a quartet of officers stood, their pendants and medallions glittering in the bright sunshine.

At that moment, a brief stirring took place in the limp sails. Jeffrey Smythe glanced toward the bow and observed a faint darkening of the water about a quarter mile ahead and to port. As he watched, the dark area moved slowly toward the *Cozy*; and within a few minutes, another brief stirring occurred in the main sail.

"A breeze," Smythe stated simply. "There's a faint wind line developing off the port bow, moving in this direction from the east. We must prepare to trim the sails if the breeze continues."

Sure enough, for the next quarter-hour a light breeze formed, ruffled the calm sea surface and puffed out the main and jib sheets. Smythe worked the sails masterfully, and soon had the *Cozy* moving forward at a snail's clip. It was difficult to determine if any measurable way was being made because of the prevailing current, but at least the boat seemed to be moving forward. As their forward motion became evident, the building swell pattern also became more noticeable, its ponderous movement flowing under the keel of the boat.

Keeping one eye on the large ship and one eye on the sails, Smythe felt a slight sense of relief that they had not already been approached. He told the others, "I think because we are flying the Jamaican flag rather than the American flag, the Cubans might leave us alone if we can continue to sail away from land."

"Let's hope so," Larry interjected. "I'd sure hate to wind up in a Cuban prison. I've heard some ugly stories about being locked up in Cuba—and that's something I'd sure like to avoid."

Soon the breeze freshened a bit more, and the *Cozy* responded like a thoroughbred to its rider—springing forward with her bow cutting smartly through the lightly dappled sea. Off the stern, the menacing gray gunship moved forward as well, keeping pace with the *Cozy* but not gaining, holding steady about a half mile astern. Nerves were tense, and fingers crossed; but after an hour of following the small sailboat, the navy ship veered to its port, came fully around, and began steaming back from whence it came. A huge sigh of relief escaped from the *Cozy* crew.

"I believe we are lucky," announced Jeffrey Smythe. The others felt the relief just as strongly if not more so. After a few moments of reflection, Smythe seemed to cheer-up. "Okay," he blurted, "let's sail to Great Inagua!"

∞

As the afternoon progressed, the breeze continued to build. The breeze warm and steady, emanating from the east, and the *Cozy* made decent headway of about five knots. The seas remained smooth and calm, although Smythe noticed that the widespread groundswell continued to build. By late afternoon, the breeze freshened to about fifteen knots. Now the others could also feel the slow rolling buildup of the swell becoming shorter in duration and steeper. The air remained hot and sultry, but the combination of the steady wind and their forward movement helped ease their discomfort.

Smythe went below and once again checked the weather reports. Conditions had deteriorated. He went back on deck and told the others what he had determined from the radio reports. The low-pressure system was shifting farther north than previously predicted. It was also deepening. The center of the tropical disturbance was now expected to pass near the Windward Passage—between Cuba and Haiti—precisely where the *Cozy* was heading. Strong gusty winds, intense squalls, and heavy seas were possible for the entire time they would transit the Windward Passage, beginning around nightfall and lasting for approximately thirty hours.

"It could become extremely rough," Smythe commented. "If the center of the low intensifies, we could be in for some dastardly weather. Let's hope it moderates; but even if the low does not deepen, the system is likely to affect us to some extent. Let's batten down everything and be prepared to shift into full storm mode if conditions deteriorate."

Following his announcement, they all worked together to get things storm ready. Kurt and Larry pulled down and stowed the bimini. Madison went below and moved all loose objects from the tables and shelves, placing everything in cabinets and drawers. Smythe went about checking all of the rigging, including the lines, sails, and winches. If foul weather developed, they were as ready as possible.

Just before sunset, Madison and Kurt went below and prepared a meal of sliced Spam, cold canned beans and chunks of bread. It was too hot to cook. They also brought out four cold Red Stripe beers to wash down the meal. Watches were established. Kurt and Larry were assigned to the first four-hour watch, between eight and midnight, with directions from Smythe to wake him immediately if anything unusual or threatening developed. Around eight, Smythe and Madison then went below for some rest.

The first hour remained uneventful.

Entering the second hour, the winds increased, as did the swell. Clouds rolled in. Soon, the *Cozy* was flying along on a steady beam reach, her rails lapping into the water and sending sheets of spray along the deck. Larry sat at the helm, and it took his full concentration to keep the boat on course as she rolled and lifted in the building wind and seas. "Looks like it's picking up quite a bit; do you suppose we should alert Smythe?"

"No," Kurt responded, "I think he would awaken on his own and come out if he thought it was getting too rough. How about you? Do you need a break?"

"Sure, it would be nice to stretch and ease the tension from my hands and fingers."

Kurt took over the helm, and he soon realized why Larry had expressed concerns over the building seas. At the helm station, it was even more evident that the sea was getting rougher by the minute, with winds now gusting above twenty-five knots and the swell building. The *Cozy* was not only heeling over at a steeper angle, but she was beginning to wallow on the backside of the swells and race nearly uncontrollably down the steep faces. He looked out into the dark night, wondering how bad the seas must look in daylight. It was difficult to tell just how rough it was, as there was no moon and a heavy dark blanket of clouds obscured the stars.

It became more and more difficult to maintain a steady course, and the seas made it physically exhausting to hold the helm steady. To compound matters, it started raining. Kurt realized that they had better drop the jib and reef down the main.

He started to ask Larry to go below and wake Jeffrey Smythe when a loud snap resounded in the night, and the jib went flying across the deck, causing the *Cozy* to jibe radically to starboard.

Pandemonium erupted as the *Cozy* spun out of control, her beam broadside to the wind and swell, and her jib sheet tore loose from the bow and flapped wildly and dangerously across the deck.

Jeffrey Smythe came rushing up out of the cabin, cursing loudly over the din. "What the bloody hell is happening?" He shouted. "What the hell is going on?" He looked around and saw Kurt trying desperately to turn the stricken vessel back up into the wind as the jib whipped and lashed back and forth over the boom and across the decks. Larry was trying to grab the flapping jib, but it whipped so powerfully by the winds that there was no way to hold it down. Smythe worked his way to Kurt's side, grabbed the wheel, and with all of his strength leaned into it and held it firmly in position. Gradually, the bow swung around into the seas, and the rolling of the hull and the whipping of the jib began to ease.

'Grab that sail. Lash it to the boom." He turned to Kurt, "What the hell happened?"

"I'm not sure. We were sailing along fine, but it was getting rough. I was just about to call you when something broke in the rigging, and the sail came flying back at us. I tried to hold course, but lost control when the sail ripped loose and the boat spun around."

Smythe looked upward in dismay. "Christ! I think we must have snapped a clew, and the jib halyard has more than likely become tangled in the topmast rigging. We're going to have to disconnect the jib from the top of the mast or we could get dismasted."

"How do we do that?" Kurt asked.

"One of us will have to go up the mast. But first, we need to secure the jib so that it will not cause any more damage, and drop the main."

At that point, Madison came up out of the cabin. Smythe saw her starting to climb out on deck and barked an order. "Get back down below. We have it under control here for now. Stay below and be available to gather up a couple of things after we have things lashed down better."

Madison, Kurt could see, looked deeply frightened, and he was too. He looked over at Larry who had managed to grab the jib sheet and lash its loose end around the boom. The jib flapped only slightly now, and the bow turned into the swell and held steady. Still, the boat lifted and dropped radically as the steep building swells rolled under her keel. While it did not seem quite as extreme now that they were hove-to, the winds continued to gust powerfully at speeds that were likely above thirty knots. To make matters worse, the rains got heavier. Kurt, Larry, and Jeffrey Smythe worked together to lower the mainsail, leaving a small section tied to its lowest point. Using the shortened main as a staysail, Kurt was able to hold the bow into the wind with much less difficulty.

The rain increased, with sheets of stinging water blowing sideways from the powerful winds. Despite the warmth of the water, the wind and penetrating wetness felt chilling. Visibility dropped to almost zero, the white-cresting foam the only thing visible in the inky blackness.

Smythe crawled over the foredeck to the bow, ascertaining that his assumption about the forward clew had been correct, it had ripped loose from the hull. Easing his way back to the cockpit, he informed the others of the problem and briefly explained what they had to do.

Satisfied that things were under control at least for now, Smythe went below to gather the tools that he would need to go aloft and endeavor to disconnect the jib from the topmast. Kurt stayed at the helm, holding the bow steady into the wind and swell. Larry asked Kurt if he wanted his 'foulies'—an item that Smythe had insisted they bring along. When Kurt agreed, Larry went below to pull them out from the forward hold. Slipping into their foul weather gear, Kurt and Larry waited at the helm for Smythe to return.

When Smythe emerged from below deck, Madison stood at his side. He held in his hands a bag containing a Boson chair, a rigging knife, two pairs of pliers, and a shoulder harness. He moved close to Kurt and Larry in order to be heard above the raging wind. In a calm authoritative voice he told them, "I need to go up to the top of the mast. Kurt, you stay at the helm and do your best to keep our bow directly into the wind and seas. Larry, I need you to brace yourself as stably as possible and use the starboard wench to help raise me aloft. I will help haul myself using the main halyard. It is going to be brutally unpleasant up there, and I'm counting on you to give it your best shot. Madison, you stand by with Larry to help in any manner that you can. If anything happens to me, I suggest you just cut loose all the rigging and hope that someone comes along to rescue you."

He said this in a matter of fact tone, making the unspoken point that if something did happen while he was aloft, he would likely not live to share in the aftermath.

Smythe then proceeded to rig the Boson chair and organize the lines for hauling him up the mast. He was dressed only in a t-shirt and tight shorts in an effort to minimize the possibility of getting lines tangled in his clothing. Looking up, the others began to realize the challenge that lay ahead. The mast stood more than forty feet tall, the top barely visible in the pelting rain and darkness. It swayed back and forth wildly in the heavy seas, moving from side to side in at least a twenty-foot arc as the *Cozy* rocked and rolled in the swell. The task would not be easy.

Ready to go, Jeffrey Smythe turned directly to Larry and asked, "Do you think you can hold me? I will also help to haul myself up; but once I'm at the top, my life will be in your hands. We will need to be careful that the sheets do not tangle, especially while I'm going up and coming down."

Recognizing that it would be nearly impossible to verbally communicate once he was up the mast, Smythe then proceeded to establish a set of signals to be used, and asked Larry if he understood the plan.

Larry, with determination responded, "I'll do my best."

Smythe nodded and moved into position.

∞

"Okay, let's go," Smythe instructed as he began to pull himself upward using the main halyard as a hauling rope. At deck level, Larry pulled on the extra jib sheet that was wrapped twice around the wench, with the other end attached to the harness of the Boson chair. Slowly, Smythe began to inch upward, his feet cleared the deck, and his body swung in unison with the swaying mast. Inch by inch, Smythe moved aloft, rising slowly into the darkness.

An eerie tension built above the discord of the storm. The constant rocking and rolling of the boat magnified the intensity of the situation. On two occasions, Smythe swung away from the mast as the swell caused the *Cozy* to lurch. With one hand on the halyard and the other reaching upward, he was unable to grab the mast for support; and his body swung away from the mast a few feet, leaving him hanging out over the deck and putting enormous strain on both mast and rigging.

Forty feet above the deck, with pounding rain, gusting wind, and a wildly swaying mast, Jeffrey Smythe finally reached the top, but sensed his energy waning. His body felt wracked and tortured even though he felt no pain. The bone-chilling wind and rain had caused complete numbness throughout his entire body.

Working with one hand only—the other was needed to hold on, Smythe pulled out his rigging knife and worked to un-jam the line from the masthead rig. One section of the line, where it stretched across to the eye strap, had knotted tightly, pulled taught by the powerful tension of the wind yanking on the lashed down sail. He worked steadily at the jammed line, prying and working the knot with the tip of a marlinspike in an effort to free it from the mast top.

The wind continued to howl, the rains dumped in relentless stinging sheets, and the seas rolled the tiny boat relentlessly in the dark stormy waters.

Smythe called down, and they heard his muffled shout, "Got it!" At about the same time, the upper end of the jib sail dropped toward the deck, caught on the wind, and wrapped the entire aft section of the *Cozy* under its blanket. The three of them in the cockpit were immediately plunged into an even deeper darkness. Madison let out a stifled scream.

"It's okay," Kurt reassured her, "it's loose up top now. We need to get this sail folded and tied down, then try and help Larry bring Smythe back down." That said, Kurt lashed the helm into place and began moving toward the bow, trying to find the end of the sail so that he could start folding or wrapping it into a manageable bundle. Stuck as he was under the canopy of the heavy sail, he had difficulty locating its edge. He reached the mast and felt around blindly, managing to secure one corner of the sail. Hauling it into the cockpit, he began to try and fold it up. Twice the wind tore it out of his hands and sent it flapping. He called out, "Madison, can you give me a hand?"

A moment later she was at his side, clinging to his shoulder with one hand. "What can I do?"

"When I get the edge pulled back in, help me hold it in place while I try to get it folded." With her help, Kurt was able to make a couple of folds. As the loose sail shrunk in size, it became more manageable. Soon they had it folded into a loose pile, and they shoved it deeply into the flooring of the cockpit, the opposite end still tied to the base of the mast.

"Okay," he said to Madison, "let's see what we can do to try and get Smythe down."

Moving to Larry's side, Kurt said, "I'm ready to help."

Larry looked at him and gave a lopsided grin. "My right hand is cramping, and I'm not sure if I can use it effectively unless I can relax it for a minute or two."

Kurt looked down at Larry's hand where he clutched the line that held Jeffrey Smythe in place. The line was wrapped once around his palm; and even in the darkness, Kurt could see that the color was not as it should be at the tips of his fingers—they were bone-white. Reaching down, Kurt told him, "I'm going to take a coil around my hand first, then you loosen your grip, and I'll take over the strain."

"Fine," Larry acknowledged, "but I'm going to keep my left hand secured and help hold on."

The maneuver worked well, and Larry released his rigid hand and fingers, attempting to wiggle them around and bring them back to life. It was not working. He continued to try and move his fingers, but they were simply not responding.

"We need to do something." Madison screamed out frantically. "He's still up there! We need to get him down!"

"Yes, we know," Kurt reassured her calmly, "but we need to be careful. If we try to hurry it too much, something could go wrong and…" He left the rest unsaid.

"I'll be ready in a minute," Larry commented unsurely, his voice wavering. "I'm starting to get some feeling back."

As Larry worked his right hand and fingers, Kurt looked up into the darkness. "Smythe, are you okay?" He called out loudly. There was no response. He tried again. "Smythe, can you hear me?" From the darkness above, they heard a faint voice call back down, "Please, get me down."

At that moment, Larry felt something different and heavier than rain splatter onto his head and shoulders. He glanced down and saw several small brownish-gray chunks of vomit speckling his shoulder. "Shit!" Larry exclaimed, "He's puking."

High above, Jeffrey Smythe was indeed vomiting, the cause more than likely due to the treacherous impossibility of the situation than seasickness. Fortunately, for those below, the winds carried the majority of his regurgitate into the storm tossed sea.

Larry nodded. "I'm ready. We can do this." He reached over Kurt's shoulder and placed his right hand over Kurt's. "We'll pull together. Just let me know if you have any difficulties."

Kurt yelled up into the blackness overhead. "Okay Smythe, we're ready to bring you down."

They began to pull, putting all of their combined strength into the rope. Nothing happened. It was solid. Kurt looked up and yelled out again, "Smythe! Are you ready?" No response. He tried again. There was still no response. They looked at each other and Larry stated dryly. "I think he's out of it and has locked himself into the rigging. I'm not sure he's hearing us or is capable of responding."

Kurt instructed Madison. "Go get the flashlight." She turned hurriedly and went below, returning in a few moments with a long gray flashlight. Kurt hit the switch and shined it into the darkness above. At first, he could not get the light focused on the mast top or on Smythe due to the pitching and swaying of the boat. The darkness and the pounding rain created odd shapes and shadows, and the rainbow effects of the light shining through the rain distorted the light. Holding the flashlight steady, the beam eventually illuminated the small limp-looking body that seemed to be dangling from the shrouds above.

"Christ, he looks like he's passed out." Kurt murmured. "What the hell are we going to do?"

"Let me try to talk to him," Madison insisted, as she moved toward the mast and stood atop the cabin, her arms wrapped tightly around the mast for support.

"Jeffrey!" She yelled, cupping her hand in an effort to direct the sound of her voice. "Jeffrey! You need to help us." Her piercing female voice sang out clearly in the dark, its pitch and intonation ringing out audibly in the tumultuous night air. She tried again. "Jeffrey! Can you hear me? You need to help us get you down! If you can hear me, move your left leg."

Staring intently overhead, all three could see a slight movement from his left leg, which hung loosely below his torso. It helped that he was wearing shorts, as his fair skin caught the glow of the flashlight beam.

"Okay, Jeffrey." Larry called up, his voice becoming hoarse with effort. "We can bring you down, but you need to loosen the line. It's stuck on something." Watching carefully for any sign from above, they saw movement from Smythe's left side, followed by a gentle tug on the line that held him in place.

"That might have done it!" Larry exclaimed. "Let's try again." Pulling together, Kurt and Larry felt the line give. They pulled again and gained a short amount of line. Nodding encouragement, both men pulled harder, and between them, they began to gain a few feet at a time. Sweat poured from their heads, although the sweat could not be distinguished from the rain. They continued to pull.

"It's working!" Madison cried out. "He's coming down!"

Without Smythe helping as he did during the ascent, it was a slow and painful descent. The lines cut into both Kurt and Larry's hands and wrists, with an ooze of capillary blood bubbling to the surface of their skin from the tension and strain. Madison still stood atop the cabin, clinging tightly to the mast, her eyes lifted into the dreary sky as she watched Smythe's drooping torso lower slowly downward. After several agonizing minutes, her hands reached up and caught his ankles. "I've got him, just a little more."

With one final pull, Kurt and Larry watched as Jeffrey Smythe's limp body came abreast with Madison, and she wrapped her arms around him. "I've got him. He's down!" She exclaimed breathlessly, tears poured down her cheeks to mingle with the rain. Kurt and Larry released their grips on the rope and straightened out to help Madison.

They undid the harness and lowered him to the cabin top and together moved him to the cockpit.

He was cold and unresponsive. His flesh looked pale blue, he was covered in tiny goose bumps, and he shivered uncontrollably as they leaned him against the cockpit wall.

"Go get some blankets. I think he's hypothermic," Kurt stated. Madison stared at him, as if to say 'I'm not leaving.' Larry saw her reaction and responded immediately. "I'll get blankets."

"No!" Madison responded. "Let's get him below where it's drier."

Together they carried him down into the cabin, struggling to keep him from being injured further as they tried to maneuver his inert body down the narrow companionway and into one of the bunks. After an awkward effort, they had him safely below and wrapped in blankets. Some hot tea or other liquid would have been nice, but there was no way they could work the stove the way the boat was rolling and pitching. After they secured Smythe into the berth and wrapped him in blankets, Kurt informed Madison that they needed to go back on deck and do some damage control. She stayed at Smythe's side.

Inside the cabin it was better, but not much. Water dripped and ran down from the portholes, from caulking cracks in the cabin top, and through the open companionway. Most of the blankets were wet, and it was difficult to remain upright, even in a sitting position, due to the extreme motion of the boat in the storm-tossed seas. Madison did her best to shield Jeffrey Smythe's inert form from the water rivulets pouring from numerous places above the bunk. She had to brace herself into position to keep from being dumped unceremoniously from the edge of the berth. With blankets wrapped all around his body, Madison ran her hands and arms over and across him in an effort to encourage circulation. Tirelessly, she toiled.

∞

Up on deck, Kurt and Larry surveyed the carnage. Loose lines cluttered the decks. The jib had loosened partway from where they had stuffed it a short while ago and was beginning to billow in the wind. The rain had increased, and the winds howled through the loose rigging. As the bow pitched up and over the steep seas, waves of water rushed over the decks, splashed against the fore cabin, and bathed them in saltwater. Their foul weather gear was ineffective, since they had had to keep their heads uncovered while they worked. Fortunately, the main held, and the mast and boom were still secure.

"Should we try to get back on course?" Kurt asked.

"No," Larry responded. "In these seas, I think we're better off just trying to keep our bow pointed into the swell."

Suddenly, they heard a cry from below. "Kurt! Larry! We're sinking!"

Leaving the lines that they were attempting to untangle, Kurt and Larry rushed together into the cabin. Sure enough, the floorboards floated in water. They looked around, and Kurt moved to the switch panel to see if the bilge pump light was on. The panel was dead. "Shit! I think we've lost all power. I'm going to go out and check the running lights."

On deck, Kurt could see immediately that the running lights were out. The usual faint red and green glow that shone off the white cabin top was not there. He went back down below. Lifting the engine hatch, Kurt informed Larry and Madison that the water was two to three feet deep in the bilge. The portholes and hatches were all leaking, causing a steady flow of water to pour into the interior from the combined effects of rain and seas. "We have to bail," he told them. "I'll get a bucket."

Going into the forward locker, Kurt came back out with one of three five-gallon buckets that they had stowed aboard before leaving Montego Bay. Somehow he knew that they might come in handy. Moving the engine hatch clear of its opening in order to make access easier, Kurt reached down and dipped the bucket into the black oily water. A slick sheen of diesel fuel and engine oil covered the surface.

"We need to form a bucket brigade to empty the bilge," Kurt said to Larry. "And for now at least, it's just me and you."

Larry nodded, moved to the companionway and positioned himself so that he could reach the bucket and lean out to empty it out of the cabin. Kurt passed the first bucket up, sloshing almost half of it into the cabin as he tried to pass it up. "We need to lighten the load. I'll try it about two-thirds full next time."

The next effort went smoother, not as awkward or heavy, and the bucket emptied without any mishap. For the next hour, the two men toiled together, passed bucket after bucket of water from the bilge to the deck and dumped most of it back into the sea. Every few minutes one of the buckets spilt due to the rolling and pitching of the boat, leaving a slippery greasy coating on the cabin sole, steps, and in the cockpit. As a result, Kurt slipped and fell forward onto his left shoulder, bruised his upper arm and caused a small gash on his temple where it struck one of the steps. Compounding the problems, an occasional surge of seawater rolled over the cabin top and into the open hatch cover, dumping as much or more water than they had just bailed out. At one point, Larry called down. "I need a break. Are we making any headway?"

"Yeah, we're making progress; but there's still a lot of water, and it seems to be coming in almost as fast as we dump it out."

While Kurt wiped the blood from his cheek, Larry looked around the boat and suggested they try to plug-up some of the worst flows of incoming water. Going forward and gathering towels, dirty t-shirts, and a few other items of cloth, Larry worked with Kurt to stuff rags into the leaking areas. Their makeshift cloth gaskets looked terrible, but they helped stem the flow.

For another forty-five minutes, the two men continued to bail. Eventually, they had the water level down to a point where the five-gallon bucket was ineffectual. They took a break.

In the meantime, Jeffrey Smythe seemed to be recovering. He had regained some of his color and was responding to Madison's touch as she continued to rub his arms, back, and shoulders in an effort to get his circulation moving again. Kurt tried not to watch the physical interaction, realizing that Smythe had nearly died from the ordeal that he had gone through.

Kurt crawled out on deck to check things out. He shook his head in angst as he took in the sight. Even in the blackness, he could see that the weather was getting worse. The swells were now so large that the *Cozy* would drop into a world of total blackness each time they fell into a trough. Rising to the crest was not much better as he looked around and saw steep combing seas breaking all around. The pitch of the wind was stronger than ever, as it screeched through the rigging and lashed across his face and arms. It was not a pretty sight. To make matters worse, the sight of the tiny little eight-foot plywood Sabot lashed to the deck for a lifeboat was a joke. It would not last a few minutes in these seas with even one person aboard, much less four of them. He gulped with anxiety, a deep dread overwhelming him. They were in a real mess.

During the next several hours, Kurt and Larry took two more turns bailing. Each time they removed approximately two to three hundred gallons of combined saltwater and rainwater. They traded places every few minutes, passing the buckets with about three gallons of water up from the bilge and dumped it onto the deck, where it flowed overboard. They counted out the dumps, planning for fifty empties with each effort.

After about two hours, Madison helped Jeffrey Smythe sit up in his bunk. He seemed to have regained his senses. His body still shook from the effects of the hypothermia, but his eyes were once again focused, and his body had returned to a more normal color. He made an effort to join Kurt and Larry in their bailing efforts, but Madison would not allow it.

"No!" She admonished him. "You nearly died. You are not going to help with anything yet!"

"But they need my help." He gave her a determined look. "They cannot continue like they are going, or they too will collapse."

"Then I will take a turn. You stay where you are."

Madison slid away from the bunk and moved out to where Kurt and Larry bailed.

"Let me help," she stated. Kurt kneeled at the bilge station with Larry seated on the first step of the companionway, dumping the buckets as Kurt handed them up. She reached down and grabbed the bucket from Kurt's hand and elbowed him aside.

With a sigh of relief, Kurt accepted her insistence, and he leaned back against the cabin wall to briefly rest. He knew she wouldn't last long at the task, but even a few moments of respite was a blessing. He counted twenty-five passes and then moved up to relieve Larry for a few minutes. After Larry rested briefly, they took over from Madison again, reducing their own counts to forty, then they allowed Madison twenty-five bails of her own. It made the task much less exhausting, and soon the water level was down enough that all three could take about a one-hour break.

Taking turns, they worked that way through the dreary night, with Kurt and Larry occasionally going out on deck to look around and ensure that all was holding together in the storm. Jeffrey Smythe stayed in his bunk, totally spent and obviously too weak to assist with anything.

They all looked miserable. They each suffered from extreme physical fatigue, but even more traumatic was the mental stress and uncertainty of their situation. Each knew that they were not far from succumbing to the power and fury of the sea, and that their boat was in serious jeopardy of going under. All it would take was the combination of a rogue wave or extremely large swell with a steep trough, and the *Cozy* could become a hapless victim of the elements. With a steel hull, a heavy bilge loaded with hundreds of gallons of water, and an open hatch cover, their boat would not likely recover from an unexpected plunge beneath the surface. Stoically, they each dug into the depths of their instincts for survival, and they somehow managed to continue.

CHAPTER NINETEEN

Daylight mercifully arrived, although the sight it brought was perhaps even more frightening than being in the dark. Their boat—which at forty-seven feet had seemed much larger when tied to the dock—bobbed like a cork on the storm-tossed seas. All around them huge boils of white foam rolled and crested on the tumultuous surface. Under the keel, the sailboat rose and fell on a swell that dwarfed her, the steep, deep troughs dropping downward twenty to thirty feet, and then rising back to the crest where the obscure horizon appeared to roll like undulating hills. During the night, the winds had increased steadily until at first light gusts were exceeding sixty knots and holding steady at around forty. Spindrift flew in sheets from the wave tops, sheared from the surface of the sea. They each questioned their survival. Their only hope was to keep bailing and keep the bow into the wind and swell. Perhaps the *Cozy* might survive the mayhem and stay afloat.

Kurt crawled up into the cockpit to look around. The sight looked horrendous. In the early morning gloom, the seas looked brutal. About every twenty seconds, huge swells rose and lifted the vessel from the depths of the trough to the apex of the crest, where the scene became even more brutish looking. From the top of the swells, a churning mass of smaller wind-created waves stirred and boiled the sea surface like a cauldron. Tinted by the gray overcast and accentuated by the turbulence, the seas took on a purplish hue that looked almost as if the ocean was taking a beating that left dark purple and black bruises where the three to five foot wind chop swirled around on the thirty-foot swells. It created an eerie looking panorama that was both frightening and spellbinding.

Gazing around, Kurt felt a rush of sour bile rising into his chest, constricting his throat and causing him to swallow rapidly and intently. 'Goddamn it!' He swore inwardly at himself, recognizing the onset of seasickness. 'Not this again.' He tried to fight it off, consciously trying to avoid the inevitable reflex that he felt constricting his entire body. It didn't work; and within a few moments, he found himself leaning out over the rail as a gush of vomit spewed out of his mouth in a violent torrent. Again and again he convulsed, each time the amount of spew diminishing in force and volume. Each regurgitate was immediately captured by the wind and flung into the churning seas. After a few last dry-heaves, Kurt wiped sluggishly at the back of his mouth with his hand and leaned back against the cockpit rail, spent and weary. Below, the sound of his noxious puking was lost in the overwhelming dissonance of the storm. He sat forlornly in the cockpit, grimacing at the bilious aftertaste that lingered in his throat and mouth. He was not a happy man.

After a while, Kurt felt a little better, although his head throbbed and his entire body felt weak and tormented. Soaked from the rain and seas, he went below, determined to put on a good face to the others. He halted in his tracks as he stepped down and looked ahead of him into the cabin. Madison knelt next to Jeffrey Smythe, her right hand gently massaging his head and neck. She had changed clothes and looked startlingly lovely in a pair of cutoff gray shorts that highlighted her round firm buttocks and a cropped blouse that clung provocatively to her full bosom. Her tan arms and legs added to the delightful look, and he felt a quick and sudden tightness in his loins.

But then he refocused on what she was doing, and a sharper animalistic pang of anger coursed through his system. His initial reaction was to roar—to attack—but his common sense prevailed. He waited for her to look up, seething as he watched her hand stroke Smythe's stringy hair.

After a moment, she saw him standing there. "Oh, look, Kurt. He's all right. In fact, he's doing much better. He wants to get up and go out on deck, but I have told him that he needs to recover more so that he does not have a relapse." She paused for a moment. "I was soaking wet and needed to change," she commented as an afterthought.

Kurt wanted to lash out, not at her but at Smythe. But he held his composure in check and responded flatly, "Glad to see you're both feeling better. It's quite a mess out there. The storm has increased dramatically, and I'm sure you are aware that we are still taking on a lot of water."

"Right-oh," Smythe responded flippantly. "I've been telling your little lady here that I need to get moving and square things up. She seems to think I am not prepared to get back to it. Do you suppose you could exert your influence on her motherly instincts?"

Kurt seethed. What a smartass. It was obvious to him that Smythe was relishing the attention and encouraging Madison to fawn over him. He felt like kicking him in his crooked English teeth. Instead, he said to Madison, "He's right. We need to get back to it. The storm is intensifying, and we're all going to have to work together to keep this little ship from going down."

She looked from one to the other, seemingly oblivious to the underlying current of animosity that existed between the two men. She shrugged and stepped away from the bunk. "Okay. What do we do next?"

Kurt said, "We need to do another bail. Both Larry and I are worn out too, and our hands are sore and bleeding from the constant effort. Do you suppose you two could take a turn?"

Madison started to say something, but Smythe cut her off. "But of course. I will pull on my rubbers and go to the deck. Madison, you pass the buckets up to me."

Madison pulled on a pair of sweatpants for the chore, since she did not bring along any foulies.

It infuriated Kurt to see Madison working with Smythe—her small cotton blouse wet and clinging to her full heaving breasts, and Smythe ogling her each time she bent down to fill the bucket and pass it up to dump. Her gray sweatpants were also soaked and stuck tightly to her buttocks. She looked like the goddess Amphitrite battling the seas with her long golden hair tied in a ponytail and tucked into the back of her blouse to keep it from dipping into the bilge.

Kurt understood why Smythe had a smirk on his face—he was front-row center to a show and enjoying every minute—while Kurt simmered in frustration. But there was not a thing he could do.

As the morning wore on, the storm continued to pound. Rainfall came in both brief and prolonged torrents, with the heaviest downpours creating a painful cacophony of noise within the tiny cabin. The rain became so intense at times that they were forced to pull the hatch closed to reduce the amount of water pouring into the interior. After each deluge, they resumed bailing. During one rain interlude, Smythe and Kurt went out on deck to assess the storm. It was really ugly. Mountainous walls of water rolled across the storm-tossed sea. Wordlessly they looked at each other, shook their heads, and went back below.

"There is nothing we can do for now except continue to bail," Smythe stated. "There is no indication of the storm weakening yet, and we have lost all communication. We will just need to work together until the storm eases."

For the remainder of the day, the four desolate sailors took turns bailing, resting for a short while between shifts. They managed to improve the stoppers and gaskets they had improvised to stem the flow of water from the hatches and portholes, but still the water found its way into the boat. Because Madison did not have foul-weather gear to wear, she remained in the cabin, passing buckets up to the others. But to Kurt's relief, she had pulled out another sweatshirt to wear over the scanty blouse.

Although it was hot and humid in the cabin and the sea and rainwater warm, the three men periodically went into mild hypothermia from the constant intrusion of water into their foulies. They had also developed sea-sores from the constant exposure to salt water and the friction of the rubber against exposed skin. Between shifts bailing, they tried to close their eyes and rest; but the ferocity of the storm and the constant pitching, bucking, and lurching, made sleep all but impossible. Throughout the long and dreary afternoon and into the night, the four miserable souls fought the effects of the storm.

Around midnight, they became aware of a slight change. The last couple of bailing efforts required less time and removal of less water. Outside, the din and clamor had diminished. Smythe crawled out onto the deck and watched the storm for a few minutes. Returning below, he informed the others, "I think we have seen the worst of it. Let's do one more bail, then try to get some rest before daylight."

Working together, they made one final emptying of the bilge and then slid the hatch closed to keep the rainfall out. In their bunks, they wedged themselves into place. Outside, the gale raged.

∞

In the morning, Kurt woke first. Dulled by the deep torpor of sleep, he was briefly unaware of where he was or what was happening. As his awareness level rose, he began to recall what they were coping with. He lay quietly and listened intently to the low muffled sounds reverberating through the boat. Gone was the insistent roaring of the storm. In its place were the more subdued sounds of sloshing water and some clanging on the decks. He tried to rise, but his body failed him. Slowly, he moved his legs and arms, becoming aware of the aches and pains in his muscles and on his skin. He lifted his arms up to where he could see them and grimaced at the sight of raw blistered-looking sea sores that oozed a pasty mustard-colored mucus. He groaned. His shoulder ached, and the side of his head throbbed from where he had struck it against the cabin step. After a few moments of methodically working his legs, Kurt managed to lower them over the edge of the bunk and lift himself into a seated position. He felt miserable. Holding his throbbing head in his hands, he sat there trying to compose himself enough to get up. He desperately needed to pee.

He attempted to stand, but found himself dropping onto his knees before he was able to force himself to a standing position. He looked down into the engine hatch and could see that another round of bailing needed to take place, but the water level was not nearly as high as it had been the prior night. Rather than try to make his way to the head (which was partially under water anyway), Kurt elected to climb out on deck. He carefully slid back the hatch in an effort to not disturb the others and crawled up into the cockpit.

Looking around, the sight still looked gnarly, but not nearly as extreme. The seas were lumpy and gray, tossed and tumbled by the aftermath of the storm; but the swell was way down. He turned in a full circle, taking in the surrounding ocean. White caps rolled from the crests of the wind chop, and an occasional comber churned from the crests of the swells, but it was vastly improved. The wind was fluky, gusting to around twenty-knots, but dropping to almost zero at times. To the west, a thick dark wall of billowing gray-white cumulonimbus clouds sat heavily on the horizon blotting out the sun, their tops glowing brightly as if illuminated from within. Only a few puffy popcorn clouds scudded overhead. He felt immense relief and sat in the cockpit and relished the demise of the vicious storm that had hammered them so harshly for the past two days. After a while, he roused himself and went below.

In the cabin, Kurt saw Jeffrey Smythe seated on the end of his berth. Kurt nodded and put his finger to his lips to indicate quiet. Smythe nodded back, rubbed his hands over his face and through his thinning hair. He shook his head slowly while looking at Kurt, as if to say, 'Whew, I'm glad that's over!'

Kurt smiled and moved to the small bench seat at the galley table.

After Smythe had climbed out onto the deck and relieved himself, Kurt joined him in the *Cozy's* cockpit.

"Way better!" Smythe exclaimed. "That was a rough one."

"Yeah," Kurt concurred, "that wasn't much fun at all." Looking out at the still storm-tossed ocean, he asked Smythe, "Any idea where we are now?"

"I will be taking a fix at noon. If it calms enough by then to get a good angle on the horizon, I should be able to determine our current position without any difficulty. I would guess that we might have drifted forty or fifty miles during the course of the storm, perhaps more. I will let you know once I have a chance to get a good reading from the sun."

Larry awakened. He too was stiff and sore, but relieved to see that the storm had abated. Smythe went below, fired-up the cooking stove which had miraculously survived unscathed, and brewed a pot of steaming coffee. Madison awoke to the commotion and inquired sleepily if the storm was over.

"It appears to be spent," Smythe replied. "There is still some residual swell and chop, but it has improved considerably."

"I'm so happy to hear that," Madison responded, stretching her own sore body in a languorous animal-like manner. Kurt greeted her cheerfully.

"Good morning sunshine." He moved to the side of her bunk, kneeled, and leaned over to kiss her on the forehead, allowing his hands to gently massage her neck and shoulders. "You were a real trooper," Kurt reassured her. "It was quite a storm, and you bore it well."

She looked up at him, a warm smile spreading across her lovely face. "Thank you. I think we all did. And I am so grateful that Jeffrey is safe. I was afraid that…" she left the sentence dangling.

Kurt nodded. "Yes. It was quite an ordeal, and we probably owe him our lives. Without the courage he showed by going up the mast, we could have been in even worse trouble."

After coffee and rolls, they all went up on deck and began to reorganize. Things were a mess, and it was still a little awkward maneuvering around in the storm-tossed seas. Moving carefully, they stowed the jib, re-secured the loose lines that were strewn around the deck, and hoisted the main to its second reef point. Setting course in a northeasterly direction, they held steady at sixty degrees until they could get an accurate fix.

As the morning progressed, the seas continued to diminish. By noon, the surface was back to near normal, with only a steady twelve to fourteen-knot trade wind in evidence. The swell had diminished to about eight feet, and they were moving at a slow but comfortable clip. Madison took the helm, while Kurt and Larry tied the bimini in place.

Smythe took his sextant on deck and got a fair reading on the horizon. The seas remained lumpy; and on the low deck of the moving sailboat, the horizon did not remain stationary for long as he gazed into the sighting tube, but he was able to obtain a decent relative angle with the sun. From that, Smythe went below and studied the chart, marking their current position as being about forty-six miles further north from their last fix. He went topside and altered their course to forty-four degrees magnetic.

Back on course, Madison turned to Smythe and inquired, "Any idea how long it might be before we reach land?"

"If the breeze holds, we should make landfall at Great Inagua Island around dark. When we arrive, I hope to be able to fire-up the engine so that we can make our way into the port under power. The entrance to the main anchorage is relatively clear and open in front of Mathew Town; so we should not have any problem arriving in the dark."

For the remainder of the afternoon, the four of them alternated helm duties, in between resting their sore and tired bodies in the still sultry and stifling heat. Shortly after lunch, they un-reefed the main and let the sail fill. Pursing out with a steady beam wind, the full main caused the *Cozy* to lean another ten degrees to starboard, dipping the gunnels into the indigo sea and increasing her speed to six knots. They reached the entrance to Man of War Bay in Mathew Town just before nightfall. Kurt and Jeffrey Smythe worked together to jury-rig the taped-up intake hose and opened the petcock to allow the seawater to feed the engine. Fortuitously, the flooded bilge did not climb above the level of the wiring harness, and the *Cozy* was equipped with an extra starting battery mounted well above the engine compartment in a watertight bulkhead. Smythe connected that battery to the starter. The engine coughed and sputtered but eventually started. The intake hose held, and they entered the calm anchorage under low idle speed. Dropping the hook in about four fathoms, Kurt played-out about one hundred fifty feet of rode, and the *Cozy* settled comfortably into the bay just as nightfall draped a star-covered blanket over the tranquil sea.

CHAPTER TWENTY

Early the next morning, the crew of the *Cozy* awoke almost simultaneously, refreshed and rejuvenated, although the lingering soreness in their shoulders and backs, and the visible raw-looking inflammation from the sea-sores were still evident on their arms and legs. Nonetheless, they were all ready and eager to put their feet onto solid land.

They launched the Sabot, and squeezed into its tiny shell, the waterline lowering to within three inches of the rails. A serene calm covered the bay; so they were not too concerned about taking on any water. They rowed ashore and tied up at a small rickety dinghy dock in Government Basin, Mathew Town, where the Customs House resided. An affable fellow with jet-black skin and a broad white smile that seemed to spread across his entire face greeted them. His strongly accented English was hard to follow, but they managed to answer all of his questions—many of which centered around the violent storm—and fill out the requisite forms needed to enter the Bahamas. It took about an hour to complete the check-in process.

Leaving the Customs House, they headed toward 'town.' Town did not consist of much, one small hotel, a quaint general store, a few shops, and a water and icehouse. Water, they would soon discover, was a valuable commodity in the Bahamas.

Most of the island's economy centered on and around the huge Morton Salt factory that operated in the island's interior, on the shores of Lake Windsor (more commonly called Lake Rosa). There, thousands of tons of salt were harvested each year and shipped abroad for consumption.

There was no pavement. Instead, the streets were covered in a solid white-sand base. All of the commercial buildings and nearby dwellings reflected colorful pastel shades, and the unique and varied architecture resulted in odd juxtapositions. Since the island was so remote, one could see how the mish-mash of construction evolved.

Happy to be on shore, the four travelers located the small general store and purchased a couple of items needed on board the *Cozy*. After walking around the town for about an hour and taking in the sights, they returned to the Morton's Main House Hotel—a rustic building with about a dozen guest rooms and a small bar/restaurant that served meals only when the rooms were occupied. On that particular day there were no guests, and therefore no food being served. They headed to the boat to fix lunch. However, as they reached the wharf, a strange-looking vehicle pulled alongside, and the driver jumped out and greeted them with great enthusiasm.

"Greetings, I am George!" He introduced himself in his infectious Bahamian accent. "I am here to serve you, answer any questions you may have, provide you with any of your needs, and take care of you in any manner of your choice."

Impressed with his gregarious attitude, the group laughed and introduced themselves, and explained that they were looking for a place to eat lunch but there did not seem to be anything open.

"That is no problem at all!" George informed them in the rich deep accent that prevailed throughout the Bahamas. "Come with me, I will take you to my home where my lovely Cecelia will prepare for you the finest conch fritters in all of the Bahamas!"

Concerned about the cost, Jeffrey Smythe asked, "What would be the cost of your transportation services and lunch?"

"Oh, cost? That is not a concern to me. We have conch in abundance, and it is only a few blocks to my home. My taxi, #5, has more than enough gasoline to get us there and back. Do not worry about the cost. If you choose to share a couple of dollars with us, we would not decline the offer of a small cash payment; however, we would like to share our table and our friendship with you regardless of your ability to pay."

They shrugged, a silent affirmation took place, and they climbed into the car with George.

Taxi #5 was one of only thirteen privately owned vehicles licensed on the island. Morton Salt had a number of their own cars, plus transport trucks, but most residents on the island walked or peddled bikes wherever they went. The car had originated as a 1960 Chevrolet, but it was now impossible to tell the make or model. Over the years, the car had been modified numerous times, using whatever parts and pieces were available. Both front and rear bumpers had come from an old Pontiac, the hood and front fenders stripped from an old Ford, the lights and grille removed from an Oldsmobile, and the seats and interior dash taken from an old wrecked Plymouth. Under the hood, the smooth-running engine came from a Ford pickup truck. The taxi was painted a multitude of colors, the primary one a bright blue; but red, green, yellow, and purple brightened the many body parts that had been replaced. A large chrome vintage Cadillac ornament adorned the hood, and a pair of bulbous Volkswagen headlights protruded incongruously from the front fenders. It was quite a vehicle.

Underway, George gave a running commentary about the life and activities on Great Inagua Island. Nearly all inhabitants either worked directly for Morton Salt, or provided some sort of service for the operation. Most were island born, and many had never left the island. His family was in its fourth generation, after his Haitian born great-grandfather had shipwrecked on the island while on a fishing trip nearly one hundred years ago.

While many Bahamian men were large of stature, George was small, thin, and wiry. His large coal-black eyes seemed lit from within, glowing like beacons inside the whites of his eyes. His features looked almost effeminate—wide set eyes, full cheeks, a narrow nose, and full puffy lips. Despite his rather delicate features, he conveyed masculinity and obviously took great pride in his manliness.

Arriving at his home, they all climbed out of the 'Chevy' and walked up a crushed shell pathway to a small bungalow painted pastel lime green with white trim. A stunning dark-skinned young girl who, at first glance, appeared to be about ten-years old met them at the doorway. On closer scrutiny, they could see that she was not a girl but a mature woman. She stood less than four-foot tall, but had an incredibly well shaped and finely developed body. Her oval-shaped face was lovely, and her large widely spaced green eyes sparkled with flecks of gold. Unusually thick eyebrows and long dark lashes punctuated the shape and luster of her eyes. Her silken black hair grew long and lustrous, flowing down to the tiny dancers' dimples on her lower back. As she turned slightly to clear the doorway, her round buttocks jutted enticingly.

Her beauty and the overwhelming sensuality of her diminutive body stunned them all.

"This, my friends, is Cecelia, my delightful and delicious wife!" George informed them proudly, bowing slightly as he raised his palms upright to make the introduction. Turning to her, he introduced his guests in turn, remembering each of their names without a hitch even though they had only become acquainted a short while before.

When Cecelia acknowledged the greeting, her face lit up like a jewel, her eyes sparkled, and her perfect white teeth gleamed brightly. The three men from the *Cozy* stood enraptured, fascinated by the doll-like woman.

Not surprised by their reaction—he had seen it many times before—George laughed lightly. "She is an adorable little beauty, right?" Pulled from their reverie and brought back to social decorum, the three men turned to George and concurred, trying not to stare.

Turning to Cecilia, George informed her that their guests were searching for a place to eat lunch, but the hotel café was closed. He asked if she could prepare a plate of conch fritters. Smiling sweetly, Cecilia nodded at them and turned to go back inside as George moved a couple of rattan chairs around so they could sit.

"Might I be of help?" Madison offered before Cecelia disappeared.

Cecelia smiled brightly, "Yes, of course. You do not need to help, but you could come inside with me and keep me company while I prepare some food." Her voice trilled light and musical and carried only a hint of the island accent. Madison went inside with her.

On a patio shaded by the tall palms that surrounded the quaint little cottage, George asked his guests to be seated while he went inside to get a pitcher of ice-cold lemonade. The lemonade proved to be one of the best-tasting cold drinks they had enjoyed in months. As they sipped, George regaled them with stories and insights into life on the remote island. He also asked them for details about the storm, their journeys, backgrounds, and ideologies. He seemed an articulate man, knowledgeable about the sea and life in general, and their conversation flowed effortlessly.

After a while, Cecelia and Madison returned carrying a platter loaded with golden-fried conch fritters and another piled with thinly sliced sweet bread. There were also two small dishes filled with homemade dipping sauces—one of them a mild mango salsa, the other a spicy yellow blend mixed from the roots of a wild island plant. The conchs were the best they had eaten anywhere, lightly breaded, tender, and full of flavor and savory texture.

They chatted the afternoon away, with Cecelia replenishing their lemonade periodically. Each time she stood to walk into the house, the men could not stop themselves from ogling her sensual little body. She looked astonishingly beautiful. George frequently complimented himself at being fortunate enough to have found her, and it became obvious that she adored him as well.

Toward evening, George invited them to dine with them. They politely refused the offer, insisting that they must return to the *Cozy* and continue with the repairs and cleanup from the storm. George, however, insisted that they return for a 'very special dinner treat' the following evening. They agreed to his offer, which would include a tour of the interior the following afternoon. They all piled back into Taxi #5, and George drove them back to the docks. Before leaving, Jeffrey Smythe offered George forty dollars American for the ride, lunch, and drinks; but George would accept only twenty—telling them that it was too much, but he did not have change for the twenty. He drove off, waved happily, and promised to return for them around noon the following day.

Back on board the *Cozy*, they each went about performing 'damage control' from the storm. Kurt and Larry worked to prepare the forward clew for repairs, straightened up the rest of the deck mess, and coiled and stored the loose lines. Jeffrey Smythe removed the broken intake hose, planning to head off in the morning to look for a replacement. Madison worked below, reorganizing things that had been tossed around, and dried out clothing and other items that were soaked from the inflow of both salt and fresh water. Some packaged food items were ruined and discarded, but nothing they could not live without.

Together, Kurt and Madison prepared a tuna noodle casserole with a small ten-pound tuna provided by one of the fishing boats anchored nearby. Afterward, they all sat in the warm evening air and discussed plans for traveling over the Grand Bahamas Bank. They knew that travel over the shallow reef-covered bank would be limited to daylight hours; and even then, some portions could be crossed only during the brightest hours of the day. They agreed to spend one more day in Great Inagua, and depart early the next day.

∞

Sleeping-in much later than usual, they got a sluggish start the following morning. After coffee and a light breakfast, Smythe went off to search for a replacement hose. Kurt, Larry, and Madison continued to reorganize and straighten-up the *Cozy*. Smythe returned after about an hour with the hose, and a used bronze deck bracket that would suffice to make repairs to the forward clew. Smythe replaced the hose while Kurt and Larry repaired the foredeck area where the clew ripped out. Satisfied that the repair was sufficient, they re-connected and hauled the jib to make sure it worked properly. The hose repair also went smoothly.

At precisely noon, George pulled up to the dock and 'honked' his horn. The honk was not a real honk, but the blare of an 'A-Ooga' horn. He hit the horn three times to make sure they could hear him.

They were not quite ready to leave; so they hollered to George that they would be a few minutes. Also, the anchorage was not quite as flat and smooth as the day before. They would need to take turns getting to and from the *Cozy* in the little Sabot, with no more than three of them in it at one time. Smythe, Larry, and Madison went first, with Larry rowing back out to pickup Kurt after dropping the other two at the dock.

Once they were all gathered at the dock, they climbed into Taxi #5 and were off on their next adventure.

George served as a good tour guide, pointed out sights and explained things along the way. The island was arid, and except for the occasional tropical depression or hurricane, received very little rainfall. A short distance inland, the imposing shape of several large buildings loomed up from the sand dunes that covered the terrain. George explained that they were looking at the buildings of the Morton Salt Company on the shore of Lake Rosa.

They rose over a small ridge and saw an incredible sight. Spread before them lay an expansive marshy bay alive with a massive flock of coral-pink flamingoes. The majestic birds stood and floated in a lime-green colored lake surrounded by a ring of white salt deposits.

From one end of the lake to the other, tens of thousands of stately flamingos stood on one or both of their spindly legs or floated in the shallow waters, their black-tipped beaks poking into the murky water, slurping algae, or searching for the omnipresent brine shrimp that make the mire their home. A few flamingos were airborne, their long graceful bodies gliding through the air with their thin stork-like legs tucked in and trailing behind their elongated bodies. It was a sight right out of National Geographic.

"Those are our pink 'flaminkos'," George announced dramatically, strongly emphasizing the 'k' sound. "They are many thousands, maybe more than one-hundred thousand. Those fine pink birds are the best secret of Great Inagua, our island's natural treasure. I have brought you here to see them; and if there are no others around when we walk down to their roosting site, I will have another special treat for you."

He put the car into gear and headed along the sand-covered road, then made a turn onto a smaller narrower road that was almost invisible in the scrub-covered landscape. That road, really more of a trail, wound its way down toward the water's edge. Pulling into a small cutout nestled behind a bank of dense shrubs, George parked and turned off the engine. "We will get out now. But walk softly, do not speak, and remain quiet." He carried an odd-shaped bag under his arm. They walked for about five minutes, paralleling the shore. On their right, the visitors stared in wonder at the beautiful gangly birds. Standing in the shallows, the pink-coral colored flamingoes looked incongruous in the way they sleuthed the water for food—their spoon-shaped beaks buried in the murk, appearing to scoop the mud in an upside-down manner. Many of the birds stood on one leg, balanced as if on a thin stick, their large oval bodies appeared much too heavy for such delicate legs. The scene moved Madison, and she yanked repeatedly on Kurt's arm to point out individual flamingoes displaying peculiar moves. Suddenly, George halted, put his finger to his lips to indicate he wanted silence. The others froze, and remained still as George moved stealthily behind one of the shoreline bushes.

Kneeling, he pulled a large 'Y' shaped slingshot from his bag and inserted a small round object into the pocket of its pouch. Pulling back on what appeared to be a v-shaped rubber tube until it touched his right cheek, George aimed and released the slingshot, firing a small round ball toward one of the unsuspecting flamingoes. The ball struck it on the head with a loud thump, and the bird collapsed into the water. He reached down and inserted another ball, took aim and released another shot. Another bird collapsed from its stance, dropping near the first bird.

George stood, walked back near the others, and waved at them to come toward him. As he rose and beckoned, his movement caused a raucous clamor from the closest flock of birds. In unison, hundreds of birds took to the air, their shrill squawks mingling with the beating of their wings as they took flight. Rising into the air in a massive display of flaming color, the startled birds sent wave after wave of other birds into the air. Soon the sky filled with pink as thousands of flamingoes flapped, squawked, and took flight toward the center of the lake.

George moved toward the two fallen birds, and waded into the shallow water about knee deep. He reached down and picked each one up by the neck, their once graceful bodies dangled from the narrow stem of their long necks. Their long spindly legs dragged in the water as George walked toward shore.

"You killed them!" Madison exclaimed. "What have you done? You killed those two beautiful birds."

George looked confused. Slipping into the island dialect, he stated simply, "They is good to eat. I get them for you to eat."

"I don't want to eat them!" She shrilled, "They are beautiful birds, and they have a right to live. Why would you do that?" Madison cried out. She turned and looked at Kurt. "Don't you have anything to say? Do you see what he did? He killed them. They were so beautiful, and now they are dead. Why did he do that?"

Kurt moved to her side, and reached out gingerly to put an arm around her shoulder. She almost violently shrugged his arm away. He stepped back and commented quietly, "Madison, he's an islander. It is their way. He is trying to do something special for us. He does not understand why you are so upset. It's his way of life, and he did it for us."

She stood defiantly, glared at Kurt, and then looked back at George. George looked dumbfounded, baffled by her behavior. He looked to Kurt, Larry, and Jeffrey Smythe as if to get their reassurance. They all looked back at him and gave him that look, a slight shrug and raised eyebrows, that is indicative of bewilderment in the male species.

"Please," George pleaded with Madison, "do not be troubled by my action. I wanted to do something special for all of you, and the flaminko is good to eat. I brought you here to see them in their environment and to share their beauty with you. Afterward, I want to have you share their delectable taste and flavor. I did not mean to upset you."

Madison looked back at the others, aware that they were siding with George. She shook her long blonde hair in a display of frustration and moved toward the car. The others followed.

During the ride back, George attempted to lighten the mood by pointing out other sights. The men responded politely, but Madison sat stoically staring out the open window with the wind and air whipping her golden locks around her head and shoulders.

At one point, George implored, "Please do not talk with anyone about this visit to the flaminko lake. It is not legal to shoot or eat the flaminko, but there are so many of them that those of us that live here eat them on a regular basis. Our government officials know that they are a small part of our national diet; so they ignore our taking of a few of the birds for our own tables. But we are not allowed or authorized to allow others to share in their delights. So please do not talk with anyone about this experience."

Kurt responded, "We will not talk with anyone."

George honked once as he approached his house. Cecilia came running out to greet them, wearing a short white cotton dress that clung to each of her splendid curves. Her smooth light-mahogany skin glowed against the bright white fabric. Dressed as she was, she appeared even more doll-like than she had the day before, and the three men from the *Cozy* were once again dazzled by her loveliness.

She went to the trunk where George was removing the two birds. He grabbed them by the neck and handed them to her. She clutched them in her small hands and held them out away from her clean white dress, as she moved toward the back of the house. "Would you like to join me?" She asked Madison.

Madison did not look at her but uttered an emphatic, "No!"

Cecelia glanced over at her husband, who merely shrugged and ushered the others into the yard.

The overall mood during the ensuing few hours was not as comfortable or as enjoyable as it had been during their previous visit. Madison turned very quiet, withdrawn and sullen, seating herself away from the others with her arms crossed tightly across her chest. George and the other three men talked, but the conversation was not as smooth or natural as it had been the day before.

Cecelia popped in and out, wearing a long blood-splattered apron. She tried a couple of times to engage Madison in conversation, and invited her to join her in the house, but Madison stubbornly declined. At one point, Cecelia asked George to help her with something, and the two disappeared into the house for a few minutes. While they were gone, Kurt took Madison for a short walk and tried to talk to her about the situation. Madison steadfastly refused to lighten up, telling Kurt to go ahead and do what he needed to do, but not to include her.

When Cecelia brought out the platter of food, Madison excused herself, and told the others that she was going for a walk. She carefully avoided looking at the steaming plate of baked flamingo.

The others enjoyed the meal. Served on individual plates piled high with steaming brown rice, the baked flamingo tasted rich, savory and delightful. Kurt compared it to turkey. Its texture and coloring was not as strong or fibrous as wild turkey, but more like the dark meat of domestic turkey.

Madison returned a while later, commenting that she was not feeling well and wished to return to the boat. The men thanked Cecelia and George profusely for the fine meal and for their hospitality, and climbed into Taxi #5 for the ride back to the docks. Once there, Jeffrey Smythe handed George forty dollars, which George steadfastly declined. Smythe insisted, but George would not accept any money, asking Smythe to please try and express his most sincere regrets for having upset Madison. Farewells were made, and the taxi headed off into the twilight.

Back on board, the men made an effort to talk with Madison, but she firmly refused to discuss the matter. "He did what he did, and all of you went along with it. I have nothing more to say on the subject. Please do not bring it up again."

CHAPTER TWENTY-ONE

In the morning, Jeffrey Smythe awoke before daybreak, and prepared to get underway. Kurt and Larry joined him shortly thereafter, but Madison remained in her bunk. Smythe sat down with Kurt and Larry in the cockpit and laid out a chart of the Bahamas.

Between Great Inagua and the island of Bimini, they would transit an area that is one of the most intriguing island chains on the planet. Consisting of seven hundred islands, about twenty-four hundred cays, and nearly one hundred thousand square miles of reef-covered terrain, the Bahaman Archipelago is a navigational challenge. Because of its shallow reef-strewn topography, sailing through the Bahamas requires extreme diligence and well-planned travel routes. Smythe laid out a tentative route that took them up and around Acklins, Crooked, and Long Islands, and into the Exumas, thus circumventing nearly one-third of the distance to Bimini. They would miss some of the more remote and pristine southern and eastern portions of the island chain, but would cut their travel time by several days. They all agreed to set a course as Smythe suggested.

They hauled anchor, set sails and started the anticipated forty-hour sail to the Exumas.

About an hour into the day, Madison came out on deck and smiled at the others. "I suppose I should apologize for my behavior yesterday, but I was really troubled by George killing those birds." She paused, and then continued, "I realize that it's a male thing to kill and eat animals, but seeing it happen was just too much for me. If I had not seen the flamingoes, I probably would not have reacted the way I did. But the whole thing was just overwhelming for me. So please, forgive my behavior, and let's put the whole incident behind us."

After her apology, the mood aboard the *Cozy* improved; and they turned their attention toward sailing the boat and enjoying the calm seas and favorable winds.

Pushed along by the steady northeast trade winds, the *Cozy* made nearly eight knots over ground. The repair on the jib clew held, and they were able to race along under full sail.

Except for the occasional sighting of sea life, the afternoon passed uneventful. The air remained warm but slightly cooler than the norm, and striated, wispy altostratus clouds blanketed the sky. By nightfall, they had covered over one hundred miles and continued to sail steadily. A half moon rose on the eastern horizon, casting a silver beam on the glistening sea. They took four-hour shifts at the helm, following the same pattern as before, with Kurt working with Larry and Jeffrey teamed with Madison.

Jeffrey Smythe and Madison were on the early morning watch, the four a.m. to eight a.m. shift, and once again Madison fell asleep just before daybreak. Her head nestled onto Smythe's shoulder, and Kurt found her that way when he awoke and looked out on deck shortly after seven. Kurt nodded curtly to Smythe, who looked up at him and smiled smugly, shrugging slightly as if to say 'What can I do?'

Madison responded to his movement and lifted her head sleepily from his shoulder. "Oh, no," she whispered, "I've fallen asleep again."

Kurt thought, 'At least she's going to sleep.'

Larry joined the others on deck. It was not yet eight, but Larry and Kurt offered to take over the morning shift. Smythe and Madison accepted the offer, with Smythe saying he was going to work on their navigational progress, and Madison went below to sleep.

The *Cozy* had covered more distance than Smythe had projected. By late afternoon, it became apparent that they would likely reach the Exuma chain before nightfall. Closely studying the charts and an old weathered copy of *A Sailor's Guide to the Bahamas*, Jeffrey pinpointed the place where he would like to set anchor. Selecting a site that appeared to be a shallow, well-protected cove on the western end of Little Exuma Island, near Williams Town, Smythe adjusted the compass heading a few degrees westward. As the sun settled over the sparkling topaz-colored water, the low-lying outline of Little Exuma came into view. After another hour, they were dropping sail and firing-up the engine to enter the shallow bay.

Without a depth sounder, Smythe instructed Kurt to go to the bow and take depth readings with a lead ball attached to a sounding line. That line was marked at five-foot increments for depth soundings. His first two soundings resulted in depths beyond the fifty-foot length of the tackle. On his third drop, Kurt called out forty-eight feet to Smythe, who sat stoically at the helm while slowly maneuvering the *Cozy* between dark areas, endeavoring to stay in the lighter colored water.

Gliding steadily ahead, the water within the cove became flat and calm. They were now within the confines of the small bay, a u-shaped enclosure about one fourth of a mile across. When Kurt called out 'thirty-two feet,' Smythe pulled the boat out of gear and allowed it to drift forward. Reaching twenty-five feet, Smythe called out to drop the anchor. As Kurt played out chain then line, Smythe slowly reversed until one hundred fifty feet of rode had played out, at which point he instructed Kurt to make it secure. At about the same time the sun dropped into the bay, the sailboat *Cozy* settled at anchor.

Celebrating their arrival at their first stop since departing Great Inagua, Kurt pulled out a bottle of Pussers Rum and mixed four tall glasses of pineapple, rum, and coconut juice. The drinks were sweet and smooth and quickly consumed. He mixed four more, then another four, until the rum bottle was emptied. By that time, they all felt happily light-headed. They sat around and talked about the next few days and their anticipated journey over and through the shallow banks of the one hundred thirty mile Exuma Sound—a journey that they expected would take at least four or five days due to the limited hours of good visibility.

There was no hurry to get underway the following morning. They would have only about an hour of travel time around the southern tip of Little

Exuma before they entered the reef-dotted shallows on the northeastern portion of Exuma Sound. Once in those shallows, it would require extreme diligence to keep an eye out for the thousands of dangerous coral heads that cover the region.

After a light breakfast, a little tidying of the boat, and a short swim in the slightly murky waters of the bay, they hauled anchor and were underway. An hour later, Kurt and Madison stood on the bow gazing ahead and marveling at the amazing clarity of the water when Kurt suddenly called out, "Reef ahead."

As the *Cozy* moved forward, the distant shadow that they had seen became more and more visible. Soon they were sailing over a gorgeous white limestone shelf dotted with small coral outcroppings. The water looked so clean and clear that the depth appeared to be only feet; however after Kurt took several depth soundings, it was discovered to be more than thirty feet deep. A little further on Kurt pointed again, this time more animatedly as a larger more visible shoal appeared. Jeffrey Smythe maneuvered the *Cozy* in the direction Kurt pointed, and they cleared the protruding obstruction without any problem.

At that point, Madison asked if they could stop and snorkel. The water looked so inviting that she wanted to jump in and explore. Smythe informed her that it would continue to be like that and probably get even better as they traveled northward, and he didn't want to stop and waste the best hours of visibility. He promised they would find a lovely spot in the early afternoon where they could stop, drop the anchor, then swim and snorkel to their heart's content.

Twice during the next few hours, the *Cozy* had to stop and alter course to avoid particularly large areas of submerged reefs. Once they needed to avoid an underwater blockade that stretched for nearly a mile. One of them had to remain on the bow without any sunshade protection, and soon all were feeling the effects of the hot tropical sun. Eventually, they rigged a lightweight canvas tarp, tying one corner to the forward stay and another to one of the side-stays and the mast, to partially block the fierce rays of the scorching sun.

Shortly after two o'clock, Jeffrey Smythe pointed at a small island to port, and suggested that they make way to that small cay and spend the rest of the day and night at anchor. Dropping the sails and altering course, they made their way toward a bright white sand beach encircling a tiny cove. Several tall palm trees swayed gently in the breeze above the beach, adding to the charm of the tiny island. Nearing its crystalline waters, they took a couple of soundings, surveyed the area for other obstructions, and dropped anchor in about twenty feet of water. Once settled, all four of them jumped into the warm clear water for a swim. There was not much to see, the bottom surrounding them was an expansive sand and limestone shelf that held little underwater beauty. But about one hundred yards to the east, an area of darker reef or coral outcroppings could be seen. Kurt, Madison, and Larry climbed into the Sabot to go explore.

As the trio got closer to the submerged reef, they glimpsed an underwater garden. First, they passed over a heavily covered sea-grass bed with numerous dark blotches visible from the dinghy. Continuing on, massive mounds of bulbous brain coral came into view, and the surrounding underwater topography came alive with vibrant shoals of reef fishes, flashing and swirling in the clear water.

Locating a small semi-circular opening in the reef structures, they dropped the dinghy's small mushroom anchor in a patch of sand. They donned facemasks, fins, and snorkels, and slid over the side. As was her custom, Madison took with her a small foam Boogie board, holding onto it with one arm.

Immediately, the surroundings came to life, the coral reef illuminated by the bright tropical sunshine. Everywhere they looked, there was a mélange of living beauty—vast stretches of assorted coral, sponges, and reef fishes.

They stayed in the water for over an hour. They saw several green sea turtles of varying sizes, as well as occasional rays and small reef sharks. Kurt and Larry located dozens of spiny rock lobster tucked under the lip of nearly every overhanging structure. They each grabbed a couple, careful to avoid those 'holes' where huge moray eels slithered. In the sea grass areas, they discovered hundreds of queen conch. Several varieties of the big mollusks, including a few large and impressive emperor helmet and triton trumpet creatures, crawled across the sea floor in search of food. They picked up a couple of the queen conch to supplement a lobster dinner.

Returning to the *Cozy*, they dropped the lobster into a game bag to keep them alive until dinnertime. They also inserted a large hook into the meat under the carapace of the conch and hung them over the side so they would relax their foothold in the shell and drop it off. Once the shell was off, the conch meat was ready to tenderize and prepare for dinner. They feasted that evening on the rich delectable seafood.

Afterward, they watched another spectacular tropical sunset, marveling at the vibrant colors of sky and clouds as the setting sun played a panorama of celestial elegance across the clear Bahamian skies.

They spent the following two and a-half weeks like that first day, working their way northward through the Bahamas during bright daylight hours, snorkeling, swimming, and exploring the numerous unpopulated islands and atolls in the morning and afternoon. On one occasion, Kurt and Madison managed to sneak off by themselves and rowed out to one of the small, unpopulated islands they had anchored near. They found a secluded spot where they could spread out a beach blanket and enjoy a romantic afternoon together.

After shedding their clothing, Kurt and Madison reveled in the thrill of being nude and making love on a remote tropical island in the shade of a swaying palm. Madison released all of her usually restrained sexual energy. She responded to his tenderness with a lack of inhibition, relishing the touch of his exploring hands, fingers, lips, and tongue; and she returned the attention eagerly and with great enthusiasm. They had always appreciated the virility of each other; but on that particular afternoon, they both reached and experienced new feelings and sensations that were fed by the tropical sunshine and voyeuristic experience.

Afterward, they went over and sat on one of the low dunes under a swaying palm. They held hands in the shade of the single palm and gazed out at the sparkling sea.

Neither spoke for several minutes. Then together, each started to say something. Laughing, Kurt said, "Sorry, you first."

She looked into his face and gripped his hand a little tighter. "We're getting close to the end of our trip. Another week and we should be in Florida."

He looked at her lovely face and saw a flicker of sadness pass over her eyes. "Yes, I was going to say almost the same thing. Our trip is getting close to the end."

"Oh, Kurt," she whispered, a forlorn expression clouding her lovely features. "I don't want it to end."

"I know. I don't either. It's been an incredible trip, and I wish it could continue. But we do need to get back to the 'real world', then we'll figure out what we do and where we'll go. Maybe we can return to here, or somewhere similar, and find something to keep us going. After all, right now, I don't think we have one hundred dollars between us and that certainly won't get us very far."

She turned her head away and started to say something, then paused and remained quiet. He kept expecting her to say something, but she did not. After a few minutes, she stood up, pulled him up beside her, and said cheerfully, "I think we'd better get back to the boat. The other two are probably starting to wonder where the heck we are."

They dressed, and crossed the small island to the skiff. They waved out to Larry, who stood on the foredeck of the *Cozy,* obviously looking around for them.

Back aboard the *Cozy,* neither Larry, nor Jeffrey Smythe questioned where they had gone. The look of contentment on their flushed faces told the tale.

∞

As expected, the remainder of the journey through the placid waters of the central Bahama Bank went very quickly. They sailed for four or five hours a day, stopping in the early afternoon when the sun dropped toward the west and its glare on the shimmering sea surface made it too difficult to spot reefs and coral heads. Once anchored, they swam, snorkeled, and explored some of the tiny deserted islands and atolls.

At one of the isolated reefs, while snorkeling a good distance from the skiff, Kurt and Larry encountered a huge menacing giant barracuda that seemed to stalk them for nearly half an hour as they cautiously made their way back to the anchored Sabot, keeping a wary eye on the barracuda the whole time. The barracuda was more than six feet long, at least a foot in diameter, and laced with dark gray blotches along its shimmering silver sides. It stayed at a distance of about fifteen feet; slowly opening then snapping shut its large and gaping tooth-lined jaws, as if demonstrating its ability to inhale an arm or a leg in one swift bite. Later they learned that the rhythmic opening and closing of its jaws is merely a reflex mechanism designed to circulate water through its gills.

At another stop, several five-foot black-tip reef sharks eyed them suspiciously, circling around them for several minutes before they were able to climb back into the skiff. Those sharks then proceeded to hover in the vicinity while they rowed back to the safety of the *Cozy*. After a few minutes, the sharks swam slowly away.

Throughout the journey, they encountered minimal civilization, although they did pass a few sailboats and see a few small fishing boats when they passed near Georgetown, the capital of the Exumas. They had sufficient supplies and enough water to get by; so they elected not to stop at any of the inhabited ports in the central Bahamas, although they did spend an enjoyable afternoon and evening visiting with a family that lived on a small island named Rat Cay. During that visit, they saw several of the huge nearly six-foot long rock iguanas that make the Bahamas home. Other than that, they did not encounter any real civilization until they reached New Providence Island, home of Nassau, the Capitol City of the Bahamas.

∞

Entering a narrow bay between neighboring Paradise Island and the northeast shore of New Providence Island, they discovered a vastly different environment. New Providence is a bustling island community that is home to nearly eighty percent of the entire population of the Bahamas. The Capitol, Nassau, rose in the distance, its high-rise buildings and widespread commercial district visible from the sea.

After navigating the narrow channel between Paradise Island and Potters Cay, Jeffrey Smythe intended to drop anchor in the well-protected bay that was appropriately called Hurricane Hole—named for its year-round shelter. A strong current flowed out of the bay, and their headway at full power lowered to about two knots.

Smythe located an anchorage space between several large yachts, and the *Cozy* settled on its hook in about five fathoms of water, less than one eighth mile from shore. The water in the bay looked clouded and murky, unsuitable for snorkeling. They did jump in, cool off, and take their customary saltwater bath.

It was early evening and the travelers decided to stay on board, then spend the following day replenishing supplies, taking on water, and exploring their surroundings. They looked forward to a day of shore-side rest and relaxation.

After a good night's sleep—except for the all-night sounds of wild partying coming from a huge resort complex on nearby Paradise Island—the four members of the *Cozy* piled into the little Sabot and rowed to shore.

Dominating the landscape of Paradise Island stood the imposing structures that comprised the Paradise Island Hotel. The elaborate hotel, lavish villas, and casino made Paradise Island very upscale and way beyond the means of the *Cozy* crew. They walked around and even went into the plush casino, but everything on the island was both high-priced and luxurious. After spending a couple of hours exploring, they went back to the *Cozy,* hoisted anchor, motored across the bay, and took on fifty gallons of water at the Nassau yacht haven at an exorbitant cost. After taking on the water, they continued on toward the east end of New Providence, where they discovered a gorgeous anchorage in Montagu Bay. Dropping anchor in about three fathoms, they spent the remainder of the day swimming and snorkeling in the clear aquamarine water.

Because everything was so expensive on the islands of New Providence, they decided not to spend much time ashore but simply picked up a few items from a small grocery store and prepared their own food on the boat. They were happy to have ice and cold beer again, and their evening was peaceful and enjoyable.

They decided to depart and try and make the island of Bimini—their last scheduled stop before Florida—at daybreak the following morning. Their option was to sail the deep-water troughs around the Berry Islands, clear the Great Isaacs Bank, and round into Bimini from the northwest— or to navigate the reefs of 'the Berrys' and spend a few more days en route. All four were feeling the effects of being on a small boat together for nearly a month and were looking forward to reaching Florida. They plotted a tentative course around the Berry Islands and thereby avoided the notoriously dangerous reefs of the Great Isaacs Banks.

∞

As daybreak cast its suffused shadows over the bustling commercialism of New Providence Island, Kurt, Larry, Madison, and Jeffrey Smythe prepared to embark on the one hundred-twenty mile journey to South Bimini Island. The morning air turned warm and balmy, with a silver-lined mass of constantly changing cumulonimbus clouds marching slowly across the distant horizon. On shore, the lights of the city glowed and sparkled, sending a distinct message that civilization was out there and would soon awaken. A couple of small fishing skiffs accelerated out of the harbor, their wakes creating a widening 'v' as they bore toward the open ocean.

"Haul away!" Jeffrey Smythe called out, and Kurt and Larry pulled up the anchor. Breezes were minimal; so Smythe started the engine and shifted it into forward after the ground tackle was pulled and securely lashed. Madison and Kurt hoisted the main, Larry cranked-up the jib, and the *Cozy* put to sea.

Setting a northerly course, Smythe motored until they reached the deeper waters of Hanover Sound. Well clear of land and reefs, they made a nearly ninety-degree change of course that set them on a more westerly heading north of New Providence Island. Soon a gentle trade wind of about eight knots filled the sails. It was pleasant to be under full sail and not worry about dangerous reefs and coral heads. The deep blue waters of the Northwest Providence Channel rolled gently in the open ocean swell. The metallic rays of brilliant and warm sunshine danced merrily on the rippled surface of the sea.

They sailed close to a cluster of large fishing boats, all setting purse-seine nets in an area where gulls and other sea birds dipped and dived into teaming shoals of baitfish driven to the surface by feeding tuna. Kurt and Larry set out trolling lines rigged with feathers, but nothing bit. It was more than likely they were not moving quick enough to entice the fast-swimming tuna. Soon they were beyond the area that looked promising, but they left the trolling feathers to drag in their wake.

After about two-hours, they altered course to a more westerly heading, setting a bearing to clear the tip of the northern Berry Islands. Fair winds continued to prevail, increasing to about fifteen knots, but the swells remained minimal at about four feet. Sailing conditions turned ideal, and they made better speed than expected. By late afternoon, they entered the narrow passage bisecting the northern edge of the Berry Islands and Great Abaco Island. The breeze remained constant, but the swell and combined seas became more confused as the winds and currents of the passage converged. Warm spray splashed over the bow, washed across the decks and sent fine sheets of spray into the cockpit as the winds shifted to a more northerly direction. They switched to a starboard tack, trimmed the sails, and made a minor southwesterly course adjustment.

As nightfall approached, Jeffrey suggested they drop the jib and reef the main. They had covered more distance than expected, and sailing through the night would be much easier on all of them without full sails. Their speed slowed to about five knots, and the ride became more comfortable as the heel lessened and the spray stopped breaking over the bow.

Kurt and Larry worked the first evening watch, anticipating that they would make another course alteration around Great Isaac Bank sometime after midnight. Smythe counted on being able to see the light beacon from Isaac's Lighthouse at a distance of about twenty miles. The area could be dangerous, unpredictable, and often turbulent due to the confluence of the Northwest Providence Channel, the Grand Bahaman Bank, and the prevailing currents through the Straits of Florida. Smythe wanted to be sure that they transited the notorious reef with caution.

The beacon from Isaac's Lighthouse came into view around eleven p.m., and the lighthouse glow brightened as they neared the lonely sentinel that jutted up out of the depths in the vast expanse of open water. As the glow increased, the distance seemed to diminish rapidly, giving Kurt and Larry some concern that they would be upon it before Jeffrey Smythe came on watch. They kept a close eye on the flashing beacon and another eye on the time. The hour of midnight arrived first. Larry went below and roused Smythe and Madison, allowing them a few minutes to wake from the deep slumber of the night.

As the *Cozy* neared the flashing light, a noticeable change in the pitch and roll of the boat became evident. The seas became steeper and more confused, sending the *Cozy* into brief plunges into 'holes' that caused the bow to lift and tilt upward at steep angles. Side troughs also began to form, tilting the hull steeply to port or starboard in a random awkward canting motion. It became very difficult to sit or lie comfortably and nearly impossible to walk around.

The commotion could be attributed to the convergence of the wind, swell, and current in the vicinity of Isaac Cay at the extreme northern end of the Bimini Archipelago. The tiny atoll, only a couple of acres in size, rises steeply from the ocean depths about eighteen miles from the nearest point of land. Like most partially submerged banks, the atoll creates a natural area of disturbed ocean even in mild weather conditions.

The boat pitched and rocked to such an extent that they all needed to cling tightly to whatever they could grasp. A sliver of a tilted moon brightened the starry sky, its subtle moonbeams danced erratically on the dark tumultuous sea surface.

Sea noises increased considerably, and the sloughing of the boat through the building seas sent sheets of spray across the decks. The winds shifted wildly, causing the sails to whip and slap as the boat lurched in the swells.

Madison, clinging tightly to one of the handrails alongside the cabin wall, began to tremble as she envisioned another storm like the one they had experienced in the Windward Passage.

Timidly, she questioned Smythe, "Jeffrey, are we in trouble again?"

He turned to her and was about to answer when she continued. "Is another storm developing?

'No," he responded emphatically. "There is no storm. We are simply caught in the vortex that is normal and expected in this particular region. It should all ease up as soon as we clear Isaac Cay and change course toward Bimini."

Madison sighed, "I sure hope you are right. I don't want to ever go through anything like that again."

"Don't fret," Smythe assured her, "It will calm down soon."

Smythe sat at the helm, gripping the wheel as he held the *Cozy* on course until they cleared the northward extremity of Isaac Cay. At that point, he informed the others that they were going to tack to port, and skirt the western edge of the Great Isaac and Great Bahamas Banks.

Their course change brought little relief from the turbulence and, in fact, made the ride even more uncomfortable as they entered the fast-flowing current of the Gulf Stream. Under a reefed main, the *Cozy* was barely making any headway. Smythe informed the others that he wanted to hoist more sail, beginning with fully releasing the main. Kurt and Larry crawled across the deck to the boom and untied the reef points. Hauling the main to full, their speed increased by about two knots. They held course for the next two hours, taking them well clear of the Isaac Bank and a few miles to the west of the Hens and Chickens Bank.

From there, Smythe made a slight shift to the east and plotted a course to North Bimini Island, approximately twenty miles distant. If the wind and current continued to hold, Smythe estimated they would reach Bimini by mid morning. When the silvery moon dropped into the black depths of the sea, the darkness seemed to magnify the veiled sailing conditions, and the seas became even more chaotic. They endured the end to a miserable, physically challenging night.

∞

The eastern sky lightened a couple of hours later and daybreak brought relief. The seas moderated as the *Cozy* made slow headway. Being able to see the choppy seas provided a better perspective on the swell and currents. The ocean began to calm down. When the sun rose in the east, the clear shallow waters of the Great Bahamas Bank lit with a celestial glow.

When they could distinguish the low outline of the islands of Bimini, Smythe altered course a few more degrees to the east, hoping they might encounter smoother conditions near the contours of the Continental Shelf. Sure enough, as they approached the edges of the steep underwater escarpment, the current moderated, as did the general grumpiness of the ocean.

Kurt and Larry were scheduled to take over the helm at eight o'clock, but Jeffrey Smythe and Madison declined to go below. So the four of them took turns at the wheel as they slowly made their approach to Browns Marina on North Bimini Island.

As the *Cozy* sailed over the prodigious drop-off that distinguishes the Bahaman Shelf, Smythe started the engine and had the others lower and stow the sails. No sooner were the sails down than they once again entered the crystal clear aquamarine waters that make the Bahamas such a visual delight. Brilliant white sand beaches interspersed with rocky volcanic outcroppings lined the shore. The sands were punctuated with swaying coconut palms and an occasional small cottage on South Bimini, while a sprawling cluster of buildings covered most of North Bimini Island.

Smythe had closely studied the charts and read the Coast Pilot carefully. He was aware that the narrow entrance to Bimini Harbor could be tricky, at best, and nearly impossible to navigate under certain wind and current conditions. Winds from the west to north made the entrance extremely difficult and combined with incoming or outgoing tides, nearly impossible. Fortunately, the winds were favorable, out of the east, and the tide was high and temporarily stationary.

On their approach, the topography of the Bimini Islands, one of the smallest yet most popular island chains in the Bahamas, looked unremarkable. The chain consists of three small Islands—North, South, and East Bimini—with a combined landmass of less than nine square miles and a population of around twelve hundred. More than eighty percent of the populace is packed into the narrow strip that comprises North Island. Its natives are descendents of slaves from the eighteenth century slave trade from West Africa, and mixed with an eclectic blend of English and American expatriates and the progeny of European traders and pirates. What makes Bimini so attractive to tourists is its proximity to Florida (less than forty miles), its pristine waters, and the prolific game fishing that surrounds the islands.

Many believe Bimini to be the source of the fabled 'Fountain of Youth,' which explorer Ponce de Leon is said to have discovered. To this day, a small well exists on South *Island* with a plaque commemorating it as the proverbial fountain.

Kurt, Larry, and Madison all stood on the bow and kept a diligent watch for coral heads, as Smythe maneuvered carefully into the channel entrance.

Inside the bay, Smythe located a small concrete abutment where they could moor. Alongside the wharf, he instructed Kurt to drop a lead line and discovered they had nearly twelve feet of depth under the keel, an adequate depth. They secured lines to a large concrete bollard, hung fenders along the starboard rail, and looked around.

∞

The tiny marina nestled at the fringes of Alice Town held a conglomeration of low rust-colored buildings interspersed with pastel-painted shops and offices. From one of the small offices, a young dark-skinned woman and a smaller even darker man emerged and walked toward them.

"Halo." The young lady called out. "Welcome to Bimini Island. I am Tyra, and this is Salvio. We operate the marina and can help you with whatever your needs might be."

Tyra looked stunning, lithe and feminine, with jet-black hair and enormous coal-black eyes set widely apart in a beautiful oval face. Her skin, the color of dark mahogany, contrasted starkly with her short white cotton dress trimmed with bright yellow. Her white teeth sparkled within her welcoming smile, and her eyes danced merrily as she glanced from person to person.

Salvio on the other hand looked thin, old, and gray—his features almost indistinguishable in a shadowy ashen-colored face devoid of expression or emotion. He seemed to shrink even more as he got closer, while Tyra exhibited a vibrant glow that seemed to light up her surroundings.

Turning to Salvio, Tyra performed a slight bow toward him and stepped aside.

When he spoke, all four of the new arrivals looked at him in surprise. Salvio, meek and bland in appearance, had a voice that resonated with a deep musical timbre that instantaneously captured their attention. "My friends," he intoned, "you are obviously new to Bimini and do not know what to expect. I can see that you are impressed with Tyra's beauty and surprised that I speak distinctively. We are accustomed to both reactions. Please relax and feel comfortable. We are your friends, and we are here to help you with whatever you may need." Salvio completed his brief talk with a sallow smile and immediately seemed to fade into the shadows again, although he remained standing in bright sunlight.

Larry broke the brief silence. "Great. We don't really need much. We're just laying over for the night before heading across to Florida. Is there anything we should know about Bimini that is not in the Bahamas guidebook?"

"Oh," Tyra offered, "there is a small café about a block down the quay that serves the Bahamas' best conch fritters. It is run by my Aunt Tessa and my three cousins."

Larry replied eagerly, "We'll definitely try it out. Will you be there?"

Laughing lightly, Tyra responded, "Perhaps, I often go there after my work is completed. Which reminds me, we will need to charge you four-dollars for the dockage. We accept Bahamian or U.S. dollars."

Jeffrey Smythe went below to get the money while Larry continued to flirt with Tyra. She tolerated his flirtations, coyly demurring to his teasing and humorous comments. Salvio stood to the side, apparently not interested in the bantering.

When Jeffrey Smythe emerged with the cash, farewells were made, and Larry reminded Tyra that he would definitely be at her aunt's café later in the evening.

∞

After tidying-up the *Cozy*, the four travelers climbed up onto the wharf to stretch their legs. Following a short walk around the harbor, they returned to the boat and discussed their plans for the passage across the Gulf Stream to Florida the following day. There was uncertainty and restraint in the conversation as they all realized that the adventure they had shared for so long was nearing its end. They popped a beer and sat gazing out over the Island and surrounding waters in subdued silence.

As the afternoon wore on, Larry commented that he would like to check out the local scenery and identify the café where they planned to meet for dinner. Before Larry headed off, Kurt kidded him about his obvious fascination with Tyra. Madison punched Kurt in the arm, admonishing him to lighten up with his teasing.

For the crew of the *Cozy*, the mere act of being on solid ground brought a welcome relief from the toss-n-tumble passage they had completed over the course of the past two days. Surrounded by the beautiful waters of the

Bimini Islands, each felt nostalgic, as they remembered their travels and pondered the reality that their adventure neared its end.

Standing, Kurt reached out and grasped Madison's hand, informing Smythe that they were going for a walk.

Heading off to the northwest, Kurt and Madison walked a couple of short blocks through a combined residential/commercial area, making brief contact with several friendly islanders. Madison looked very pretty in a flowered cotton dress, her long golden hair radiated in the sunlight and her shapely browned legs skipped along lightly in her sandals. Kurt felt exuberant, overjoyed at having such a beautiful woman by his side and happy to be on dry land.

Madison, on the other hand, appeared somewhat subdued. Kurt assumed her somber expression was due to the fact that their journey was almost over. He gripped her hand more firmly and smiled down into her pensive eyes. She smiled back, but did not speak.

When they neared a white sandy beach, they stopped and sat atop a low stone-built wall overlooking the lagoon. After a few quiet moments, Madison leaned her head on Kurt's shoulder and commented wistfully, "It has been wonderful, Kurt."

Tilting her head up so that he could look into her eyes, Kurt smiled, "Yes. It has been wonderful. I think we both feel really blessed to have shared such an incredible experience together."

Madison thought for a moment, and then laughed lightly. "There were so many fun and amazing times. From the first interactions we had in Ensenada Harbor right up until today, we have really shared some incredible experiences." She raised her eyes and looked at him.

"It has truly been an amazing experience to share, hasn't it Kurt?" The question was rhetorical, and she continued.

"Remember Mazatlan and getting stuck in the mud? And the day you rescued Larry at that little Island in Manzanillo? The good times in Acapulco and the day Linda nearly drowned? Tiona and all of her drama, especially the day she jumped off the ship? All of the beautiful places we saw and visited." She paused for a moment, her face animated by the joy of her memories.

She started rambling again. "I'll never forget Acapulco, the Panama Canal, and the storms, rains, mosquitoes, and trips by bus. Jamaica, Negril,

Great Inagua, the Bahamas, coral reefs, gorgeous sunsets, snorkeling and playing on pristine beaches, the Cuban gunboat, the horrible storm, and the flamingoes… and," she paused, shaking her head slightly before continuing, "Yes, even that, although it was painful, was a memory to cherish."

Kurt laughed at her jumbled reflections. "Yeah, they were incredible times, and it was you being there with me that made it so perfect."

Madison gazed deeply into his hazel eyes. "Oh, Kurt. I love you so much. Thank you." She paused momentarily, and then continued before he could respond, "Thank you. A thousand times, thank you. I have enjoyed these past couple of months more than anything or any time in my life. It has been incredibly fun, exciting, and enlightening. I will always cherish the memories of this trip, and I love you so much. I feel that we have become closer than we ever were."

Kurt tilted her face up to his and kissed her deeply, savoring the sweet taste of her lips and the subtle quiver of desire that soon became evident in her response.

Reluctantly, he pulled away, realizing that if he continued the embrace he might find it difficult to restrain his urges.

"Madison, you are the love of my life, and I should be the one thanking you for giving all of this to me." He kissed her lightly once again, then pulled back and said, "But I think we should move along before I lose it completely and ravish you right here on the beach."

She laughed and stood up. "Okay, let's walk on the beach for a while."

Kurt reached out to help Madison over the short wall and onto the sand. Then using his left hand for leverage, he athletically hopped over the wall, yelped and collapsed onto the sand when his left foot landed on a partially buried rock. Madison turned around immediately and knelt at his side.

"What happened?" She asked.

"My foot," Kurt replied, grasping his foot. "I landed on a rock when I jumped over. My foot twisted. I might have broken something. It hurts like hell."

"Let me help you." Madison reached under his arm to help him up so that he could sit on the rock wall. Then she knelt before him, removed his sandal, and lifted his foot to inspect it closer. Gently massaging and turning his ankle, she looked up into his eyes and asked if it hurt.

"A little, but I don't think it's too bad. Let me just sit here for a minute and see how it does."

She lowered his foot onto the sand, and he slowly and carefully moved it back and forth, up and down, grimacing slightly with each maneuver. "I don't think I broke anything, but I probably have a moderate sprain. Let me see how it feels if I try to walk."

Carefully Kurt stood, shifted most of his weight onto his right side and then transferred weight onto his left side. At first it seemed okay, but suddenly he winced deeply and grabbed onto Madison's shoulder, balancing on his right foot only. "Crap! It really hurts when I put full weight on it. I don't think I can walk without your help."

"Well then," she smiled up at him, "I guess I'll just have to help you back to the *Cozy*. But, maybe we should try to find a doctor."

"No." Kurt stated emphatically. "No doctor. First of all, we don't have any money to pay for a doctor. And secondly, I really don't think its anything serious. I think it's just a sprain. Some ice, rest, and a couple of aspirin and I should be fine."

Madison looked at him skeptically but bowed to his obstinacy. She assisted him back over the wall, helped with his sandal, and together they began hobbling back toward the wharf.

It wasn't easy. Kurt seemed to do fine when he kept the majority of his weight on his heel; but whenever he shifted forward, his ankle hurt, and he leaned heavily on Madison's shoulder. They slowed even more so that Kurt was not tempted to transfer weight onto his toes, and made steady progress back toward the dock. When they reached the residential area, one of the islanders they had encountered earlier saw them hobbling along. He approached and offered to help. For both Kurt and Madison, walking was awkward, the differences in their height making it difficult for both of them. The man who offered to help was about the same size as Kurt; so when he traded places with Madison, the hobble became easier for Kurt to endure.

When they reached the boat, the nice gentlemen offered to deliver some ice from his home, which he explained was nearby. Instead, Madison went back to his house with him, returning within a few minutes with a large bag of ice. She put most of it into the cooler, then packed some into a towel and wrapped it around Kurt's foot and ankle. She gave him a couple of aspirin and sat with him in the cockpit.

Neither Smythe nor Larry was aboard. A short while later Larry returned to the *Cozy*. He looked at Kurt and commented, "Oh, Christ! What happened?"

Madison looked up and smiled wanly. "Kurt jumped over a wall and hurt his ankle. It's a little swollen and hurts him to walk, but he doesn't think it's serious and does not want to see a doctor."

Larry shook his head sadly, "Well shucks, brother. That was a dumb thing to do."

Kurt looked up at him and grinned sheepishly. "Yeah, it was. But what the heck, we've all made it this far without anything bad happening. I suppose one little foot sprain is not that big a deal."

"Can you walk?" Larry asked.

"Not without help. But I really don't think it's too bad. I should be fine after ice and a little rest. I guess I just won't be able to get out and about much tonight."

Larry sat with them for a while, and they talked about their adventure, reminiscing fondly as each recalled bits and pieces of the trip that had left indelible memories in their minds. Larry popped a couple of cold beers. There were only four beers left aboard, so they each drank one, then the three of them shared the last.

A short while later, Jeffrey Smythe returned to the boat. After explaining to him what had happened, they discussed their plans for the evening. Larry, of course, intended to visit the café down the road; but it was about a half-mile away, and Kurt did not want to try and walk that far. They agreed to fix Kurt something to eat and bring back a couple of beers for him, then Larry, Madison, and Jeffrey Smythe would head to the café and try the conch fritters.

∞

After showering and fixing Kurt a bite to eat, the three others prepared to head out to 'Aunt Tessa's.'

Kurt really did not like Madison being alone with Smythe; however, Larry would be with them, so he said nothing. He did his best to conceal his angst. He knew this was their last night in the Bahamas, and he did not want it to end on a sour note. He took a moment to snuggle up to Madison.

She spoke to him softly. "Darling, don't worry. We're just going out for a while to try the fritters. If Larry 'connects' with Tyra—or anyone else, for that matter—I'll have Jeffrey walk me back to the boat, even if he wants to stay out longer."

Kurt looked deeply into her eyes and smiled. "It's okay. I trust you."

She smiled broadly back at him. "I love you so much."

He nodded. "Yeah, I love you too. In fact, why don't you try to persuade Jeffrey to just walk you back to the boat and then go back without you? I'd love to spend a little time with you alone tonight."

She laughed lightly, "Oh sure, should I just tell him that we want to have sex?"

Kurt chuckled. "No, I don't think that would be good. Just tell him to go out and have some fun, and you'll stay on the boat and play nursemaid to me."

"Yeah, right."

When Larry and Jeffrey Smythe came out on deck, they chatted idly for a few minutes, and Madison kissed Kurt goodbye. He watched them walk down the wharf.

CHAPTER TWENTY-TWO

Kurt sipped on a cold Red Stripe beer, watched the purple sunset and listened to the wavelets slap the side of the *Cozy*. It was a magical time of evening, and he wanted Madison at his side sharing the moment with him—the tropical sunset, the colors, the warmth, the smells and beauty of the sea. Kurt sat pensively in the cockpit of the *Cozy* watching it unfold; while a half-mile away, Madison, Larry, and Jeffrey Smythe enjoyed a similar vista from the barstools at 'Aunt Tessa's' café.

∞

Madison seemed to be in her own little world, oblivious to the bustling activity around her. She stared out over the ocean. A pensive smile creased her brow as she absorbed the beauty of the sunset. Abruptly, the deep thumping of Bongo drums echoed on the balmy air.

Madison turned to see a trio of Calypso musicians had setup and begun playing music on a stage near the back of the small café. Soon the café throbbed to the beat of Reggae tunes, and several couples danced together on the stage.

Madison saw Larry smile broadly as he watched Tyra walk through the front door. Tyra's short red dress, cut fashionably low at the bosom, accentuated a white seashell necklace that rested on her glowing dark brown skin. Tyra turned, saw Larry staring, and her lovely face lit up with a sparkling smile. She lifted a finger toward him, indicating just a moment, and she went behind the counter to give Aunt Tessa a hug. After that, she sought out two of the young pretty waitresses, her cousins who were serving the customers, gave each of them a hug and chatted with them briefly. Her greetings completed, Tyra walked over to the table where Madison, Larry, and Jeffrey Smythe sat, and greeted them as if they were old friends.

"Halo. I was hoping you would be here," she offered sweetly, touching both Larry and Smythe on the shoulder, and then she leaned over to give Madison an affectionate hug. "You are so beautiful!" She exclaimed unpretentiously to Madison. "Your hair is so beautiful, and your skin is so smooth and delicious."

"Oh, please," Madison demurred, "You are the one who is beautiful." She looked at Larry and Jeffrey who were both ogling Tyra like teenage boys.

Madison took charge. "Please, won't you join us?" She asked, gesturing to one of the chairs at the table. Larry and Jeffrey Smythe almost tripped over each other trying to pull the chair out for her. Larry succeeded in reaching it first. Both Madison and Tyra giggled at the awkward gallantry displayed by both men. Tyra sat, and they began an animated session of getting to know one-another, with Larry garnering most of Tyra's attention.

For the next couple of hours, they talked, drank, and danced. Larry and Tyra took to the dance floor first, where Larry did his best to sway to the beat despite his lack of rhythm or skill. Tyra—not too surprisingly—proved to be fluid and graceful, as she swirled around the dance floor with ease and sensuality; and all eyes in the small room were focused on her swinging and swaying curves. As she moved around the dance floor, Larry followed to the best of his ability, grinning broadly and obviously pleased to be dancing with such a beautiful woman.

After three dances, Larry persuaded her to return with him to their table. A group of appreciative Europeans from another table purchased a round of drinks for the Americans and the talented native dancer, and soon the café patrons became even more festive and boisterous.

Two more rounds of drinks materialized as the group talked and listened to the musicians, and Tyra convinced Madison and Jeffrey to join her and Larry on the dance floor.

∞

Madison, although not as talented as Tyra, garnered her own following of gawkers because of her all-American beauty and femininity. She and Jeffrey actually moved well together, complementing each other's more conservative yet subtly immodest gyrations, much to the appreciation of those watching.

Madison was happily intoxicated. She was enjoying the evening immensely and had experienced only brief—quickly cast aside—recriminations of guilt for enjoying herself with such abandon without Kurt at her side. But she also felt very light-headed, and her next attempt to gyrate on the dance floor nearly caused her to fall over. She returned to the table and told Jeffrey that she should probably return to the *Cozy*.

Larry chose that moment to ask Tyra to walk with him on the beach, an offer that she readily accepted.

Smythe paid their bill, they said their goodbyes to the entire roomful of new friends, and the four of them walked outdoors.

Larry told Madison and Jeffrey Smythe that he and Tyra were going to head toward the ocean. He asked Smythe if he would escort Madison back to the boat, and Smythe assured him that he would.

Madison and Jeffrey began walking toward the wharf where the *Cozy* awaited. After walking a short distance, Jeffrey turned to Madison and asked if she would like to continue on a while longer in order to walk-off some of the effects of the evening libations. Realizing that Kurt would probably not appreciate her returning 'three-sheets to the wind,' Madison agreed; and they headed off in the general direction of the lagoon.

Upon reaching the sandy shoreline, Jeffrey suggested a walk on the beach. They removed their sandals, and he reached out and held her hand to help her over the low rock wall. On the beach, he continued to grip her hand. When they reached the water's edge, they stopped and stood gazing over the placid lagoon. It looked lovely and entrancing, and Madison felt mesmerized by the tranquil beauty and serenity, but she also felt confused. She dropped Jeffrey's hand and suggested that they head back to the boat.

He looked at her intently; and before she could say more, he leaned over and kissed her on the mouth. Her first response was to pull away; but as she stepped back, Jeffrey Smythe reached out and pulled her toward him, placed both hands behind her neck and tilted her head upward.

"Oh Madison," he whispered huskily, "I have waited for this moment way too long." He kissed her again.

She felt a warming begin to course through her body, and found his lips surprisingly soft. At first she did not respond, but she allowed him to hold her against him and felt his lips pressed tenderly against hers. Then his hands moved down her back, along her hips, and over her rounded buttocks.

When his hands cupped her breasts, her body responded instinctively, a delightful tingling sent shivers down her spine and into the core of her femininity. She moaned, responding to his kisses and pressed her body tighter against his. Alarm and uncertainty flitted through Madison's conscious thoughts, but the effects of the alcohol lowered her inhibitions. She did not respond with eagerness, nor did she resist.

Jeffrey wore a lightweight windbreaker and a long-sleeved button-up shirt. He casually removed the jacket and shirt and laid them out carefully on the sand. He eased Madison down onto the garments, while at the same time unzipping the back of her thin summer dress. As usual, she did not wear a bra. Her firm full breasts glowed tantalizingly in the starlight. He unbuttoned his pants, removed them, and slid her white panties down over her hips and legs. As he pulled them down over her ankles, his lips found the thick furry mound of her golden curls. She moaned again.

Their coitus ended quickly. When he entered her, she became vaguely aware that he was not as well endowed as Kurt, the only man she had ever known sexually—other than the forgettable assault she had endured from her stepfather when she was a teen. This intercourse was not at all gratifying for her, partly because it was over so quickly and partly because she did not feel the fullness and power that she always felt with Kurt.

The act completed, she could not believe she had allowed it to happen. Mortified by her infidelity, she closed her eyes and laid her head back against the sand. She slipped rapidly into an alcohol-induced slumber.

Jeffrey Smythe recognized that she had fallen asleep; and he leaned on one elbow and gazed intently at her young supple curves, his smug, self-satisfied smile indicated that he had finally fulfilled his longtime fantasy.

∞

On board the *Cozy*, Kurt felt disappointed that he was unable to go out with Madison, but his foot was still quite sore. He reflected on how much Madison meant to him. She was everything he had ever wanted in a woman—smart, wholesome, and intoxicatingly sexy. He determined then and there that he would ask her to be his wife when they returned to southern California and their lives became 'normal' again.

Later, after waiting for another hour or so, his loving thoughts began to turn slightly darker. He did not like the fact that she was out and about with Jeffrey Smythe, who he did not trust, and he became increasingly anxious. For what seemed like an eternity, he sat in the cockpit of the boat listening to the distant music, the peals of laughter and gaiety wafting across the calm tropical air. There was not much taking place anywhere else, and the sounds of partying, although distant and muted, dominated the night.

He desperately wanted to get off the boat and go get Madison, but his sore foot prevailed. He sat quietly and endured the misgivings that coursed through every fiber of his being.

With each passing minute, his anxiety built. When the music ended and the sounds of partying stopped altogether, he breathed a sigh of relief in anticipation of her arrival. His mouth felt dry, and his head began to pound as time slowly dragged on. After a while, he could endure it no longer; and he climbed out of the cockpit and onto the wharf. His foot felt better, and he tested it gingerly. He found that he was able to walk without too much discomfort as long as he did not move too quickly. He walked a few yards, stopped, and pondered the situation.

His head spun in bewilderment, his thoughts in turmoil. 'What the hell could she be doing? Why hadn't she returned? Was she alone with Jeffrey Smythe—that slime ball of an Englishman?'

He walked back and stood on the dock next to the *Cozy*, not knowing what else to do.

It was nearing three a.m., and Kurt was becoming frantic. He felt worried that something bad had happened—that she had been accosted, attacked, injured, raped, murdered. It was all he could do to keep from shouting out into the night.

∞

Madison shivered, the night air chilling her awake. She looked over to see Jeffrey leaning on one elbow, staring down at her, a possessive, hungry look in his eye. He spoke throatily, "Ah, my little beauty has awakened." He leaned down to kiss her. She spun her head away, feeling horribly guilty, ashamed, and dirty.

When Smythe attempted again to embrace her, Madison said coldly, "Stop! I should not be here. I should never have allowed this to happen. Please, just give me my clothes and get away from me."

Jeffrey seemed surprised by her reaction. He reached out to touch her hair, speaking quietly as he said, "Madison, listen to me..."

"No!" She cut him off abruptly. "No! Just don't say anything."

She reached down and picked up her dress, slipped it over her shoulders and down over her nakedness. She stood and moved away from Smythe. After a few steps, she turned back to him and stated simply yet firmly. "I am going back to the boat. I would like you to stay away for a while."

Smythe looked at her, deep disappointment evident on his face. "Sure. I understand. I will just walk around for a while."

"Thank you," she mumbled. She turned away from him and walked slowly toward the boat. With each step, her thoughts changed. 'What can I tell him? How can I face him? What will he do and say?' Her footsteps slowed, her feet heavier and more difficult to lift.

As she rounded the last building before walking out onto the wharf, she looked up and saw Kurt standing slump-shouldered alongside the *Cozy*. Even in the darkness, she could see the worry on his face.

Kurt looked up and saw her walking toward him. Her movements slowed even more as she got closer. At about twenty feet, she stopped and broke into tears.

∞

Kurt stood immobile, unsure, confused. He felt an immediate urge to rush to her and wrap his arms around her, to console and comfort her. But he also felt trepidation—an inner feeling that her breakdown was the result of something dark and sinister, something that he did not want to know.

As she stood there sobbing, Kurt became aware that her tears could only be from guilt. His senses told him that she was crying out of internal despair, not because of innocuous events.

For a long time, the two of them stood rooted in place, neither moving, and nothing being said. Finally, Madison looked into his face, and through sobs whispered quietly, "Oh, Kurt, I am so sorry."

Kurt stared at her in shock, his gut wrenched painfully. He knew what had happened without her having to tell him. But he also needed to hear it, as painful as it would be.

"Tell me what happened."

She started to move toward him.

"No! Stay where you are. Just tell me what happened."

Madison slowly shook her head back and forth. Her mussed golden hair caught the dim lighting of the stars and glowed like a halo around her face.

'How beautiful she is.' Kurt found himself thinking.

She started to speak, faltered, and stood still again.

Softly Kurt demanded again, "Tell me what happened?"

"I fell asleep on the beach."

An all-encompassing quiet filled the air.

"And?" Kurt prompted her quietly.

"And I slept with him."

The silence and abject misery were noticeably palpable. Nothing moved, nothing could be seen, heard, or felt, other than the painful silence of the night.

Time stood still as Kurt stood there looking at her. He wanted desperately to rush to her, wrap his arms tightly around her and pretend that this was not happening. But it was, and his feelings of pain, anger, disbelief, and despair pounded through the night air with the intensity of a hurricane. When Kurt gulped deeply, he realized that he had been holding his breath.

His reaction broke the spell, and Madison's head slumped forward, her deep wracking sobs filled the oppressive night. Kurt stood rooted in place, watching Madison. Had it been anything else, anyone else, he could probably have dealt with it better, but not Jeffrey Smythe.

"Where is he?" Kurt asked her abruptly, a malevolent expression clouding his face.

"I don't know. I asked him to stay away for a while," she responded miserably.

Kurt raged. He had always disliked Smythe, and now that dislike had turned to outright hatred. If Smythe were there, Kurt realized, he would kill him.

∞

Time continued to creep. Madison's weeping quieted to heavy breathing, interspersed with sniffles and deep sighs. She looked up at Kurt, feeling profoundly lonely and remorseful. 'Why?' She thought to herself, 'Why would I be so stupid? How could I do this to him, to us? What have I done?' That thought moved her to another round of sobbing as she realized that she had changed their lives forever. She knew that Kurt would never forgive her for this, and she knew that there was nothing she could do or say to make it better. Flashes of beautiful memories coursed through her mind as her thoughts tumbled randomly from the present to the past. She could not focus, she could not think clearly; and the more she tried, the more painful the effort became. Regrettably, she realized that it was like that for Kurt also. He was such a good man, they were so good together, and they had so much to look forward to. But she had ruined it all. Now as she looked at him, her realization of how deeply she loved him made it even worse. She broke into deep sobs once again.

∞

Kurt gradually began to focus. He could feel the torment distorting her lovely features. He could hear the pain dripping like teardrops from her voice. He realized that he had been standing there looking at her for a very long time when he looked up and noticed a faint lightening of the night. Daylight was nearing, and he thought 'soon it will be tomorrow.'

He tried desperately to pull his thoughts together, knowing that he could not bear to stay where he was or interact with Jeffrey Smythe.

Larry was still missing—Larry who was supposed to protect Madison.

"Where is Larry?" He asked Madison.

"I don't know. He went off with Tyra, and I haven't seen him since they left the café together."

Kurt felt a sudden surge of anger and resentment toward Larry. He had trusted his brother to keep Madison safe and out of trouble. Now he was angry that Larry had let him down. No, it wasn't Larry's fault—it was Madison's. She did what she did, and no one was to blame except her. And Smythe. The slime ball Limey bastard had ruined everything. With a determined effort, Kurt shook his head as if to shake the madness out of it and turned his back on Madison as he moved ponderously toward the *Cozy*. As he reached the boat and stepped over the rail, he heard Madison ask, "What are you going to do?"

"I'm leaving." He stated simply. "Please, just leave me alone."

Engulfed in the deepest, most profound misery he had ever known, Kurt pulled together his belongings, and stuffed his clothes and personal items into a travel bag. He pulled out Madison's handbag and discovered that they had about sixty-five dollars between them. He knew it would not get him very far, but hoped it would at least get him back to the States. He put the money in his pocket.

He could see Madison sitting slumped atop one of the large concrete bollards on the dock, her sweet angelic features contorted in despair. Each time he glanced her way, he quickly tore his eyes from her so as not to succumb to her pitiful appearance and rush to her side to console her. Each time he glanced her way he also saw the imagined shadow of Jeffrey Smythe standing behind her with a smirk on his pockmarked face. That image tore at his guts, impelling him to get away as quickly as possible.

Taking a last look around, he realized that there were a couple of things that he wanted to take with him but did not think possible under the circumstances. One of them was the large hand-tied green-glass fishing net-float that he had gotten from the Japanese fishing boat back in Panama. The other things were the assortment of conch shells that he had found while free diving in Jamaica and in various stops throughout the Bahamas. He thought, 'I really need to talk to Larry before I leave.' But he did not want to wait around with Madison—it was too painful. Also, even though one part of him wanted desperately to confront Jeffrey Smythe, his overall common sense made him realize that murdering the slimy bastard would ruin his life more than it was already ruined. He grabbed his bag, stepped off the boat, and began walking awkwardly away.

"Kurt!" He heard her anguished cry. "Kurt. Please, Kurt." She sobbed. Purposefully, doggedly, and painfully, he continued to walk.

Her pleas turned to a wail. "Kurt. Oh, please Kurt. Don't go. I'm sorry. I'm so desperately sorry! Please. Please. Kurt. Kurt. Kurt." Her voice faded with each word, each painful step.

As he got farther away, her pleas lessened, quieted and turned to sobs. Stubbornly, he continued to walk away, resigned to not turn around or to succumb to the desperation in her plaintive cries.

∞

After a few minutes and by far the most difficult and tormented steps of his life, Kurt paused. He ran his hands over his face, ears, neck, feeling the pain and suffering emanating from every pore of his being. He breathed deeply, sighed, and looked around.

Everything looked blurry. He saw things, but he couldn't see anything. It was like he was looking through the lens of a camera that was out of focus. He sensed the early morning sun begin to rise, but there was no warmth in his being. He sensed that he was standing on a dock and that he was alive with blood coursing through his veins, but something inside of him seemed to be whispering 'death.' He felt helpless, forlorn, a hollowed out husk. Where there had been joy and warmth yesterday, there was now only cold remorse. Where there had been hope and optimism, there was now an empty glass.

A stupid rock buried in the sand. Who would think something like a rock buried in the sand could shatter a person's life?

He pulled his aimless thoughts into focus and asked himself the disturbing question, 'Why would she do this to me, to us?'

He stood there in the balmy morning air, on a concrete dock on the Island of Bimini, and felt as though the essence of the man that had been Kurt Decker had been erased.

He was only vaguely aware of time, space, or reality. Briefly, he broke out of his despondent funk and thought, 'It's only a dream, a nightmare. I will awaken soon, and it will all go away'. But he looked down at his hands, blinked a couple of times, forced a dry swallow down his throat, and realized that it was real, that he was where he was, and that he needed to do something. He breathed deeply and looked around. He refocused.

He really wanted to find Larry, but he had no idea where to look. He assumed Larry must have connected with Tyra last night and was somewhere with her. But where that might be, he had no idea. Trying desperately to think clearly, he decided that he should probably find a spot where he could watch for Larry to return. He circled around a couple of commercial buildings and found a spot where he could see most of the wharf and the bow section of the *Cozy*, with very little likelihood of being seen by Madison or anyone else. When he sat down atop an overturned shipping crate, he realized that an even worse scenario would be to see Jeffrey Smythe. He sat there for several long and agonizingly drawn-out minutes before a man walked out from behind one of the distant buildings and moved toward the *Cozy*. It was Jeffrey Smythe.

Seeing Jeffrey Smythe immediately clouded his thoughts again. Hatred, pure, thick, raging hatred, pulsed through his veins. He could feel his body leaning forward, his primal urges compelling him to react, to attack. But something stronger and more rational deep inside of him kept him in check, held him back.

Madison stood near the edge of the wharf, looking forlorn and defeated. Smythe walked slowly toward her; but before he was too close, she held her arm straight out, palm extended, and cried out, "No! Leave me alone!"

Smythe froze in his tracks about ten paces away. Kurt saw that he was speaking, but could not hear his words. Again, he saw Madison look up at Smythe briefly, holding both hands and arms in front of her as if to say 'keep back.' Smythe stood very still, staring at Madison, who eventually dropped her arms to her side and again let her chin slump to her chest. Silently, Kurt watched their interaction unfold. One part of him wanted Smythe to make a move toward her—in which case he would have the provocation he needed. But nothing happened. They both stood there like statues as the tropical sun rose in the pastel blue sky and warmed the morning. From out of the corner of his eye, Kurt caught the movement of another person, Larry. He was walking down the wharf from the direction of Aunt Tessa's Café, and the rising sun cast a long shadow ahead of him. Kurt waved his arms, trying to get Larry's attention, but to no avail. Larry was obviously wrapped up in his own thoughts, a happy bouncing gait to his steps.

Kurt reached down, grabbed a large pebble, and tossed it toward Larry. It struck a few feet away. Larry stopped and looked around. He glanced toward the distant figures of Madison and Jeffrey Smythe standing near the *Cozy*, looking odd and incongruous. He also spotted Kurt, standing off to his right in the shadow of one of the nearby buildings. Obviously confused and bewildered, he looked back and forth between the three shipmates.

Madison and Jeffrey Smythe were not looking his way, and Kurt was beckoning somewhat frantically, so Larry headed toward him.

∞

Larry felt great, his mood ebullient. He had just spent an incredible night with an even more incredible woman, and he was feeling really good. As he got closer to Kurt, his exuberance waned as he noticed Kurt's stiff posture and the gaunt haunted expression on his normally jocular features. He stopped and asked quietly, "Kurt, what's wrong?"

Looking up with a discernable amount of difficulty, Kurt responded dully, "She spent the night with him." He paused briefly before finishing. "Madison slept with Jeffrey Smythe."

Larry was quiet for a long thoughtful moment, and then whispered, "Aw Christ, Kurt. I'm sorry."

Kurt looked directly into Larry's eyes, his anguish palpable. He shook his head slowly. "Yes. I'm sorry too." He managed to respond quietly.

Standing together on the edge of the wharf on Bimini Island, in the shade of a metal-roofed warehouse, the two brothers looked into each other's eyes. Larry saw the pain, suffering and disillusionment his brother carried in his heart. For Larry, it caused an immediate and profound reversal—one minute he had been alive and aglow in the pleasures of life and the next he was plummeting into a state of compassionate remorse. He knew instinctively that Kurt felt as though his world was destroyed, and he felt a growing pang of guilt for having allowed it to happen.

As if reading his brother's thoughts, Kurt said quietly, "Larry, it's not your fault. It was Smythe. That Limey bastard has been waiting for the opportunity to do this, and he finally found it." He added pensively, "I really want to kill the bastard."

Larry nodded slowly. "Yeah, I understand. I would feel the same way. But, you can't. You know that don't you?"

"Yes," Kurt replied. "But it sure…" His words tailed-off, and he sighed deeply. "I need to go, Larry. Will you help me with a couple of things?"

"Of course, you know I will. But what will you do? I know you don't have much money, none of us do."

"No. But I took what we had, and I think it might be enough to get me back to Florida. From there, I'll just have to try and figure something out." He paused. "Will you try to keep my glass-ball with you and the conch shells that we gathered?"

"Sure. I'll figure out a way to get them back to California. But what about Madison?"

Kurt looked at his brother for a minute. "Take care of her will you? I know there's not much you can do; but if you could get her away from the Limey bastard, I would be grateful."

Larry nodded, watching his brother seethe, and understanding the pain that he was going through. He wished he could do or say something to ease Kurt's pain, but he knew that only time could really do that. He moved to his brother and put his hand on his shoulder. Kurt stood there, looking out at the bay where just the bow section of the *Cozy* was visible, with Madison standing woefully on the concrete wharf, her head slumped, and Jeffrey Smythe staring at her a few yards away.

Kurt reached out and hugged his brother, then picked up his bag and walked away.

EPILOGUE

Later that day, Kurt caught a 'puddle jumper' flight out of Bimini to Miami for thirty-four dollars. From there, he called his sister Susan in California, and she wired him the money to catch a flight back to L.A. Fortunately, he still had his little house in Hermosa Beach; and his landlord agreed to let the rent go for a while longer so that Kurt could re-established his life. His pickup truck had a dead battery but started with a jump-start from a neighbor. He discovered that his boss welcomed his return, and there was plenty of work available at the warehouse. He doggedly buried himself in work, trying to avoid contact with people that would ask questions about his trip, and about Madison.

∞

Jeffrey Smythe, Larry, and Madison, sailed the *Cozy* across to Miami the day of Kurt's departure. For Madison, it was a miserable ordeal that took place in a fog. She immersed herself in self-pity, refusing to interact or communicate at all with Jeffrey Smythe, and only minimally with Larry.

It was an easy crossing of the Gulf Stream, and they arrived in Ft. Lauderdale at Berth 66 in time to clear Customs the same day. That evening while Madison stayed aboard by herself, the owner of the *Cozy* met Jeffrey Smythe and Larry at a nearby restaurant, thanked them profusely for making a safe delivery of the boat, and gave them a five hundred dollar bonus for their efforts.

They stayed aboard for one more night, an awkward evening during which Madison continued to avoid almost any interaction with the two men. The following morning, Smythe gave Larry and Madison three hundred cash, and they said awkward farewells to each other.

Smythe caught a flight back to England later that same day.

Larry came up with the idea of looking for a car-delivery to California. After several hours of research, he located an individual who needed his Lincoln Continental delivered to San Francisco. A deal was struck, and the following morning Larry and Madison began an eight-day drive across country from Miami to San Francisco. From there, they caught a Greyhound bus back to Los Angeles.

∞

Tiona and Charlie married two weeks after returning to San Diego. They settled into a comfortable life of fun and leisure.

Sanford returned to trucking, moved to San Francisco, and eventually started a family with a woman trucker that he met at a truck stop in Barstow, California. She gave up her job to be a mother to their two kids.

Guillermo went home to Montana, found a spicy little blonde who owned and operated a local bar in Billings, and moved in with her.

Captain Ellis and Dawn settled in the Bahamas where they accepted positions operating a 'Barefoot Cruise' ship.

None of the other passengers had any further contacts with either Kurt or Larry, and presumably returned to their 'real' lives in 'the real world.'

Back in Huntington Beach, Larry found that Marcos had settled back into his normal routine of life at the apartment they shared. Marcos announced that he and Linda were engaged and were talking about an October wedding, but he would continue to share the apartment with Larry until the wedding took place. Larry went back to his moving job.

Madison returned to Hermosa Beach, where she found Kurt living in their same little cottage and back at work on his furniture projects. Madison offered to pack her things and go to Brawley to live with her mother. While she was packing, Kurt suggested that they try to work things out. By midnight, and after a lot of tears and difficult dialogue, they agreed to stay together and try to put the pieces of their lives back together.

Their effort lasted about a month. Madison went back to work at the restaurant. They both tried. Despite the fact that they were getting along and had rekindled their intimacy, the reconciliation simply did not work.

After trying and realizing that it just was not the same, Madison moved to San Diego where she started another relationship with an old friend. That relationship was short-lived. A few weeks later she met another guy—a musician. They moved away together to Hawaii, and she found a job working on a dive excursion boat.

Kurt moved to Florida. He bought a boat, started his own charter fishing business, and met and married a fiery little raven-haired beauty that stood four foot ten and weighed ninety-nine pounds sopping wet.

Kurt never forgot lying naked on a white-sand beach, under a palm tree, in the warm tropical sun.